The Nowhere Girls

Alex Urquhart

ISBN: 0-692-89031-9
ISBN-13: 978-0-692-89031-8

TABLE OF CONTENTS

ACKNOWLEDGMENTS

Thank you to everyone who has offered words of encouragement during the production of this book. Mom, Dad, Alyssa and Raven, your support and enthusiasm made me work diligently every day to create something that you would be compelled by. The Nowhere Girls is for you.

1

Katie downed the double shot of whiskey in a single swig. Careful not to pay too much attention to the burning sensation in her stomach, she set the shot glass back onto the wooden table and glanced in the direction of the door. A tall man with salt-and-pepper hair draped around his face lumbered through the doorway. She frequently saw him at the bar, although she didn't know his name. With a nose that overshadowed the rest of his features like a beak, the man reminded Katie of a crow. His large forehead proliferated the congruence of his eyebrows, which were barely a centimeter apart, and he had hollowed cheeks that gave off the impression of someone who had experience with amphetamines. Katie watched him saunter over to his favorite stool and plop onto it rather unceremoniously. He was one of a select few people whom she saw so frequently at this tavern that if Katie were to visit and notice his absence, she would think that something was terribly wrong.

Katie withdrew her gaze from the man and honed her focus

back onto the table she was sitting at with her friend Charles. It was typical of a small town bar to often have the same people in it, but Rip Tide's in Newport, Oregon, took this quirk to another level. Even people like Katie who only went to the bar once every couple of weeks were considered regulars due to the dearth of new faces.

"Up for a smoke break?" asked Charles, leaning in with a smile.

Katie glanced at him, brushing the ever-falling hair out of her eyes. He was one of those friends who wanted to go for a cigarette every ten minutes.

"Ugh, fine," said Katie.

The pair rose and made their way in the direction of the door, weaving in and out of drunks and designated drivers alike. When Katie passed the tall man who reminded her of a crow sitting at the bar, he gave her an odd scowl. Katie frowned, unaware of any transgression they would have committed, and kept walking toward the door.

When they were outside and out of earshot of the man, Katie turned toward Charles. "That was fucking weird."

"What?"

"That guy in the black coat at the bar gave me a weird look when I walked past him."

"He probably thought you were cute."

Katie gave Charles a one-fingered salute as she pulled out a pack of menthol cigarettes and he laughed.

"You sure it wasn't Anthony?" continued Charles gleefully.

"Screw you," Katie said without smiling. Charles guffawed. He took every opportunity to get in a shot at Anthony Mason, Katie's irascible and eldritch boss with whom she had a checkered past.

"Mind if I bum a smoke?"

"You asked to smoke, but you didn't have any cigarettes?"

"I knew you would." Charles gave her a sheepish smile.

Rolling her eyes, Katie withdrew two cigarettes and handed one to her friend. She lit the end of hers with the bright orange lighter that had been in her pocket, and gave that to Charles too.

Newport was a beautiful town when the weather was nice. The problem was, nice weather was rare. When it wasn't raining from November to May, it was overcast, and the hot days in the summer weren't even very hot. It was currently late August, meaning the rain would start to become more frequent again in the coming months. Katie didn't mind it; she always preferred the cold to the heat.

In between puffs on his cigarette, Charles talked about some show on Netflix that he had been watching, and although it looked like she was listening, Katie tuned out. Her mind wandered to work tomorrow the next morning. She had been a barista at Mason's Coffee for three years, and it had become monotonous to say the least. Even when it was busy, the job didn't hold her full attention.

Charles was droning on about some monster show that apparently was a perfect homage to the eighties when Katie's phone vibrated in her pocket. Once she pulled it out, she saw that her grandmother, Teresa, was calling her. Katie held up her index finger, signaling to Charles that she needed a moment, and he looked somewhat miffed that his rant had been snuffed out.

"Hello?"

"Hey, Katie. Are you coming home soon?"

Katie sighed and rubbed her eyes aggressively, trying to ebb away her frustration.

"I have literally been out for less than an hour."

"Well, it's Sunday night," Teresa said.

"This is one of the only days me and Charles can hang out. I have to work tomorrow anyway, so I won't be out long."

Teresa sighed and muttered, "I am going to go to bed soon, so just be quiet when you come in."

"Okay."

Katie hung up and took the longest drag on her cigarette yet. Sometimes she regretted choosing to stay in Newport with her grandmother after her parents had moved to Northern California after she graduated high school. Every time Teresa tried to reel her in when she was out at the bar, it made her question the decision.

Katie snuffed out her cigarette on the ground and threw it into the designated bucket outside the bar. She motioned to Charles that she was going back inside, and he followed her in.

After two more drinks, and enough of a buzz that she felt happier than she was when she had gotten off the phone, Katie told Charles that she was heading home. Her grandmother, although pretending to sleep, was probably in bed worrying about Katie. Instead of acting like a noble gentleman and offering to walk her home, Charles said that he was going to stay inside for a couple more drinks. Feeling a little unnerved that she had to walk by herself, Katie said good-bye to him and stumbled toward the door, feigning more sobriety than she felt. Work tomorrow was going to be rough, but hey, she was young. She could take it. Teresa's house was only four blocks away from Rip Tide's anyway.

Katie walked out of the bar and staggered up Third Street, careful to avoid tripping on the cracks in the sidewalk. It was somewhat of a climb as the street sloped up toward Highway 101. She walked underneath a streetlight and noticed that all the light did was make her more aware of how dark it was outside. It was always an eerie thing to walk by herself, but the alcohol usually helped sooth her trepidation. However, tonight the liquor seemed to heighten her awareness of the fact that she was alone as she walked two more blocks in the direction of her house.

Katie saw movement across the street in her peripheral vision and noticed the same crow-like man from the bar walking in her same direction. Her heart pounded at the sight of him; she hadn't expected to see anyone at this late hour. He must've left Rip

Tide's immediately after she had. Katie quickened her pace, but it seemed as if the man did not notice her anyway since he was staring down at the screen of his phone. Although somewhat unnerved, she simply turned at Pine Street toward her home.

Katie glanced back again over her shoulder. The man had stopped walking and was staring at her from afar. He held his phone aloft in his hand, as if he were about to send a text or make a call. Katie again heightened her pace and gazed back at the man instead of looking in the direction she was walking. Dread was bubbling in the pit of her stomach, mixed with anger at Charles for not walking her home. The man maintained his eye contact for a few seconds and then went back to looking at his phone. *Fuck you, dude,* thought Katie. He had given Katie the creeps inside the bar, and now that she was walking alone with him not far behind, her unease had reached a new level. She was probably imagining it, but as she was moving, she heard quick footsteps behind her.

Katie froze. She did not know what made her stop, but it felt like something was totally out of place. The hairs on the back of her neck stood up. She turned to look for the man who had been behind her, but he had vanished. Katie angled her vision toward the street. The only thing she saw was the normal set of houses she frequently walked past, a massive Douglas fir tree, and a Jeep with tinted windows parked next to the sidewalk. She stayed motionless, waiting for something she felt but could not see.

Katie fumbled for her phone and attempted to use the light from the screen to illuminate the darkness. She slowly leaned to the side, looking for anything unusual. Hopefully her brain was just playing tricks on her. With a start, she noticed the bushes on the other side of the street seemed to dance for a second, yet she did not feel a breeze.

Katie couldn't even find her voice. Glacially moving in front of the Jeep, she kept her eyes glued to the spot where she had seen movement. It seemed as if some unspeakable horror was waiting in the darkness.

The headlights of the Jeep turned on, almost blinding Katie as she shielded her eyes. She didn't even have time to process the light before someone grabbed her from behind.

2

Jonah Carr sat on the edge of the leather couch, listening to the old man ramble on. The few stray white hairs on the top of the man's glistening bald head stood straight up like they had been petrified in the upright position. The man was spindly and thin, which reminded Jonah of a stock character from any animated Tim Burton movie. He spoke with a slight lisp and spitted on certain words. An audio recorder sat in front of him, capturing his every word. Jonah attempted to scribble down the man's physical description in his notepad, although it was doubtful it would make it into the story. People didn't care what the man looked like. They cared about how he kept fifteen ferrets in his garage.

Jonah had been sent by the *News Times,* a small paper in Newport, to write a feature story about Clive O'Hara, a man who used his house as a ferret shelter. O'Hara received calls from around the county from locals who found the animals, and he would take them in. Occasionally he would offer them up for adoption as pets to anyone in the community who wanted them, but the market for ferrets was not exactly thriving. Jonah's publisher, Randy Marks, told Jonah before he went for the interview that he realized the assignment was "total bullshit," but it was Newport. Nothing ever happened, and cute sells.

"Sometimes I name them after *Star Wars* characters," O'Hara said with a grin from ear to ear. "This one here is Yoda!"

Jonah stared at the snow-white ferret in the man's hands and thought he had never seen anything that reminded him less of Yoda. However, he smiled.

"There is no try," Jonah said wryly.

"What?"

Jonah stared at the man for a few seconds. He had a complete look of befuddlement on his face.

"Nothing. So how long have you been doing this?"

O'Hara briefly mulled over his answer. "Shoot, I started doing it about ten years ago. It didn't really become a thing until the last few years, though."

"When you say 'a thing,' what do you mean?"

"I mean, it just started as a hobby and sort of suddenly became a job. I turned into the Lincoln County Ferret Guy." He let out an odd giggle.

"And we thank you for your service," Jonah replied. O'Hara then released a mad cackle and pretended to tip an invisible cap in Jonah's direction.

Jonah had been refining his interviewing technique for the past two years, and one of the best methods for success was building rapport with your subjects. Though interviewing respondents was something that was emphasized in a couple of Jonah's journalism classes, it really just took practice to become proficient at building an amicable interaction with an interviewee.

"I didn't think they would actually send anybody out here." O'Hara smiled. "What I am doing really ain't that special."

"Oh, I think people will be interested in this. It might even bump up the number of adoptions."

O'Hara shook his head. "Ain't that many people reading the *Times.*"

Jonah smiled. *Ain't that many people who give a shit about ferrets,* he thought.

After ten more minutes, Jonah wrapped up the interview, thanking O'Hara for his time, and gathered his audio recorder and notepad. He told O'Hara the story should be printed the following Wednesday and shook his hand. Jonah then went out to his late-model Toyota Corolla that was parked outside.

Once the engine fired up, Jonah pulled out his phone and checked the time. It was just past eleven in the morning. He had only spent an hour interviewing O'Hara, and he didn't have any more interviews for the rest of the day. He had barely gotten five hours of sleep the night before, so he decided a coffee was in order and pointed his mental compass toward Starbucks.

"Yeah, can I have a medium caramel latte?" Jonah spoke up into the drive-through receiver minutes later.

"You mean a Grande?" Jonah didn't miss the grit in the barista's voice.

"Yeah, thanks," Jonah said, irritated at being corrected as though the employee he was speaking to didn't understand what he meant. He then quietly muttered, "You *Grande*, twat."

When Jonah pulled up to pay, the obese blond kid who apparently took his order was leaning out of the window like Jonah was moving his car far too slowly. The kid looked like an interspecies combination of a duck and Ellen DeGeneres. Jonah smirked as he handed him a five-dollar bill. After receiving his change and his coffee, Jonah drove off. While pulling away he distinctly heard the kid say, "Have a nice day too, you *Grande* twat."

He resisted the urge to put his car in reverse and drag the kid out of the window WWE-style, and let the remark slide.

Jonah pressed the gas pedal downward with vigor as he drove in the direction of the lookout cliff called Jump Off Joe's. It was a spot that hung precariously over the Pacific Ocean and gave onlookers a spectacular view. He frequently visited the spot for coffee breaks after interviews so he could enjoy his latte with some quiet before heading back to the office. Turning left onto Eleventh Street, Jonah drove as far as he could without plunging over the abyss into the sea below, so that he could attain the best view possible.

The first thing he did after his engine was off was text his friend Wesley. Jonah sent him a link to a GIF that he had found on the Internet that morning that had amused him. It was a clip of several Korean men conducting a failed miniature rocket launch and then applauding as if it had been a sterling success. Chuckling at his own wit, Jonah looked back over the cliff. He often pondered why it was called Jump Off Joe's. Perhaps a man named Joe had enough Oregon rain one day and committed suicide via hurling himself over the brink, but it didn't seem like an efficient way to do the deed. You would die, sure, but your remains would be splattered all over Nye Beach and the main course for a seagull Thanksgiving. Not to mention the area below was rarely free of bystanders. If you were going to do something as idiotic as killing yourself, at least spare other people the trauma of seeing it and the mess of cleaning it up.

Jonah gazed out over the blustery ocean. He frequently thought about how very remote the Oregon Coast was. In many ways, it was the edge of the earth; a form of exile for its residents. However, there was great beauty in it too. Sprawling sandy beaches and massive rock structures next to the canvas of thousands of trees made for spectacular aesthetics. Jonah took delicate sips of his scalding-hot latte and listened as the dulcet tones of Jack Johnson sifted through his car's speakers. One thing you could find in Newport, Oregon, unlike many other places, was peace.

Jonah's phone vibrated in his pocket. He pulled it out and saw that it was his editor, Randy Marks.

"Jonah?"

"Yeah, what's up, boss?"

"I need you to get down to the docks as soon as you can." Marks sounded tired and on the verge of a cold.

"Like the bayfront?"

"Yeah. They found a body in the water. Coast guard is pulling it out now. I know you don't usually cover stuff like this, but I want as many of us down there as possible."

Jonah paused, his heart starting to beat rapidly. "Any idea who it is?"

"No confirmation, but the rumor getting out is that it is a young woman named Katie Deeds."

3

Jonah watched from the end of the pier as the forty-five-foot coast guard response boat slowly pulled into the harbor while rain cascaded down into Yaquina Bay. He stood among a crowd of twenty people or so, all watching avidly as the boat drew closer. Several police vehicles were parked along the sidewalk behind the crowd, and cops congregated at the reception area where the coast guard would return. A whisper steadily began to break out among the crowd as the front-most onlookers could see the shape of a body bag on the boat's aft deck.

Several men on the boat in full coast guard regalia noticed the watchers and arranged themselves to block what was apparently Katie Deeds's body from view. Silently cursing himself for forgetting his *Times*-issued camera in his car that was parked three blocks away, Jonah withdrew his phone and took as many pictures as possible. Three of his colleagues, Micah Thrash, Jim Nevins, and Carla Smith, were intermingled with the bystanders. Only Carla had brought an official company-owned Nikon camera.

Newport was not the smallest town on the Oregon Coast by any means, but it was a tight-knit community. When something of significance happened, everyone seemed to come together like seagulls swarming to discarded crumbs of bread. In a less friendly town, a random event like the one Jonah was currently probing might go unnoticed. But here, where the residents clung together like schools of fish, an untimely death brought about a large swath of curious bystanders. Jonah saw many people in work uniforms milling about. He assumed they were supposed to be working shifts at the various businesses that ran along the bayfront, but Katie Deeds's death had beckoned them away.

Jonah began to snake his way through the crowd, trying his hand at a better angle to view the oncoming boat. He passed a tall man with a large nose and hollowed-in cheeks who seemed to be completely absorbed with the action on the water. All Jonah managed to do was to get to the third row of people before his path was cut off by a large man wearing a police uniform.

"Sorry, Carr, you can't get any closer," Josh Hernandez said.

Jonah had had a couple of interactions with Hernandez over the past year, as he had covered three or four other breaking stories when the other reporters were not available, and Hernandez had been at the scene a couple of times. He had always struck Jonah as a power-hungry dick.

Jonah appraised Hernandez, giving him a critical stare. "Why the hell not?"

"Because we don't want blown-up pictures of the girl's body all over the front of the newspaper," said Hernandez with a snarl.

"So you can confirm that it is a girl?"

Hernandez frowned. "You know I can't get into details."

Jonah gave a shrug. "I had to try."

"No you didn't," Hernandez said with such ferocity that Jonah was surprised flames didn't sprout from his nostrils.

"Where is Rick?"

"Ask him," Hernandez said, getting an inch away from Jonah's face and snarling.

Jonah took several steps back from Hernandez and dialed Rick Casey's number on his cell phone. Casey was a sergeant on the police force and had developed somewhat of a relationship with Jonah over the past year after the *Times* ran a profile on him. Jonah noticed with annoyance that Hernandez hadn't even bothered preventing Jonah's colleagues from getting closer to the scene.

After several rings, Casey answered.

"Hello?"

"Rick, what's up?"

Casey sighed heavily. "Do you really think I have time to talk to you right now? This is a clusterfuck."

"I just need you to give me something, Rick. We need to get ahead of this. You know Randy won't give a shit what my excuses are if I come back with nothing on something as big as this."

This was only partially true. There were people at the police station who were designated for talking to the press who would probably speak to one of the other reporters from the *Times.* Jonah was trying to assert a bit of imaginary leverage to see where it got him.

Casey sighed again.

"Where are you, Rick?"

"I'm still at the station. We have been fielding calls all morning."

Jonah paused. "Can I meet you there this afternoon?"

Casey considered this in silence for a few moments, before responding, "I'm not going to be seen with you at the station the day of a public suicide. People will start to catch on to the fact that I am your source. We need to meet in private."

Jonah pulled into the Nye Beach turnaround, carefully scanning for signs of a squad car. After several moments, he saw the black-and-white vehicle that was parked in the row closest to the beach, on the far end, away from eyesight. Jonah parked right next to Rick Casey's car, got out of his car, and approached tentatively.

Casey leaned over and opened the door, motioning for Jonah to get in. Jonah slid his slim figure into the front passenger seat and looked over at Casey with apprehension. The man was in his fifties. His skin looked like rough leather or a pirate's treasure map after years of exposure to the sun. His forehead was massive, jutting over a pair of bright blue eyes. The buzzed hair on top of Casey's head was bleached blond. His massive stomach and red complexion seemed to call attention to the fact that Casey could never stop sweating.

"Look, Jo, I really shouldn't be doing this. You know how much trouble I would get in if I give you any information that the PR guys don't give out."

Jonah looked at him with a supplicating expression on his face. "You know that if we use anything you tell me in a story, we won't use your name. That has always been our agreement."

"I know, but it's a small fucking town. Anonymous sources are never really anonymous here, and people already know that me and you have a relationship. The only reason I agreed to it was because I needed to get the hell away from the chaos at the station for a few minutes, and with something as big as this, you guys are going to get all the information eventually anyway. And I needed a cigarette." Casey exhaled a long and rattled breath.

"Well, go on then." Jonah gestured to him. "Light up."

"In my squad car? Yeah, right. I'm going to wait until you leave."

There was a momentary lapse in the conversation, as Jonah and Casey were both not exactly sure where to begin.

"I do appreciate this, Rick."

Casey gave Jonah a slight nod and turned to face the ocean, which was thrashing about wildly. In the past half hour, the rain had become heavier and the wind had started to blow in stronger gusts. It was a tiny bit rare to experience a mild storm in late August, but not unheard of. Jonah pulled out his small notepad from within his heavy coat, as well as a pen. He knew Casey wouldn't allow him to record their conversation, so he just opted to take notes.

"So what do you know, and what don't you know? Bear in mind that there are some things that I am not at liberty to discuss yet."

Jonah carefully processed his next words. "All I know is that a young woman named Katie Deeds was pulled out of the water this morning. The first time I heard it was a suicide was from you when we were on the phone. I was down at the docks for about a half hour, but Hernandez wouldn't let me see anything. Apparently, there wasn't much to see anyway. The people who were down there got a glimpse of the body on the aft deck of the response boat, but the coast guard got it to the station before anybody could get a real look. The crowd dispersed pretty fast after that. I talked to a couple of people, but like I said, nobody really saw anything."

Casey looked at him with his brows raised, apparently surprised at how little Jonah actually knew. He leaned forward, taking a deep breath before launching into his explanation. "Well, you have the name right, so that is something, I guess. Twenty-one-year-old Katie Deeds jumped off the Yaquina Bay Bridge at approximately five o'clock this morning. The coast guard found the body after about six hours of searching. No witnesses on the bridge, but there were some people crabbing off the dock from down below who saw the body hit the water. They were the ones who called it in."

"Where did you get her name?"

"Her grandmother called 911 at three this morning. Katie had gone out last night for a drink with her friend and never came home. The woman, Teresa Deeds, had gotten three texts from Katie that indicated that she was planning on killing herself."

Jonah frowned. "What did the texts say?"

"You know I can't tell you that."

"Did Teresa say that she had been feeling suicidal before last night?"

"Well, she was a bit frantic. But no, she sounded like it had totally came out of left field."

"I don't get the timeline of the whole thing."

Casey looked at Jonah. "What do you mean?"

"Well, doesn't it seem a bit odd to go out for drinks with your friends and then commit suicide directly afterward?"

Casey looked at Jonah and scrunched his forehead. "If you're asking if I think it's odd for a drunk person to have suicidal ideations, no, I don't."

"But she obviously had planned to kill herself. It isn't a spur-of-the-moment thing. So why would you go out drinking beforehand?"

"Hell if I know. Maybe she was trying to build up the courage to actually do it. Maybe she was saying good-bye to her friend."

Jonah considered this, then continued, "Have you sent anyone to interview the people she was communicating with last night?"

"Well, Teresa Deeds has been at the station all day. We only interviewed her for a little bit, though. She didn't have much to say. She was in shock. We haven't interviewed the friend who was with her yet. He left for Corvallis this morning to visit a friend, but he should be back soon."

Jonah turned over the information in his mind, until he clung to another detail that perplexed him: the age.

"Shit, man. Twenty-one years old? Why would a twenty-one-year-old girl jump off a bridge? You would think that would be past the age of teenage angst and way before a midlife crisis."

Casey shook his head. "Not a clue. Didn't leave a note, and

her texts didn't really explain anything."

"Did her grandma say this type of behavior was typical for Katie?"

"She has never killed herself before, no," said Casey, pursing his lips.

"I know that, but has she ever done anything wild before? Or unpredictable?"

"Well, that's the thing," said Casey. "Her grandmother did say that Katie tended to be impulsive. Sometimes irrational. She said that the girl once paid a hefty fine and did some community service for keying an ex-boyfriend's car."

Jonah's eyes bulged. "Shit."

"Yeah."

"But I mean, I don't see the relevance of that in terms of the suicide," Jonah said, thinking out loud.

"And what is that supposed to mean?"

"I just mean that those two things aren't really correlated. Just because she went nuts on an ex doesn't mean she was a suicide waiting to happen."

"Well, she *was* a suicide waiting to happen, because that's what did happen."

Jonah looked back toward the ocean and nodded slowly. "Yeah, I know."

Jonah walked unabashedly through the front door of the *Times* at the corner of Eighth Street and Benton, later than he was supposed to but undeterred by his tardiness. It was shockingly quiet inside, almost to the point of being unnerving. There were only two or three people at their desks, and Jonah realized that everyone else must be in the war room.

The war room was a small, claustrophobic area with a round conference table in the center. When Jonah ducked in, he saw that Micah Thrash, Carla Smith, and Jim Nevins were already sitting around the table, along with two other of their colleagues. At the head of the table was their editor, Randy Marks. Behind Marks was a large whiteboard with details of the case that Marks's subordinates had already provided him scribbled all over in dry-erase.

Randy was a short man with a beer gut and thick brown hair that took the shape of a dome around the crown of his head. Jonah often thought that Marks looked like someone who would fall asleep while working at a tollbooth. His appearance was not to be confused with his demeanor, though. He was a tough guy and a bit of a hard-ass.

Marks looked over at Jonah with a scowl as he walked in. "Where the hell have you been?"

Jonah held up his hands in defense. "I was talking to the police."

"So have we, if you hadn't noticed," replied Marks, pointing in the direction of the whiteboard.

"I wasn't talking to the PR guys; I was talking to an actual cop."

"And I am sure you have the same information as the rest of us."

"I guess there is only one way to find out, isn't there?" Jonah said with a little more force than he meant to.

Marks looked like he wanted to throttle Jonah, but refrained. He paced around the room for a moment, lost in thought. Abruptly, he launched into a detailed annotation of the writing that was on the whiteboard.

"Katie Deeds was a twenty-one-year-old local. She lived with her grandmother here in town, and worked at a coffee shop that's run by a man named Anthony Mason. Last night, at approximately seven thirty, she went out for drinks with her friends and never came home." With every point in the story, Marks would gesture to a corresponding word scribbled on the whiteboard.

"The grandmother, Teresa Deeds, said that she had fallen asleep when she received a text from Katie in the early morning that indicated she was planning on killing herself. Teresa called 911 and dispatch sent two units out looking for her. Two hours later, the cops received the call from eyewitnesses on the bridge who saw her jump. The coast guard spent several hours trying to recover the body before they located it at about eleven thirty," finished Marks with one last jab at the whiteboard.

Jonah waited for a few moments to make sure Marks was done. "The general outline I have is the same, with a couple of significant differences. First, my source says that Katie sent three texts, not one. Second, I was told the witnesses were on the docks down below, and that there wasn't anybody on the bridge itself."

Marks furrowed his brow and looked at Carla Smith. "Fuck me," he said. "Those are some pretty huge discrepancies. We need to call the station and talk to Tony Burke and double-check what he said. Are you positive he said one text and that the witnesses were on the bridge?"

Carla cowered back from Marks. It was a small move no one else saw, but Jonah noticed. She was a thin blond woman, with a mousy face and pale skin. "Uh, yeah. Regarding the texts, he wasn't specific in the amount of them that were sent. I guess I just assumed it was one. Sorry."

"That sure was fucking stupid," Marks said with a snarl.

Smith looked like she wanted to slide underneath the table. "I'm sorry, Randy. As for the witnesses, I am positive that Burke said that they were on the bridge."

"Like I said, we need to call him again. There is a chance the mistake there was on his end. Or that it is bad info from Jonah."

Jonah smiled and shrugged his shoulders. "Unlikely."

Marks then looked around the room, letting his displeasure with the variances simmer. The silence hung like it was its own entity. When he finally spoke, his tone was much calmer and deliberate.

"Jonah, since you seem to have more of a handle on this, you're going to write the story that will run on Wednesday. I want you to talk to Tony Burke immediately and try and set up an interview with Teresa Deeds or Anthony Mason tomorrow to get some background on Katie and some quotes."

Jonah wasn't exactly enthralled to have to talk to the grandmother of a deceased young woman. Speaking with the bereaved was never fun, especially when the death in question is unexpected. Also, the turnover for Wednesday's issue of the *Times* was fast, but the opportunity to write a story as big as this was enticing. He nodded in Marks's direction.

"Well, that fucking settles that," said Marks.

Jonah trudged up the stairs of his apartment building, exhausted. What had started as a routine Newport day had turned into a proverbial shit show. After his meeting with Marks and the others, he had immediately called Tony Burke. Burke, the public relations coordinator for the Newport Police Department, had confirmed the information from Casey: Katie sent three texts to her grandmother in the early hours of Monday, August twenty-ninth. He also had said that he had communicated the wrong information to Carla Smith earlier that day; the witnesses had actually been on the docks, not the bridge. Burke had profusely apologized and said that he was glad they had caught the mistake before they ran the story.

The rest of Jonah's afternoon had been spent coordinating interviews with Anthony Mason and Teresa Deeds. Mason was kind of a prick about it, but had agreed to meet Jonah at noon the following day. As for Teresa, the call had been awkward. Jonah, after identifying himself and his employer, had told her he was sorry for her loss. She did not respond. After Jonah had told Teresa his intentions, she had become somewhat angry. "I don't want to talk to any damn reporters," she had said. However, after Jonah had explained that the story was going to run regardless of whether she spoke to him or not, Teresa had conceded to an interview to make sure Jonah didn't "screw anything up." She didn't sound like the grieving grandmother of a dead young woman, but then again, Jonah had only spoken to her briefly.

Finally, Jonah had begun to write the first draft of the story that would appear on Wednesday, August thirty-first. He had simply assembled the factual who-what-when-where information he had received from Tony Burke and Rick Casey and would fill in the why and the biographical bits about Katie after the two interviews he had scheduled with Mason and Teresa.

Jonah walked through his front door and sat down on the couch that resided in what doubled as his living room and his kitchen. Withdrawing his phone from his pocket, he scrolled through texts he had exchanged with a woman named Daisy earlier in the day. Jonah had met her at the bar several weeks ago, and they had met up a few times. It wasn't anything serious. Jonah wasn't even sure he liked her yet, or if he just liked having someone to talk to. He tended to think it was the latter.

After sufficiently meditating on the flirtatious texts, Jonah prepped for dinner. Tonight seemed like a good night to make tacos. They were easy, and he wouldn't have to spend eons wasting away in hunger while some extravagant dish broiled or baked. As his mind began to wander, Jonah thought of the interview he had conducted with Clive O'Hara earlier in the day. The experience seemed so far away, like it had occurred several weeks ago. He had always thought he had preferred artsy, small-town stories like O'Hara's, but now, it was like the flame for writing cutesy features had been extinguished and had been replaced by a gnawing hunger: a craving to know more about Katie Deeds.

4

The man leaned against the hood of the Jeep, smoking a cigarette and mulling over the events of the last twenty-four hours. The months of planning and stalking the girl had satiated his appetite for hunting. It wasn't exactly easy; it had been five years since his last kill, and he was a bit rusty. The vetting process was the most difficult part. It was incredibly strenuous to maintain a job while also stalking a potential victim in a small town. But he had been successful. He had studied the girl's behavior and found the most plausible explanation for her death—suicide. She was wildly erratic and impulsive. Once the man had followed her and watched as she drove drunk through an urban neighborhood, swerving every few minutes. He had also seen her go home with men she had met at the bar on two separate occasions, and had quietly observed as she had left their houses in a drunken stupor in the wee hours of the morning. Those closest to her would be devastated; the man felt certain that they wouldn't think suicide was out of the question for a girl as unpredictable as Katie.

The man flicked his cigarette butt onto his lawn, squashing it with his massive size-thirteen boots. He often pondered his mental state. He knew that clinically, he would be defined as a sociopath. The man sometimes wondered if it was common for others who suffered from this specific form of psychosis to be aware of their condition, or if the defining trait of a sociopath was to not know that he or she was one. But the man did know, and he was comfortable with it. His lack of empathy for other people was natural. In fact, it seemed strange that people could spend time dwelling on the pain of others. However, it was not difficult for him to feign being sympathetic. He had spent most of his fifty-plus years studying his peers and mimicking their emotions. What they said. What their faces did when they said it. It was not difficult to imitate.

The man knew from his time stalking her that Katie Deeds would go to the bar once every couple of weeks and would almost always stumble home to her grandmother's, inebriated beyond belief. He could have easily taken her before last night, but where was the fun in that? The hunt was as much of a thrill as the kill.

He had not spent much time toying with Katie. Only a few hours. He had kept her tied up in the Jeep, waiting in a parking spot in a lot near the bridge that was nowhere near a street lamp until he was certain that no cars were approaching from either direction. Highway 101 on either side of the bridge was pretty much a straight shot, so the man could see vehicles coming from far enough away that he could estimate an approximate amount of time he had to perform his task. There was always the risk that someone on the north side of the bridge could turn from a side street onto 101 and surprise him, but that was why he had picked the wee hours of the morning. Traffic was extremely sparse. Plus, if there wasn't any risk involved in what he was doing, the thrill would be nonexistent.

The reason he had picked the bridge was because it was

within comfortable walking distance of Rip Tide's, where Katie was last seen leaving, so it was in the realm of possibility that she could have walked. The Oregon Department of Transportation kept cameras on the bridge that were controlled remotely. There was no way for the man to suddenly disable them without raising suspicion. Instead, the man had spent many random nights over the past few months casually walking underneath the camera that would capture the spot where he would throw Katie off, and spraying a simple salt solution onto the camera's lens. The salt built up on the lens would blur any image it captured. That way, it appeared as if the camera had just deteriorated over time. If a cop had somehow tried to file a subpoena for the footage, all they would find was a distorted picture. The man had made sure to do it at irregular intervals and in the dead of night when nobody was there to witness him. He also had made sure to stay just out of the cameras range, so he was never captured using the spray. By the time ODOT realized they needed to replace the camera, Katie Deeds would be long dead.

He had rehearsed his plan hundreds of times in his head. The crabbers were down below on the edge of the dock, as he had made sure they would be. He had carried Katie onto the bridge as fast as he could, and quickly cut the rope around her hands. After removing her gag, he had placed his hand over her mouth until the moment just before he threw her over. It would make sense to hear screams from someone committing suicide as they fell, but the suspension of disbelief would be broken from the witnesses below if they heard her scream before she went over the rail. The man had watched her fall, his heart pumping with excitement. Once he had heard the crack of her body hitting the water, he had broken into a full sprint back to his Jeep. It had taken him the span of a couple minutes to commit the crime.

The man had made sure to keep his headlights off while driving away on the specified route he had laid out for himself, just as a precaution. When the cops canvassed the area looking for witnesses, they would never receive the description of a forest-green Jeep fleeing the scene.

It was almost too perfect. The man had to marvel at his genius as he looked around the wooded area surrounding his home. The true brilliance in his plan was the randomness of it. Long ago, he had had a modus operandi, and it had nearly gotten him caught. Since then, he had made each murder look as different as he could, so that the cops would never connect them. He had become a master at evading suspicion. Getting away with it was almost as intoxicating to him as committing the crime. And he had been getting away with it for thirty years.

5

Jonah heard the ding of a bell as he opened the door to Mason's Coffee. As soon as he walked into the building, he bumped into one of the many tables cluttered around the room and felt claustrophobic. There were several places where there was only a small walkway to maneuver through as he twisted and turned around chairs. The walls were decorated with abstract paintings, and soft jazz wafted in the air from the old-looking radio propped upon the counter that stretched along the entire left side of the room. Also on the counter was a silver espresso machine that stood in front of a cute brunette barista who was making some sort of extravagant drink. The only other person in the tiny shop was a buff man who sat at one of the many tables. The man was completely bald and had a thick hooped earring that dangled from his left ear. On his chin was a grey goatee that contrasted with his dark skin, and his forehead held heavy eyebrows.

The man rose as Jonah approached and held out his hand. He had a deep, booming voice. "You Jonah Carr?"

"Yeah."

The man held out his hand for a shake. "Anthony Mason."

"Nice to meet you."

"Likewise." Mason motioned for Jonah to sit in the seat opposite him at the table.

"I really appreciate you taking the time to do this. I know when this kind of thing happens it is not fun to talk about." Jonah took out his recorder and notepad. "I am truly sorry about Katie."

Mason nodded. "It is pretty raw. I don't really think I have begun to process it yet. I didn't get much sleep last night. But I appreciate the sentiment." Mason's eyes had bags underneath them, and he had a giant cup of coffee in front of him.

"Right. Well, let's make this quick. I don't want to take any more of your time than I have to," Jonah said.

"Thank you."

Jonah was slightly taken aback by how polite Mason was acting. When scheduling the interview, he had come off as abrasive, to say the least. Perhaps his lack of sleep had zapped all his ability to be an asshole.

"Do you mind if I record this?"

"Nah." Mason sniffed.

"Thanks." Jonah pressed the red *record* button at the center of his audio device.

"So how long did Katie work here?"

"About three years. She was my longest-tenured employee. She started part-time at the end of her senior year of high school, then transitioned to full-time as soon as she graduated."

"So she went to Newport High?"

Mason raised his eyebrows. "Uh, yeah. Would've thought you already knew that."

"Well, my boss said she was a local, but that is one of the reasons I am speaking with you. We are sort of scrambling to fill in the blanks."

The cute barista behind the counter was using the rag in her hand to wipe the same spot over and over, and she appeared to be glancing at the pair of them in her peripheral vision. Jonah assumed that the girl must have worked with Katie and had some sort of relationship with her. Perhaps he would get a quote or two from her as well before he departed.

"So she worked for you for the last three years?"

"That's what I said."

"What was she like?"

Mason considered his next words carefully. "She was a good kid. Spunky, you know? Fun to be around."

"Did she ever strike you as emotionally unstable?"

Mason smiled in a dry way, and Jonah saw he had a single silver filling on the right side of his grin. "That is an interesting way to phrase that. If you are asking if I thought she was depressed, no, I didn't. When I heard the news, I couldn't believe it. Still don't."

"I'm sorry."

"Yeah."

Jonah glanced down at his notepad, observing some of the basic topics he had written down to remind himself to ask Mason about. "So, did she ever strike you as unpredictable?"

Mason shook his head and briefly raised his hands. "Not in my experience."

"Can you think of any reason why she would do this?"

"Honestly, no . . . It doesn't make any sense. She never seemed unhappy. But I guess that's the thing. Everyone has a cross to bear. Some people's are heavier than others."

Jonah was struck by how profound and sudden this transition into existential philosophy was from Mason. "Any ideas what sort of issues she might have been internalizing? Since she wasn't outwardly upset."

"I just told you, no," snapped Mason, bobbing his head forward aggressively like a turkey. "But I mean, look at her situation. Twenty-one-year-old girl whose parents are in another state and living in a shit-hole like this where it rains nine months out of the year. No college plans, no career goals. I can see why she might have been depressed."

"But you just said she wasn't depressed, Mr. Mason."

Instead of snapping at him again, Mason just stared judgmentally. "I said she didn't seem unhappy. What something seems like and what it is actually like are not one and the same."

Jonah ruminated on Mason's answer. As he was thinking, he observed a strange decoration next to him. A set of knives inside a plastic frame was hung precariously on the off-yellow wall. The knives were placed in the shape of a square with the sharp end of each pointing toward the next. Odd.

"How would you categorize your relationship with Katie, Mr. Mason?"

Mason's eyebrows rose so far that it looked as if they would start levitating into the air. "Are you a reporter or a detective?"

The asshole that Jonah had spoken to on the phone the previous day had returned.

"I'm not trying to insinuate anything; I am just trying to get more of a grasp on what Katie was like."

"Our relationship was pretty standard. Nothing inappropriate. I was just her boss."

It surprised Jonah that Mason had raised his outer defenses so fast. Jonah hadn't even been trying to say that Mason and Katie had an inappropriate relationship. It seemed like the man was being a little overprotective of himself.

"That isn't what I was saying, Mr. Mason."

"Well, then, what were you saying?"

"I wasn't saying anything. I was asking."

"Ask about something else."

Jonah stared at the man, perturbed by his behavior. If he was experiencing such grief that he wasn't sleeping, why was he being so defensive?

"Okay. I guess just talk more about her personality." Jonah was a little shaken from Mason's attitude, and even though he knew this remark sounded silly, it was the first thing he could think of.

Mason shook his head. "What else is there to say? She was a good kid."

"Did everyone else get along with her?"

"Yeah, everyone loved Katie."

Jonah turned to look at the brunette girl behind the counter at the exact right moment. The girl's eyes widened and her lips collapsed inward. This expression was indicative that Mason's statement wasn't exactly on par with reality. However, instead of immediately pursuing this angle, Jonah focused his attention back on Mason, determined to get another good quote for the story.

"What's it going to be like with her no longer here?"

Mason rolled his eyes. "What are you? Diane Sawyer? What do you think it is going to be like?"

"I don't know. That is why I asked. I'm just trying to get a feel for what she meant to you."

Mason stared at Jonah. More than ten seconds passed before he spoke. "Let's wrap this up. I have to do inventory." He stood up, apparently finished with the interview.

Jonah got the point. It was time for him to leave; attempting to speak to the brunette behind the counter would be asking for trouble.

Jonah quickly pulled his business card out of his pocket and set it on the table. "Okay. Well, here is my card in case you need to talk. Thank you for your time, Mr. Mason."

As he got up, Jonah glanced in the direction of the barista. They made eye contact for several seconds, and she had a mysterious look on her face. Jonah nodded at her, and then left.

Jonah knocked gently on the door of the small white house on the corner of Pine and High Street. The bushes lining the base of the house were overgrown and the knocker on the front door was rusted. Judging from the dilapidated exterior, the house had been built many years ago.

A few moments after Jonah had knocked, the door creaked open, and behind it stood a frail old woman. Her gray hair was unkempt and a pair of thick-rimmed glasses tilted down on the edge of her nose, ready to fall off. Her thin lips and small nose rested above a chin that peeked out a bit further than the rest of her facial features.

"You're the reporter, I'm guessing."

"Yes, I am, Mrs. Deeds. Jonah Carr." Jonah held out his hand. Teresa grasped it briefly.

"You are more handsome than I pictured."

Jonah flushed red. He knew it was common for the elderly to say things that were forward, but it still caught him off guard when it happened. He shuffled from foot to foot. "Thank you."

Teresa scowled at him and shook her head. "Well, come on in. Let's get this over with." It looked like Jonah was about to conduct his second awkward interview of the day.

The interior of Teresa's house was worse than the outside. There were random items scattered on the floor, and the carpet was stained in several places. The smell of the place reminded him of cat urine mixed with burnt pea soup. Teresa sat on the nasty-looking brown couch in the living room that was in front of a bulky TV. The only other place to sit down was a dark blue love seat that contrasted jarringly with the brown couch. Jonah plopped himself down onto the love seat and withdrew his recorder and notepad from his jacket. Instead of looking at him, Teresa stared out of the window with a faraway look in her eyes.

Jonah fiddled with the edges of his notepad. As he glanced over to his left, he noticed a picture of Katie hanging on the wall. She was very attractive, with a radiant smile. His stomach seemed to drop a little as he tried to broach the elephant in the room.

"I don't even really know where to begin. I am so terribly sorry for your loss."

"You said that on the phone, but no, you aren't," Teresa replied candidly. "How could you be? You didn't even know her. I don't hold it against you though."

Jonah froze, unsure of how to continue. "I realize you probably haven't even begun to process the shock of all this."

Teresa rolled her eyes and looked away. He was afraid she might cry, but she didn't seem to be close to tears. It was a weird custom to treat the bereaved as if they had caught some terrible illness that was contagious, but that was how it always was. Jonah tried to express his sympathy once more.

"No one should have to go through what you are going through."

Teresa continued to stare at him.

Jonah swallowed. "Do you have any notion as to why Katie might have done this?"

"Done what?"

Perhaps Teresa was a bit senile.

"You know,"—extracting the words from his vocal cords was painfully awkward— "commit suicide."

"Katie didn't commit suicide."

Jonah's voice seemed to catch in his throat, and for a fleeting moment, he wondered if it would ever return. "What did you say?"

"She didn't commit suicide," Teresa repeated.

Jonah's eyes bulged, and he felt a chill running down his spine.

"What exactly do you mean?"

"She was murdered."

Waves of shock crashed over Jonah. Was this woman serious?

"Mrs. Deeds—"

"No need to call me that. My husband is long gone. And we don't need to be all formal anyway. Call me by my name."

Jonah paused. "Teresa—"

The woman gave an exasperated smile while shaking her head. "Here we go."

"What?"

Teresa glowered at him over the top of her glasses. "I know you're going to tell me I'm crazy, and to be honest, I really don't care what you think."

"That certainly wasn't my intention. Is there any particular reason why you think this?"

Teresa glared at him. "Because Katie would never harm herself."

"Have you told the police that you suspect it wasn't suicide?"

"No, I haven't." She spoke as if every other person in the world should automatically know her reason for doing everything.

"Why not?"

"Because I know how it sounds. They would just tell me I'm nuts."

Jonah let this sink in for a second.

"So you think your granddaughter was murdered, and you don't want an investigation into her death?"

"There wouldn't be an investigation, at least not from the cops. Like I said, they would just take it as some bullshit rationalization from a grieving relative. Someone else will have to find out what happened."

Again, Jonah found it difficult to contain his surprise. He had no idea what Teresa meant by "someone else." Perhaps she was thinking of contacting a private investigator. It was so ridiculous that Jonah couldn't believe he was having this conversation. He knew that this was far too outlandish to publish. Teresa was right, the cops and everyone else would think exactly what Jonah thought: Teresa was still recovering from the surprise of losing a relative and was justifying her granddaughter's suicide by telling herself that there was no way Katie had wanted to hurt herself. He didn't want to continue down this path. He had a job to do.

"Let's talk about Katie for a minute. Who she was."

Teresa gave Jonah an appraising look. They had both come to a silent understanding. Jonah thought her theory was ludicrous, and she looked almost relieved to not have to try and convince him further. Then she honed in on what Jonah had just said.

"Was," Teresa repeated. Past tense. Her upper lip began to quiver. Finally, a sign of proper grief.

"Alright," she said in a quiet voice after several seconds of silence.

"What was she like?"

"She was wonderful. One of the most genuinely good people I have ever known. She had her moments, like we all do. But underneath it all, she was so pure. She just wanted what we all want. Love." As she finished her sentence, her voice cracked.

"I am so sorry, Mrs. Deeds." He now had gone from feeling flabbergasted to feeling incredibly sorry for the woman.

Teresa clenched her jaw in frustration and pointed aggressively at Jonah. "I told you, don't call me that."

"I'm sorry."

"And stop apologizing."

"I—okay."

Teresa nodded, wiping at her eyes and turning her head toward the window again.

"So I understand Katie went out with her friend and never came home. Do you know the name of this friend?" Jonah asked tentatively.

"Charles Johnson."

Jonah quickly wrote the name down. "And then, as I understand it, you began receiving texts from Katie that woke you up?"

"From Katie's phone, yes."

There it was again. The insanity. Moving past this, Jonah asked the question he was most curious about. "What did the texts say?"

"The first one said, 'I'm sorry, Grandma. This isn't your fault.'"

Jonah scribbled it down verbatim, even though his audio recorder picked it up as well.

"A few minutes later, the second one came. It said, 'I have to do this. I don't expect you to understand. But I am going to die tonight.'"

"And the final text?" Jonah asked, not thinking. He obviously already knew that Katie had sent three texts, but he wasn't sure how Teresa would respond to him already possessing this shred of information. Apparently though, she thought nothing of it.

"It just said, 'Good-bye.'" Teresa's eyes welled with her tears again.

"I'm sorry," Jonah repeated for what felt like the millionth time of the conversation. Teresa did not reply this time.

"What was your immediate reaction when you received these texts?"

"What do you think? Panic. I didn't know what they meant at first."

That didn't make much sense to Jonah. It was utterly apparent that Katie had meant she was going to kill herself. Unable to contain his curiosity, Jonah asked the question that was suddenly burning inside him. "Why do you think that Katie didn't send those texts?"

"Because, for one, she never called me Grandma. She called me Teresa."

"Your granddaughter called you by your first name?"

Teresa nodded rhythmically. "It was something she picked up from her mother. Mary always felt that calling me Mom made me not special, since everyone else called their mother that. So, she called me by my name."

Realizing that Mary must be the name of Katie's mother, this sparked another prompt from Jonah. "Obviously, I assume you have informed Katie's parents of what has transpired. If you haven't, I imagine the cops have."

"It was one of the hardest things I have ever had to do."

"I can only imagine."

"No, you can't."

Jonah took this in stride. "So are there any other reasons why you think Katie wasn't the one who texted you?"

"Because it just doesn't fit. I can't imagine any circumstance where she would ever want to kill herself. And even in some bizarre alternate universe where such a scenario would exist, she wouldn't tell me she was going to die tonight. That is about as subtle as a brick."

"So you called the cops and told them you thought Katie had been kidnapped or something?"

"No, I told them that Katie hadn't come home, and I had received those texts from her phone. They automatically just assumed it was suicide."

"They asked you this when they interviewed you at the station? When did you hear the news?"

Teresa gave Jonah a dark and brooding look. "Right after it happened, obviously. It was the worst moment of my life."

"I'm so sorry."

"When are you going to stop saying that?"

X

The rest of the interview was spent gathering biographical information about Katie from Teresa. Katie had been somewhat of an athlete in high school, playing on the varsity volleyball and soccer teams. She enjoyed writing, and kept several diaries in her room, most of which contained poems. Katie had been somewhat ambivalent regarding her job as a barista. She didn't hate it, but it didn't exactly spark a deep passion.

Personality-wise, Teresa followed suit in describing Katie as "spunky." Teresa also said she had a hard outer shell, but that Katie was more sensitive than she let on. Teresa spoke of her granddaughter as if she were still alive, which made it more depressing. However, Jonah was taken aback by how little the woman expressed grief. Aside from the crack in her voice at the beginning of the interview, she talked about the whole thing in a matter-of-fact manner, including when she suggested Katie had been murdered and when she relayed her experience at the morgue identifying Katie's body from the day before. It was a tad bit strange. Perhaps she was still in a state of shock.

After about a half hour, Jonah thanked Teresa for her time and departed. The strangeness of what Teresa had said initially about Katie's disappearance lingered on, but they had not broached the subject again. This wasn't *CSI: Miami*, or *Criminal Minds*. Homicide didn't happen in Newport. Especially a homicide as elaborate as kidnapping a young woman, texting her closest relative that she was planning on killing herself, and then throwing her off a bridge. Even just thinking about it was strangely amusing to Jonah. He supposed it was sad that Teresa had to tell herself that Katie had been murdered to avoid the thought that Katie had been unhappy. But to entertain the idea of murder seemed outlandish. The whole thing had piqued his curiosity somewhat, but if he started spouting off crackpot theories that emanated from grieving relatives and they turned out to be totally false, he would be laughed at personally and professionally.

Ten minutes after Jonah had left Teresa's house, he pulled into the parking lot of the *Times*. It was essentially empty. They were understaffed anyway, and he was sure that all the *Times*'s employees were currently out doing some last-minute reporting for stories that would run the next day. Even when you worked for a paper that prints only on Wednesdays and Sundays, some interviews got pushed to the last minute.

As Jonah walked through the front door into the main newsroom and sat at his desk, he felt his phone vibrate in his pocket. He pulled it out and saw that it was Daisy, the girl he met at the bar recently. *Beers tonight?* read the text. Jonah didn't immediately respond. He did want to drink, but he wasn't sure he wanted to do it with Daisy. He knew that they would both end up getting too drunk and going back to his apartment to have sex. The more times that that happened, the more likely he was to get too attached, and getting attached to a woman who wasn't in it for the long haul had been a problem for him over the past couple of years. He typed the words *I don't think so*, but didn't send the text. After thinking for a bit longer, he deleted the four words and replaced them with two: *You bet.*

Fuck it, he thought. He needed to get laid anyway. As he opened his laptop and clicked on the Word document that contained the first draft he had written of the story, he reflected on the two interviews he had conducted earlier in the day. He was feeling a bit of mild embarrassment regarding his interview with Anthony Mason, and trepidation for when Teresa would read the story and see that he had not given any credence to her ideas about what had happened to Katie. On top of it all, whenever he thought of the picture of Katie that was hanging in Teresa's house, he felt a pang of sadness. She was so young, and seemed to be full of vibrant life. With the culmination of these unpleasant feelings, Jonah was definitely ready for a beer.

6

The Sand Dollar was at the end of the Abbey Street Pier, down on the bayfront where Jonah had been the day before. The wind howled through the cavalcade of shops and tourist attractions that formed the bayfront, and a light drizzle of rain fell on the ground. Jonah held his hood over his head and opened the door to the Sand Dollar for Daisy.

Daisy was short and petite, with bleached blond hair that lost its color at the roots. She was extremely pale, but it added to her attractiveness, making her appear more indie and mysterious. She had purple gauges in her earlobes and wore black jeans that would look far too tight on most people, but not on Daisy.

Inside the Sand Dollar was a massive throng of people. Tuesday night was their local special: You got each beer for a dollar less than the original cost. It wasn't that much of a bargain, though. The beer was somewhat pricey. However, the atmosphere at the Sand Dollar on Tuesdays was what made Newport what it was: a quiet town with a sneaky-good nightlife.

Daisy motioned for one of the few empty tables that lined the large windows on the south side of the bar. Outside there was a beautiful view of the water. Fishing boats sat stocked against the docks, packed as tight as sardines. On the far side of Yaquina Bay was a gargantuan blue sewage plant that erupted upward on a spit of land that stretched across the water. With an eerie feeling, Jonah remembered a young girl had died yesterday on this very water, hitting it like it was cement after jumping from the 246-foot-tall bridge above.

Jonah pulled out a seat for Daisy, and she perched herself daintily on the edge of the chair. Jonah remained standing and looked at her expectantly, waiting for her to tell him what kind of beer she wanted. It was loud and crowded inside the bar, so he leaned in to hear her.

Daisy looked up at him with a start, as if she forgot that the entire reason she had come was to drink beer. "Oh yeah, just get me some sort of pale ale or something."

Jonah nodded and walked up to the bar, getting in line. The noise was booming inside the Sand Dollar as people chatted away, unaware of anyone's troubles but their own. When Jonah got to the front of the line, he observed the bartender. The man was tall and thin with dreadlocks stretching down his back.

"Wassup, man?"

"Uh, yeah, can I get a Conde Blondie and a Brutal IPA, please?"

"Definitely, man." The bartender nodded with an enthusiastic smile. Jonah thought to himself that the guy probably paid way too much attention to horoscopes and astrological charts. The dude pulled the lever of the tap for each of the beers, holding them just long enough so that the beverages frothed as high as it could go without tumbling over the edge of the glasses.

"Fourteen bucks." The bartender placed the drinks on the bar.

Jesus, thought Jonah as he handed the bartender his debit card. "Keep it open," Jonah said, referring to his tab. He walked back over to the table and placed the beer in front of Daisy before sitting down.

"Have you tried the cider here?" she asked, attempting to make some sort of alcohol-related conversation.

"No. I'm not really a cider guy."

Daisy looked a little crestfallen at her failed attempt to start a back-and-forth about drinks. This was one of the reasons Jonah knew it was a short-term fling that he had with Daisy. Their ability to hold a conversation with each other was not strong. They liked similar things, but they just didn't have the corresponding personalities to communicate properly.

"So you are writing the story on the girl who died?" Daisy asked bluntly. Jonah had told her as much via text.

"Yeah, I am. Did two interviews for it today."

"With who?"

"The girl's grandmother and her boss."

"How did it go?"

"Not too bad," said Jonah. "Her boss was kind of a dick. Only let himself be interviewed for about five minutes. The grandmother was a colorful person, to say the least. Was as emotionally distraught as you would expect. That conversation went to some strange places."

"How do you mean?"

Jonah stopped, mulling over whether he should tell Daisy. The last thing he needed was for the town to be beset by gossip because of his inability to keep secrets. However, he decided that Daisy was trustworthy enough to keep it between them; he had entrusted her with secrets about a story before and she had not spread it around, as far as he knew.

"Well, please don't tell anyone this."

Daisy's eyes lit up and she placed her hands on the table as if she was bracing herself. "I won't."

"The grandmother seems to think that it wasn't a suicide."

Daisy's mouth fell open. "What on earth? Like she thinks she was murdered?"

"Yeah."

Daisy shook her head. "Wow. I can't believe that."

"It's bullshit. There is no way."

"Yeah, I mean, didn't people see her jump?"

"Well, no. They just saw the body hit the water. But the girl texted the grandmother three different times, telling her what she was about to do. Like, there is no way someone kidnapped the girl, texted the grandmother from her stolen phone, and threw her off the bridge. Even saying it out loud makes me feel silly."

Though Jonah said this, something in the deep recesses of his brain stirred, as if it might be more plausible than he was willing to admit.

"Grief is a powerful thing," said Daisy. "Makes people rationalize things. She probably can't bring herself to admit that the girl was depressed."

"That's what I am thinking."

There was a lull in their conversation, as Jonah contemplated suicide and irrational grandmothers.

"Did she tell the cops that?"

"No, I don't think so. She just told the cops that the girl was missing and read them what the texts said. She was afraid that the cops would just think she was a nut if she told them what she really thought. Then again, I feel like the police probably should have asked her about it." Now that he thought about it, it seemed odd that Teresa had spent an entire day at the station and the police hadn't gotten any sort of notion from her that she didn't think Katie had killed herself.

Daisy leaned forward with a morose expression on her face. "That is actually really sad. That she has to tell herself that."

"Yeah."

Jonah and Daisy spent several more minutes discussing the peculiarity regarding Teresa's theory. Part of Jonah remained a little curious about the whole thing, but he couldn't rationally bring himself to consider foul play for more than a couple seconds. Half of it was the fact that it seemed impossible, and the other half was that he didn't want to get laughed at by his colleagues for stirring up drama if it turned out to be patently false. Eventually, there was another break in the dialogue. Daisy looked a little sad. Jonah thought maybe she could tell at times their relationship wasn't going anywhere.

"I have to go to the bathroom." Daisy rose from her seat.

"Okay. I'll be here."

Daisy slithered in between the tightly packed tables, heading toward the restrooms. Jonah pulled out his phone and scrolled through his Facebook feed. He then overheard a shred of conversation from a nearby table.

"No, that isn't what I am saying."

"Yes, it is, Sherry. It is exactly what you're saying."

"I'm just saying she fits the MO of the guy."

"That was twenty years ago, Sher."

Jonah sat up straighter in his chair, listening. The woman, apparently named Sherry, looked a little like white trash. She had on a camo coat and blue jeans. Her thick, curly black hair cascaded well past her shoulders. Her teeth were brown and her voice was hoarse. The man matched her in hillbilly attire, donning a heavy Carhartt jacket and a filthy-looking baseball cap with some sort of deer insignia on it. The couple appeared to be at least in their fifties.

"You got a problem there, son?"

Jonah almost jumped when the man addressed him. He was so engrossed in their conversation and their getups that he hadn't realized he was staring at them and had fallen into a bit of a stupor. "No, sorry."

"See, you say things like that, and people begin to stare," said the man.

"I really don't care," Sherry said, although her facial expression seemed to counter the words that came out of her mouth.

"Anyway, that has nothing to do with the Deeds girl," the man said.

Time froze as the weight of the man's statement pressed down upon Jonah. Had the couple overheard his and Daisy's conversation and started a similar one of their own?

"What doesn't have anything to do with the Deeds girl?" Jonah asked before he could stop himself. For a moment, the man only looked at him.

"Nothing. Show some respect."

"Earl—"

"Don't 'Earl' me." The man stood from the table suddenly. "I'm getting another beer." He stomped to the end of the line, evidently extremely irritated with his wife.

Jonah looked at Sherry with an apologetic expression. "I'm sorry about that, I didn't mean to intrude."

"It's fine. He's just a bit of a hothead," said Sherry. "It wasn't a big deal anyway. When things like this happen, people are going to talk."

Jonah considered her, wondering whether to proceed. Finally, the curiosity in his gut got the better of him. "So what were you talking about?"

Sherry glanced over to the bar at Earl. "Well, he's right, it probably doesn't have anything to do with this," she said.

"What doesn't have anything to do with this?"

"Those girls in the nineties."

Jonah had no idea what the woman was talking about.

"Which girls?"

"The ones who were murdered."

7

Jonah couldn't help but choke on his drink. He coughed incessantly for fifteen seconds as Sherry repeatedly asked if he was alright.

Jonah waved off her concern.

"Are you sure?"

"Yeah." Jonah coughed. Finally he cleared his throat. "There were girls who were murdered in Newport?"

"Yeah. By a serial killer. Five of them, in the eighties and nineties. Never caught the guy. The cases went cold, but the DA reopened them together about eight years ago. They still didn't find anything."

Jonah's mind started whirring at light speed. "How on earth have I not heard about this?"

Sherry shrugged. "Well, it was more than twenty years ago."

"How did they conclude that it was a serial killer?"

"Because of the type of victim. All five girls had disappeared while walking alone late at night. And they were all teenagers.

They found the skull of the first girl in an abandoned car."

Jonah suddenly felt nauseated. "The skull?"

"Yeah, they found it over by the reservoir. They didn't find it until ten years after she disappeared neither. She went missing in eighty-four, and they found the skull in ninety-four."

"What about the other girls?"

"Two of them were camping when they left their tent and vanished in ninety-two. The other two were last seen walking by the highway three years after that."

"So all of the girls but the first were abducted in pairs?"

"That's right."

Jonah was left speechless as he thought. "I still don't know how I haven't heard about this."

"Are you a local?"

"No, I grew up in Portland."

Sherry nodded, raising her hand a little to accentuate her point. "There you go."

Jonah still thought it was strange that this subject was new to him. "Did they ever have any suspects?"

"For a while they thought it was a guy who died in prison. Bobby something-or-other."

"Bobby," repeated Jonah.

"Yeah, but they backed away from that theory pretty darn quick."

"I wonder why."

Sherry shrugged again.

"Do you remember the names of any of the girls?"

"I think one was named Kylie," Sherry said.

Jonah then remembered how this whole topic had come up in the first place. "So you think this is connected to Katie Deeds?"

"No, it probably isn't. I'm just saying, she fits the description. Young girl, walking alone at night."

"But didn't the other girls just disappear? They weren't found the following day like Katie. And Katie sent those texts." Jonah began to doubt Sherry's credibility.

"I'm not saying it totally fits," said Sherry, turning a little pink in the cheeks. "I'm just saying it's weird."

"Yeah," said Jonah, internally judging Sherry for sounding like a conspiracy theorist.

Sherry looked up as Earl approached the table, returning with a beer in his hand. Jonah turned away, hoping the man would not make any rude remarks after Jonah had clearly been talking to his wife.

"Got myself the hazelnut." Earl lifted his beer to show her.

"That sounds good." Sherry smiled.

Jonah stayed still, taking small sips of what remained of his beer. He felt the warmth of his buzz in his brain as he contemplated what Sherry had said. Surely it was all an exaggerated campfire story. If there ever had been a serial killer in Newport, he would have heard about it.

Jonah wondered what was taking Daisy so long. He was eager for her to return so that he could cross-check Sherry's statement about the murdered girls. Just when he was beginning to worry about her, Daisy reappeared.

"Sorry, I just redid some of my makeup. I didn't realize how crooked my eyeliner was until I got into the bathroom."

Jonah hadn't noticed Daisy's eyeliner, but he decided to let the moment pass. He then looked directly at her.

"I have something I want to ask you about."

"Uh, okay."

"Can we go outside so you can smoke or something?" Jonah glanced at Earl.

"Uh, sure." She looked nervous, as if she suspected Jonah were about to break it off with her. As they shuffled to the back patio of the bar for the designated smoking area, Jonah looked back. Earl was staring at him with narrowed eyes. He ignored this and stepped outside.

Daisy rubbed her thighs awkwardly as she faced Jonah. "So,

what's up?"

"This isn't what you think," said Jonah, half laughing.

"I don't think anything."

"Okay. Well, this is going to be random."

Daisy chuckled and tucked her hair behind her ear. "I love random."

"Yeah, you're probably going to think it is weird that I pulled you outside to ask you about this, but I just want to know if you know anything about any teenage girls who went missing in the nineties."

Daisy looked immensely relieved, which was somewhat amusing considering Jonah had just asked her about murder victims. "Well, there were those two girls who were found out by Moolack Beach."

"Just two?"

Daisy gave him a side eye. "Yeah, why?"

"There was a woman in there sitting next to us who started talking to me about it when you went to the bathroom. She said there was five victims, and that the police thought it was the work of a serial killer. Her husband apparently thought it was offensive that she brought it up. That's why I wanted to come outside."

Daisy raised her eyebrows. "No, I hadn't heard all of that. I just remember the two girls. Why did this get brought up? Do you usually swap stories about serial killers with strangers in bars?"

Jonah laughed. "I try not to, but it does happen on occasion. I know this sounds far-fetched, but the woman brought it up because of Katie."

Daisy initially looked shocked, but then her face morphed into an amused expression. "What the hell?"

"Yeah, I know."

"Like she thinks that Katie didn't commit suicide? That she was murdered by the same person who killed those girls?"

"I told you it sounded far-fetched."

"Man. First what you told me about the grandmother and now this. Is everyone in this town on drugs?"

"Guess so."

Daisy removed a purple lighter from her coat pocket and lit the end of the cigarette she was holding. The light drizzle had stopped, but the wind had picked up. It was starting to get cold outside. Jonah looked out over the bay, and again with a shiver down his spine, he imagined Katie's body hitting the water.

"So there were actually two girls found at Moolack beach?"

"Not on the beach itself, but in the woods nearby, yeah." Daisy blew out a puff of smoke.

"When was this?"

"Shit, I don't know."

Jonah let this sink in for a minute. He wasn't sure what to make of it. He didn't put any stock into the cold cases being in any way related to what happened to Katie, but he was curious to know more about them. He watched as Daisy took gigantic drags on her cigarette, letting the cancerous fumes fill her lungs.

"I still can't believe I didn't know about this," said Jonah.

Jonah and Daisy returned to their table, and Jonah noticed Sherry and Earl had gone. He would've liked to have spoken more in depth with Sherry, but it wasn't to be. Jonah and Daisy spent the next half hour drinking another beer each, before deciding to depart. Jonah figured it probably was not safe to drive with more than two beers in his system anyway.

As they left the Sand Dollar and made their way back to Jonah's car that was parked up the hill from the bar, Jonah looked across the street. Poseidon's Nightclub shook from the deafening music playing inside. Outside was a group of young adults in a semicircle. They all seemed to look slightly forlorn, but perhaps that was just reflective of how Jonah felt as he walked alongside Daisy.

He knew she would ask to come back to his apartment. Before he had even gone out that night, he had hoped that they would end up next to each other in his bed, but the night spent with Daisy seemed to have eradicated that desire. Not because she was undesirable; they just didn't have the chemistry, and Jonah didn't like to sleep with a woman if he was sure he didn't have a connection with her. He knew it in his heart that she wasn't right for him, but he felt conflicted. He wasn't ready to go back to the lonely existence of having no one to speak to, and he wasn't sure how to tell Daisy. It was quite the conundrum.

As they approached his car, Daisy looked at him. "So, back to your place?"

Jonah didn't respond, letting the silence speak for him.

Daisy frowned a little. "Or not?"

"I'm sorry, Daisy, I just don't think it's a good idea tonight."

Daisy stared at him, raising an eyebrow.

"Okay."

Jonah was surprised. In fact, he even felt a slight twinge of annoyance. She was supposed to protest and act heartbroken, as if her carnal desire for his sweet lovemaking had been withdrawn viciously from her grasp. His ego roared in protest.

Without another word, Daisy hopped into his car. On the drive over to the apartments where Daisy lived, the pair remained completely silent. Jonah could tell that she was eager to be rid of him as she tapped her foot and refused to look in his direction; apparently, denying her sex was the ultimate sin. When he went to drop her off, she sprung out of the car without a good-bye. As Jonah flipped a U-turn and sped back toward his own apartment, he was officially pissed. Although it was his decision to negate the relationship, he had not expected her to act like such a petulant child. In his heart, Jonah knew that getting angry was pointless; he would likely never see Daisy again anyway. And yet, it still ate at him. It wasn't that he wanted her.

It was the fact that he wanted to be wanted by her. He desired validation, yet she acted like his decision to end things with her wasn't a big deal to her at all. It made him feel insignificant.

Once Jonah arrived at his place and began trudging up the steps of his apartment in Agate Beach, he started to reflect on the day. Overall, it was a pretty shitty experience. He had conducted two awful interviews, and although he achieved a state of ambivalence for a while due to the alcohol, his buzz had worn off thanks to Daisy's shortness. He opened the door to his living room and kicked off his shoes with more ferocity than was probably necessary. Plunking himself onto the couch, he let his eyes lose their focus.

The only upside to his night was the realization that the story he had written about Katie would be printed tomorrow in a quick one-column report. He would probably receive several texts from his friends after the story ran, wondering if he knew any more about why Katie had killed herself. He might reply to a couple of them.

On the floor he noticed his laptop. *Oh, what the hell,* he thought. He picked it up and flipped it open. Distracting himself from his anger was probably a good thing anyway. It was time to find out more about the girls who had been killed.

8

The rain outside fell in heavy sheets and the wind howled angrily. A full-blown storm had broken out, making Jonah feel much more alert as he begun typing.

The first thing he searched for was "missing girl's skull recovered Newport, Oregon," and the initial hit on Google was an archived story from *The Oregonian*. It was a piece written by a man named David Browning and was printed on June 7, 1994.

> *The remains of Kylie Desmond were recovered on Monday in Newport, Oregon, where the girl went missing nearly a decade ago in August 1984. Desmond's skull was found in an abandoned 1987 Ford Taurus early on Monday morning by a team of forensic investigators, following a tip received from a transient who had been traveling east on Big Creek Road.*
>
> *Desmond, 14, was last seen at the theater in Newport at*

a showing of the movie Red Dawn *on August 12, 1984. She had been walking home alone on Highway 101 after the movie when she went missing.*

"I am completely devastated," said Kenny Desmond, Kylie's father. "Even after all this time I still held out hope that she was alive."

Though they have no solid leads, authorities believe Desmond's death may be associated with the May 13, 1992 disappearances of 16-year-old Felicity Sanders and 15-year-old Shelly Schwartz, who were last seen near a phone booth on Highway 101 after leaving their tent while camping at Beverly Beach State Park. Their bodies were recovered five months later, 20 miles east of Newport.

"There is no definitive proof, but we think the two cases might be connected," said Sheriff Tim Connely.

The recovery of Desmond's remains brings to end a mystery of nearly ten years. Desmond was beloved in the small coastal community of Newport, says Connely, and her disappearance shook the town to its core.

"It didn't end the way we wanted it to, but I am just glad that we can give the family and friends some closure."

Sources say the next step for police is using the evidence recovered in the abandoned car to establish a link between Desmond's murder and the list of preliminary suspects that was created in 1984.

"Hopefully our guys can find something that will help us

> *bring the killer of an innocent 14-year-old girl to justice," said Connely.*

Jonah stared at the screen for a good thirty seconds after he had finished reading. Sherry hadn't just been blowing smoke. In fact, Jonah was surprised at how accurate the woman's recounter of the facts had been. For being such a random person, Sherry had provided a hefty amount of detail. Perhaps it was common in small towns for the facts of a case to spread like wildfire.

Jonah began to feel uneasy. A killer in Newport? And one who targeted teenage girls? Everything he knew about the coastal community countered the possibility something as malignant as this could ever exist in such a benign place, even twenty years previously. The rain that slammed against the window of Jonah's apartment seemed to get louder. It was as if the elements outside had turned sinister.

Jonah scrolled up the page and clicked the *back* button on the browser. He erased his previous search and typed in "missing girls Moolack Beach." Again, the most relevant result in Google was a story from *The Oregonian* by Micah Morris. It read, "Bodies of Teenage Girls Found North of Newport." It was from June 11, 1995.

> *The bodies of Jenna Eason, 16, and Cara Lee, 14, were found in the woods near Moolack Beach on Saturday afternoon, according to Newport police. Eason and Lee disappeared approximately two weeks ago while walking north on Highway 101 about a mile from where their bodies were recovered.*

> *Newport police located the bodies after a 12-day search of the area. The young girls, who attended Newport High School, had told their friend that they were planning on returning to Eason's house after visiting*

her, and headed toward the family's home in Agate Beach on foot. They were walking along the highway when they were last seen by passing motorists at 2 a.m. on May 29.

"We are deeply saddened by this tragic turn of events," said Sheriff John Paxon. "Our thoughts and prayers go out to the families of these beautiful young girls."

Though Coroner Aaron Dobbs, who conducted the autopsies, was not ready to estimate a time of death for the two girls, he did say that they appeared to have been strangled.

Paxon says he realizes the surrounding community will be quick to associate the girls's deaths with those of Felicity Sanders and Shelly Schwartz, who also disappeared while walking alone on the same highway in May of 1992, but he urged residents to not jump to any conclusions.

"We realize the circumstances are similar," said Paxon. "But we have absolutely no evidence that these deaths are related yet."

Sanders and Schwartz were also found buried in a secluded wooded area, and had been strangled.

Instead of automatically focusing on suspects, Paxon says to be empathetic to those in the community who knew the two girls.

"I get that we all want to know who did it, and no one more so than me. However, let me remind everyone that

the families of these girls will never be the same. Focus on them, and not on the monster who so recklessly disposed of these children," said Paxon. "That's what they were. Kids."

Paxon said that as of Saturday evening, the police had no immediate suspects in the deaths of Eason and Lee, though they were working around the clock to try and apprehend the perpetrator.

"We will find who did this," said Paxon. "I promise you that."

Jonah realized after he finished reading that he had been holding his breath and let out a long exhale. He withdrew his hands from the keyboard and found that they were perspiring heavily. Zoning out for five minutes, Jonah processed what he had just read. It was abundantly clear to him that the two pairs of girls who had been killed were done so by the same person. A set of two girls last seen walking alone at night, found strangled to death in a wooded area sometime after? To pretend that the two cases weren't connected was ridiculous.

Jonah felt in his gut that Kylie Desmond, the first girl whose skull had been found by the reservoir, was also the victim of the same killer. She had to be. She also had been walking alone on Highway 101 when she was abducted. The killer had covered his tracks better with Desmond than he had with the other girls, though. Ten years was a long time to go missing. With an eerie feeling, Jonah wondered if the killer had intentionally planted Desmond's skull in the Ford Taurus to taunt the police. *I'm still here. You have stopped thinking about me, but I haven't stopped thinking of them.* That's what it seemed like the killer was trying to say.

Sherry hadn't just been musing about an urban legend. She

had been telling a shockingly accurate version of events. Jonah tried to dive into the depths of his memory and retrieve the conversation he'd had with Sherry verbatim. What else had she said about the missing girls? What other details had she provided? Jonah quickly withdrew a pen and his notepad and began to sketch out the details to try and make further connections.

With a jolt, Jonah remembered that she said that the district attorney reopened the cases together somewhat recently. He again deleted the terms of his last Google search and typed in "district attorney Newport reopens murder case." It wasn't the top hit in the search results this time, but it didn't take him long to find the *Oregonian* story that a woman named Cheyenne Blue had written. It was dated January 24, 2009. "DA Reopens Five Homicides From the '90s in Newport," read the headline. The piece was more like long-form journalism than a breaking-news story:

> *In the early hours of a rainy May morning in Newport, two teenage girls left a friend's house and began to trek home. They were never seen again. Two weeks later, police found the bodies of Jenna Eason, 16, and Cara Lee, 14, in a forest north of town. The girls had been strangled.*
>
> *This May will mark the 14th anniversary of their disappearance.*
>
> *Now, Dan Jenkins, Lincoln County's longtime district attorney, has reopened the case, along with four other unsolved homicides that spanned from 1984 to 1995. Jenkins is hopeful that advances in DNA technology will be able to substantiate new clues and direct police to the killer.*

It also may answer a question that has haunted local police in Newport for more than two decades: Is there a serial killer in the small coastal town?

"We all have been thinking about that question for years," said Daryl Close, a retired Oregon State Police detective.

Since 1984, there have been five unsolved homicides of teenage girls in the area. All the cases bear similarities and two of them are close to identical.

In separate cases, there were two victims who were friends. In each, the girls were last seen north of town late at night or very early in the morning, and all four were found strangled. The bodies of all the girls were also recovered in two heavily-wooded areas.

Investigators say their best hope of finding the culprit is with the evidence found on Eason and Lee, because their bodies were discovered only two weeks after they had disappeared, while the other girls had been missing for five months, and in one case, ten years.

"I have been waiting a long time for the technology to do this," said Close. "These girls deserve justice."

Kylie Desmond, 15, was the first to vanish. She was last seen walking north on Highway 101 after a showing of the movie Red Dawn *in August 1984. For ten years, no one knew what had happened to her. In June 1994, police were notified of an abandoned car at the Newport Reservoir. Inside, they found Desmond's skull.*

In 1992, Shelly Schwartz and Felicity Sanders, both residents of Lincoln City, 20 miles north of Newport, went camping at Beverly Beach State Park on May 13 with Sanders's family for a weeklong camping trip. However, after one night, the two girls disappeared. The pair had left the family's tent and were last seen at a pay phone on Highway 101.

Five months later, on October 10, their bodies were recovered in a forest near Eddyville, a town 20 miles east of Newport.

Three years after, Eason and Lee were watching videos at their friend Maya Leslie's house on Northwest 63rd Street at approximately 1:30 a.m. As they prepared to leave, Lee asked Leslie whether she could call her and said that if she didn't hear from her in an hour, she should call the police. Lee and Eason were never heard from again.

Leslie had reportedly asked Lee why she heeded the warning, but Lee refused to tell her.

"It was like she knew she was in danger and she shouldn't be walking home by herself. To this day I think her killer had been stalking her before then, and Cara had noticed something weird," said Leslie. "She sensed someone was hunting her."

When the girls were found two weeks later, it was a grisly scene. The bodies were found, one on top of the other, covered with brush and debris. An autopsy revealed that the girls died from asphyxiation.

> *Jenkins says that finding the killer is something that still keeps him up at night.*
>
> *"To think about what happened to these innocent young girls makes me sick to my stomach," says Jenkins. "Even after all these years, I still sometimes lose sleep over what happened to them. I have faith in our new technology that we will be able to solve these crimes and give the community some much-needed closure."*

There it was. The truth staring back at Jonah in a perfectly linear and clear fashion. There had been a serial killer in Lincoln County, that much was clear. Where the person was now being the real question.

Jonah felt somewhat disturbed sitting alone in his apartment. To think that at this very moment there could be a dormant killer living within a few miles of him made his skin crawl. The rain continued to beat down aggressively on the pavement outside. He looked uneasily out the window. The darkness outside threatened to envelope him if he stared for much longer, so he looked away. He supposed he ought to close his blinds.

What was equally as baffling was the fact that Jonah had lived and reported in the area for two years, and this story had eluded him the whole time. Sure, it had taken place two decades ago, but the fact that he had heard about it from some hillbilly at the bar made Jonah question his ability as a reporter. If he didn't have a nose for an ordeal such as this, what other stories had he missed?

Jonah tried to reflect more on what Sherry had said about the case. He suddenly remembered that she had told him that the only clear suspect they'd had was a man named "Bobby something-or-other." Jonah erased his Google search for the third time, and typed in "Bobby serial killer Oregon." The name Bobby Ray Foles popped up as the first hit. Jonah clicked on the man's Wikipedia page.

> *Bobby Ray Foles (June 12, 1940 - May 15, 2006) was an American rapist and an alleged serial killer in the United States and Canada. He died in prison of prostate cancer during a 15-year sentence following a conviction for rape, kidnapping and attempted rape in Newport, Oregon, in 1996.*
>
> *Foles was a construction worker who was known to travel extensively around North America. He lived in a total of eight states, including Florida, Iowa, Louisiana, Texas, Oregon, South Carolina, Tennessee and Washington.*
>
> *In 1970, he was charged with murdering a couple in Texas, but was never convicted of the crime. Foles spent the majority of the '70s and '80s in British Columbia, Canada, where he was known to have committed several violent offenses.*

Jonah scrolled down to a section on the page that was titled *Suspected Victims*. It said that Foles was a suspect in at least fifteen murders, dating as far back as 1970.

> *Highway of Tears: Foles is a suspect in the Highway of Tears murders. His DNA was found on the body of Carrie McDonald, one of the presumed victims. Foles is also suspected to have killed both Gale Woods and Pam Fisher in 1973. He is believed to have killed as many as 10 of the other victims and possibly as many as 20.*

Potential Canadian victims include those reported missing from Highway 16, a roadway nicknamed the "Highway of Tears" due to the high number of murders and disappearances of women on the road in the 1970s.

So Foles was a person of interest in a famous serial-murder case from the 1970s. However, it said nothing on the page about Foles being in any way connected to the murders of the teenage girls in Lincoln County. Jonah could see why Foles would have been a suspect. A semi-famous serial killer who was arrested in Newport for rape a year after the final victims had been found. That seemed like more than just a coincidence.

But according to the timeline of Foles's activity, he would not have been in Newport when Kylie Desmond disappeared in 1984. Was Jonah to believe that a teenage girl who had been murdered after walking alone on Highway 101 was not connected to the four other teenage girls who had been killed in the exact same fashion?

Another thing that bothered Jonah while he was examining other elements of the webpage was the fact that Foles had probably murdered at least ten women in their twenties and thirties during the seventies. But not teenage girls. Never someone as young as fourteen-year-old Kylie Desmond.

If it wasn't Foles, did the real killer just go dormant for twenty years? Had he died or just lost his appetite for killing? The latter seemed unlikely. The most disturbing possibility was that the real killer had continued killing unbeknownst to the police.

Jonah began to dwell on Katie Deeds. He was still inclined to think that her death was a suicide. However, he had to admit that there were some similarities between Katie and the other girls. All were local to Lincoln County, and Katie had also been walking by herself when she disappeared. But Katie was twenty-one and the other girls had all been under seventeen. Katie had been found the day after she vanished, while the girls had been found weeks, months, and even years after. Most importantly, there were the texts. If Katie had been abducted by the same killer, he would have had to completely change his method of operation to send those texts.

Still, something gnawed at Jonah's stomach about the case as he began to close the tabs of his browser and shut his computer. He knew that it would take him awhile to fall asleep as his mind revolved around the murdered teenage girls. The eerie possibility that a serial killer was still in Newport seemed to bear down on Jonah like an evil spirit.

Jonah started shuffling through the pages of his notepad, looking for his notes on the interview with Teresa Deeds. He finally located what he was looking for: a name scribbled onto the upper right corner of the notepad. Charles Johnson. Jonah still had not begun to accept the possibility that anything suspicious had happened, but talking with one of the last people who had seen Katie Deeds alive couldn't hurt.

9

The man entered the shed, ducking to avoid hitting his head. He fumbled in the darkness for the string to the light, eventually locating it and pulling. The shed became illuminated, and the man moved toward the table in the center of it.

On the table sat twelve items: a compass, a musty-looking water bottle, a package of gum, a silver earring, two bracelets, a tampon, a bottle of pepper spray, a gold necklace, two rings, and a bright orange lighter. The man picked up the lighter with his gloved hand for a moment and felt himself getting hard.

He set the lighter back down on the table and approached the opposing wall. Nailed to the wall was a photograph of Katie Deeds. The man had taken the photograph several months ago when she was walking into Mason's Coffee. She had been crossing the street and glanced back toward the parking lot, frowning at the "tourist" who was pointing his camera in her direction. The thought that Katie had seen the man several times without thinking anything of it aroused him.

The man had kept the photograph of Katie hung on the wall ever since he began targeting her. It was a source of inspiration for the man—a way to motivate him to keep working to accomplish his goal even through all the late nights walking across the bridge and following Katie to different spots around Newport.

The photos were tradition, after all. Over the past thirty years, whenever he had set his sights on a new target, he would hang her picture on the wall of the old shed, letting it incubate until the girl was dead. When he had accomplished his goal, he would tear down the picture and burn it.

The first few kills had been the most difficult. He was almost embarrassed to remember his time as a fledgling killer. He had thought that burying them in secluded areas would be sufficient, but it obviously had not been. Combine that with his preference for strangulation, and he had almost gotten caught.

Ever since that damn woman had come to interview him, he realized he had to change his tactic. The woman had never suspected him, but she had pieced together far more than he ever thought was possible. He had to commend her for that. But he needed to change. Unlike most killers, he did not want credit for his crimes. He couldn't spend the rest of his life in a cell. Therefore, he had evolved. Every kill since Jenna Eason and Cara Lee, he had used a different method to do the deed. He had begun to put all his effort into making them look like accidents, runaways, and suicides. The man had always waited for a certain amount of time to pass between crimes, in case the police had gotten on his trail. If the kill had gone smoothly, he wouldn't wait as long. If not, he would go dormant for a while.

The man tore down the photo of Katie from the wall and took his lighter from his pocket. A brilliant thought then came to him. Instead of looking further for his own, he grabbed the orange lighter off the table and used it to ignite the corner of the photo. *It's better this way,* he thought. He smiled greedily as he watched it burn in his hand, before dropping it to the ground.

The man reached inside his coat and withdrew a nail and the photograph of the young blonde he had taken earlier that day. He had never had this quick of a turnaround before, but the death of Katie had gone so well that he felt like he could risk it. He shoved the nail into the wall, pinning the photograph of his new target against it.

10

The phone rang several times before Teresa Deeds picked up. Her voice sounded weak. Perhaps the grief had begun to set in.

"Hello?"

"Hi, Teresa?"

"Yes, who's this?"

"Jonah Carr, from the *Times*."

"Yeah, I saw the story. Read it first thing this morning. You did a good job."

Jonah was taken aback. "Thank you, Teresa, but that actually was not why I was calling."

"Oh," she said, sounding apprehensive.

Jonah waited, unsure of how to phrase his next question. "The reason I was calling was because you mentioned Katie was with someone named Charles Johnson the night she died."

"Yes… And?"

"Do you have any contact info for Charles?"

There was a long pause.

"And why would you need that? The story is already published."

"I know, I am just piecing together her night," Jonah said, offering a feeble explanation. It was as if he could hear Teresa's frown through the phone.

"Piecing it together? Why would you need to do that for?"

Jonah was stumped. He couldn't figure out how to explain his reasoning for needing to speak with Charles without sounding like an idiot. Heck, he wasn't even sure *why* he wanted to talk to Charles. He knew that if he gave in and told her that he was questioning the nature of her death she would provide him with the information he sought. But, again, if this all turned out to be a false trail he didn't want to get her hopes up.

"I just need to make sure of something."

"Make sure of what?" The woman was making this very difficult.

Fuck it, thought Jonah. "I am just trying to make sure that she really did leave in the direction of the bridge."

Teresa gasped.

"Look, I didn't find anything, and I have no reason to think it wasn't a suicide. I am just making sure we cover our tracks."

"I don't know if I have any contact information for Charles."

Jonah heard her scrambling around.

"He came over here a few times. He and Katie were pretty close. But I can't think of any reason why I would have his phone—Wait! I don't need his number. He works at the brewery. You should be able to find him there."

The Rogue Brewery. That was what Teresa meant.

"Thanks, Teresa, I really appreciate it. I will let you know if anything comes of it." Jonah hung up before Teresa could get in another word.

An hour later, Jonah swung his car into the lot of the brewery on the south side of Newport. It was an odd structure. Three massive spheres jutted awkwardly into the air, and the word "Rogue" was horizontally emblazoned in a gargantuan font on the side of one of the spheres. There were three large parking areas outside of the building that were almost completely empty. The brewery sat next to the bay, within shouting distance of the bridge, which towered over the water below. It was an overcast day, and the water appeared murkier underneath the cloud cover.

Jonah got out of his vehicle and approached the entrance to the building. One of the spheres proffered a small archway, which was where patrons could enter. He passed underneath the archway, and came into a huge hallway with a roof that had to be at least thirty feet high. There was a black arrow that was plastered to the nearby wall, pointing toward a door. Underneath the arrow, a sign said Offices.

Jonah walked into the main office and saw a gruff-looking man sitting at a desk. His thick arms contrasted jarringly with his tiny head. He had the beginnings of a beard, as if he hadn't shaven in a couple of days. His facial structure reminded Jonah of an orc from *Lord of the Rings.*

"Hey, I'm looking for Charles Johnson," Jonah said without any introduction.

The man narrowed his eyes and looked him up and down, apparently deciding if Jonah was worthy of speaking with Charles.

"One sec." He rose from the desk, and Jonah noticed that he was incredibly tall as he lumbered out of a back doorway. He returned two minutes later followed by a weaselly-looking kid with shifty eyes.

"Hi, are you Charles?"

"Yeah."

"Nice to meet you." Jonah held out his hand. Charles grasped it briefly before relinquishing his grip, as if touching Jonah's hand might give him a terrible illness.

"I was wondering if you had a few minutes to talk to me about your friend Katie Deeds."

Charles's eyes bulged. "Are you a cop?"

Jonah smiled and shook his head. "No, I work for the *News Times.*"

"What do you want to know?"

"Mind if we step outside?"

"Can I smoke?" Charles leaned against the outside of the building.

Jonah looked at him, bemused. "I'm not your father. You could light a joint for all I care."

Charles gave him a sheepish grin, displaying a wide array of crooked teeth. He gave off the faint onion-like scent of body odor. Withdrawing a cigarette from the pack he pulled out of his pocket, Charles started struggling to light it. The wind had picked up outside.

"Here." Jonah offered his hand to cup the lighter so that it would produce flame. The fire sprouted and touched the tip of Charles's cigarette. He inhaled deeply.

"Thanks, man," he said.

"No problem."

The two stood in silence for a few seconds, listening to the sounds of the surrounding coastal dwelling. Seagulls cawed loudly, and in the distance, Jonah could faintly hear sea lions barking. The only other noise was the tide splashing against the rocks, just on the other side of the brewery.

"I understand that you were with Katie the night she died."

Charles looked up at him with a stony expression. "Yeah."

"I realize how difficult this must be for you."

"Yeah," Charles repeated in a monotone voice, looking at the ground.

"You and Katie were close?"

Charles's eyes seemed to dampen. "She was my best friend, man."

Jonah felt a pang of sympathy for the kid. No one that young should have to deal with the tragedy of losing his best friend.

"I'm really sorry."

"Yeah."

Jonah wasn't quite sure what to say next. "Did she seem okay when you were hanging out?"

Charles nodded his head and looked at the ground sadly. "Yeah, man, totally. She seemed completely fine. She always was. I can't believe she wanted to do what she did."

"Suicide is always a shock. I am sorry that you have to deal with this."

Charles didn't say anything. He just continued to stare at the concrete.

"She never gave off any sort of signs that she was depressed? I know it's tough to think about, but please try and remember, Charles. This is important."

Charles looked up at him, evidently confused. "Are you writing her obituary or something?"

It was somewhat funny to Jonah that Charles had just thought of this question now, after he had already begun to give an interview. He clearly wasn't thinking straight.

"No. I already wrote the story that ran in the *Times* today."

"Then why is it important to you to know if she was depressed? She killed herself, man. Obviously, she had to have been depressed."

"I guess I just want to know if you noticed anything unusual that night."

Charles glared at Jonah. "Unusual? What the hell? What do you even mean by that?"

Jonah maintained an even tone while he replied. "I just want to know if you noticed her acting strange, or if you encountered anybody that night who struck you as odd."

Charles looked for a second as if someone had hit him over the head with a hammer. "Anyone acting strange?" His voice rose. "Man, are you saying what I think you're saying?"

"I'm not saying anything," Jonah said quickly, although he knew it was too late. Charles had already gone down a dark path in his head. His eyes began to shift rapidly back and forth as the wheels in his head began to turn faster.

"Are you saying that you think it wasn't a suicide?"

"No, of course not. I'm just trying to get a grasp on how that night went down."

"Man, I ain't stupid," Charles said, although his syntax seemed to counter that proclamation. "You wouldn't have come here to ask me this if you think . . . Wait a second."

"What?"

"There was that weird guy at the bar."

Jonah's stomach did a mini-somersault. "There was a weird guy at the bar?"

Charles nodded fervently. "Katie said he was looking at her funny when we went outside to smoke."

Jonah considered this. It was probably nothing, but there wasn't any harm in seeing if it led anywhere. "What did this guy look like?"

Charles screwed up his forehead as if he were looking directly at the sun, trying to concentrate. "Shit, man, I don't know how to describe him. He had long black hair—"

"How long?"

"Like, to his shoulders about."

"What did his face look like?"

"Like he had been on drugs before."

"What do you mean by that?"

"I don't know, his cheeks were all caved in. And he had like, shadows under his eyes."

"Shadows?"

"Yeah."

Jonah had been writing every word Charles was saying onto his notepad. "Do you know anything about this man?"

"No, not really. I see him a lot."

"Where do you see him?"

"At Rip Tide's. He's there pretty much every time I go there. It's like he lives there."

Jonah interviewed Charles for several more minutes, although he didn't say anything else of consequence. Charles had stayed at the bar after Katie left, so he didn't have any information about what had happened after their rendezvous at Rip Tide's. Katie had gone by herself.

The man with long black hair was the peak of their conversation, and it was a shaky lead at best. Jonah didn't have the man's name, and all he knew was that the man spent a lot of time at Rip Tide's and that he had given Katie a funny look. Not exactly a lot to go on. However, Jonah didn't have to return to the office until later that afternoon, so he decided to swing by the bar and see if he could find the man or ask someone about him. Jonah wasn't even sure why he was pursuing this angle. He knew logically this was going to be pointless. But a slight knot in his chest had developed, as if there were something more that he needed to discover about what had happened that night. He kept thinking of the photograph of Katie on the wall. The image of her radiating smile propelled him forward, motivating him to make things right. He wasn't sure if anything was even wrong, but he had questions. Perhaps this man could provide answers.

Ten minutes later, Jonah pulled into the Nye Beach Turnaround, where Rip Tide's was open for business. He parked near the same spot he had when he had interviewed Rick Casey on the day of Katie's suicide. The bar was not very far from the spot.

The ocean was calm today, as if it were recovering from the

storm the night before. The tide was slowly pulling the water closer to the beach. Jonah ambled up the short hill to the bar. He noticed an elderly couple walking by and gave them a small smile as they passed. The old man and woman were the only other people perusing Nye Beach, which seemed out of place for the summer, even in late August. Usually this part of town was packed with people.

Jonah scoped a white bucket sitting on the ground, doused in cigarette butts. To the left of the bucket he saw the entrance to Rip Tide's and pulled the door open. Jonah had been to the venue several times before, but not in a long while. The place was sort of a dive; he usually didn't mind this, but he felt that Rip Tide's seemed to be perpetually on the precipice of a bar fight.

There were only three people in the bar. One of them was a thin older man who had a handlebar mustache and white hair. The other two were women. Nobody matched the description that Charles had given him. Jonah hadn't expected to find the man, anyway, with as little as he had to go off. Perhaps he could ask the bartender about the man. But he didn't want to just start questioning this person out of the blue, so he decided to order a drink. He perched himself on a flimsy wooden stool and waited for the bartender to come around. Jonah noticed that the bottom of the bar underneath the liquor bottles was covered in what appeared to be large stickers that offered quirky mantras. One of them read, "If you run into an asshole in the morning, you just ran into an asshole. If you run into assholes all day, then you are the asshole." *How profound,* thought Jonah.

The bartender, who was somewhat famous in these parts, slid into Jonah's vision. Even Jonah knew that her name was Patty. She had gleaned a certain level of recognition around Newport because she had been at Rip Tide's for over thirty years and treated everyone who came through as though they had been friends forever. She had short, silver hair that was pulled into a ponytail. Her face was somewhat wrinkled, but she had kind green eyes.

"Hey, what can I get for you, honey?"

"Can I just get a rum and Coke?"

"Is well rum fine, honey?"

"Yeah, that's fine."

Patty withdrew a glass from under the bar and mixed the cocktail. She whipped it up in a matter of seconds. "Thanks," Jonah said as Patty passed him the glass.

Jonah sipped on the beverage for a couple minutes, taking in the scenery around him. A jukebox across the bar was playing some terrible Creed song. *Nothing like an afternoon of rum and butt rock,* thought Jonah. On the ceiling of the bar were several banners that sported the logos of different National Football League teams and there were five flat-screen TVs plastered in various spots around the room. It was still too shoddy to consider Rip Tide's a sports bar, but at least it was trying to be something. Jonah started pondering how to begin questioning Patty as he sipped on his cocktail.

The door to the men's bathroom swung open, catching Jonah's attention. Out of it wandered a tall man with long black hair and hollow cheeks.

Jonah's stomach dropped and his mouth went dry. He stayed frozen for a minute, unsure of what to do next. This man was clearly who Charles had been describing. He looked rather like a crow, with his large nose taking the shape of a beak. It was difficult to guess his age, but Jonah would estimate he was somewhere north of forty. He wore a long trench coat that draped around his feet. Jonah looked him up and down. He had to admit that there was something about the man that made the hairs on the back of his neck stand up. It was as if a sixth sense Jonah possessed was firing off some sort of disturbance signals.

The man meandered across the bar and didn't notice Jonah looking at him. He walked right out of the front door. Trying to act normal, Jonah got up from his stool, threw some cash on the counter to pay for his drink, and followed him out. He had no idea what he was going to do. Hopefully he could catch up to the man and just ask him a few quick questions. The worst that would probably happen was the man refusing to talk to him. He likely didn't have anything to hide and would not hesitate to speak with Jonah.

As Jonah pushed through the door, he was startled to notice his target had only traveled a few feet outside the bar. He stood next to the white bucket and was attempting to light a cigarette. Why did everyone smoke in this town?

Jonah didn't know how else to approach him, so he threw caution to the wind. "Hey, I'm Jonah." He extended his hand.

The man looked Jonah up and down with a surprised expression on his face. For a moment it seemed as if he wouldn't say anything at all, but surprisingly, he clasped his hand with Jonah's.

"Leighton."

Jonah was caught off guard for a second at the strangeness of the name. The man seemed to be middle-aged, and unlike the younger generation, unique names were not as frequent for someone of his age demographic. Gathering himself, Jonah quickly said, "Nice to meet you."

"You too." He had a deep, methodical sounding voice.

"You're probably wondering what the hell I want," Jonah said, attempting to make the man laugh. However, Leighton kept a straight face.

"Thought maybe you wanted a smoke."

"No, no, I don't smoke." Jonah waved his hand around to emphasize his point.

Leighton appraised Jonah, looking unsure of his intent. "Oh."

"I don't want to waste your time, so I'll just get right to it. I work for the *Times*, and I wrote a story on the girl who committed suicide on Sunday night," Jonah said, a little bluntly.

"I know this was the last place she was, and I'm just doing a little follow-up looking for witnesses who may have seen her that night."

Leighton's eyes widened. "What girl?"

"I just said. The girl who jumped off the bridge."

Leighton blinked rapidly, staring at Jonah. He was clearly debating what to say. Instead of answering, the man became suddenly distracted. He had focused his attention on a spot behind Jonah, looking at something in the distance. Jonah look behind him for what had caught the man's eye, but he saw nothing. When he turned back, Jonah's heart stopped. Leighton had taken off running in the opposite direction.

11

Jonah stayed still for a few seconds in complete bewilderment. He was in such a state of shock that his body seemed to be detached from his mind. He couldn't believe what was occurring. When retroactively looking back at what had happened next, Jonah could never rationally explain in his mind why he had chosen to do what he did. But for some reason, he began to run after the man.

Jonah saw Leighton loop around the corner, passing underneath the giant archway that read "Nye Beach Turnaround." The man was a good fifteen feet ahead of him.

"Hey! Wait!" Jonah shouted, finding it hard to summon the air to yell. Leighton looked over his shoulder at Jonah and sped up. Sprinting down the block, he turned to duck down a ramp that led underneath the building to his right. An underground parking garage.

Jonah stopped when he got to the garage entrance. Every cell in his body was on alert, warning him of following. Chasing a scary man through an underground parking structure? It was like the beginning of a nineties slasher flick. Curiosity began to overtake logic, and Jonah ducked down through the entrance way.

It was much darker down below than on the street. There were a couple of lights that were intended to illuminate the structure, but they were feeble at best. Jonah wished he had superhuman vision. There were several vehicles in the garage, but no sign of the man. Jonah's heart thumped at a supersonic pace. Where had Leighton gone? The stark possibility he was lurking behind one of the parked vehicles made Jonah's blood pressure rise higher and higher. Jonah fumbled in his pocket for his phone. He accessed the flashlight app and pointed it in front of him. The man was still not visible.

Jonah craned his neck slowly to the left and right, looking everywhere for where Leighton may have gone. Up ahead the light showed a door tucked into the far left corner of the garage. It was open. He sped up again while putting his phone back in his pocket and then burst through the door.

It took his eyes a minute to adjust to the new setting. He wasn't outside again, but rather indoors. He was surrounded by delicate picture frames and porcelain figurines stacked eloquently on revolving glass structures. It appeared the employee parking structure he had just run through was connected to a gift shop. Judging by the large loop that he had chased Leighton in, he was probably right back at the Nye Beach Turnaround.

Standing behind a cash register on the right side of the shop was an old, bewildered-looking man with brown skin and slanted eyes.

"Which way did he go?" Jonah was barely able to get the words out through his ragged breathing.

The man couldn't seem to find the words to respond, so he just pointed toward the front door. Jonah didn't even apologize for the ruckus that he and Leighton had created as he brushed by him. Jonah wondered if he would call the police, as two strangers had just burst through the back door of his shop at high speeds.

As Jonah pushed his way out of the front door, he immediately recognized his surroundings. Rip Tide's was across the street and twenty feet to the left. Leighton had indeed led him in a circle. The question was, had the man gone right or left when he left the gift shop? Jonah had to make a snap decision, and thus, he went left toward the parking lot, toward his car. He slowed his pace, as he had no idea if he was going in the right direction.

Movement ahead signaled that he was indeed on the correct path. An old, red Ford Mustang sped out of the lot in front of Jonah, barreling toward him. He saw that it was clearly Leighton behind the wheel. For a moment he considered getting in front of the vehicle to see if the man would stop, but he quelled the thought immediately. As Jonah rushed out of the way, he saw Leighton make eye contact as he drove past. Jonah tried to get a glimpse of the license plate on the Mustang as it rumbled up the hill, but he could just make out the letters VXF before the car turned right. There was no use following now. By the time Jonah had made his way back up to Third Street, the Mustang would be out of sight.

Jonah stopped and placed his hands on his head, trying to open his lungs and gather all of the air that he could. If his heart started to beat any faster, it would likely explode. What on earth had just happened?

Jonah walked directly up to Patty, taking no notice of anyone else still in the bar. The atmosphere was still pleasant. Apparently, everyone was unaware of the wild chase that had just happened outside.

Patty leaned in with a warm smile. "Hey, honey, did you want another drink?"

"Hey, Patty." Jonah was still breathing heavily. "No, I don't need another drink. I just want to ask you if you can identify somebody for me real quick."

She frowned and pursed her lips before replying. "Identify somebody?"

"Yes, somebody that was here just moments ago. He comes here frequently as I understand it, so I'm sure you would at least recognize him, if you don't know him personally."

"Okay," Patty said, cautiously.

"He was the man who just left through the front door a few minutes ago. He has long black hair, and he is tall."

Patty's eyes lit up as a lightbulb seemed to turn on in her head. "Oh, you must mean Leighton!"

"Yes, Leighton. Do you know his last name?"

"Jones. Leighton Jones. Been coming here for years."

"Leighton Jones."

Patty nodded. "Yup."

"Thank you so much. Can I ask you something else?"

Patty looked at him with an apprehensive expression on her face. "Uh, sure."

"Do you know if he was here on Sunday night?"

Patty gave a disapproving look in Jonah's direction, as if he had crossed some invisible line. "I'm not sure if I should tell you that, hunny. Leighton is one of our most loyal patrons."

Jonah shrugged his shoulders in frustration. "That's fine, I just want to know if he had any interaction with a girl that was here too."

Patty shook her head. "Sorry, I don't want to give out that information. If you need to know that, you're going to have to ask Leighton himself."

Jonah shook his head in irritation and left without another word. All Patty had cost him was time. He was sure he could find out all he needed to know about the man called Leighton Jones from Sergeant Rick Casey.

12

Jonah drifted back toward his car with his mind whirring so fast that he was surprised it wasn't making noise. Before getting in the driver's seat, he had to pause for a second to gather himself.

Back in college, Jonah had had a philosophy professor named Andrew Quarles who had told him that in life there are going to be moments for everyone where there is a *before* and an *after*. Moments that drive you forward and make you choose a path that will define your life in the immediate future. Jonah had a sneaking suspicion that Leighton running away from him was going to be one of those moments. What was purely a knot in his stomach before had become something much more. Leighton's reaction to Jonah mentioning Katie clearly told him something was terribly wrong. If not directly pointing to foul play, it at least communicated that it wasn't the open-and-shut case that everyone in Newport thought it was. Why else would the man run? There was no logical explanation for it other than Leighton knowing something about Katie Deeds's death.

Jonah still couldn't believe what had just happened. Questions needed to be answered, and they needed to be answered quickly. He needed to come up with a plan of action. There were people he had to speak with about this turn in events. Randy Marks was high up on the pecking order, as Jonah knew he needed to find some sort of cover story for why he was going to be using his time interviewing people connected to Katie Deeds in the immediate future. There was no way Marks would let him dedicate his efforts to this if he thought Jonah was investigating whether an apparently clear suicide was actually a suicide. Marks always encouraged his reporters to ask questions, but he also always told his subordinates, "Report on the news, don't make the news." Perhaps Jonah would feign that he was doing a long-form feature story on the aftermath of Katie's death and the impact of losing someone everyone knew in a small community. That way he wouldn't have to lie to Marks about what he was doing, but he would have an ulterior motive for why he was doing it. Jonah obviously wouldn't tell him about the insanity that had just occurred in Nye Beach, even though he was dying to recount the story. It would be detrimental to his efforts, because Marks would catch on to what he was doing, and if he came to the conclusion that Jonah was wasting his time, he would actively try and put a stopper on it.

This sentiment would hold true for Rick Casey, as well. Jonah needed to talk to Casey, but he thought it was probably smart to withhold the fact that he had just run after a stranger through a private parking lot and the back door of a gift shop. Casey would ask Jonah why the hell he approached Leighton in the first place, and what he was planning to do if he had caught the man—an answer he didn't have. However, Jonah needed to get as much information as he could about Leighton. He just wouldn't tell Casey that it was related to Katie Deeds.

Jonah thought of anyone else he might need to speak to. It seemed like Marks and Casey were the most important. He exhaled slowly as he opened the door to his car and folded himself into the passenger seat.

With a start, he remembered the man in the gift shop. If the man had indeed called the police, it wouldn't be long before a unit pulled into the parking lot, looking for the source of the disturbance. It was probably best to leave now and hope that the shop didn't have cameras. He pulled out of the turnaround and turned right. His heart was only now starting to slow down from the chase.

As Jonah headed down Third Street, he saw a police car driving North in the direction that he had just left. *Good timing,* he thought. He knew the officer would just take the report from the gift shop guy and move on with his day. Nothing had been stolen or damaged. The only crime that had been committed was possibly trespassing, and Jonah knew the cops wouldn't waste their time with a subpoena for camera footage on something like that.

After the police car passed, Jonah pointed his car left down Ocean Avenue, back toward Highway 101. It was less than a five-minute drive back to the office. In his car, he pulled out his phone and dialed Casey's number. The Bluetooth emitted the sound through his speakers. The phone rang twice before Casey answered.

"Hello?"

"Hey, Rick, it's Jonah."

"Hey, man, what's up? I saw the story. Way to go. I think you managed to phrase everything in a way that won't get my ass canned," Casey said, half-sarcastically.

"Thanks, Rick. Appreciate that."

"So what's up?"

"Yeah, so, I'm working on another story, and I need some information on a guy. I was thinking you could maybe run a name and see if any outstanding warrants come back, or if he has any criminal history."

Casey's voice reflected surprise. "Wow. Not the kind of thing you usually ask for."

"I know. This is a different type of story." Jonah knew it sounded like a lame excuse.

There was dead air on Casey's side of the phone before he said, "You know I could lose my job for providing you with information like that. I get cops do this kind of thing all the time, but don't think that just because I agree to this once I will always agree to it in the future."

"Deal."

"What's the name?"

"Leighton Jones."

"Leighton? Interesting name," Casey muttered. "How is it spelled?"

"L-E-I-G-H-T-O-N, I think."

"Last name Jones?"

"Yeah," Jonah said.

"What are you thinking about this guy?"

"I don't really know yet."

"Uh, okay. So is that all?"

"Could you give me an address on the guy too?"

"Jesus, Jonah," Casey said, irritably.

"I won't tell anyone where I got it."

"Are you going to go try and interview him?"

"Something like that."

"We'll see. No promises," Casey said in a flat tone. "I'll call you with what comes back in a bit. I'm on my lunch."

"Okay."

Jonah hung up. He pulled into the lot of the *Times* and turned his engine off. Two minutes later, he was inside the building, knocking on Randy Marks's office door.

"Come in," Marks said gruffly.

"Hey, Randy." Jonah slid through the door.

Marks looked at Jonah, scanning him up and down while he

wrote down something on a printed document in front of him. His eyes always looked beady to Jonah. "Did you come to get my congratulations on the story? Perhaps a celebratory blow job?"

What a charmer, thought Jonah. Marks had a dry sense of humor and frequently made comments that could be taken in the wrong way if you weren't familiar with his brand of amusement. He was usually pretty good about knowing his audience, and Jonah wasn't easily offended.

"As appealing as that sounds, no, I didn't." Jonah closed the door. "I actually came to run a potential story by you. I know you would usually give out assignments in a couple of days, but I wanted to run this by you before you did."

"Oh, you found a story all on your own, did you? Man, I am going to have to just sit here for a minute so my boner can subside," said Marks sarcastically.

Jonah chuckled and shook his head. "Before you get too aroused, let me run the story by you first."

The corners of Marks's lips twitched for a second as he repressed a smile. He was one of those men who seemed to respect you more if you could play along. "Okay, shoot."

"Well, it is sort of a follow-up on the Deeds girl. I want to do more of a feature-style type piece on the aftermath of her death. Interviewing coworkers, friends, and whatnot. Kind of put into perspective what effect a tragedy like this has on a small community, you know?"

Marks looked a little taken aback at first, as if he was surprised that Jonah would bring Katie up so quickly after the first story had ran, but then his eyes fogged over as he thought. "Usually that sort of thing works a little bit better a few months down the road, I think. Like, 'Six Months Later, Impact of Teen's Suicide Lingers On,'" he said, proffering an imaginary headline.

"I know, but I want to get reactions while they're still fresh,"

Jonah said, scrambling a little. He was trying his best to hide all social cues he was lying about his intent.

"Hmm. Maybe," Marks said quietly, chewing his lip.

"What were you thinking of having me do instead?"

"Truthfully, I wasn't really sure."

Jonah gave Marks an enthusiastic smile and leaned in with his palms facing the ceiling. "Well there you go!"

Marks reclined in his chair, and as he started speaking, he did so slowly and cautiously. "I don't know, Jonah. This kind of thing might be able to work since stories like this are so few and far between in Newport, but I'm a little hesitant to run something like that. Might rub people the wrong way."

"How do you mean?"

"Because it literally just happened a couple of days ago."

His explanation didn't make much sense to Jonah. The proposed story would be about the town's grief, so how could it rub people the wrong way? Perhaps Marks was just hesitant because the idea didn't come from him.

"Okay, but it wouldn't run until next week at the earliest."

Marks paused again, contemplating. "Fine. But tread lightly. And if this story sucks, it will be the last time you decide your own assignment."

"You got it, boss."

"Now get the fuck out. I have to pretend to do things."

Jonah chuckled and left the office. He was somewhat caught off-guard by how smoothly that had gone. Marks was in a much better mood than when he was in the war room on the day of Katie's death. Hopefully he would stay off Jonah's back for the next few days while he interviewed different respondents. If his reporting went anywhere, and he found any sort of proof that Katie Deeds's death was not as it seemed, then he would bring the truth to Marks. Marks would probably be pissed that he had lied, but he also would be enthralled that Jonah had broken such a crazy story.

Jonah sauntered over to his desk and turned on his computer. He was still a little perturbed due to the corybantic chase that had taken place in Nye Beach less than twenty minutes ago, and he was also finding it difficult to not tell anyone. For the sake of secrecy now that Marks had cleared his idea for the fake piece, he knew that sharing the wild story would be detrimental to his oncoming exploration of Katie's death. There wasn't a single colleague of his who wouldn't immediately tell Marks what had happened, and then Marks would bust Jonah for lying to him. As Jonah opened his email account, he clicked through messages, trashing most of them. After deleting what felt like a hundred, he began perusing different websites, letting the time pass while waiting for Casey to call him. Within a half hour, he felt his phone vibrate.

"Hey, Rick."

"Hey, man. You owe me one."

"What did you find?" Jonah asked quickly.

"Your man doesn't have any current outstanding warrants. However, he does have a record. I ran a criminal history, and in 1997 Leighton Jones was busted for domestic battery against his ex-wife. Spent six months in prison for it."

"Okay." Jonah was a little unimpressed. Domestic violence was a terrible thing, but not all that uncommon.

"It gets better. Or worse, I guess. In 2002 he was booked for stalking and the attempted rape of a nineteen-year-old girl who got him with pepper spray before he could penetrate her, according to the police report that I found on file. His attorney cut a deal with the DA, and he only served two years for it."

"Wow." Jonah's heart started beating quickly again.

"That isn't all either. Sounds like this guy has been accused of several crimes that were sexual in nature. He was arrested three times for sexual assault in the last five years. However, in two cases, the charges were dropped by the victim for unknown reasons. In another case, the accuser died of a heroin overdose before it was brought to trial. We are looking at a probable serial sex offender that has been able to skate on luck and circumstance."

"Jesus fucking Christ."

"I know," Casey said.

"Do you have an address for me?"

For a few seconds Casey didn't say anything. "Yeah, I do, but before I give it to you, I need your word that if anything comes of it, you can't tell anyone you got it from me."

"Of course."

"Alright then. It's 452 High Street."

Jonah's voice stuck in his throat and a shiver ran down his spine. The address that Casey provided was within a block of Teresa Deed's house and not far from where Katie was last seen.

13

Sierra jumped into the passenger seat of the Ford Bronco. It was an old vehicle, either made in ninety-six or ninety-seven; she couldn't remember which. Kyle put a pinch of chewing tobacco into his bottom lip and adjusted his blue baseball cap with the Newport Cubs paw logo just above the bill.

"I really wish you would stop chewing," Sierra said in a small voice. "It is so disgusting."

"Babe, how many times are you gonna say that?"

"However many times it takes you to quit."

Kyle rolled his eyes and drove down Eads Street, away from his house. He turned left on Seventh and continued up a steep hill that took him past the cemetery. He was pushing fifty-five miles an hour, about thirty miles too fast for a residential area. But Kyle wasn't concerned. Police never came up this road.

Kyle swerved around a sharp corner, causing Sierra's blond hair to fall into her eyes. "Fucking slow down, Kyle!" she shouted.

"Sorry, babe," he said, pumping his foot softly on the Bronco's brakes.

The road expanded into a clearing, and Kyle turned the Bronco down Duke Avenue. It was an exceedingly narrow road. Although it was supposed to be two lanes, if separate cars were approaching each other in opposite directions, one of them would have to pull off the road to allow the other to pass. The Bronco cruised its way down the hill, until Kyle found what he was looking for: a spot to the side that was large enough for his vehicle to fit. He put the truck in park and turned off the engine. They were now deep in the woods.

As soon as the engine was off, Sierra pulled out an orange pipe from her purse. She spent several seconds digging around until she located what she was after: a Ziploc bag with several clumps of marijuana inside. Sierra fingered the bud until she closed her hand around a tiny nugget that she picked away from the rest. Daintily setting the nugget inside the empty sphere of the orange pipe, Sierra began smashing it down with the butt of the lighter she had brought. She pressed the end of the pipe gently against her lips, ignited the lighter, and inhaled.

Kyle reached halfheartedly for the pipe, waiting for his turn. Eventually, Sierra passed the paraphernalia in his direction and he snatched it out of her hand. He spit the remainder of his tobacco into the empty beer can between his legs. After a hit for himself, he set the pipe down onto the dashboard and turned to look at Sierra. She had large, beautiful green eyes, and high, rounded cheekbones. Kyle smiled at her. With a spark of passion, the two began kissing.

This was their favorite spot. The couple had started dating in May, and several times every week that summer they would drive out to this place, smoke pot, and have sex. Both of their parents were somewhat strict, and being that they were both seventeen, it was difficult to find a place to release their pent-up sexual frustration without getting caught. Kyle had discovered this spot accidentally when he was running.

As the two began to maneuver their bodies against each other, feeling the heat and anticipation of impending sex, neither of them noticed a forest-green Jeep parked fifty feet behind them or the man inside who was watching them through his binoculars.

14

Jonah spent the rest of the afternoon writing the piece on Clive O'Hara and his ferrets. The story had originally been slated for release on Wednesday, but Katie's suicide had pushed it back a week. Next to him he had Leighton's address scribbled on his notepad. He knew the subsequent step for him investigating Katie's death was to go to the man's house, but he was nervous of doing so. If Leighton was tied to Katie in any way, would he become violent? The man's history of sexual assault clearly showed that he was completely unstable. And what if he just ran again when he saw Jonah?

As Jonah scanned his notes from the O'Hara interview, looking for one last quote to add to the story, he decided to put off going to Leighton's place until the following day. He would mull over how he was going to do it and try to build confidence to be prepared for some sort of confrontation.

Jonah decided to text his friend Wesley and see if he wanted to grab a drink in the evening. He still had not shared the details of his frenzied pursuit of Leighton, so he was looking forward to confiding in someone. Almost immediately after Jonah texted him, Wesley replied with an affirmative. It was probably his favorite quality about Wesley; he was so easygoing and laid back, and was almost always up for an adventure. Jonah texted back and told him to meet him at a pub downtown called Moby Dicks at seven. It was even more of a dive than Rip Tide's, but it had sort of a cult following.

Jonah spent one more hour refining the story on O'Hara before he emailed the document to Randy Marks. The story was just about 800 words, somewhat short for a profile. Jonah shut his computer and prepared to leave the office, relieved at being done for the day. He was very much looking forward to his evening with Wesley.

The music was far too loud as the two friends ducked through the doorway of Moby Dicks later that night. Some middle-aged woman who was terribly overweight was singing some of the worst karaoke that Jonah had ever heard.

"Do you want to touch me there? Where? There! Yeah!" caterwauled the woman in a husky smoker's voice, singing an old Joan Jett song.

After each getting a drink from the grumpy male bartender, Jonah and Wesley sat at a bar table with some wobbly stools in the middle of the bar. They were far enough away from the karaoke stage that they wouldn't get rained in the drunk woman's spit as she blasted out eighties' hits from her tar-addled lungs.

Wesley drank his cocktail of rum and Coke in an alarmingly fast fashion. He was a thin, good-looking man who knew his way around an alcoholic drink. His light brown hair was longer than most men's, dropping down so that he had to tuck strands of hair behind his ears. He had brown eyes and deep dimples when he smiled. Wesley was one of the most agreeable men Jonah had ever met. He was almost too kind and never gave you negative feedback. When you complained, he would always assert that your position was obviously the correct one to have.

"So, how you been, dude?" Wesley asked genuinely. They had briefly exchanged pleasantries when they had met each other outside, but this was the first time they had gotten to have an actual conversation.

"I've been good. Had a wild last couple of days, though."

"What do you mean?"

"I don't know if you heard about the girl who jumped off the bridge a couple days ago."

"Yeah, man, I saw it on Facebook. Just awful." He said it as though Katie had been his close friend. As far as Jonah knew, they had never met.

"Yeah, it is. I had to write the story we ran yesterday."

"Shit, that must have been tough to do. Did you have to interview any family members or anything?"

"Yeah. I talked to the grandmother that she lived with. And her boss."

"How did that go?" Wesley asked anxiously, as though the answer would cause him great personal relief or distress.

"Eh, they went okay. Her boss was kind of a dick. The grandmother was fine. Didn't seem to have hit her yet. She did share something pretty shocking with me, though."

"What?"

Jonah decided to just say it. "She, uh, thinks that Katie was murdered."

Wesley's mouth fell open. "What? No fucking way," he said, stretching out the A in *way*.

"Yeah, that's what I thought at first too."

"Wait, at first?" Wesley's eyes widened.

"Yeah. I don't even know where to begin," Jonah said, building up the suspense. "In fact, I think we need a shot of something so I can loosen up before I spin you this thrilling tale."

"You got a deal." Wesley grinned.

They both approached the tired-looking bartender, who seemed less than pleased to be graced with their presence again. After a brief back-and-forth discussion, they came to a consensus that their best option was tequila. They ordered Jose Cuervo and returned to their table once the bartender had doled out the two shots.

Wesley held his shot glass aloft with a casual smile on his face. "What should we cheers to?"

"Hmm. Cheers to tequila?"

"Hear, hear." Wesley raised his glass. Both downed the tequila in one gulp and they each made a face that was akin to one you would make if you had just received a surprise enema.

"Jesus, that is rough." Jonah wiped his mouth with his sleeve.

"Yeah. Like drinking tangy gasoline or something," Wesley replied. They both roared with laughter. "So, take me down your rabbit hole. This story sounds like it could be life-changing."

"Yeah, it just might be." Jonah smiled. He said it as though he were joking and tried not to let on that he actually concurred with that sentiment. What had taken place over the last day looked like it was at least going to change one life: his. Part of him was bubbling with anxiety, knowing how big of a stepping stone this could be for his career and that the consequences would be dire if he screwed it up. No one would ever take him seriously as a journalist again if he flubbed. However, there was also a part of him that was just yearning for the truth. That was why he had decided to become a journalist: to expose what was really happening and hold people to account. He wasn't sure where the whole thing was going, and there was a chance that it could still be a suicide. But he was positive about one thing now: He didn't have the whole truth. Not yet.

Before he began, Jonah decided to preface his story with a

warning. "Now, this goes without saying, and I completely trust you, but you obviously can't tell anyone what I'm about to share with you."

"Of course."

"So, first, I guess I'll start with the friend. I went to interview this guy named Charles, who was with Katie, the girl who died, the night she jumped. They were drinking at Rip Tide's. I talked to him after the story ran. I didn't need to. There was just something that was bothering me about the whole thing."

Wesley leaned on his elbows, digesting every word that Jonah uttered. "Anyway, Charles was a weaselly little twerp and didn't have much to say, other than mentioning this weird guy who had given Katie the creeps at the bar. Now, I obviously didn't think the guy that had given her the heebie-jeebies was much of a lead, but I decided to try and find him anyway. Charles told me that he always hung out at Rip Tide's and that I could find him there."

Jonah paused to take a sip on the first drink that he had ordered, a still unfinished rum and Coke. "So I looked for a guy who matched Charles's description of the man, and I found him right away, right where Charles said he would be."

"What happened?"

"Well, I approached him and asked him about Katie." He let a dramatic pause hang on the air before continuing, "The guy ran away."

Wesley's mouth dropped open for the second time that night. "What the fuck?"

Jonah nodded vigorously. "Yeah. And I chased him."

Wesley's jaw stretched so far that he looked like a snake trying to devour a mouse whole. "No you didn't."

"Yes, I did."

"Why did you do that?"

"I don't know, man. It was just kind of an instinct. Like I knew that he had done something wrong."

"Jesus Christ, dude. Did you catch him?"

"No. We kind of made a big loop around Nye Beach. I followed him through that gift shop across from Rip Tide's. I lost him for a minute, and he was able to get to his car and drive away before I could catch up."

Wesley's mouth was still ajar. "What were you going to do if you caught him?"

"I honestly have no idea."

"Why would he run?"

Jonah gave a little shrug. "I'm still trying to figure that out. But here's the thing. I got the guy's name from the bartender, and then I talked to a friend on the police force and got him to run a criminal history. Turns out the guy's been arrested several times for rape, and once for domestic battery."

"Holy fucking shit," Wesley blurted. "So if he ran, he must know something about the girl?"

"That was my thinking, as well."

"What's his name?"

"Leighton Jones."

"Leighton? Kind of a weird name."

"Yeah, I know. And here's the real kicker. His address is right by where Katie Deeds was living. And not too far from where she disappeared."

"No fucking shit," said Wesley with his eyes flooded with wonder. "So what are you going to do now?"

"Well, I got the guy's address, so I might just show up at his house and see what happens."

"Jesus," Wesley said. He went quiet for a while, processing everything he had just heard. His expression was beyond ridiculous; he looked terrified, excited, disturbed, and incredulous all at the same time. It was almost too many emotions for one face to express.

"You think this girl might have been murdered?"

"I think it's possible. Even saying that feels wrong because it sounds so wild, but I mean, what was just an inkling in my gut now has some pretty damning evidence to support it. Why else would Leighton run?"

"I literally can't believe you may have uncovered a murder. Are you going to go to the police?"

"If this visit with Leighton yields anything, then yes."

Wesley shook his head in disbelief. "Wow."

Jonah spent another ten minutes going over all the details several times, as Wesley wanted to make sure he understood every nuance of the story. Wesley seemed to dwell the most on the fact that Jonah had chased Leighton, as it was the most baffling segment of the whole thing. He knew Jonah to be docile, easygoing and not conflict oriented. Not someone who would chase after a stranger for a story.

By the time Jonah had finished, he had started to feel a heavy buzz. The alcohol numbed the shock of the events of the last forty-eight hours, and he began to relax. Wesley wanted to keep talking about how crazy it was that Jonah might have uncovered a homicide in little old Newport, Oregon, but after another fifteen minutes, Jonah's focus was finally elsewhere. He tried to shift the conversation to Wesley's work. Wesley was employed at a small company called Newport Rental that leased landscaping equipment to anyone who needed it. It was heavy manual labor, and Wesley was in very good shape because of it. However, the last thing he wanted to talk about was work, and he pushed the topic of conversation back onto Jonah and his investigation.

After answering a couple more questions about Leighton, Teresa, and Katie, Jonah suddenly remembered the missing girls in the nineties.

"Oh, and there is something else that I totally forgot to tell you," Jonah said, interrupting another question from Wesley. "Sorry to interrupt."

"No problem, go ahead." His personality dictated that, unlike most people, he truly wasn't agitated at all when interrupted.

"So I was at the bar the other night with Daisy."

"Do you think you guys are going anywhere?"

"No. In fact, I think we're done. We just don't connect. We kind of had a bit of a falling out the other night. Anyway, this story isn't about her, it's about these cases that I was looking up the other night."

Wesley sipped off of his drink tentatively. "Okay."

"When I was at the bar with Daisy, I overheard a lady talking about several girls who had gone missing, one in the eighties and four in the nineties. I had never heard about the cases before, and I asked her about them. She gave me a lot of details, and at first I thought she was blowing smoke. But then I went and I looked up the cases on the Internet and everything she was saying was true."

"Are you talking about Kylie Desmond and Cara Lee and those girls?"

"Yes, exactly! You know about them?"

"Of course." Wesley nodded. "It was a big deal around here when I was a kid, even in the years after it happened."

"I'm surprised I never heard about it," Jonah said, again marveling at his own incompetence.

"You aren't from here," Wesley replied empathetically.

"True," Jonah said. "But still."

"Anyway, why are you bringing that up?"

Jonah didn't reply, but looked at Wesley with a meaningful expression. It took Wesley a moment to realize what Jonah was insinuating, and then, once it clicked, his eyes bugged out.

"No way. You don't think—"

"They probably aren't connected," Jonah added quickly. "It's been thirty-two years since the first victim, and twenty-one years since the last. I'm just saying. Young girl, walking alone at night by herself."

"Yeah," said Wesley. "But those girls were just teenagers.

Wasn't the Deeds girl in her twenties? And they found her right away. The other girls weren't found for a while after, I think."

Wesley had reiterated all the points that Jonah had made when Sherry had first told him the theory in the bar. But, unlike Sherry had done, he simply concurred with Wesley.

"Yeah, like I said, I don't think they're connected."

The husky-voiced woman had stopped singing, to the joy of everyone inside. A small man who was apparently the karaoke host walked on stage and took the microphone. "Okay, who's next?"

Wesley looked at Jonah with an expression on his face that hinted he would like to go on stage.

"No way, man. You can go up there by yourself, but I would rather stick my nuts in a ceiling fan."

Wesley laughed. "Fine. I was sort of joking. I would be so off pitch that only dogs would be able to hear me, anyway."

Jonah giggled and finally finished off his rum and Coke. The alcohol had begun pulsing through his veins, and his vision had lost focus. His mind gravitated back to the girls in the nineties.

It was eerie to him that a serial killer had ever existed in Newport. The fact that they had never caught the suspect was the most troubling. Everything he had learned from police procedurals on TV told him that a serial killer doesn't just stop being a serial killer. In all likelihood, the killer had probably died or left town. But for some reason, the small chance that the culprit could still be in Lincoln County gnawed on Jonah's conscience. It was as if some unforeseen boogeyman lingered just out of view, watching him from afar.

Jonah decided to stop drinking for the rest of the night and watched as Wesley consumed another beer. Time passed more quickly, and the rest of the night they spent talking about sports. It was nearly the first game of the college football season. The Oregon Ducks looked to be in the middle of a rebuild, but Wesley was such a big fan that he ignored the experts' prognostications. He was one of those fans that thought the Ducks would win every game, no matter the odds.

In total, Jonah and Wesley spent about two hours at the bar before they decided to call it a night. Jonah was still a little buzzed, although not as drunk as he had been. He figured that he was sober enough to drive, and after saying good-bye to Wesley, he walked back to his car.

When Jonah got back into the driver's seat, he started to consider things. It was only eight thirty, and he wasn't quite ready to go home. He shuffled through his options. There was only a limited amount of things to do in Newport anyway, so potential destinations were sparse. As his mind landed on one prospect, he inwardly scoffed. *What a terrible thought. That is the last thing that you should be doing right now,* thought Jonah. *No good can come from that. You could lose your job.* His better half rose up and was trying to quell his inner daredevil. He knew full well that it would be a mistake. But for some reason, Jonah couldn't stop himself. It was the alcohol. It lifted his spirits and gave him courage to do things that were folly. And he knew what he was considering was in fact incredibly stupid. But for some reason, he turned on his car and headed for Leighton Jones's house.

15

The brush on the other side of the street seemed to rustle mischievously as the wind floated through it. High Street was one of the filthiest places in Newport. The neighborhood was a total ghetto, and the houses had been built long ago. The road was cracked in several places, and the trees hung over the pavement as if they were guarding it. It would be a good place to go trick-or-treating on Halloween night, as the spookiness that radiated from the street hung over Jonah like a rain cloud.

Jonah looked at the musty-looking home from where he was parked down the street. The rusted numbers 452 were stuck precariously against the side of the house. The bushes in the front yard were overgrown and the garage door was covered in dirt. A wind chime tinkled softly as a breeze drifted by the front door. The noise was chilling.

In the driveway, the old red Mustang that Leighton Jones had fled in was parked. As soon as Jonah had seen the vehicle, it was as if all the liquid courage the tequila had given him had suddenly melted away.

Jonah opened the door to his car and climbed out like a spider. He began walking slowly across the street. With every step he took, his heartbeat increased. He exhaled from his diaphragm, but it was difficult for him to catch his breath. His palms were sweating profusely. Jonah tried to keep as silent as he could, in case he couldn't summon the courage to knock, and he also tried to remain in the shadows as much as possible. That way Leighton Jones would never know he had been there.

Climbing the three steps to the front porch, Jonah stood still and waited. Instead of knocking, he pressed his ear to the door. He could hear the noise of what sounded like a television. He listened for several more moments before withdrawing his head.

For some reason, Jonah was unable to muster the bravado to knock. This was proving more difficult than he thought it would be. It was as if the very fiber of his being was urging him to run back to his car and speed off. But if he did that, he would just have to return here tomorrow. Jonah needed to find out what happened to Katie Deeds, and the next step was Leighton Jones. Jonah could feel it in his gut.

Jonah clenched his hand into a fist and brought it up to his eye level, ready to knock on the door. He held his arm in midair, as if some extraterrestrial force was holding it back. The sound of the television was still audible.

With one swift motion, he knocked on the door three times before he convinced himself to do otherwise. After a few seconds, the sound of the television ceased. Jonah heard heavy footsteps coming in his direction. His heart beat faster than it ever had in his life. Suddenly, he noticed a small peephole on the door. He felt a chill run down his spine as he knew he was being watched through the hole.

Jonah expected the door to open, but it didn't. Instead, he heard the footsteps walk away. *Strange,* thought Jonah. It took him a minute to arrive at the conclusion that perhaps Leighton was running away again, through a back door or something. He leaned to the side over the porch rail to try and catch any movement from the back of the house, but he couldn't see anything.

Without warning, the front door swung open. A tall man with long black hair and a face that looked like a crow stood motionless behind the threshold. He was holding a shotgun.

"Get the fuck off my property," Leighton Jones said through gritted teeth.

Jonah was so surprised that he almost fell backward off the porch. It took him a few moments to regain his balance, and then he started retreating.

"I don't mean to cause any trouble, Mr. Jones. I just want to talk."

"What makes you think I want to talk to you?" Leighton snarled. "Was me running away not clear enough for you? How did you find my house anyway?"

Leighton pointed the barrel of the shotgun in Jonah's direction. Jonah had never had a gun pointed at him before, and he couldn't say he enjoyed the experience.

"I can't tell you that," said Jonah, standing up straighter and trying to inflect strength into his voice, feigning bravery that he did not feel. "Point is, unless you are planning on abandoning your home, I know where you live now, and it would be easier to just talk to me now and get it over with."

"How about option number two? I shoot a man who is trespassing. You bleed out on my front lawn, and when the cops come, I will tell them it was self-defense."

"And how will that work out for you?" Jonah raised his voice a little. "I'm unarmed." He raised his arms in the air, motioning for surrender. "With a record like the one you have; you think you'll get away with it?"

Leighton's face, which was showing anger before, suddenly morphed into anguish.

"You talked to the cops?"

Jonah nodded, keeping his hands in the air.

"You know whoever you talked to could lose their job for that."

"But still, the point remains. If you shoot me, you will spend the rest of your life in a cell, which you probably should be doing already with all you've done." The shock at being held at gunpoint had subsided, and his temper was starting to rise.

Leighton lowered the shotgun. "Who the fuck are you anyway?"

"I told you yesterday. My name is Jonah Carr. I work for the *News Times*."

Leighton's face melded into a humorless, sarcastic smile. "The last person I would ever want to speak to is a reporter."

"Would you rather speak to the police?"

There was a long pause as Leighton's black eyes burrowed into Jonah's blue ones. He seemed to be debating what to say. After several more moments, Leighton finally spoke.

"I know what you're thinking. But I didn't do anything to the girl."

Jonah's mind started racing, trying to find the best question to ask next. "What girl?"

Leighton rolled his eyes impatiently. "The Deeds girl."

"Then why did you run?"

Leighton looked away and said quietly, "Because."

"Because why?"

"Because of the things I've done."

Jonah opened his eyes wider and his stomach dropped. "I thought you said you didn't hurt her?"

"I didn't!"

"Then what do you mean, *what I have done*?"

Leighton just looked at him.

"Put the shotgun down so I can talk to you without worrying that you're going to blow your own door off its hinges."

Leighton jumped slightly. He didn't put the gun down, but he backed up a couple feet.

"Here's what I know," said Jonah. "You've been arrested several times for sexual assault. You're a rapist, Mr. Jones. I don't know why, but the women you have hurt over the years all have dropped the charges against you or died. Frankly, it disgusts me that you could be out and walking around in society. But here you are. So perhaps you could see why I think it's a little odd that a sexual predator such as yourself would run when I mentioned Katie Deeds's name."

Leighton's face seemed to lose some of its color; Jonah's harsh words had surprised him. He started to back away and cower even further. This made Jonah rise more. It was as if he was the one holding the shotgun.

"Did you hurt Katie, Mr. Jones?"

"No," he whispered.

"Don't lie to me."

"I'm not."

Jonah looked at the man and began thinking. He knew that if Katie had been murdered, whoever had done it was smart enough to spend a copious amount of time planning it out. Hell, if someone had stolen her phone and sent three texts that alluded to suicide, and then thrown her off the bridge, this was likely a plan that had been metastasizing for a long time. The culprit would have picked the time and the place when he wanted to do it. Leighton's presence in this equation felt totally random. Although he was a predator, he just felt like a bystander here. Perhaps he hadn't attacked Katie. But then why had he run? If he didn't do anything wrong, he wouldn't be behaving in such a frightened manner. Jonah was clearly missing something. Suddenly, it clicked.

"Were you planning on hurting her?"

Leighton looked at Jonah for a few seconds, and then, shockingly, he nodded. Jonah was so flabbergasted at the fact that Leighton had willingly copped to planning a crime that it took him a few seconds to reorganize his thoughts.

"Did you follow her when she left the bar?"

Leighton nodded again.

"She didn't go in the direction of the bridge, did she?"

"No," said Leighton. Jonah felt a leap of excitement.

"Which way did she go?"

"She was only a couple blocks from here. She was going down Pine." Leighton sounded ashamed.

"So a serial sex offender follows a young, attractive woman out of a bar as she heads home. Were you going to rape her, Mr. Jones?"

Leighton looked at the ground. It was all the confirmation Jonah needed.

"So *that's* why you ran from me. But you didn't rape her, is that what you're trying to say? You followed her, but you didn't get a chance to attack her like you had planned to?"

Leighton gave Jonah a steely glare.

"If that's true, why didn't you follow through, Mr. Jones? Why didn't you do what you have been doing for twenty years and victimize a woman who had no hope of defending herself?"

"Because I couldn't bring myself to do it," said Leighton. He tried to inflect empathy into his deep, methodical voice.

"Bullshit. You expect me to believe that?"

Leighton started to snarl and he hurled his next words at Jonah like they were an insult. "I don't care what you believe."

"You *did* rape her, didn't you, Mr. Jones?"

"No! I ran!"

Staring at Leighton in disgust, Jonah wanted to throttle the man. "You ran? Why would you—"

In a split second, it hit him. All at once, waves of understanding crashed over him. Fear, excitement, and disgust bubbled up inside his gut.

"You saw something, didn't you?"

Leighton froze. The expression on his face made the hairs on the back of Jonah's neck stand up.

"You saw someone else when you were following her, is that what you're telling me?"

Leighton's nostrils flared and his eyebrows raised.

"And this person scared you off? Did they not see you?"

Leighton swallowed and looked down.

"Who did you see, Mr. Jones? You must tell me."

At first, Jonah thought Leighton wasn't going to answer. For a moment, he was afraid that the man would shrink back into the house and slam the door. But he didn't. After several more silent beats, Leighton finally responded.

"A man. A man in a mask."

16

Jonah could hear his own heartbeat as his most vital organ slammed against his chest ferociously. “A man in a mask?”

Leighton’s voice dropped a few octaves, making his response more ominous. “Yes.”

“Where did you see this man?”

“He was standing behind a tree. He looked like he was hiding from the girl.”

“Hiding? Or waiting?”

“Both,” said Leighton.

“And she definitely didn’t see him?”

“No. She saw me, though,” responded Leighton quietly. The shotgun that was cradled in his arms drooped sadly toward the ground.

“She saw you following her? What did she do?”

“I don’t think she knew that I was . . . you know, following her. I was pretending to be on my phone. But anyways, she sped up.”

"And what did you do?"

"I sped up, too, but then I saw him."

Jonah leaned forward, trying to keep his ear as close as he could to Leighton's quiet tone. "Did he see you?"

"I don't think so. He was looking in the other direction around the tree."

"Did it look like he was going to do something to Katie?"

Leighton paused. "Yes," he said, his voice barely above a whisper.

"And then you ran?"

"Yeah."

Jonah felt truly repulsed by Leighton. The fact that the man could a see a young, innocent girl about to be attacked and flee without even thinking of helping her was stomach-churning. But then again, if not for the man in the mask, Leighton would have been the one to attack her. So, it wasn't exactly surprising.

Jonah pressed on. "Describe this man for me, please."

"I don't know. I didn't get a good look at him. He seemed tall. Very tall. Thick. Like buff, you know? He wore a heavy jacket and gloves, I think. And like I said, the mask. A black ski mask. I only caught a glimpse of him for a few seconds. It scared the shit out of me, so I got out of there."

Jonah took a step forward, trying to urge Leighton into action. "You are going to have to talk to the police. You're going to have to tell them this."

"Fuck that." Leighton regained a bit of the angry disposition that he had first held when he opened the door. "What am I going to tell them? How am I going to explain what I was doing?"

"You don't have to tell them anything about what you were doing," said Jonah. "You can't get arrested for thinking about committing a crime." He felt disgusted with himself that he was offering a way out for such a horrible human being. But the police needed him.

Leighton raised his voice and barked at Jonah viciously. "Listen, if you go to the cops and they force me to talk, then fine. But I sure as hell am not going to go to them first."

"Well, alright then," replied Jonah.

Leighton's jaw cocked to the side in anger. "Are we through?"

Before Jonah could answer, Leighton slammed the door in his face.

X

There it was. Jonah had proof that Katie Deeds hadn't committed suicide. She had been walking home and had been set upon by a creature in a mask. Leighton Jones had witnessed the real devil hiding in the shadows. The masked man must have abducted her, stolen her cell phone, and sent those texts before driving her to the bridge and throwing her off. As unbelievable as it was, Teresa had been right. Katie had been murdered.

Jonah couldn't believe it. A killer in Newport? And one who had devised an elaborate plan to capture a girl, sent text messages that made it look like a suicide, and then had thrown her off the bridge in the presence of witnesses down below so that it looked like she jumped? Jonah shuddered as he realized how intelligent the killer was. He had clearly waited for the perfect time to take Katie, a time when she would theoretically be alone in the darkness. Unluckily for him, Leighton was also on the prowl. Jonah supposed that it was lucky in a strange way that Leighton had decided to do what he had. The only way that a hunter who had isolated his prey could be stopped was by another hunter who was targeting the same unwitting quarry. If Leighton Jones had not followed Katie, no one would ever have gotten a look at her killer. And yet, Jonah was still disgusted by him. He thought of Teresa Deeds and how she would feel if she knew someone was attempting to rape Katie, and anger boiled inside him.

Jonah withdrew his phone immediately and found the contact he was looking for. It was a tiny bit late, but Rick Casey would answer. He always did. After three rings, Jonah's theory was proven correct.

"Hello?"

"Rick, it's Jonah."

"I know who it is. I have caller ID," said Casey rudely.

"At least you weren't surprised then," Jonah snapped back.

"It's a little late, don't you think?"

"Yeah, sorry," said Jonah. "But this is really important. In fact, this may be the most important phone call we have ever shared."

Casey laughed. Jonah stayed silent.

"Holy shit, you aren't joking."

"Nope. We need to meet as soon as we can. Tomorrow morning if you can swing it."

"Wow, uh, okay then. What time? And where?"

"Somewhere private." Jonah looked over his shoulder in his car as if someone could somehow be tuning into their conversation at that very moment. "Let's say nine—at the turnaround like last time."

"Okay," said Casey. "Shit, Jonah, this is serious, isn't it?"

"I would be lying if I said it wasn't."

"Can you give me any hints as to what it's about?"

"I'd rather not say it over the phone," replied Jonah. "But I can tell you that it is a violent crime."

"Jesus."

"Just be there at nine."

"Okay," said Casey.

Jonah hit the *end call* button on the screen of his phone. He looked over at house number 452 and almost wet himself. The blinds were pried open, and Leighton's ugly face was pressed against the glass, staring at Jonah. He felt the strong urge to flip the fucker off, but he refrained, and turned his engine on. Part of him wished he could find a way to nail Leighton, too, but there were more pressing matters on his mind now, thanks to what Leighton had seen. Perhaps when this whole thing was over, he would look into Leighton Jones and see why he was able to skate free after all he had done. But that was a mystery for another day. One thing was for sure: Leighton had not killed Katie Deeds. It was just a coincidence that he lived so close to Teresa.

Jonah started his car and drove down the street. He decided to turn in the direction of Teresa's home before heading back to his own apartment. The road was a dead end, so he flipped a U-turn once he hit the last bit of pavement and observed his surroundings. To his left he passed the rustic-looking house where he had come to interview Teresa earlier in the week. Jonah had to travel about thirty feet farther before he saw the spot that he thought Leighton had depicted for him. A massive Douglas fir tree jutted out of the ground across the street from the sidewalk. Jonah stepped on his brakes for a second, realizing with a shudder that he probably was only a few feet away from where the predator in the mask had waited in silence to capture Katie Deeds. What truly disturbed Jonah was his next thought: Teresa Deeds had been asleep only a block away from where her granddaughter was captured. If Katie had just made it a little bit farther she might still be alive.

X

The next morning, Jonah got into Rick Casey's squad car in Nye Beach, not far from the spot where he had chased Leighton. It was blustery outside but not raining. The first signs of fall were emerging as a thick layer of clouds made for an exceedingly gray morning. The ocean, which was only twenty feet in front of them, was oddly tranquil that day. It reflected how Jonah felt, bracing himself for later storms to come.

Casey looked tired. His large forehead was speckled with beads of sweat. Even though the sun was nowhere to be found, he wore a pair of expensive-looking shades. He intermittently sipped on a Starbucks coffee as Jonah spoke.

"He didn't really provide any information, but he rubbed me the wrong way," he said, speaking of Anthony Mason. Jonah had decided to start at the very beginning of his investigation and walk Casey through the people he had talked to linearly.

"Anyway, so yeah, I talked to Mason and then I talked to Teresa, the grandmother. She didn't tell the police this, but she thinks that Katie didn't actually commit suicide."

Casey's forehead crinkled at this, and although Jonah couldn't see his eyes because of his sunglasses, he felt that they were probably being rolled.

"Like she thinks she was murdered? What a kook."

Jonah bobbed his head from side to side. "That was my initial reaction too."

"Why would she not tell us that?"

"I think she was concerned that you would have the reaction you're currently having."

Casey looked put off by this remark, but Jonah ignored this. He explained to Casey about how Teresa had told him of Charles Johnson and how he had gone to interview Johnson. He phrased it as though he had conducted the interview for his initial *News Times* story.

"Charles mentioned how Katie had gotten weird vibes from a guy at the bar the night that she died. I didn't think it meant anything, but I went to the bar and looked for him, just to cover loose ends, and that's how I found Leighton Jones."

Casey's mouth opened slightly in a confused expression.

"Wait, Leighton Jones the rapist that you called me about? What the hell? I thought you said that was for a different story."

"I lied," said Jonah.

Casey frowned.

Jonah held out his hands to try and placate him. "I don't think you're going to be angry when you find out what I got from the guy."

Unlike in his conversation with Wesley, Jonah left out the part about how he chased Leighton around the block. There wasn't any point in sharing something like that with someone on the police force; Casey wouldn't care for a random citizen attempting to be a vigilante. Therefore, Jonah spun a slightly different tale.

"Leighton initially refused to talk to me at the bar, but it felt like he knew something that he wasn't sharing. After I got his address from you, I went to his house and tried to talk to him there. He answered the door with a shotgun and tried to scare me off, but I eventually got him to talk."

Jonah let a long, drawn-out dramatic pause penetrate the air.

Casey leaned in expectantly. "And?"

"And after talking to him I think Teresa was right. Katie was probably murdered."

Casey's forehead wrinkled so much at this that it looked like a Hershey's Kisses wrapper that had been crumpled up.

"Jesus, Jonah, tell me you're joking. You can't believe that."

"Hear me out first, Rick," pleaded Jonah. "So Leighton was at Rip Tide's that night, and he saw Katie leave. He said she didn't even walk in the direction of the bridge. He knows this because he followed her."

Casey took in a sharp breath. "Wait, he followed her? Why?"

"Because he was going to rape her."

And then his mouth fell open.

"He told you that?"

"Yes."

"Jesus Christ." Casey shook his head.

"He followed her and was going to attack her, but he didn't get a chance to."

"Didn't get a chance to? What do you mean?"

"Well, this is the part that is most important. While Leighton was following her, he saw a man in a mask hiding behind a tree near where Katie was walking. The man didn't see him, but Leighton said that it looked like he was there specifically waiting to do something to Katie."

Casey looked confused. "A man in a mask? What kind of mask?"

"A ski mask."

One of Casey's nostrils was now raised in befuddlement. "And what did Leighton do when he saw this man?"

"He fled."

Casey looked out at the ocean as he processed the information. Jonah waited for ten long seconds for him to reply. When he did, it wasn't what Jonah was expecting.

"So you believed him?"

Jonah stared, aghast. "Believed him? Of course I believed him. Why wouldn't I believe him?"

"Because what you're suggesting is that this masked man kidnapped Katie, texted Teresa fake suicide plans, and then chucked the girl off the bridge. Do you realize how fucking crazy that sounds? You think someone wanted Katie dead that badly?"

"But why would Leighton lie about that? Why would he willingly confess to planning a rape of a girl who died the same night that he saw her if he didn't actually see someone in a mask?"

"Fuck if I know," said Casey. "Point is, you have to take everything with a grain of salt from someone like this. A lifetime sex offender who, in all likelihood, is on drugs or has been on drugs before, judging from the mug shot I saw on file."

Jonah rolled his eyes. Casey was reaching.

"Okay, well, I do believe him. Combine that with what Teresa said—"

"A grieving relative who is trying to rationalize why her granddaughter would kill herself."

Jonah pumped his fist in the air in fury as he yelled at Casey.

"Come on, Rick!"

"Jo, you can't jump to wild conclusions like this. For one, Teresa thinking it wasn't suicide is completely explainable. She basically lost her own child and can't bring herself to admit that Katie was unhappy," said Casey bullishly. "Secondly, how could someone have pulled off that kind of crime? Carrying a twenty-one-year-old girl onto a public bridge and throwing her off without anyone seeing him doing it? Lastly, you have the suicidal texts. This isn't a movie, Jonah. People don't kill people and make it look like suicide like that. Especially not in Newport, Oregon."

Jonah was completely baffled at Casey's response. He thought what he had provided was irrefutable evidence. It was extraordinary that Casey couldn't see the obvious fact that whoever this man wearing a ski mask was had taken Katie. To ignore testimony from someone who claimed to have seen someone hiding and waiting to abduct a girl who had died in an apparent suicide? It was mind-boggling and offensive.

"You have to go talk to Leighton Jones. You have to see for yourself."

"I don't have to do anything. I *will* go talk to him just because I like you and consider you a friend, but this is a total waste of time. The fact that we are having this conversation gives me a headache." Casey rubbed his eyes. "I wouldn't be surprised if Leighton didn't even see her leave. With things like this, people like to get more involved than they really are."

"People like to get involved in suicides and pretend they're murders for shits and giggles?"

"Don't be a smart-ass. I already said I would go talk to him. Don't make me take it back."

"When will you talk to him?"

"When I have the time."

"This is important, Rick. I'm telling you, Leighton is telling the truth."

"We'll see, I guess," replied Casey.

X

Jonah left Nye Beach extremely frustrated. To him, it seemed as if Casey was being extremely cavalier about the information he had provided. He had just proffered a witness who had given a story that clearly countered the police's conclusion about Katie's death. Casey had always struck Jonah as a decent and well-meaning cop, but he was being very thick in this situation.

Jonah pulled into his personal parking spot at the *News Times* and turned off his engine. The only person left Jonah thought of who might be able to help was Teresa. Perhaps she could provide some shred of information that she hadn't already given in the first interview that would further aid the police in opening an investigation.

Before heading into the office, he pulled out his phone and searched for Teresa's number. The phone rang only once before Teresa answered.

"Hello?"

"Teresa, it's Jonah Carr from the *Times* again."

"Did you talk to Charles?" Her voice trembled.

"Well, yes," said Jonah. "And some other people."

"Other people? Who? Did you find something?"

Jonah paused. He knew it was risky to share everything he had found with Teresa, as she could become obsessive and start to get overly involved in the case. But he threw caution to the wind.

"Yes, I did."

"What did you find?"

"I think it's best if we meet face-to-face again."

17

Jonah was back in the same musty-looking house that smelled like soup and cat litter with his notepad and pen in front of him, as he had been when he interviewed Teresa earlier in the week. Teresa had agreed to an interview that afternoon. Being that she was retired, her schedule was completely open. And she was obviously very eager to receive the information Jonah had about her late granddaughter.

Teresa came out of her kitchen carrying two cups of coffee and set them on coasters on the table. Jonah grasped the mug that was intended for him and took a sip. Immediately, he recoiled. The coffee was scalding hot and tasted like someone had thrown a stale burrito into hot water.

Teresa sat down across from him and leaned forward in anticipation. "So, what did you find?"

Jonah looked at the elderly woman and felt a pang of sympathy at her expression. Nothing that he was about to tell her could bring her Katie back from the dead, which was the true tragedy.

"Through Charles, I was able to locate another witness at the bar who saw her leave. He left at the same time Katie did. He was walking home too." He had decided to exclude the part about Leighton's true motivations.

"And? He must've seen which direction she went." Teresa's eyes flitted back and forth over Jonah's face.

"He did. She didn't go in the direction of the bridge. She was on her way here."

"I knew it. I fucking *knew* it."

The cursing from an old woman like Teresa was jarring, but Jonah pressed on.

"Also, he saw something else."

Teresa's eyes widened. "Oh Jesus. What did he see?"

Jonah gulped. "This is going to be a bit of a shock. And keep in mind that this might not necessarily be true. I don't know what reason he would have to lie, but he could have. My source was walking in the same direction as Katie, and he saw a man in a ski mask hiding behind a tree, near the corner of Pine and High Street."

Teresa drained of all her color. Her lips moved but no sound came out. She looked woozy, as if she might pass out.

"Are you alright, Teresa?"

Teresa couldn't form the words to respond. All she could do was stutter. Finally, after ten more seconds, she repeated what Jonah said. "A man in a ski mask?"

"Yes."

"Oh my God," exclaimed Teresa. "Oh my fucking God." Her chest rose and fell more rapidly as her breathing spiraled out of control.

"I know."

"What did he do when he saw this man?"

"It scared him. He left."

Teresa's mouth went agape and her face suddenly flushed

red in fury. "He left? He saw a masked man hiding behind a tree while Katie was walking by, and he didn't even try and warn her or help her?"

"My source, uh, isn't exactly the heroic type."

"What a fucking asshole!" Teresa shouted indignantly. "I can't even believe . . . Katie . . . and he could have saved her." She looked like she was on the verge of a panic attack, breathing rapidly and shaking.

"I know. I felt the same way when he told me."

Teresa placed her head in her palm, rubbing at it while she continued to shake. When she next spoke, her voice was much weaker. "Did you tell this to the police?"

"Yes, I did," Jonah responded. "They are going to talk to my source soon."

"Holy hell. I knew it. I just *knew* it."

After a few moments of trying to regain her breath as well as her composure, Teresa looked up at Jonah with an expression of complete exhaustion.

"Is that all?"

"Actually, no. I also wanted to ask you a couple of other questions."

"Other questions? What else do you need to know? Don't you have what you need?"

"Well, perhaps. The police might start investigating right away after they talk to him." Jonah tried to say what he meant without actually saying it. Teresa instantly caught on to what he was insinuating.

"Wait, they might? What do you mean they might? You found a witness who saw that Katie was not only not walking in the direction of the bridge, but who also saw a man in a goddamn ski mask hiding behind a tree, and they *might* start investigating? What the hell are you talking about?" With every word her voice got louder.

"Here is the thing: In situations like this, where everything they have so far clearly points in one direction, something that would normally be irrefutable becomes not so if it points in the other direction," said Jonah delicately. "With the texts you received, and the fact that Katie was prone to unpredictable behavior on occasion, and the way she died—it all points to suicide. I'm not saying they won't look into it, but they might start to doubt the credibility of the witness more than they normally would. And if they don't find anything else to support his claim, then justice will not be served."

Teresa had fire in her eyes. "That makes zero sense. The police wouldn't just ignore someone who saw something like that. Are you sure you aren't coming here to ask me more questions because you want to be the hero who finds whoever did this instead of the police?"

It was Jonah's turn to be irritated. It might have been because Teresa had gotten to the truth of the matter, but he was still aggravated by this comment.

"Listen, I'm just trying to help. And if you didn't notice, without me, we wouldn't have gotten this far in the first place."

Teresa rolled her eyes and took a giant swig of her coffee.

"So would you be willing to answer a couple more questions?"

"It depends on what they are." Teresa pursed her lips.

"Can you think of anything unusual that has happened lately with Katie? Has she ever mentioned anything about anyone that struck her as odd? This can be as far back as a month or two ago."

Teresa looked annoyed at first, as though his question had a patently obvious answer and was not worth asking. Then she began to consider what Jonah had asked her.

"Not that I can think of off the top of my head."

"Can you think of anything Katie might have told you in the past few weeks that she thought was strange? Or anything that made her feel threatened?

"Threatened? No. I think I would have already brought that up if I—"

Teresa abruptly stopped mid-sentence, and her eyes glossed over, hit by the weight of her memories.

"I think I do remember something."

A wave of goose bumps erupted on Jonah's arms.

"What?"

A look of fear and uncertainty washed over Teresa's face. "Four or five weeks ago, she came home from work, and we had an odd conversation. She told me that on her way home she felt like she was being followed."

Silence dominated the room for what felt like an eternity. Jonah and Teresa sat speechless, both of them realizing the significance of what had just been said.

"She felt like she was being followed? She didn't see someone actually following her though?"

"No, she didn't see anyone. I can't remember the exact conversation, but she conveyed to me that on her way home she felt like she was being watched. She didn't see who it was, but she was fairly certain someone was following her."

Jonah felt a concoction of different emotions stir in his belly. Part of him was frightened and part of him felt excited. The fear emanated from the deeply disturbing thought of the killer stalking Katie for a prolonged period of time. The excitement was due to something else, but he wasn't quite sure what it was. In the deep recesses of his brain, it was as if something seemed to click.

"Did you take any precautions after this?"

"Honestly, no. We kind of just forgot about it. I think Katie felt like she must have imagined it."

Why did people constantly do that? Ignore their instinct because it didn't seem logical? Now that he knew about the man in the ski mask, it seemed altogether possible to Jonah that Katie had been vetted by her killer. In all likelihood, she *had* been followed at some point.

"Why didn't you mention this to me in our last interview?"

"I didn't even think about it," said Teresa defensively. "It happened a while ago, and like I said, we forgot about it because she thought she had imagined it."

"I see."

Before Jonah could assemble another question, his phone vibrated in his pocket. He pulled it out and saw that it was Rick Casey.

"Excuse me just one moment," he said to Teresa. She didn't even respond. She looked green.

"Hello?"

"Hey, Jonah," Casey said.

"Hey."

"Bad news."

Jonah sat straight up. "What?"

"I already went and talked to Leighton Jones." Casey's voice was strained.

"And?"

"He said he didn't even remember seeing a girl matching Katie's description on the night in question."

18

Jonah had been worried that this might happen, but it was still a little surprising nonetheless. Leighton had retracted his story. Not only had he told Casey he didn't follow Katie home, but he had even said he didn't remember her from the bar that night. It was a complete reversal of what he had relayed to Jonah. Jonah had pleaded with Casey and told him that Leighton must have just gotten cold feet, but the officer shook him off in a matter of seconds. "There is nothing I can do about this Jonah," Casey had said.

Jonah had to figure out how to try and explain the inexplicable to Teresa Deeds.

"That was my friend on the police force, and I'm afraid I have bad news."

Teresa looked deep into Jonah's eyes. "Whatever you're going to tell me, it can't be worse news than what I received the other day."

"You're right," Jonah admitted. "But it's still not going to be pleasant. The police went and talked to the witness, and he presented a totally different story than what he did to me. He said now that he didn't even see Katie that night."

Teresa's mouth fell open. She was at a loss for words for a few moments.

"What? Why would he do that?"

"I'm not sure. Maybe he got scared. The witness has a bit of a criminal record himself, and perhaps he didn't want to get too involved with the police. Maybe he realized if they ever found a suspect that he would have to testify in court. I honestly don't know why he would do this."

Teresa looked on the verge of tears. "What are we going to do now? Are you going to go talk to him again and try and convince him to tell the police the real story?"

"Yes," Jonah said. Perhaps he could persuade Leighton to do the right thing. Maybe he could reinforce the point that the man hadn't actually committed a crime by following her and *planning* to rape her.

"What if he won't do it?"

"Then we'll move on to our next option."

"Which is?" Teresa folded her arms.

"I'm not sure."

Jonah began gathering his notepad and pen that were scattered out over Teresa's coffee table. He had planned on taking notes of their conversation, but he hadn't gotten around to it.

"I'm going to go over to his house. I'll call you after I meet with him."

"Okay," Teresa said faintly.

Jonah grabbed his coat and headed toward the front door.

Less than five minutes later, Jonah was outside of Leighton's front door. His surroundings were a lot less eerie since it was light outside. He supposed that held true for most neighborhoods.

After Jonah knocked several times, he heard rustling from inside. It sounded like Leighton was milling about, getting up to answer the door. Jonah heard heavy footsteps as the man appeared to be approaching. The door opened, and Leighton stood there menacingly with his hands balled into fists. His long, frayed hair was draped around his face like curtains.

"I don't want to talk to you." Leighton scowled. "I have nothing to say."

Jonah shook his head with an exasperated expression on his face. "You could try explaining to me why you changed your story."

Leighton smiled malevolently. "I don't know what you're talking about."

"Don't play games with me. I know you changed your story about the night Katie disappeared when you talked to the police."

"Did I?" Leighton rocked back on his heels, clearly mocking Jonah.

"Fuck you," Jonah said, seeing red. "A girl was killed, you asshole. Think about her family."

"I don't know anything about Katie Deeds." He flashed an ugly, mocking grin.

"Yes, you do. I don't know why you're afraid to talk to the police, but nothing is going to happen to you. They will care far more about catching the man you saw."

"What man?" Leighton again showed his yellowing teeth as he grinned. "I didn't see a man."

For a second, Jonah felt a strong urge to punch Leighton right on the bridge of his massive nose, but withheld. He held his fists at his side.

"If the police find whoever did this, and they realize you were lying, you could be arrested for obstruction of justice."

"No one saw me. If this girl was murdered, how would the perpetrator be able to prove that I knew something and kept it a secret if he didn't even know I was there?" This was actually true, and Jonah didn't have an answer for it.

"You just admitted again that you did see the man," Jonah said through gritted teeth.

"What man? The girl committed suicide."

Leighton again grinned in a disturbing way and slammed the door shut in Jonah's face.

Jonah immediately called Teresa and informed her of what had happened. She sounded heartbroken by the news. However, Jonah lied and told her he would keep trying to get Leighton to change his mind to try and assuage her feelings of despair. But he didn't. He knew that Leighton wouldn't speak to him anymore.

What was next? There was no one else who could provide him with new information that might be able to give him a lead on the man in the mask. The police had no reason to subpoena for the footage from the bridge on the night of Katie's death that would show her either jumping off or being thrown. Without a material witness, there wasn't any reason to watch the recorded video. Jonah had to start to face the truth: He had hit a dead end.

As he drove back to the office, Jonah was enveloped by anger, gripping the steering wheel until his knuckles became white. An innocent twenty-one-year-old woman had been murdered, and it was looking more and more likely that her killer could get away with it. He didn't know what to do. All his means of furthering the investigation into Katie's death were currently exhausted.

When he entered the rows of cubicles in the office of the *News Times*, Jonah saw Randy Marks lurking by his desk.

"What's up, boss?"

"How's the story coming?"

"It has only been a couple of days, so . . . fine, I guess, considering."

Mark's weird bowl haircut seemed to quiver as a slight wave of anger pulsed through him. "Don't be a smart-ass. I'm only hovering because it's my ass on the line here too. If this project isn't going well, you need to tell me."

"It is going swimmingly, thank you," said Jonah.

"Go fuck yourself," Marks said at the sarcasm, and he stomped off.

Great, Jonah thought. Now he had to deal with a boss who was constantly going to be over his shoulder. What was he going to do if he didn't have the story that he had planned on writing? Write the one that Mark thought he was? Penning a story that depicted the aftermath of teen suicide in a small town seemed impossible due to the fact that Jonah was certain it wasn't a suicide.

What next? Jonah couldn't just stand by and let a murder go unnoticed, especially now that he had spoken with the bereaved family and friends and gotten the true scope of Katie's death. He kept picturing the photograph of the beautiful young girl on Teresa's wall, while also imagining Teresa herself shaking back and forth and looking ill at the news of what Leighton Jones had seen. These people who were left behind deserved justice, as did Katie herself.

It felt as if there was something he was missing. Some thread he couldn't quite grasp that would lead him somewhere promising. But what was it? Jonah tried to visualize Teresa's words from their conversation earlier. When she told him about how Katie had thought someone had followed her, it was as if something had clicked. Like a piece of the puzzle fell into place. But he didn't know why. Jonah concentrated with all his being, trying to make it simmer to the front of his consciousness.

Suddenly, he realized what it was. The night that he had

gone home from his disastrous date with Daisy and looked up those cases from the nineties, the article had said that one of the girls, Cara Lee, had been at a friend's house the night she disappeared. Before she left, she had warned the other girl to call the police if she didn't hear from her. Her friend—Jonah couldn't remember the girl's name—had said that it was like Cara had known someone had been following her. Like she had sensed she was being hunted. It seemed the same exact thing had happened to Katie.

19

The man was scared. As he looked from the driver's seat of his Jeep, his heart thumped rapidly against his chest like a bird trying to escape from its cage. He couldn't believe it. After all his research and reconnaissance, how could he have let this come to pass? The one thing he had never let happen before, and the one thing that could possibly foil him, had finally occurred.

He was parked in the familiar neighborhood. His surroundings reminded him of Halloween: large trees reaching over the street with their claws and nails, while shadows dominated the area. The night was far more sinister than previous nights, perhaps because of his recent discovery. Normally, the man would remain calm, cool, and collected, even in the face of turmoil, confident in his prowess and the ability to wiggle out of a corner. But this was different. Things had changed.

The man wasn't even sure what he was going to do. If the police found the body, they would almost assuredly make the connection. Whoever it was that had found the witness would likely go to a different person with the information, and they would start to investigate the lead. If the man was going to do what he was considering, he had to make absolutely sure that it would just go down as a missing person.

The man would have to abandon stalking Sierra Bunker, at least for now. There was at least one person hot on his trail, and the last thing he needed was for this mysterious individual to be given more fuel to pursue him. Perhaps the man could fulfill his goal of taking Sierra after this threat was taken care of.

The man hadn't been told who was connecting the dots. Whoever it was that had found the witness hadn't gotten far enough to warrant him doing anything about it. The anger deep in his stomach boiled over while thinking of this faceless devil that was looking for him. Perhaps it was that damn woman who had spoken to him several years ago. That fat bitch who had no idea how close she had gotten to answers.

Sweat seeped underneath his armpits as he watched through his tinted windows, looking at the house. He wouldn't do anything yet. If he started killing everyone who could be a threat to him immediately after he discovered them, he would spend the rest of his life in a cell. This was purely a mission to discover the creature who had seen him. It would benefit him to know what he was dealing with.

The front door to the house opened. As an instinctual reaction, the man ducked down in his seat, although he couldn't be seen regardless thanks to the tinted windows. The man watched as a tall figure ambled out of the door with his head down. The man felt unsettled as he looked at the figure. Leighton Jones closed his door and was completely oblivious to the Jeep parked across the street.

20

It didn't seem like it could have been possible twenty-four hours ago. But as Jonah sat in his cubicle at the *Times,* he had to face facts: The killer of those girls in the nineties had never been caught. It wasn't totally out of the realm of possibility that the same man had killed Katie too. There were so many similarities between the first five girls and Katie that to neglect the idea of it being the same culprit would be foolish. All of them had been walking either by themselves or in pairs late at night on, or near, Highway 101. They were all somewhat close in age. And as Jonah thought about it, he realized with a chill that they all looked somewhat similar. They all had light hair, pretty smiles, and they were usually short and petite.

Of course, there were differences in the cases too. Katie had had witnesses to her death and had been found the day after. Kylie Desmond hadn't been found for ten years, and two of the other victims weren't found for five months. Katie had died from her fall off the bridge; she had not been strangled like the other victims. But the similarities had become more than uncanny. Jonah had finally begun to accept the possibility that they were all linked.

In the story about Kylie Desmond, it mentioned the two girls who went missing in 1992. Those girls, whom Jonah knew less about than the rest, were named Felicity Sanders and Shelly Schwartz. Jonah didn't cling to any new details about these girls he hadn't already processed when he read the story the first time. The girls had been camping in Beverly Beach and had left their tent. They were last seen walking by themselves near a phone booth by Highway 101. Jonah made a point to look up more about Sanders and Schwartz later.

Jonah switched the tabs on Google Chrome and brought up the page with the story that synthesized the five cases, including those of Cara Lee and Jenna Eason. He focused on the passage that spoke of Lee's friend, Maya Leslie. Jonah gobbled up the words on the screen voraciously as he reread the key sentences:

> *Lee asked Leslie whether she could call her, and said that if she didn't hear from her in an hour, she should call the police. Lee and Eason were never heard from again.*
>
> *Leslie had reportedly asked Lee why she heeded the warning, but Lee refused to tell her.*
>
> *"It was like she knew she was in danger and she shouldn't be walking home by herself. To this day I think her killer had been stalking her before then, and Cara had noticed something weird," said Leslie. "She sensed someone was hunting her."*

That seemed to be the exact same scenario that Teresa had depicted when talking about Katie. He knew it could be possible that it was just a coincidence, but Jonah felt in his heart that it wasn't.

Jonah minimized the tab with the story about Eason and Lee and brought up the first story about Kylie Desmond again. He reread about how the girl's skull had been found in a Ford Taurus ten years after she had gone missing. This detail seemed crucial. It was as if the killer had wanted Desmond's body to be discovered, and when it wasn't, he had left the skull in the car in a public place to get credit for his crime. But why wait ten years? To let nature destroy any viable evidence left on the skull?

The other girls had also been found relatively easily, covered lightly in brush in wooded areas. It was like the killer had only halfheartedly hidden them. He wanted them to be found. In the hypothetical scenario that the same man who killed the girls in the nineties *was* also responsible for Katie's death, why had he changed his modus operandi? Perhaps the police had gotten close to finding him, and the man had been forced to change. Maybe he had continued killing, but he had stopped doing it in a manner that would taunt the police and had started covering his tracks. Perhaps the real thrill for him was simply getting away with it.

Jonah wrote down the names of notable people in the story. There was Kenny Desmond, the first victim's father. Jonah already dreaded speaking with this man. Talking to one devastated family member of a dead young girl was enough. Next, there was Sheriff Tim Connely. Jonah guessed Connely probably had been retired for a long time. He scribbled down the name anyway. It likely wouldn't be as difficult to get in touch with Connely as it would with other people involved in the case. And yet, even if Jonah made contact, there was no guarantee that Connely would be willing to speak with him. Why would a retired PD want to talk to a reporter like him?

Jonah clicked over to the story from 1995 that specifically focused on Eason and Lee in another tab on his browser. The notable names in this story were Sheriff John Paxon, who must have immediately succeeded Tim Connely, and Aaron Dobbs, the coroner who had conducted the autopsies of Eason and Lee. Jonah wrote down the two names on the same sheet of paper. He guessed that Paxon wouldn't be difficult to locate, but Dobbs might be.

Finally, Jonah again brought up the story from 2009 that talked about all five girls as the work of a serial killer. This was the most helpful story, because it gave all the details of the cases chronologically and in a straightforward fashion. There were three more important names in this piece: Dan Jenkins, the District Attorney at the time; Daryl Close, a retired state policeman; and obviously Maya Leslie, Cara Lee's friend. Jonah consolidated the names onto his list.

Jonah probed the story again, looking for anything that stuck out. Dan Jenkins, the DA, had felt hopeful that advances in DNA technology over the years would assist in substantiating new clues on the cold cases. Obviously, that hadn't worked out. That, combined with the fact that the person had evaded police for thirty years, led Jonah to believe that whoever the killer was, he was highly cautious. To leave no viable DNA evidence on five separate victims was quite a feat.

Other than the scant DNA clues, there was nothing that jumped out at Jonah upon rereading the archived *Oregonian* piece. He had the seven names saved and would start attempting to track them down. Jonah knew it would be difficult work. But hopefully at least one of them would get back to him and help him answer some questions.

The fact of the matter was, he didn't have anyone left to talk to regarding Katie. Leighton wouldn't speak with him again. Charles had nothing else of significance to say. Anthony Mason was almost irrelevant. Teresa was more ignorant than Jonah was about who might have done it, and the crabbers on the dock who had seen Katie fall to her death had already left town, according to Rick Casey. The only thing Jonah could do was look into the cold cases and try to establish a corresponding link to Katie Deeds. Even if it wasn't connected, he could at least try to bring the families of Newport the peace they had been seeking for three decades. Maybe these old cases just needed a fresh set of eyes. It was time to start making calls. Jonah's investigation into this serial killer from the 1990s had begun.

21

Randy Marks had been the editor at the *Times* since 1990 and was an incredible asset in assisting Jonah as he began his search. Through Marks's network of colleagues, Jonah could locate the phone numbers of David Browning, Cheyenne Blue, and Micah Morris, the authors of the respective articles on all of the girls, in a matter of twenty minutes or so. Marks had jumped at the opportunity to use his prowess in the field to find their contact information when Jonah had asked. He hadn't even questioned why Jonah had wanted the emails or phone numbers of the three reporters, and didn't seem to have any idea that it was connected to Katie Deeds. Jonah suspected that his boss was just eager to show that he was useful in more than just a small-town paper setting.

Before he had become an editor, Marks had worked for a paper in Portland, Oregon, *The Willamette Weekly,* as a writer in the eighties. He attended many press conferences and media scrums with reporters from *The Oregonian* and had made several friends at the rival Portland paper, including the long-term publisher of *The Oregonian,* Ian Jackson. Jackson had served as the boss of Browning and Morris, and his successor was Cheyenne Blue's superior. Browning was retired, but Morris and Blue still worked for *The Oregonian.*

Jonah first called Browning and asked him for an avenue to speak with Sheriff Tim Connely, his first name on the list. Jonah had told Browning that he was doing a follow-up on the cold case from 1994. Unfortunately, Browning said that Connely was now retired and living in South Florida, and thus, he no longer had the updated address or phone number for the man. However, Browning could provide a number for Kenny Desmond, the father of the first victim. Apparently, Desmond still lived in Newport after all these years.

Next, Jonah dialed Micah Morris, the reporter who had written the initial story on Jenna Eason and Cara Lee. Morris answered immediately. After a brief aside about who he was and what paper he worked for, Jonah asked Morris for any information on the former sheriff, John Paxon, and the erstwhile coroner, Aaron Dobbs. Unfortunately, Morris only had a slight recollection of who Jonah was talking about and definitely didn't have addresses or phone numbers for Paxon or Dobbs. "I have written so many damn stories over the years that a lot of sources tend to blend together," Morris had said. Jonah thanked him anyway and moved on.

Finally, Jonah called Cheyenne Blue, who had written the most recent story from 2009 that asserted that the five girls had been killed by the same person. Blue was a perky-sounding woman, with a high-pitched, slightly creaky voice. Like he told Browning and Morris, Jonah conveyed to Blue that he was simply writing another piece on the cold cases, even though he didn't have new information on the girls. This explanation seemed to suffice. Jonah could tell that Blue was still extremely curious about what had actually happened to the victims.

Blue was able to retrieve a personal cell phone number for Dan Jenkins, Newport's district attorney. However, Maya Leslie, Cara Lee's friend to whom Lee had heeded the warning, had died in a car accident in 2012. Also, Daryl Close, the former state policeman, had passed away from a heart attack less than six months before. Jonah couldn't quite believe his luck, but he was thankful that Blue had passed along the information regardless.

Out of the seven names on his list, the only two who he was able to get phone numbers for were Kenny Desmond and Dan Jenkins. Jonah called Desmond first to get it out of the way. He didn't fancy speaking to Desmond about something that had obviously ripped the man's world apart, but he had to.

"Hello?"

"Hi, may I speak to Kenny Desmond, please?"

"Yeah, one second," the man said with his gruff, gravelly voice. After a bit, a new voice started to speak. The voice was wheezy and dry.

"Hello?"

"Is this Kenny Desmond?"

"It is."

"Hi, Mr. Desmond, this is Jonah Carr. I am a reporter for the *News Times*. I am currently writing a story that revolves around several teenage girls who were murdered in the 1990s. As I understand it, your daughter, Kylie, was killed in 1994?" Jonah asked, all in one breath.

There was a long pause before the man responded.

"Kylie was killed in eighty-four. She was found in ninety-four," Kenny said. "But yes, I am her father."

"Ah, yes, that's what I meant. Well, I am deeply sorry for your loss, Mr. Desmond."

"Thanks," Kenny said quietly.

"Right, well, I'm doing a follow-up piece on your daughter and the other victims, and I was wondering if you would be able to sit down with me for an interview. It would be extremely helpful."

There was another pause. "A follow-up piece? What do you mean?"

"It is difficult to explain. It would probably be easier to convey if we were face to face."

A long bout of silence followed this, and Jonah was only assured that Kenny hadn't hung up by the sound of his labored breathing through the phone receiver.

"I'm not sure about this."

"Trust me, Mr. Desmond. This will be worth your time. New evidence has come to light, and I want to get your take on it."

It seemed as if curiosity got the better of Kenny. "Hmm. Alright," he said in his wheezy voice.

Jonah gave a small pump of his fist in triumph. "Great! Where and when should we meet?"

"I'm busy today. Got a lot of work to do. Maybe tomorrow?"

"That sounds perfect. What time tomorrow? And where?"

"I guess noon would work," Kenny said. "And my house is fine."

"Great! Where do you live?"

"I live out off the bay road. My house is on Deer Avenue. It's about two miles east of Newport. There will be the water treatment plant to your right. Deer Avenue to your left. Turn there and the road will slope upward and there will be a twist at the end of the street. My driveway is just around the corner. The house number is 455."

"Got it, thanks. I guess I will see you then. Thank you for your time, Mr. Desmond!" Jonah said, too upbeat for the gravity of the interview topic.

"Don't mention it. See you tomorrow."

X

Jonah made the long, winding trip down the bay road the next day. It was aptly named, as the road was only a few feet from Yaquina Bay. On the non-water side of the street, there were sloping hills that made their way back up to Highway 20, which traveled east. Several upscale-looking houses were sprinkled onto the hills. Surrounding the houses were gargantuan trees that jutted into the air from every angle. The bay looked more like a swamp, with thick vegetation and lily pads growing in its shallow bits.

Jonah had traveled two miles down the winding road when he saw Deer Avenue to his left. To his right was the massive off-teal water treatment plant, letting him know that this was indeed the correct street, so he turned. The road climbed upward and curved sharply into the woods. There was a DEAD END sign that was posted just before the curve that Kenny had described. As Jonah's car rounded about the twist, a huge house came into his line of vision.

The building was light blue with two stories. It was perfectly kept; no dirt or cracks in the foundation could be seen. In the driveway was a black BMW, and judging by the shine of the paint, it was probably brand new. The garage was white and formed about one-fourth of the house. Jonah wondered if any other nice cars were parked inside of the garage.

Kenny Desmond's place exuded wealth. Jonah had briefly researched Kenny's background, and found that the man operated a landscaping business. A business mogul in this neighborhood was not uncommon; most of the homeowners were upper class and took part in some sort of entrepreneurial venture that usually involved the fishing industry.

Jonah parked his car next to the BMW. He hopped out of his seat, shut his door, and made his way up a beautiful wooden deck that led to the front entryway. He rang the white doorbell twice.

Within moments, the door swung open. A tall, well-built man with short black hair and gray eyes stood looking at Jonah.

"You must be the reporter," the man said gruffly.

"Yes, are you Kenny?" Jonah held out his hand.

"Nah, I'm his brother. Name's Brendan." He grasped Jonah's hand. "Come on in." He led Jonah through a gorgeous living room with furniture in it that looked as if it had never been sat in before.

"So are you just here visiting Kenny?" Jonah asked, trying to make conversation.

"What? No. I live here too. We operate the business together," Brendan muttered.

"Oh, okay. Yeah, I knew that he ran the business. I didn't know that anyone else was a part of it, though."

"Yeah. I am. You can sit on the couch. I'll get Kenny." Brendan left the room as Jonah sat down. As he withdrew his recorder and notepad, Jonah marveled a bit at his surroundings. Coming from a dinky little flat, he couldn't imagine what it was like to stay in a place like this. It would almost be too blissful. When Jonah was a child, he and his parents had all been crammed into a tiny two-bedroom apartment. Eventually, they had upgraded to a house, but it too was small. They had lived right above the poverty line for his entire childhood. Jonah had never known opulence, nor comfort. It almost made him feel out of place to be sitting among it.

From the couch, Jonah could see out of the window across the room that showed the backyard. There was a huge, sprawling lawn that angled down, forming a slight hill. At the bottom of the hill was a thick forest of Douglas firs. From the height on which the house was built, there were magnificent views of the bay just above the bundle of trees. The sun shone spectacularly that day, which only enhanced the aesthetics.

Jonah's stupor was interrupted by a squeaking noise. He

turned toward the hall from which he heard the sound and saw a grizzled man in a wheelchair rolling toward him. The man had shoulder-length, unkempt brown hair that was doused in a heavy amount of gray. A mini-beard sprouted a couple of inches down his face. His gut sagged over his tiny legs, which looked like they had atrophied from his time in the wheelchair. His voice was raspy as he began to speak.

"I'm Kenny. Nice to meet you." He took his hand off the right wheel of his wheelchair and held it out into the air.

"Jonah Carr." Jonah shook the man's hand as he stood up. He was surprised by Kenny Desmond's appearance. David Browning hadn't said anything about him being disabled. And though Jonah had done some brief research on the man, nothing had indicated his paralysis.

"Sit down, sit down." Kenny waved his hand toward the couch. Jonah immediately plopped back down and couldn't help but stare at the man for a few seconds.

Kenny narrowed his eyes. "Yes, I know I am in a wheelchair."

"I wasn't—"

"Got in a car accident back in ninety-four. Broke my neck. When it happened I told the doctors I was going to walk again, but they just kept telling me I was paraplegic and that it doesn't reverse itself. Been trying to prove 'em wrong ever since. Even called my doc when I felt a tingle in my legs two years ago and tried to argue with him. Told him he was wrong about me not walkin'. He told me I didn't have a leg to stand on."

Jonah's mouth twitched.

"You can laugh, kid," Kenny said with a wry smile. "It was intentional."

Jonah smiled widely. "I imagine it's important to keep a sense of humor about it."

"It is important to keep a sense of humor about everything." Kenny grinned.

"Agreed."

Kenny looked him up and down. "So, what is it that you're working on? You mentioned the gist of it on the phone, but I don't really know what you meant."

"Ah, right. So, as I'm sure you're aware, a young woman named Katie Deeds died of an apparent suicide early on Monday morning."

It took Kenny a few seconds before he answered. "Yes, I am aware of it. It is terrible." He looked away, forlorn, and sat back a little in his wheelchair. The man looked incredibly feeble, and Jonah saw his left hand droop down off his lap, shaking. Jonah wondered if the man was purely cold or if he had some sort of neurological disorder.

"Yes, it is," agreed Jonah.

"But why are you bringing that up? I thought you wanted to talk to me about Kylie."

"Yes, well . . . I have reason to believe that Katie Deeds didn't commit suicide."

Kenny frowned at Jonah, apparently confused by what he had said. "Wait, what?"

"I think she was murdered," Jonah said more bluntly.

Kenny's pupils dilated in shock. "But . . . I . . . How could that be possible? I don't understand. Weren't there witnesses that saw her jump off the bridge?"

"Well, there were people who saw her hit the water. They didn't see her jump. Anyway, I have encountered a witness who ran into Katie earlier that night and saw something that seems to rule out the possibility that she jumped of her own volition. I'm not sure I should tell you exactly what this person saw for your own safety."

"Why are you telling me this?"

"Well, I don't have definitive proof—"

"Wait," said Kenny, rocking forward in his wheelchair with his mouth ajar in wonder. "You can't be saying what I think you are saying."

Jonah nodded. "Yes, I think I am."

Kenny looked positively bewildered. "No way. That isn't possible. It was that Foles guy that killed Kylie. And he is dead."

"Bobby Ray Foles?"

"Yes, him," Kenny said while nodding.

"Why do you think it was him?"

"I don't think it was him. The police think that it was him. That is what they told me like seven or eight years ago."

"I see," said Jonah gingerly. "Right. Well, I don't have any proof that there is a connection. It is what you might call a hunch. To be frank, even though I have accrued circumstantial evidence that Katie Deeds was murdered, I have sort of hit a dead end in terms of starting a police investigation. The witness who is key to this case has changed his story, out of fear, I suppose. Anyhow, there are significant similarities between what happened to Katie and what happened to Kylie and the others, so I am sort of following my instinct here."

"Well, not to be rude, but I really don't think that's possible," Kenny said, sounding exasperated.

"I know you don't, but just humor me. I won't take up much of your time. I just need you to answer a few questions about Kylie."

Kenny looked out the window for a moment as his eyes glazed over.

"You know, it has been thirty-two years since she went missing, and I can still feel the pain right in my chest. Not a day goes by where I don't wonder what I could have done differently," said Kenny with his head drooping down. "You know what I think about the most? The things I have missed. Her graduating high school. Going away to college. Getting engaged. Dancing with me at her wedding."

Kenny's eyes glistened with tears.

"I am truly sorry, Mr. Desmond," said Jonah awkwardly.

He had never been good at consoling people in pain. Having never experienced real tragedy himself, it was hard to relate to someone like Kenny and offer words of solace.

"And what that monster did to her. Leaving her sku—you know." He couldn't say the world skull. "Out in public like that. I can't think about it without feeling like I am going to puke. But more than anything it makes me angry. If I ever got my hands on Bobby Ray fuckin' Foles, there's no tellin' what might have happened to *his* skull."

Jonah nodded, thinking it best to just let the man continue speaking.

"It is still hard to talk about, but then, sometimes I feel like it is the only thing I want to talk about. I guess I can answer your questions, but I really don't think it is going to help you."

"Well, I appreciate it."

"So what do you want to know? Keep in mind, like I said, it has been thirty-two years. The details aren't exactly, uh, fresh in my mind."

"I understand," said Jonah. "So first, just take me through that night all those years ago when she went missing. As I understand it, she went to see a movie?"

"That's right." Kenny slumped in his wheelchair. "*Red Dawn*. Never seen it, never will."

"That's understandable. So, she went by herself?"

"That's right." He nodded. "That was my first mistake. I should have insisted that she go with a friend. But Kylie was kind of a loner. She didn't have many friends."

"Was her mother here? Did she have a problem with Kylie going alone?"

"God, no. Kylie's mom ain't been in the picture since Kylie was a baby. She lived with me and Brendan her whole life."

"So you and Brendan have lived here since the eighties?"

"No, we didn't have this house built until 1999. We used to live in a smaller place in Agate Beach when Kylie was a kid."

"Ah, okay. Anyway, so she walked to the movies by herself?"

"No, of course not. I gave her a ride. I was going to pick her up too, but I took too long for her, I guess. I was a half hour late. She called the house several times from a pay phone, but I didn't answer. I wasn't home. I was still going to pick her up, though. I just got distracted. So she started walking. We didn't live very far from the theater."

Kenny paused. His raspy voice had cracked when he said the word "theater."

"I'm sorry. I just can't get over how bad of a parent I was that night. Sometimes I think that I deserved this," Kenny said, fighting back tears.

"No parent should ever have to bury their kid." Jonah put a consoling hand on Kenny's shoulder. Kenny put his own hand over Jonah's, accepting the gesture.

"So you showed up to the theater, and she was gone?"

"Yes." Kenny wiped at his eyes.

"What did you do?"

"I called the police and drove everywhere around town looking for her. Was looking all night."

Jonah nodded. "And you didn't hear anything for ten years?"

"I was in constant contact with the police for the first few months. But no. I never heard nothin'."

"I imagine that was very difficult," Jonah said sympathetically.

"They were the hardest years of my life. Up until the day that they found her over there by the reservoir, I never gave up hope."

Jonah felt his stomach drop in pity. "Did you ever hear from the police about any sort of DNA evidence left at the scene? Like, did they have anything that they could link to possible suspects?"

"Not that I heard. Seems like Foles did a real good job cleaning up after himself. The cops said that the other girls were strangled. I guess that is what happened to Katie too. That is something I will never get over."

Jonah didn't say anything. He wasn't sure what Kenny meant.

"This might seem weird to you, but I always wonder what Kylie must have been thinking while he was choking the life out of her. It takes more than a few seconds to strangle a person, you know? I can only imagine the thoughts running through her head. Maybe she was wondering, *Where's my dad?*" Kenny said weakly. As soon as he finished this sentence he broke down, sobbing.

All Jonah could do was rub Kenny's arm, trying to comfort him. What could you say to a man who had been completely broken, literally and figuratively? The sight of a bawling, bereaved father in a wheelchair was one of the most pitiful things Jonah had ever laid eyes upon.

"I am so so sorry, Mr. Desmond."

"Call me Kenny."

"Okay."

There was a long break in the conversation, as Kenny worked to control himself. He wheeled himself over to the coffee table and reached for a box of tissues. Jonah gazed at the man, a little hesitant to continue. Would he be overstepping his bounds if he continued his line of inquiry? He felt a little strange asking more questions. Then again, he hadn't gotten what he had come for yet. Jonah needed more, and no matter how much distress it caused Kenny, he had to keep going.

"So, Kenny, let me ask you. I know it has been a really long time since she disappeared, and I am sure the police asked you this back then, but can you remember Kylie ever telling you about anyone unusual or threatening she may have interacted with in the days or months before her death?"

Kenny smiled, although he was clearly more exasperated than he was amused. "Listen, I get why you would ask that, but of course not. If I had, the police would have caught the guy, don't you think?"

"Probably, yes, but you are right, I had to ask."

Kenny looked away, nodding.

"So, how certain are you that whoever killed Kylie killed the other girls too?"

Kenny looked back at Jonah, his eyes red from crying. He looked surprised at the question. "I mean, beyond all doubt. Don't you think so?"

"Wouldn't be here if I didn't. Just wanted to get your take on it," Jonah said matter-of-factly.

"They have to be all connected, don't they? They were all teenage girls. They were all walking alone on the highway. I mean, yeah."

"Have you ever talked to anyone else about it being the work of the same killer?"

"The police obviously. And the DA."

"Dan Jenkins?"

"That's him." Kenny raised his index finger in acknowledgement.

Jonah scribbled down a couple of words on his notepad about how Dan Jenkins kept cropping up. "Right. Anyone else? I am just trying to get a lead on who else I might be able to talk to that might point me in the right direction."

Kenny mulled over Jonah's question, and then his face lit up. "There was that lady who came by here."

"A lady? What was her name?"

"Oh geez, I don't remember. She gave me her card. It is in a drawer in the kitchen somewhere, I think." Kenny pointed in the direction of the kitchen.

"What was this woman's profession?"

"She was a private investigator."

"Do you remember who she was hired by?"

"Hired? No, I don't think she was hired. I think she was just interested in the case. Obsessed is more like it."

"Obsessed? Why would you say that?"

"Oh, I don't know. She had already talked to a bunch of people before me. She had a giant notebook full of notes and pictures. And newspaper clippings. She called me several times after I talked to her in person, and kept askin' me more stuff. Eventually I got tired of it and stopped answering when she would call," said Kenny, shaking his head. "I was happy to talk to her the first time, but she was just really relentless after that."

"And you don't remember her name?"

"Marie, or something. I really can't recall."

"I would really appreciate it if you could find that card."

X

It took Kenny almost fifteen minutes of scrounging around his kitchen drawers before he found the business card. It was more difficult for him than it would be for a non-disabled person, as he was constantly restrained to a seated position and had to reach further to dig in drawers. Finally, he withdrew what he was looking for from the bowels of a drawer that was filled with letters and other miscellaneous items he semi-discarded.

"Here it is." Kenny sounded triumphant as he held the small card. He handed it to Jonah, and Jonah flipped it over to observe the printed font. It read *Maryanne Wiggins, Private Investigator.* Underneath this, it listed her phone number and her email.

"May I keep this?"

"Go for it. I ain't got no use for it."

Jonah tucked the card away into his pocket, and the two men headed back to the living room, Jonah walking, Kenny wheeling.

"Where were we?" Jonah sat back down on the couch.

"You were askin' me about if Kylie ever interacted with

anybody suspicious and what not."

"Right. Did anything else strike you as strange about the night she disappeared?"

"Strange? Besides the fact that my daughter was abducted?"

"Yes, well, I suppose I phrased that wrong. I meant anything strange that you saw before that," said Jonah, rubbing his temple awkwardly.

"No. Like I said, I was preoccupied." He sounded strangely ashamed of himself.

Jonah squinted his eyes in concentration. "What exactly were you preoccupied with?"

"A woman." Kenny dropped his chin.

"Ah."

"It was just a fling. Never saw the chick again after that night. Never wanted to."

"I see."

After a minuscule interlude of silence, Jonah went to pursue a new angle. "Were there any other men that Kylie frequently interacted with in her life? Especially in the year before her death? I know that sounds weird, but a lot of times in situations like this, the victim often knows or has seen their killer before they are taken. I don't know how applicable that is since we are likely dealing with a serial killer, but anything you can remember helps."

Kenny looked a little uncomfortable, but answered anyway. "Not really. Not that I know of. Kylie didn't interact with a lot of people in general. She didn't have a lot of friends. The only people who she spent a lot of time around was me and my brother Brendan. And before you even go there, he wasn't even in town when she disappeared," Kenny said, his tone flat.

"I wasn't going to—"

"I know, I know." Kenny brushed off Jonah's excuse. "I just had to say it anyway."

Jonah looked at his notepad and examined the list of topics

he wanted to ask Kenny about that he had assembled before the interview.

"In terms of how Kylie was found, do you think the killer was trying to send a message?"

Kenny frowned. "What do you mean?"

"Doesn't it seem strange that whoever placed her remains in that car waited an entire decade to do so? Doesn't it seem like a taunt?"

"What? Foles had a personal vendetta against me or something?"

"No, like the killer was trying to remind the police that he was still out there."

Kenny got a strange gleam in his eye, as though he were disturbed and fascinated at the same time. "I have never thought about it like that. Maybe so."

It wasn't exactly the hot take that Jonah was looking for, so he looked back down at his notes, and moved on to the next topic.

The rest of the interview lasted approximately fifteen minutes. Kenny didn't provide anything else that would help Jonah on his quest. As much as Jonah tried to focus the conversation on the days leading up to her death, and who she might have interacted with, Kenny just kept talking about Kylie as a person: who she was, how she was special, and how he revered her innocence. It was incredibly depressing to listen to. This killer, whoever he was, had ended two lives when he took Kylie's.

When it got to the point that Jonah felt like he wasn't getting any further, he gathered his things.

"I appreciate your time, Kenny. I know this was difficult to talk about."

"Yeah. Well, I hope it helped," he responded, holding out a shaky hand. Jonah grasped the hand and shook it, noticing the strength Kenny possessed and the fierceness with which he bore into Jonah's eyes.

"Listen, I don't think there is anything here. I know in my gut that Foles killed my daughter. But if by some tiny chance you are right, and it wasn't Foles . . . you better help me catch that fucker."

"Yes. I better."

X

Jonah reflected on the interview as he sat in his car. He supposed it had been helpful, in that he had gained more perspective on the night that this whole thing had started thirty-two years ago. It was all such a tragedy. The fact that Kenny had to be stuck with a lifetime of guilt because he had pursued a woman's affection in his loneliness was a damn shame. As Jonah thought of the broken man in his wheelchair, he was filled with a new resolve.

Jonah pulled the small business card out of his pocket and turned it over in his hand. He decided he had nothing to lose. This Wiggins woman probably didn't have anything to share that Jonah didn't already know, but it was worth a shot. Jonah dialed the number.

The phone rang so many times that Jonah thought it was going to go to voice mail. However, at the last second, a voice that sounded wrought with phlegm answered.

"Maryanne Wiggins."

"Yes, hi, my name is Jonah Carr. I am a reporter at the *News Times*. I have been working on a story about a young woman who allegedly committed suicide this past Monday morning. I don't know how to say this, but I have questions about the circumstances surrounding her death, and I was wondering if I could speak with you about it. It could have a connection to something else that I think you may know something about." He knew his explanation sounded clunky.

The line was silent for a good five seconds. Jonah briefly wondered if the woman had hung up.

"Hello?"

"You think something else may have happened to her?"

"I know it sounds crazy, but yes."

There was more silence. Jonah just waited, anticipating the woman's response.

"Mr. Carr, I think we need to meet."

22

Maryanne Wiggins's office looked tiny from the outside. It sat above a shop called Sandcastle Toys, looking anything but welcoming. The paint was a stale kind of gray, and the storm that was raging outside made it appear even drearier. Jonah supposed that it was very Newport to have a private investigator's office be directly above a toy store.

It was the day after Jonah had met with Kenny Desmond, and the weather had taken a turn for the worse. The heavy cloud cover made the entire town look several shades darker, and the wind blew fiercely, pushing the rain sideways. Jonah sat in his car, as he had arrived slightly earlier than he told Wiggins he would.

When Jonah got out, he was surprised he didn't blow away as the gusts of wind slammed against him. He had a bit of difficulty shutting his car door against the wind but managed it and headed for the front door of Sandcastle Toys with the hood to his rain jacket pulled over his head. As he pulled the door open, a bell rang in response to his presence.

An old woman who looked like an owl peeked over the top of her glasses from the stool behind a desk. She had so many wrinkles on her face that it was difficult to see her eyes.

"Hello, dear." The old woman smiled.

"Hello," Jonah chimed. "Sorry to disturb you, but I am looking for Maryanne Wiggins."

"Ah, yes," said the woman. "Maryanne mentioned something about a reporter. She's upstairs." The woman pointed in the direction of a dusty-looking staircase that was behind several shelves of toys.

Jonah waved his hand appreciatively. "Thank you."

He trudged up the staircase slowly. It was so steep that his thigh muscles burned while climbing. At the top of the small flight of stairs was an oak door with a plaque plastered onto it: MARYANNE WIGGINS, P.I. Jonah knocked several times and waited.

"Just a sec," shouted a husky voice from inside. Within a few moments, the door was pulled open, and Jonah looked upon Maryanne Wiggins for the first time. Instantly, he was reminded of a hobbit. She was very short, and somewhat overweight, although Jonah would not describe her as fat. Her hair was dark brown and her eyes were bright green. Jonah guessed that she was probably in her fifties. She was wearing a black pantsuit that fit a little too tightly around her belly.

"You Jonah Carr?"

"Yes, nice to meet you," Jonah said, extending his arm.

Wiggins shook his hand, eyeing him up and down. After measuring his appearance, she appeared to blurt out the first thought that entered her head.

"Anyone ever tell you you look like Owen Wilson?"

"Uh, no, actually."

"Well, shit. Maybe you don't."

Jonah stared at Wiggins, feeling a strong desire to laugh,

although the woman kept a straight face.

"Well come on in."

Wiggins limped back through the door frame. Her wide hips and large rear end moved as though on a swivel, and her left leg gave way a little bit more than her right whenever her feet struck the ground.

When Jonah had made his way into the room, he briefly thought that he was back out in the storm. It looked as if a small hurricane had ravaged the office. Random sheets of paper were scattered everywhere and boxes were sat haphazardly all over the floor. It was a small room with a door on the right side and a desk inside that was cluttered with folders and notebooks. Wiggins weaved around the objects on the floor, limped her way around the desk, and sat down onto a comfortable-looking chair. She indicated the less welcoming seat that was across the desk, motioning for Jonah to sit.

"Sorry about the mess," Wiggins said. "I realize it looks like a bomb went off in here, but fortunately, I remember where everything important is."

"Oh yeah, no problem at all. This isn't even that bad." Jonah sat down.

"I hope that is the last time you lie to me over the course of this meeting."

Jonah smiled awkwardly.

"So, let's get right to it," Wiggins said simply.

Jonah was surprised by how sudden this plunge into the subject matter was. There was no small talk offered, nor pleasantries exchanged. Wiggins gave off the air that she did not care the least bit about such things.

She pulled out a small notepad and a pen, ready to take notes. Jonah looked at her writing tools, before slowly pulling out his own from his coat pocket.

"Will it be strange if we both take notes on what the other is saying?" Jonah said, trying to crack a joke.

"On the contrary, I think it will be more efficient in terms of organization, which, as you can see from my office, is one of my strengths," said Wiggins sarcastically. Jonah laughed out loud, but Wiggins's expression remained stoic.

Jonah looked around uncomfortably and then said the next question that came to mind. "Do you mind if I record this conversation?"

"Yes, I do."

"Uh, what?"

Wiggins's face suddenly looked defiant. "I do mind. I don't want you to record. You can take notes, but don't record electronically."

"Uh, okay." He had never had anyone not allow him to use his recorder before.

"It is just a privacy issue, Mr. Carr. If someone were to steal your phone and find the recording of our conversation, they would know all the details and nuances of everything I am about to share with you. With notes, you will likely use some form of shorthand and a potential thief wouldn't be able to glean much from them."

Jonah sort of understood the logic in this, but was also slightly miffed, because it would be more difficult to categorize everything later. However, he decided to let it go.

"So where should we start?"

"First, I need to know everything you have discovered about what happened to Katie Deeds. I want to hear about every single person you talked to and what they told you. I need you to reiterate your witnesses' stories as close to verbatim as you can. Be as thorough and as detailed as possible. We are entering into the realm of speculation and circumstance, and it is important that we stick to the facts." She had stopped looking at him and zeroed in her focus on her notepad, poised to take notes.

"Uh, okay." He felt like it was going to take forever to explain to her every single thing he had learned so far, and he wasn't sure what to include and what not to include. Instead of trying to filter out anything superfluous, he simply started talking.

He began by telling Wiggins that he had been assigned to write the story about Katie's death for the *News Times* and how he had first interviewed Katie's boss as a way to fill in background information for the story and gather possible quotes. Wiggins scribbled down Anthony Mason's name.

He then spoke of Teresa Deeds and relayed to Wiggins how Teresa had thought that Katie didn't commit suicide. As soon as he told Wiggins this, she interrupted him.

"Why did she think that?"

"Because she says that Katie wasn't depressed and because of the texts."

Wiggins frowned, looking confused. "The texts? What texts?"

Jonah was surprised the woman hadn't heard this crucial part of the story yet. Then again, he remembered that nobody else in the community was as immersed in this case as he was, and though Wiggins had likely heard of what had happened to Katie, she would have no way of knowing about the texts.

"Teresa Deeds received three texts on the night of Katie's disappearance from Katie's phone. They strongly suggested that Katie was going to commit suicide," Jonah said. Wiggins immediately asked what exactly they had said, and when Jonah told her, she came at him with more questions.

"And why did Teresa Deeds think that Katie didn't send those texts?"

"The main reason was that Katie didn't call Teresa grandma. She called her by her given name." Jonah expected Wiggins to think this was strange, but she didn't. She just made another note.

Next, Jonah recounted his conversation with Charles Johnson and explained that Charles had told him about a strange man who was a regular at Rip Tide's and had given Katie the creeps. After Jonah elaborated on the first encounter he had with Leighton Jones, including how the man had ran away from him, Wiggins interjected once more.

"You chased him? Why? What were you going to do?"

"I'm not sure." Jonah tapped his foot impatiently. How come people kept asking him that?

The woman didn't say anything. Jonah continued and told her about his friend on the police force, Rick Casey, and how Casey had run a criminal history on Leighton. Wiggins furiously took more notes when Jonah told her that Leighton had committed several sexual assaults, intent on saving every word that he said.

Eventually, Jonah spoke of his second encounter with Leighton, and how he had gotten Leighton to admit that he was planning on raping Katie. Wiggins didn't express any visible shock at this, although she did seem to write with more fervor. When Jonah finally got to the masked man, Wiggins stopped him almost immediately.

"A man in a mask?" repeated Wiggins, with her eyes widening ominously.

"That's right," Jonah said calmly. "Hiding behind a tree."

"What kind of mask was he wearing?"

"A ski mask," Jonah said, a little annoyed. *That* was the first question she asked?

"What did Jones do when he saw this man?"

"He ran away."

Wiggins wrote down several more words. "Did Jones describe the build of this man?"

"He said he didn't get a clear look, but that the guy looked tall and somewhat muscular."

"How many people have you shared this information with?"

"Rick Casey and Teresa Deeds. That's it."

"The police officer?" Wiggins quirked her brows, surprised.

"Did he go and talk to Jones?"

"Yes, and Jones already changed his story. He told Casey he didn't even remember seeing Katie that night."

Wiggins inscribed this word for word on her notepad. "Did you speak with Jones again and try and get him to tell the real story to the cops?"

"Yes, but he was being a real prick. He pretended like he didn't know what I was talking about," said Jonah, shaking his head as though he were ridding himself of a particularly irksome gnat.

Wiggins reclined back in her chair and looked at the ceiling. After five or six seconds of meditation, she spoke once more. "Well, it looks like our path ahead will be simple, won't it? We must get Jones to go to the police. If he saw a man who appeared threatening to Katie on the night that she allegedly committed suicide, then he simply must talk."

"I know that logically that seems like the way to move forward, but I really don't think it will be that easy," replied Jonah. "I already warned him about obstructing an investigation, but he doesn't seem to care. Since the man in the mask didn't see him, we have no proof that Leighton was even in the vicinity, other than his personal testimony. But like I said, he has changed it."

"What is Jones's address?"

"Uh, 452 High Street. But I really don't think—"

"If the only other evidence you have that Katie Deeds didn't commit suicide is the suspicion of a grieving grandmother, then how else are you going to proceed other than finding a way to make Jones talk?" Wiggins talked over him while she wrote down Leighton's address. "Unless you have another witness who might have seen this masked man, then Jones is our primary option."

Jonah rolled his eyes.

"Either we go talk to Jones, or you try to convince the

police that it wasn't a suicide without him."

"Rick Casey already—"

"Go to a different cop."

Jonah shook his head and he flushed red. "Look, if you don't want to help, fine. I am just saying I have already tried to go to the police."

"Of course I want to help, but you already have more than enough information to get the ball rolling here. I don't get why you need me."

"Because I think this is connected to another case, and Kenny Desmond told me that I should speak to you about it."

A dark expression came over Wiggins's face. She looked at Jonah in awe, narrowing her eyes and opening her mouth slightly.

"Kenny Desmond? The father of Kylie Desmond?"

"Yes. I have reason to believe that Katie was killed by the same person who murdered his daughter."

Wiggins seemed to turn a little pale.

"And what reason is that?"

Jonah recounted what Teresa Deeds had said regarding the day that Katie had felt like someone was following her home.

"I had already begun looking into the numerous girls who were killed in the nineties before Teresa told me that. I didn't think it could possibly be connected to Katie, but I considered it anyway after some lady at the bar mentioned that there might've been a serial killer in Lincoln County who was never caught. Anyway, when I was researching, I read an online archived news story about two of the girls, Jenna Eason and Cara Lee. Apparently, Lee felt like someone was possibly stalking her before her death, just like Katie."

Wiggins's nose twitched, and her eyes were wide.

"Once I was told about Katie feeling like she was being followed, I reconsidered the commonalities between her and the other victims. Young girls walking alone at night near Highway

101? It became too uncanny to ignore, so I spoke with Kenny Desmond. He mentioned your name in passing and said that you had spoken with him some time ago. He also said that you already knew a great deal about the case and the other five girls who were killed," Jonah said, trying to be as succinct as he could.

Wiggins held her index finger in the air as if to stop him right there. "Five?"

"Uh, what?"

"You said five girls."

"Yes, the other five girls that were murdered in the nineties," said Jonah slowly.

Wiggins considered her next words carefully. "Kenny is right about one thing. I have worked extensively on this case, to say the least. To call it an obsession would be a bit of an understatement."

Jonah stared, unsure of how to react to this.

"This may come as a bit of a shock, Mr. Carr, but there aren't just five girls. There are likely at least twelve."

23

Jonah looked at Wiggins in horror. For a fleeting moment, he thought he had heard her wrong. "Twelve?"

Wiggins nodded simply. "Yes."

"But how—"

"Excuse me for a second." She stood and walked to the black bookshelf that was propped up against the wall. Instead of books lining its shelves, there were rows of three-ringed binders. Wiggins pulled a thick black one from the second shelf down, limped back over to the desk, and dropped it with a thud. On the side of the binder there was a piece of masking tape with the words THE NOWHERE GIRLS written on it in Sharpie. Wiggins looked up at Jonah and back down at the binder.

"This is a good chunk of my life's work."

Jonah couldn't find the words to respond. He was still in a state of confusion mixed with shock.

"We are about to go down a rabbit hole together. I want you to pay as much attention as you can. Because if you are right, and Katie Deeds was killed by the same person, then what I am about to tell you is absolutely vital," Wiggins said, making piercing eye contact and holding her voice steady.

"Okay." He prepped his pen, ready to record.

"Like I have said, this case has been more than an obsession to me. I have spent many years investigating the ins and outs of this thing. I may not know everything that there is to know, but I do know a great deal. I have spoken with countless family members, friends, and people who I have, however briefly, considered suspects. Recently, I have become somewhat resigned to the fact that I may never catch the son of a bitch who killed these girls, but I will keep trying until the day I die."

Jonah nodded.

"This binder contains everything I have found. Notes, documents, pictures, and even transcripts of conversations I have had."

She held up the binder and turned it sideways, displaying the words "The Nowhere Girls" written on the masking tape.

"If you are wondering why I wrote this, there is a fairly simple explanation. As you can see, I have thousands of pages of notes on this shelf." She nodded toward the entire black bookshelf. "I have to find a way to organize them by each individual case. Where I got the designation for this one is fairly simple."

Wiggins paused to take a deep breath. Jonah's mind was whirring and felt a little strained. Just from what she had already told him, he knew that the story he was writing had just become much bigger.

"These girls have been, in many ways, forgotten. The town doesn't care anymore. Too much time has passed. Most of its residents have never even heard of these girls. This killer has made all memory of them evaporate. They are nowhere, physically and figuratively. And I want to remind people."

Jonah was a little unsettled by this. It was pretty eerie to think of the dead in the context that she was providing. It almost made them feel like ghosts hovering just on the edge of his periphery. However, he simply nodded again for her to continue.

"Before we dive into the seven that are unconfirmed, we should go through the five confirmed kills." She opened the binder, giving way to at least a hundred pages. Wiggins rifled through the first chunk of the pages until she came to a picture. She turned the notebook so that it was right side up to Jonah, and he recognized the pretty face in the photo almost immediately.

"This is Kylie Desmond, the daughter of Kenny. She is the first known victim. As I am sure you know, she went missing on August 12th, 1984. She was last seen walking home from a showing of the movie *Red Dawn*. Her skull was found ten years later."

"Right," Jonah said while staring at the picture of the girl.

Wiggins flicked through about ten more pages of documents and arrived at a page with two more pictures.

"These are Shelly Schwartz and Felicity Sanders. They were last seen leaving Beverly Beach on May 13th of 1992. Five months later, their bodies were discovered twenty miles east of here near Eddyville. They had been strangled and left in a forest."

Wiggins passed through several more pages before stopping at yet another sheet with two additional photographs.

"These are Jenna Eason and Cara Lee. They were walking from a friend's house in the early morning hours of May 29th, 1995, when they were last seen. Their bodies were found two weeks later by Moolack Beach. They also had been strangled and discarded in a heavily wooded area."

Wiggins looked up at Jonah. "These are the five that you know about. They all bear obvious similarities and were always viewed as the work of the same killer. All five last seen walking on Highway 101 late at night. Four of the five we can confirm were strangled. It was initially a very open-and-shut case. It was just a matter of finding the guy. But they never did and after ninety-five is where things get murkier."

Wiggins flipped through the binder once more. "According to the DA, Dan Jenkins, the killer simply vanished after disposing of Jenna Eason and Cara Lee. Since there were no solid suspects and no viable evidence left on the bodies, the cases went cold. Jenkins reopened the cases in 2009, but it yielded nothing."

Jonah frowned. "But what about that Foles guy?"

A gleam of appreciation sparked in her eyes, as she was apparently pleased that Jonah already knew Foles's name. "I said *solid* suspects. Yes, it is quite the coincidence that a known serial killer was arrested in Newport only a year after the last confirmed kills, but there were always gaping holes with the theory that Foles was the guy. He resided in Louisiana in 1984 when Kylie Desmond disappeared. And he was in a Colorado prison in 1992 when Shelly Schwartz and Felicity Sanders were killed. He *was* in Newport when Eason and Lee were abducted, but unless you believe that Foles killed only two of the five girls, then he is ruled out."

"What did Dan Jenkins think about Foles?"

Wiggins reclined in her chair with an amused expression. "Don't get me started on Dan Jenkins. How that clown ever became the district attorney of anything is beyond me."

"That doesn't answer my question," said Jonah, trying to be patient. He didn't want to upset Wiggins and have her decide against sharing the details of the case with him.

"I know, I was getting there. Jenkins always seemed to think it was Foles, even back in the nineties. The whole reason he reopened the case in 2009 was because he was hoping advances in DNA technology could link Foles to one of the girls. But of course, it didn't."

Jonah had been taking notes but ceased for a few seconds. "So, you said things began to get murkier after Jenna Eason and

Cara Lee. What exactly did you mean by that?"

Wiggins limped around the room for a few seconds, apparently gathering her thoughts. "Look, the killer clearly had a preferred method. He would abduct young girls, strangle them, and leave them in areas that weren't very difficult to find. I bet even Kylie Desmond was buried someplace where the culprit thought she would be found, and when she wasn't, he revisited her burial site and put her skull and in a more public place so that she *would* be found."

Jonah got a slight chill at this, as this sentiment was the same thing he suspected, as well. He thought of the picture he had seen of Kylie on the Internet when he was first researching the case, and it left an unpleasant feeling in his gut to imagine her as a prop for the killer's pleasure.

"Anyway, I think that the police were close to catching him. I think that if he continued to do what he had been doing, he would have been caught. Therefore, he drastically changed his MO. Or, at least, he made sure he no longer had an MO. That is what I mean by murky. You have to look a lot harder to find the traces of him in the last fifteen-plus years. But if you do look closely enough, you'll see that he didn't just vanish, like Dan Jenkins thinks. He stayed right here, and he continued killing in far more elaborate, planned-out, and meticulous ways," said Wiggins balefully, and as she finished her sentence, her voice seemed to lose volume. It was like she was concerned that someone might be just outside the door, tuning in to the conversation they were having.

The woman flipped through at least thirty of the documents in the binder before she came to a photo of a girl that Jonah had not yet seen. She was blond and thin with large teeth. "This is sixteen-year-old Riley Reid. She drowned in Olalla Lake in July of 2001."

Jonah felt queasy as he looked at the picture. He swallowed. "She drowned?"

"Yes. She went with three friends to the lake out in Toledo, six miles east of here, in the summer of 2001. According to the police report, Reid and her friends were hiking in the woods surrounding the lake. Reid told her friends she had to urinate and went to a secluded spot about thirty feet from where her friends were, near the shore of the lake. She never came back. A half hour later, her friends found her body floating in the water."

Another chill ran down Jonah's spine. For some reason, he briefly pictured Katie Deeds lifeless and sallow, floating in the bay. Then he imagined Teresa's face, and the disturbance in his chest morphed into sorrow.

"When they found her, she was in her bikini. She had been wearing clothes over her swimsuit when she left the group, so the police concluded that she had spontaneously gone for a swim. Reid wasn't a good swimmer anyway, and she was found near a thick clump of seaweed that she could have gotten tangled in, so drowning seemed to be the thing that made the most sense to the police."

"I found Reid when I searched for any young girls who had died in Lincoln County in the last twenty years, and the story never made sense to *me*. Why would a young girl who isn't a good swimmer randomly decide to go for a dive when she was by herself?

"This was the first of the unconfirmed kills that I took a flier on, and I interviewed several people who knew the girl. Her mother, Tara, was absolutely convinced that something else must have happened to Riley. What persuaded me that this was the work of our guy was when Tara told me that two weeks before Riley died, she came home from volleyball practice and told Tara that she thought she was being followed by someone."

Jonah couldn't help but let out a sound of audible shock. The noise came from deep within his stomach and was guttural and strange. It seemed to catch Wiggins off guard.

"Problem?"

"It's just, the same thing happened with Katie."

"What do you mean?" Wiggins asked immediately.

"Teresa told me that about a month ago, Katie came home and told her that she felt like she was being stalked."

Wiggins got the same dark expression on her face that had appeared when Jonah had first mentioned Kenny Deeds's name.

"And the whole reason I made this connection in the first place was because this sort of thing seemed to happen to Cara Lee back in ninety-five."

"You know about that?" Wiggins asked, surprised.

"Uh, yeah. I already said that."

"Oh. Yeah. Sorry, it's just, a lot of what I have on these other girls is based on that."

"What do you mean?"

"The idea that Cara Lee was being stalked. I don't think that was unique to her or Riley Reid. I think this guy vets all his victims heavily. I think he probably follows them for months before he abducts them. He takes notes on the people in their lives and the places they go. He plans for the best time to take them. Hell, I wouldn't be surprised if some of the girls actually saw his face," Wiggins said. "They probably didn't know it, but I bet they did."

Jonah bobbed his head, attempting to nod but doing it too quickly.

"What happened to Cara Lee was my reference point when I looked into Riley, and when I began to look into all of these other girls. The thing is, when someone is being stalked for a prolonged period of time, they will often notice that something is off. They may not be able to place what it is or what exactly is happening, but they will tell someone close to them something along the lines of what Cara told her friend, or what Riley told her mom."

"Or what Katie told her grandmother," Jonah added.

Wiggins nodded and flipped through several more pages

before coming to a picture of a beautiful girl with curly blond hair. Jonah was now noticing a definite pattern. The killer seemed to prefer girls who were blond.

"And that is what brings us to our next victim. In 2005, fifteen-year-old Evelyn Sizemore was reported as a runaway. She had been living with her mother and her stepdad and went missing in December of that year. The family filed a police report, but Evelyn was not found in the days following her disappearance. Eventually, the mother, Jane, came to the conclusion that Evelyn had gone to stay with her biological father in Oklahoma. Jane never actually spoke with her ex-husband because she no longer had his contact information, but she received a postcard from Oklahoma with Evelyn's signature on the back, so she told the police to stop their search. Truthfully, I got the impression that Evelyn and Jane didn't have the best relationship, and Jane was glad to be rid of her in a way. She became someone else's problem."

Wiggins inhaled for a few seconds, and then continued, "Evelyn was the second name that I found. I immediately had my suspicions about her disappearance. She fit the age and type of victim for our guy. So, I put all my resources into attempting to contact Garrett Sizemore in Norman, Oklahoma, to confirm my theory. The problem was, he was not in Oklahoma and hadn't been for quite some time. He currently lives in Sarasota, Florida, and was there when Evelyn disappeared from Newport, so why would Evelyn send a postcard from Oklahoma?"

"And if her and her mother had such a rocky relationship, why would she even send a postcard?" interjected Jonah.

"Exactly. Anyway, I was finally able to contact Garrett Sizemore in 2010, and I confirmed that Evelyn had never lived with him, nor had she even reached out to him. When I passed this information along to Jane, she did not even seem surprised. I think she knew the entire time that Evelyn hadn't run away to Oklahoma. But I think she was just glad that she didn't have to take care of her anymore."

"So wait. The postcard came from our killer then? Like he knew that Jane Sizemore thought that her ex was living in Norman? And after he abducted her he forced Evelyn to sign the card?"

"Yes, exactly."

"Did you tell the police this?"

"Nope." That was all she was giving him. She didn't even bother telling Jonah why.

"Anyway, Jane's son and Evelyn's brother, Michael, was the one who led me to officially add Evelyn's name to this binder," Wiggins said. "He told me that two months before Evelyn disappeared, he caught a man in a ski mask peeking through the window of their living room. It happened on Halloween night, so he thought it was just a prankster trying to scare them. But I believe otherwise."

Jonah's mouth opened involuntarily when Wiggins mentioned the ski mask. That was why she had been so interested in the exact type of mask that Katie's abductor had been wearing.

There was a brief lull, as Wiggins apparently was done introducing Jonah to Evelyn and was moving on to someone else. She made her way through another clump of pages before coming to a photograph of a pale girl with light brown hair.

"This is sixteen-year-old Lacy Larson. In May of 2007, she drove off the road and plunged down a fifty-foot cliff. She was killed instantly."

Jonah looked up from his notepad. "Wait, she got into a car accident? How could she possibly have been killed by our guy then?"

Wiggins waved her hand impatiently. "I am getting there. The accident happened in the wee hours of the morning. Larson was driving home from a party. Since it was so early, there were no witnesses. Her car wasn't even found until seven a.m. the following day."

"I still am not following," said Jonah slowly. If this was one of the Nowhere Girls, why did it just sound like a car accident?

"Maybe if you stopped interrupting, you would," Wiggins snapped. "The spot where Larson plunged over the cliff is directly across the street from the steepest hill in Newport, 66th Avenue. Larson was traveling down 66th, heading home from the party. Investigators arrived at the conclusion that she had attempted to turn left onto the highway at the base of the hill, but had been going too fast and hydroplaned over the slick road and went over the cliff."

"Well, yeah, that makes sense." Jonah doubted the validity of this particular story in terms of their killer.

"No, actually, it doesn't. The tire tracks left on the road indicate that Larson's car hadn't moved even slightly to the left at the base of the hill. She had gone on a straight line across the street. She hadn't tried to turn at all."

"So, what? Someone ran her off the road?" Jonah said skeptically.

"No, I think someone cut her brake lines."

"Her brake—"

"Yes," Wiggins said quickly. "The party which she was coming from was at Stacy Prevot's house, which is at the top of 66th Avenue. According to the other partygoers whom I spoke with, Lacey's car was parked facing down the hill. She wouldn't have attempted to brake until the stop sign at the bottom of the hill, which she blasted through.

"Now with modern cars, cutting someone's brake lines won't work as well because they have a dual-circuit system. If someone were to cut the brake lines of my Audi, I would likely feel it when I started driving, but the other two wheels would be able to stop my momentum. However, Larson didn't drive a modern car. She drove her father's 1972 Ford Mustang. Cutting the brake lines would be an efficient way to do the deed."

"But surely there were people at the party who would have seen a suspicious man hacking away at Larson's car?"

"I don't think so. When have you ever seen a teenager at a party observing what was happening outside?"

Jonah thought of all the parties he had attended as a teenager, and Wiggins had a solid point. However, he continued to play devil's advocate. "Well, they were obviously observant enough to notice where her car was parked."

"That is because she took several friends with her to the party."

"And she didn't give them a ride home?"

"No," Wiggins said. "Larson didn't drink that night and had dance practice early the following morning, so she left the party. The people who were with her when she arrived stayed at Stacy Prevot's house."

"But wait, so that would indicate that our killer knew that Larson would be alone in the car on the ride home."

"Like I said, I think he vets his victims heavily. I think he knew Larson's schedule well enough to realize that she wouldn't be staying overnight at the party."

"But that still runs the risk that someone else could have been in the car when she went home."

"A risk that I think he was willing to take," Wiggins replied.

"But what would he get out of it? Doesn't this type of killer get pleasure in physically taking the life from his victims? This looks more like a mob hit or something." Jonah shook his head.

"Like I said, I think he evolved after Cara Lee and Jenna Eason. I think he realized that he couldn't continue to make every death look the same or else he would run the risk of getting caught. I think the real thrill for him is not getting caught. But he obviously still maintains a similar type of victim."

Jonah shrugged. "I don't really get why you think this one is connected. Not every teenage girl who has died in Newport in the last thirty years was killed by this guy, right? Unless you have some sort of testimony from somebody that Larson thought she was being followed too."

"No, I don't."

"Well alright then."

"Listen, I realize this is the shakiest of the possible connections. But I wasn't presenting them to you in the order of plausibility. I was just showing you each girl in linear fashion."

Jonah nodded, but remained skeptical. "Okay. Then which girl is next?"

"Which girls *are* next," Wiggins said, correcting Jonah. "The next two are a pair, much like Shelly Schwartz and Felicity Sanders, or Cara Lee and Jenna Eason. And this case is the most unique, because it also includes the death of a middle-aged male."

"Holy shit," said Jonah, with his mind running a mile a minute.

Wiggins had difficulty locating the next page she was looking for. Eventually she reached a triple photograph of a blond-haired, blue-eyed Caucasian girl, an overweight Asian female, and what looked like a dark-haired man in his forties. *One of these things is not like the others,* Jonah thought.

"This is sixteen-year-old Kelsea Craft." Wiggins put her finger on the girl's picture. "And fifteen-year-old Serena Wu. They disappeared on a hiking trip in the wilderness of the Siuslaw National Forest while they were with Kelsea's father, Ken." Wiggins pointed at the picture of the dark-haired man. "This was in June of 2009. Ken and Kelsea were avid hikers, and frequently went on similar trips around the state. Wu was Kelsea's friend from school and accompanied her and her father on this particular trip. They had made plans to camp three days in the forest, although they didn't have an exact spot in mind, according to Kelsea's mother, Linda."

Jonah started to bite his lip anxiously. He had a feeling he knew where this was going,

"A day into the trip, Linda received a voice mail from Ken that he and the girls had gotten lost, and to contact the authorities. When Linda tried to return the call, it went straight to his voice mail. Ken's phone had died. Linda immediately called the police, and a search party was sent into the woods that evening. They tried to use the GPS in Ken's Blackberry to determine their precise location, but the phone seemed to have been destroyed or disabled. Ken, Kelsea, and Serena were never found."

Jonah was so caught off guard that he briefly stopped taking notes. "They never even found their bodies?"

"No," Wiggins said. "Linda was able to determine that Ken and the girls turned off Highway 101 just past mile marker 56, onto Greenberry Road. It is an old logging road that runs through the forest. However, Linda had no idea where they went after that, and the forest stretches about 630,000 acres. They searched for weeks and were never able to find them."

"So, isn't it possible they just got lost? Like you just said, Siuslaw is huge."

"It is possible, but in my eyes, unlikely. In an interview with Linda, I was told that Ken and Kelsea had been on more than twenty hiking trips together, and they had never gotten lost before. Ken was extremely cautious and always made sure he marked his route on a map before he left. It does *look* like they just got lost, but I think that was how it was *made* to look." When she said the word *made*, Wiggins jabbed her index finger at Jonah to accentuate the point.

"But what evidence do you have?"

"For starters, the voice mail. The message that Linda received from Ken is still on Linda's computer. She listens to it frequently. She showed it to me during our interview, and I can tell you that it does not sound like someone who is just lost in the woods."

"In what way?"

"Ken's voice sounds extremely strained. And he sounds oddly robotic, like he is reading off a script."

Jonah considered this before replying, "So what—the killer followed them into the woods, took them hostage, and forced Ken to call Linda and relay that they were lost?"

"Yes."

"And then he killed all three of them? Even Ken?"

"That's correct." She nodded.

Jonah processed this. It was very peculiar and more likely that they all had just been unable to find their way home. Ken Craft's death stuck out like a sore thumb.

"I don't know," Jonah said finally. "It just seems odd that our guy would kill someone who differs drastically from his usual type of victim just to get to the girls."

"Are you saying you don't think he is capable?"

"No, not at all. I mean, it's strange that two more teenage girls just vanished with their last known location being Highway 101, like the five girls from the nineties. But on the other hand, it kind of seems like you just found teenage girls that died in Lincoln County the last couple of decades and convinced yourself that they were murdered by the man you are looking for."

Wiggins mulled this over for a minute. She didn't seem to be irritated as Jonah thought she would be. In fact, she appeared totally calm.

"I respect your opinion. Honestly, there have been days when I have thought the exact same thing. That I am inventing stories in my own head. But the more I think about it logically, the more I think that my gut is right."

Jonah raised his palms in the air to indicate that he wanted her to explain her position further.

"Newport is not a big town. There are only 10,000 residents here. You say I'm just finding girls who have died in the last twenty years and attributing them to our killer, but let me ask you this: How many teenage girls do you think have passed away in Newport since 1984?"

"I have no idea," Jonah said querulously.

"Seventeen."

"Okay," Jonah replied, nonplussed.

"Then look at a town in Oregon of similar size. Astoria. How many teenage girls do you think died in Astoria since 1984?"

"Beats me."

"Three."

Jonah couldn't help but show his surprise, with his eyebrows ascending and his mouth dropping like his jaw had become unhinged. "Wow."

"Seventeen is an astronomical number for a small town over that time period. The way I look at it, if there is even a hint of suspicion behind a young girl's death in Newport, then we have to consider the possibility that it was our guy."

Jonah saw the logic in this argument, but he was still somewhat dubious. Wiggins went back to riffling through her binder. She came to the next photograph she was looking for in a matter of seconds. It was a pretty girl with a warm smile, brown hair, and freckles.

"This is fourteen-year-old Mariah Beckham. To me, hers is the most intriguing case of all the girls I have shown you, and that's saying something."

"Yes, it is," Jonah agreed.

"Mariah died in February of 2010. She was found with her wrists slit in the garage of her family's home. A suicide note was discovered next to the bed in her room. Her mother confirmed that it was her handwriting."

"However, this is where things start to get really interesting. Mariah had never shown any signs of being suicidal in the months before her death. In fact, she had so many things going for her that her death looked suspicious right off the bat. She was dating the quarterback of the varsity football team, who was two years older than she was. She had been named homecoming queen the previous fall as a freshman. She was involved in several school plays, in which she was often the lead. Her parents were wealthy, and she was a very privileged kid. Everyone who knew her said that she was one of the most happy-go-lucky people they knew."

"Then why—"

"Mariah was home alone when she allegedly committed suicide." Wiggins pretended Jonah hadn't said a word. "When the cops started looking into it, they first scoped out the house for signs of forced entry. They found that the window to the living room had been left open. To make sure they covered all of their bases, the forensics team ran a sweep of the house to rule out any signs of possible foul play. On the carpet of Mariah's room, they found DNA that didn't belong to anyone who lived in the Beckham household."

"Jesus Christ," exclaimed Jonah, rocking forward in excitement.

"My thoughts exactly. The blood was run through several criminal databases but no matches were found."

"Isn't it out of character for our guy to leave traceable evidence behind at the scene of the crime? And why would his blood be on her carpet anyway?"

"In all likelihood, Mariah put up an initial struggle, but he was able to restrain her. At least enough to force her to write the suicide note. Maybe she scratched him before he put the gun to her head or the knife to her throat," said Wiggins. "There weren't any of his skin cells or blood underneath her fingernails, however. As for your first question, I cannot be sure. Perhaps he got rattled by the fact that she fought back, and he didn't notice the blood."

Jonah reflected back on the other cases for a moment. In terms of covering his tracks, the killer had seemed so meticulous; no other girls had any sort of forensic evidence left behind. But there was with Mariah. So their guy was not infallible after all.

"What happened after?"

"Nothing. The amount of blood that was found was so minuscule that it would have been difficult to assert that it had come from a struggle between an attacker and a victim. The police also claimed that the blood could have come from any number of Mariah's friends, as the girl had had several people over the day before she died, and they didn't want to allocate resources to run blood tests on a bunch of freshman girls. There was no other evidence to support the idea that Mariah hadn't killed herself, and the case was pretty much forgotten. The parents maintained for awhile that there was no way Mariah had killed herself. But since the police had concluded suicide and they weren't inclined to hire a PI, nothing ever came of it."

Jonah had become a little overwhelmed now. There was so much information being shared that he was experiencing sensory overload, which produced short, empty answers. "Wow," he said.

"What is most interesting to me is what happened after this. Or rather, what didn't happen. Our guy seemed to go dormant in between 2010 and 2015. Perhaps the fact that Mariah's death had almost yielded an investigation sparked a change in his behavior. Anyhow, there are no known deaths in those five years. Throughout the three decades of this thing, our guy seems to go through lulls. There are periods of four and five years where he just seems to go off the map."

"Perhaps he bases each kill on how well the previous one went? Like if it went smoothly, then he doesn't wait as long?" Jonah suggested.

"That was my thinking as well."

The woman leaned forward in her chair, bringing her eyes closer to the photo of Mariah, as if getting nearer in proximity would yield answers to the mystery.

"And the final girl?" Jonah asked.

"If you are right, and our guy killed Katie, too, the next would be the second-to-last girl."

"Yes, okay, the second-to-last girl."

Wiggins flipped to the last page in her binder. It contained a picture of a girl with white blond hair. She had slightly crooked teeth and dark hazel eyes. She looked a tad older than the other girls.

"This is twenty-year-old Wendy Gordon. Wendy drowned on January 16th, 2015."

Jonah suddenly recognized the girl. He had been at the *Times* when she had died, and one of his colleagues, Jim Nevins, had written the story. He had skimmed it over, but didn't remember the details of what had happened.

"She was last seen leaving The Bay Haven on the Bayfront after having drinks with a young man."

"Wait, having drinks? I thought you said she was twenty."

"I did, and she was. She had a fake ID."

"Ah."

"Anyway, Wendy was found dead in Yaquina Bay underneath the Abbey Street Pier. The autopsy showed that she still had a considerable amount of alcohol in her system the following morning, meaning she must have had near toxic amounts of the stuff in her body the night before.

"The examination also yielded blunt force trauma to Wendy's head. The coroner said that the wound came from a sizable rock. Therefore, the story that police put together was Wendy had gone for a walk down the pier, drunkenly fell into the water, and hit her head on a rock. She was knocked out and drowned in the water. As you can imagine, there were no witnesses to the incident."

"Who have you spoken with regarding this?"

"Among other people, the guy she met up with at the bar.

Young man named Isaac Reynolds. He told me Wendy was walking in the opposite direction of the Abbey Street Pier when they departed from each other's company."

"Of course she was." Jonah shook his head. The deeper he got into this, the more he realized how poor of a job the police had done. It was like they weren't only incompetent, but grossly negligent.

"The one thing that was different about Gordon was her age. Obviously, all of the other girls were in their teens."

"Except Katie," Jonah added.

"Yes. Except Katie."

Just then, a flash of lightning illuminated the room. Jonah and Wiggins made eye contact, wondering at the same time if the other had seen it. Several seconds later, a loud rumble of thunder crackled across the town.

"Some weather we are having," Jonah said.

"Yeah." Her eyes had begun to mist over, as she was apparently lost in thought. It was sort of an abrupt stopping point, so Jonah asked another question.

"Is that all you have?"

Wiggins looked at him like he was the most foolish person in the world. "All I have? Dear God, if I were to tell you everything I have, you would be here for days. I don't have any desire to read you the transcripts of every interview I have conducted. I was just catching you up on the most rudimentary elements of this case."

Jonah began to respond, but before he could, another loud roar of thunder erupted overhead. As Jonah looked out the window, he noticed that the rain was falling harder than he had ever seen it in his life, and the wind was gusting furiously.

"Have you ever had any leads? Or suspects?"

"Never solid suspects. For a while I considered the possibility that it really was Bobby Ray Foles. But it just seemed too implausible."

Jonah lifted his chin up and ran his fingers through his dirty-blond hair. "Is there anyone else who could lead us to our man?"

Wiggins paused. "Well, there is *someone* . . . but it is a dead end."

Jonah looked at her expectantly. "Who is it?"

Wiggins gazed at the window, observing the elements outside. The juxtaposition of the chaos of the storm and the calmness of the office was striking.

"The closest I ever got to breaking this case open was via a woman named Joanne Fellner in December of 2011. Fellner is currently serving an eleven-year prison sentence for possession and distribution of methamphetamine. She is a repeat offender, hence the extended sentence."

"Sounds like a real charmer," said Jonah sarcastically, flashing half of a smile.

"I found Fellner through an old high school classmate of hers named Kaitlyn Conroy. They went to Toledo High School in the sixties. Conroy had spoken with Fellner years ago, and when she heard through the grapevine what I was looking into, she pointed me to Fellner."

Jonah looked at Wiggins, apparently missing something. "And where does a drug addict fit into all of this?"

"Well, she may have slept with our killer."

Jonah was almost at the point where he was no longer surprised when the case took even darker twists and turns. Almost.

"She *what?*"

"I think she may have slept with the killer," Wiggins said again.

"But . . . how?"

Wiggins sighed. She reopened the binder she had just shut and once again was on the hunt for a specific page. When she located it, she pushed the binder closer to Jonah. The woman, Joanne Fellner, as delineated by the two words scribbled above the photo, was rough. Her mouth had the distinct look of someone who had spent years doing meth. Her complexion was rough and splotchy, with patches of red and irritated skin all over her neck. Her hair was messy and the makeup on her face had been applied far too heavily. Jonah made an involuntary noise of disgust.

Wiggins gave him a judgmental look. “Does her appearance disgust you, Mr. Carr? Perhaps you wish I had found a key witness who was a nine or a ten?”

“No . . . I—sorry,” said Jonah, bowing his head sheepishly.

Wiggins pressed forward. “Fellner and her boyfriend were busted in August of 2008. They sold drugs to what feels like the entire county over a five-year period starting in oh-three.

“Anyway, Kaitlyn Conroy ran into Fellner at the bar in 2006, two years before she was arrested. Conroy’s niece was Evelyn Sizemore, the ‘runaway’ whose mother had received a postcard from Oklahoma.”

Jonah closed his eyes briefly, trying to follow along.

“Conroy and Fellner began discussing Evelyn’s disappearance. Conroy was obviously distraught and full of suspicion. She didn’t believe Evelyn had gone to Oklahoma for a second. When Conroy hinted that she thought that Evelyn may have been abducted, Fellner told her something that completely changed how I was pursuing this investigation.”

Wiggins stopped speaking for a moment to let out a breath, and then continued, “Before she knew the boyfriend that she got busted with, Fellner was apparently sleeping with anybody who had a pulse. Fellner told Conroy that in May of 1995 she met a man while out drinking and went home with him. The two had sex and fell asleep. Fellner woke up early that morning and went to use the man’s restroom. She mistakenly opened the door to a closet. In the closet, she found a shirt that was covered in blood.”

Jonah stopped taking notes again and looked up.

"Fellner told Conroy that the shirt looked like it belonged to a girl. Naturally, curiosity struck her and she searched the rest of the closet. The next thing she found was a small box full of pictures of Jenna Eason and Cara Lee. She recognized them immediately because the story about the missing girls had run in the paper just a few days before."

Jonah covered his mouth with his hand, absolutely flabbergasted. "Oh my God. What did she do?"

"I'm not sure. She wouldn't tell Conroy anything else. Not even the name of the man. Conroy asked her the same question you just asked me, and she wouldn't answer. She said it was like Fellner suddenly realized that she had said too much. All I know is, Fellner didn't go to the police."

"Why not?"

"I can't be sure, but I think that she must have confronted the man, and he threatened her. Conroy said Fellner seemed extremely afraid of him. Whoever he is."

"What the hell? We need to go talk to her!" said Jonah earnestly.

Wiggins again looked at Jonah like he was stupid.

"I have obviously attempted to speak with her several times. I met with her in prison the day before Christmas Eve in 2011. We talked for a bit about Kaitlyn Conroy, and how they knew each other. Then I asked about the conversation she had with Conroy in 2006. She pretended she didn't know what I was talking about. Now she outright refuses to see me again."

Jonah's mouth was agape. He tried to form words, but he struggled to assemble a coherent sentence. "But . . . I mean . . . we have to do something!"

"What can we do? You can't make someone talk to you. And I don't even know if the story is true. Perhaps Fellner is telling the truth, and she really has no idea what I am talking about."

"But why would Conroy lie?"

"I don't think she would, but who knows?"

Jonah looked out the window, frustrated. If this was not a false trail, and they had a direct line to the killer, there was no way he could just stand by and let it be.

"And Fellner never told Conroy the man's name?"

"Nope," Wiggins replied. "Conroy didn't get far enough to ask before Fellner shut down."

Jonah straightened his posture and spoke boldly. "I'll go talk to her."

"What?"

"I'll talk to Fellner."

Wiggins looked at him with an expression of exasperation and shrugged her shoulders.

"I mean, you can try, but I really don't think she will agree to it. If she wouldn't speak to a private investigator I don't think she is going to speak to a reporter either."

"Maybe, but I need to try."

Wiggins looked at him, and then nodded. "Okay."

"What prison is she staying at?"

"Coffee Creek Correctional Facility in Wilsonville."

Jonah wrote it down and underlined it on his notepad.

The rest of their meeting was spent discussing the girls in more detail. Jonah made Wiggins go through each of the seven unconfirmed kills one by one again and took notes that were more in depth than his first attempt. He made sure to ask every question he could think of, although he knew it would be difficult to glean everything he needed to know. He just needed to acquire a rudimentary understanding, like Wiggins had said.

Other than the shocking reality of twelve possible victims as opposed to five, the main takeaway from the interview was the fact that he was now certain he was on the right path in terms of finding Katie's killer. Now that Wiggins had shown him these "Nowhere Girls" and the manner in which several of them had died, via apparent freak accidents, disappearances, and suicide, it now seemed laughable to think that Katie wasn't killed by the same person. A young girl, walking alone late at night? That was identical to the first five girls. And the fact that her killer had likely dreamed up an intricate scheme that made it look like suicide? That was akin to the last seven.

Jonah and Wiggins began to wrap up their conversation. Jonah wished that he could stay and gather even more details about the case, but he needed to get going.

"I will try to get a meeting with Fellner in the next week," Jonah said.

"Okay. I know you won't be able to, but if you *can* get her to talk, make sure to contact me immediately. What is your number, by the way?"

Jonah gave it to her, knowing that he would likely be speaking to her again soon.

"I am sure we will be in touch," Wiggins said. "Do you mind giving me your address?"

Jonah was a little flummoxed by this request. "Uh, I guess."

"In case I try to contact you and don't hear from you."

"I still am not quite following."

Wiggins's eyes bore intensely into Jonah's. "To make sure you are safe."

Jonah was unable to withhold an amused expression from breaking out on his face.

"I don't want to frighten you, and you may think it is silly, but just humor me. This person we are hunting is obviously willing to do anything and everything to not get caught. If he finds out who you are and what you know, you may be in danger."

Jonah inwardly scoffed at this, but begrudgingly wrote down his address on a piece of paper and slid it across the table to her.

Wiggins grabbed the paper with a small smile. "Don't

worry, you didn't just gain a stalker."

Jonah laughed and lifted himself out of the chair. "Well, I appreciate your help with all of this."

Wiggins remained stoic. "Yes, I'm glad you brought what you have to me. What happened to Katie is a tragedy, but we can only hope our guy made a mistake this time."

"Mm-hmm," Jonah said as he walked toward the door. "I guess I will probably talk to you soon."

"Yes, I'm sure. We are in this together now."

24

Leighton was bleeding profusely. As he hid in the shadows, his heart seemed to be skipping every other beat. He tried to keep absolutely still as the blood rushed down his forehead.

He didn't know exactly where he was. He had torn through several backyards before he had found the shed he was currently squatting in. His pursuer had been close behind him at first, but Leighton lost him as he clambered over a third fence and sprinted down the side of a house into a new yard where the shed was located.

Leighton used his hands to try and put a stopper on the gash, but his efforts were fruitless. The blood seeped heavily through his fingers and drenched the sleeves of his black coat. He felt slightly woozy, but he couldn't concentrate on the pain. All his attention was drawn to keeping silent and motionless.

He wasn't sure what the man had even hit him with. He had been walking home from Rip Tide's on High Street when he noticed a shadow behind him. As he had turned around, something large and heavy had smacked against his head, knocking him to the ground. When he looked up, he saw the man in the ski mask towering over him. Leighton was convinced the man had attempted to knock him out, and thus, was surprised when he had scrambled away from him on all fours, still conscious. But the man had kept close pursuit.

The thump of Leighton's heart against his chest seemed to magnify, and for a moment, he was irrationally worried the thumping noise would give away his location. He looked around the shed, scoping it for a weapon he could use to defend himself. There was a shovel propped up against the wall, and Leighton enclosed his bloody fingers around the wooden handle.

A dog barked in a nearby yard, and the noise was so loud that it drowned out everything else. Leighton willed in his head for the dog to be quiet, but it only seemed to get louder. In fact, the dog's barks seemed to get angrier and more vicious, as if it felt threatened. Without warning, he heard a distinct *thunk,* followed by a blood-curdling howl from the dog. Another *thunk* rang out and silence ensued.

Leighton placed his face against the crack of the two doors of the shed, trying to see what had happened. Nothing was visible as blood leaked into his corneas. He retreated farther into the shed, gripping the shovel as if his life depended on it. Closing his eyes, he listened intently, but no more noise came.

Leighton's hair was sopping wet with a mixture of blood and sweat. His breathing was so rapid that he was on the verge of hyperventilating. He tried to gain control of his lungs, focusing on exhaling and pushing all the air out before inhaling again. Slowly, his pulse dropped a little as the adrenaline subsided.

There was still no noise coming from the exterior of the shed. Leighton wished that he had kept running instead of finding a place to hide. He felt like a sitting duck, waiting to be preyed upon by some malevolent force.

Creeping back up toward the door of the shed, he used one

hand to push it slightly forward so that a small crack allowed him to see into the yard. He knew that if his pursuer were in the immediate vicinity, this motion would give him away. However, nothing charged at him, so he decided to push the door open even farther.

The yard was massive and empty, apart from a couple of lawn chairs and a white round table. There was a sliding glass door to the brown house that the yard connected to and a porch light illuminating part of the yard. This was more than fifty feet away, as the property he was on seemed to expand well beyond the normal area for a yard. Leighton considered knocking on the sliding glass door and calling for help. But then he would have to explain why he was trespassing onto their property covered in blood. If the people inside were armed, he would likely get shot before he had a chance to explain himself.

Leighton looked around, trying to see where the best escape route would be. He scanned the closest fence and moved toward it, ready to scale. The fence was only about six feet high and wouldn't be difficult to climb over. He set the shovel on top of the fence and began to lift himself up.

Just then he saw it. Fifteen feet away across the yard on the other side of the fence, a masked figure stood like a sentinel, not moving a muscle. Leighton could tell that the man's eyes were zeroed in on him.

"Oh fuck! Oh fuck!" Leighton shouted. As soon as he yelled, the man charged forward like a bull. Leighton ran back, leaving the shovel sitting precariously on the fence. He sprinted across the grass, heading for the thick bramble of bushes that lined the gate at the back of the yard. Leighton burst through the gate at full speed and headed into the trees nearby.

There wasn't much of a path through the forest, but Leighton shoved his way through blackberry bushes and branches alike. He ran faster than he ever had in his life, finding speed he didn't know he had. The forest sloped down into a slight ravine with a small stream of water running through it. Leighton splashed through the stream, internally cursing the noise that it made. He didn't bother to turn his head. He could hear the masked man crashing through the wilderness not far behind.

At the edge of his vision, Leighton saw the trees start to part. There was a road that ran just beyond the small forest. If he could only make it to the road, he would be able to flag down a passing car. His salvation drew nearer and nearer.

Suddenly, his foot caught on a root, causing him to trip and fall forward into the dirt. He tried to scramble back onto his feet, but he knew his fall had cost him dearly. Before he could regain his balance, something thudded against the back of his head and he was propelled back toward the ground.

Leighton rolled over onto his back with pain erupting all over his body. He looked at his attacker towering over him. He tried to scream, but the pain emanating from the back of his head extinguished his ability to use his vocal cords. Leighton got a glimpse of the weapon hanging next to the man. It was a crowbar drenched in blood.

He raised his hands to try and cover his face. As his gaze moved up, Leighton saw that the man was smiling through the mask. It was a humorless smile, an evil, taunting leer. That was the last image that he ever saw. The man swung the crowbar so forcefully that when it made contact, it popped his left eye out of its socket. Blood spurted out onto the ground, and with one more brute swing, the man cracked Leighton Jones's skull.

25

The row of women filed out, all dressed in orange. They were walking single file, with two guards on either side of them. Jonah sat in an uncomfortable chair that was teetering on the edge of collapse. He scanned each woman, looking for the one he had come for.

It had been five days since he had met with Wiggins. It had been a pain in the ass trying to organize the meeting with Joanne Fellner. He had had to contact Fellner's attorney, Joe Damascus, and request visitation. Damascus had been leery about granting Jonah what he had requested, but eventually he had caved. Jonah hadn't exactly fabricated his reason for wanting to speak with Fellner, but he hadn't been totally transparent either. He had just told Damascus that he wanted to talk to his client because he had a suspicion that Fellner had information that could assist him in a solving a cold case. Damascus had probed further into what Jonah was referencing, but Jonah told him that for security reasons it was best to keep it between him and Fellner.

Damascus had told Jonah he would ask Fellner about it, but there was no guarantee she would want to talk. Surprisingly, Fellner had agreed to the meeting almost immediately.

Jonah had made the long drive to the Coffee Creek Correctional Facility that morning. The road on Highway 20 that led to Interstate 5 was long and winding, and the drive was borderline treacherous. The rain had still been falling heavily as he drove through to Corvallis, making the pavement slick—remnants of the storm that had lasted the past several days. When Jonah arrived in Wilsonville, it had taken him fifteen minutes to find Coffee Creek. It was an old-fashioned building, reminding him of a prison from an earlier decade. The first thing that greeted newcomers was a behemoth tower that protruded menacingly out from the ground. It was reminiscent of a lighthouse, albeit much more sinister looking. Beyond the lookout tower was the large four-story block that contained thousands of female prisoners, including Joanne Fellner.

As the women continued to file inside the visitation area, Jonah finally made eye contact with the woman he recognized. She was short, thin, and looked to be in her fifties. Her face had deteriorated even more since the picture that Wiggins had shown him was taken. Her complexion was still rough, and she was as white as a ghost.

Fellner approached her intended stool and sat down while gazing upon Jonah. Her eyes were steely and intense as she stared through the glass that separated them. Fellner's hand gripped the phone in front of her, and she pressed it to her ear. Jonah did the same.

"You Carr?"

"Yes." He scanned her up and down, his attention absorbed by a tattoo of a sprawling black cobra on the inside of Fellner's wrist.

Fellner raised one eyebrow. "The fuck you lookin' at?"

"Oh, sorry. Just your tattoo."

"Never seen a tattoo before?"

Jonah looked up and saw hatred in the woman's eyes. "Not of that variety, no."

"Hmph." Fellner pouted bitterly.

Jonah was unsure of how to start the conversation. He decided blunt would be the best route.

"Ms. Fellner, I need your help."

"Yeah, that is what Joe said. I can't imagine with what. I have been in here for so damn long, I don't even know my elbow from my ass anymore."

Jonah snorted, trying to withhold laughter.

"Listen, if you are trying to bust somebody on the streets, I ain't your gal. I ain't been usin' or sellin' in five years."

"Ms. Fellner—"

"Joanne."

Jonah swallowed. "Alright, *Joanne*. This has nothing to do with drugs."

Fellner looked flummoxed.

"But Joe said you were a reporter looking for help on a case?"

"An old case."

"But it ain't got nothin' to do with sellin' drugs?"

"No," Jonah said. "It has to do with a murder. A murder that happened a long time ago."

There were several seconds of confusion painted on Fellner's face before her expression morphed into something much more ominous.

"Who told you about me?"

"That isn't important," Jonah replied, his tone flat.

"It was that woman, wasn't it? She sent you here?"

"It doesn't matter who pointed me to you. What matters is the information you possess."

"I don't possess no information, and I sure as hell don't have to talk to you."

"I know you don't have to speak with me, or anyone else. But if you do, you could finally bring peace to the families of these girls."

"What girls? I don't know what you are talking about," replied the woman defiantly.

Jonah sighed. He had expected this.

"I think you know exactly what I am talking about."

She lifted her chin. "What makes you think I will talk to you? That woman told you that I wouldn't talk to her, right? What makes you think you'll change my mind about talkin'?"

"Change your mind? I thought you didn't have any information to share."

"I don't."

"Kaitlyn Conroy thinks you do. She thinks you slept with the man who killed Jenna Eason and Cara Lee." Jonah thought if he were to be bold, perhaps it would fluster the woman into talking. He was wrong.

"I don't give a fuck what that crazy bitch says. She's makin' it up!" Fellner shouted into the phone receiver. The prisoners and guards surrounding her looked over.

"And what reason would she have to make it up?"

"Fuck if I know. Listen, I ain't talkin' about this. Don't try and contact me again. I'll tell Joe that you are harassing me if you do." She made a move to hang up the phone, but Jonah stopped her.

"Wait!" Jonah put his hand on the glass. "Hold on! Please don't leave. Just hear me out. Just . . . wait. Relax for a second." He tried to inflect a soothing tone into his voice. Fellner didn't hang up, but glared at him.

"Listen, I know whoever this man is must have threatened you. I know that you must be scared of him. But if you help us catch him, we can make you safe. And besides, he can't get you in here anyway."

Fellner still didn't say anything. Her expression softened,

though.

"I don't want you to get hurt, Joanne," Jonah said. "That is the last thing I want."

Fellner looked down and rubbed her forehead in exasperation.

"Look, you have a chance to make things right. You have made mistakes in your life, like we all have. But you can rectify that if you help me. Please, Joanne. He killed another girl two weeks ago."

Fellner looked up.

"Please help me. Who is he, Joanne? What's his name?"

Several long seconds passed as she kept quiet.

"Joanne?"

For a fleeting moment, Jonah thought that she was going to get up and leave.

"I don't know his name," she whispered.

"Huh?"

"He never told me his name."

Jonah's heart rate skyrocketed. He couldn't believe that she was confiding in him. Jonah suddenly felt much more tense.

"He didn't tell you his name?"

"No. We had been drinkin'. We talked all night, but I was so drunk that I never asked for his name."

"You went home with him, didn't you? And you slept with him?"

Fellner nodded.

"And then you fell asleep and woke up in his bed sometime later?"

Fellner nodded again.

"And you went looking for the bathroom? But you stumbled upon his closet?"

Fellner didn't nod this time, but her pursed lips and pale complexion gave Jonah all the confirmation he needed.

"And that is where you found the bloody shirt?"

Fellner didn't respond. She looked absolutely terrified.

"And then you found the pictures? How certain are you that they really were Jenna Eason and Cara Lee?"

"I'm positive," Fellner murmured. "The story had just been in the paper like two days before that." Her gaze flitted around the visitation room, as if she were frightened that somebody would overhear her.

"What did you do after that?"

Fellner looked away.

"Did you confront him?" asked Jonah.

When the woman turned back toward him, her face was truly haunting. She didn't answer Jonah's question.

"Did he threaten you?"

"Not me," Fellner spoke so quietly that it sounded like she wasn't speaking at all.

"What?"

"He didn't threaten me. He threatened my daughter."

"Your—"

"I can't say any more. He will kill her. Please. Leave it alone. Just leave it alone," Fellner pleaded.

The conversation was moving at a hundred beats per minute, and Jonah struggled to keep up. "Ms. Fellner, I can help you. Please let me help you. Think about the families of all the other girls. For years, they have been feeling exactly what you fear the most."

Fellner looked at Jonah as though he had slapped her. Without warning, she hung up the phone and stood up from her stool.

"Guard!" Fellner shouted. The prison guard that had been standing in the background accompanied her out of the room. She gave one frightened glance back to Jonah and was gone.

"I have good news and bad news," Jonah said into his cell phone.

"Go on," Wiggins replied.

"The good news is, Fellner basically confirmed everything that Conroy told you."

"What?" she shrieked.

"Yeah. She admitted that she had slept with the man and had found the shirt and the pictures of Eason and Lee. However, she said she didn't know the man's name."

"She didn't know his name?"

"She said they talked all night, but she was so drunk that she never even asked his name."

"Jesus," Wiggins breathed.

"Yeah. And then she confirmed that she found the shirt and the pictures in the closet."

"What did she do about it?"

"She didn't tell me. All she said was that the man threatened her daughter," Jonah said.

"Her *what*?"

"Her daughter."

"She has a daughter?" Wiggins sounded bamboozled.

"Apparently. I thought you must have known and just didn't tell me because you thought it was irrelevant."

"No, I had no idea," Wiggins responded in awe.

"Ah, well, yeah, she said that he threatened to kill her daughter if she told anyone about him."

"I wonder how he knew she had a daughter."

"Maybe it came up when they were at the bar?" Jonah offered.

"Yeah. Maybe."

"Anyway, she looked like she wanted to talk to me more about it, but she was clearly scared. She abruptly got up and left after she told me that the guy had threatened her kid. That's the bad news."

There was a long pause on the other end of the line.

"Well, it's definitely a step in the right direction. I can't believe you got her to talk. She rebuffed me at least seven times over the last five years." Wiggins sounded impressed.

"It wasn't that hard, to be honest. She looked relieved to finally admit the truth." Jonah said, trying to downplay his heroics.

"Well, still."

"So what's the next step? I don't think she will agree to talk to me again. Like I said, she looked pretty spooked."

"I think the first step is to find out who her daughter is. I can do some digging on that. As for what comes after, let me think it over. Do you want to come to my office tonight for a tiny bit so we can discuss a plan?" Wiggins asked.

"Yeah, sure. I'm still in Portland, but I should be over there around six."

"Oh, and good job, kid."

"Thanks." Jonah was surprised at the sudden warmth from Wiggins.

"Talk to you soon."

Jonah stayed in Wilsonville for the rest of the day. He had no desire to spend three hours driving for a five-minute conversation, only to turn around and drive three hours back, so he stayed and did some shopping and met a friend for lunch, as he was only fifteen minutes from where he grew up. Wilsonville itself was a beautiful town with many upscale houses. Where Jonah was from was a lot less lavish; poverty was more rampant in the suburb he had grown up in. When he had told his parents he had wanted to be a journalist, they had feigned enthusiasm, but he could tell that they were disappointed. He knew that they had been furtively hoping for him to choose a career that was much more financially stable. In his heart of hearts, he realized that his parents both possessed a tinge of regret for having to raise him in such a destitute environment. But he was dead set on proving them wrong. Jonah believed that if he was successful in his field, he could do very well for himself. And though most of him just yearned for the truth about the Nowhere Girls, part of him was also excited for the opportunity to make his parents proud.

After lunch with his high school friend, Jonah had made a call to Randy Marks. It had now been over a week since Marks had assigned him the story, and his patience was running thin. Jonah had asked for a deadline extension, and Marks had reluctantly agreed to it. Jonah didn't even know what he was going to do now. The case obviously encompassed much more than he had originally thought, and there wasn't a close end in sight. He thought he might have to confess his true intentions to Marks. Maybe with all the evidence he had amassed, Marks would be a little more lenient, but Jonah doubted it.

Jonah made the lengthy drive back to Newport at four in the afternoon. It was a beautiful trip, but it was three hours from Newport to Wilsonville, so he had spent more than six hours total in the car for the day. When he finally got back to the coast, his legs were so stiff that he felt like he had aged a few years in the time he had spent driving. He turned left on Rose Street, which would take him to Wiggins's office.

Five minutes later, he was packed back inside the cluttered room, and Wiggins was hobbling around the desk in front of him, aiming to sit down.

"I still can't believe you got her to talk," said Wiggins, again sounding impressed with Jonah as she slowly lowered her posterior into the chair.

"Maybe time had weighed down on her, you know? Like now that some years have passed she is more inclined to talk."

"Or maybe she was just more inclined to talk because you are a young, attractive man, and I'm a middle-aged, overweight woman with a limp and the body of a lethargic hamster."

Jonah burst out laughing, and immediately felt bad.

Wiggins, however, did not look the least bit offended; she simply remained straight-faced and her eyes misted over like she was thinking. She seemed to not have any insecurities about her appearance.

"So what's the plan?"

Wiggins picked up a pen and began writing on a small sticky note in front of her. "Well, I have a friend at the Hall of Records here in town who should be able to confirm the identity of Fellner's daughter, so I am going to pursue that angle. If I can get an address and she is still in Newport, I am going to go talk to her. As for you, I want you to be Leighton Jones's new shadow."

Jonah shook his head like a fly had just flown in front of his eyes. "Huh?"

"Bug him. Find out where he works and show up there. Go to Rip Tide's and try and have a chat. Just be persistent. I want you to try as hard as you can to get him to change his mind about talking to the police."

"But if he decides he does want to talk to the police, won't that kind of make us obsolete?"

"Not you," replied Wiggins. "You will still have the inside track to the story. You would have leverage on the cops, since you will be the only reporter who knows about this whole thing. Unless they want your story published now and have it affect the investigation, they will have to share details with you."

"But you won't be the one to catch this guy."

Wiggins shook her head vigorously. "I don't care about that in the slightest. I'm not doing this for the glory. Hell, I am not even getting paid. I want this bastard in prison no matter the means. If you had interviewed all the families of these girls, you would to."

Jonah nodded silently. "So if the Leighton Jones angle doesn't prove fruitful, what else should I do?"

"Well, the next step in this would be interviewing people

around Katie Deeds and see if she ever spoke with any older men. There is a ninety percent chance that Katie saw or interacted with her killer in the months before she was killed."

Instead of making Jonah disturbed, this sentiment just made him furious. Once more, he envisioned Teresa Deeds, now emotionally fractured. And it was all because of the sick fuck who had chosen Katie as his next victim.

"But first things first. Pursue Leighton Jones. Get him to talk to you in whatever way you can. You seem to have a natural talent for getting people to confide in you. And you're a smart cookie. You will find a way."

Jonah's chest suddenly felt lighter due to the compliment. He wasn't sure why, but Wiggins's praise was actually invigorating. Perhaps it was because she seemed so clever and worthy of respect herself. "Thank you," he said.

The pair spent a couple of minutes ironing out the details of their plan, and Jonah relayed the ins and outs of his work schedule so that they could coordinate the best times for future meetings. Wiggins also informed him that she would send a text as soon as she heard back from her friend in the Hall of Records.

"It should be sometime tonight or in the morning."

"Okay. I will be waiting," Jonah said, rising from his chair and readying himself to leave.

"Alright. Have a good night. Again, good job on the Fellner front. You really showed some good initiative. Maybe you should consider a career as a PI."

Jonah chuckled. "Yeah. Maybe we should get to know each other a bit more before I consider switching fields to become your partner."

Wiggins gave him a small smile. "Deal."

It was usually a ten-minute drive back to Jonah's apartment from the neighborhood where Wiggins's office was, but since it was well after rush hour, traffic seemed to be sparse and the commute was much shorter. As Jonah headed down Highway 101, the clouds above had parted and light was peeking through. The sun was beginning to set and a plethora of colors were painted beautifully against the remaining clouds. Jonah took it all in, appreciating the beauty he was immersed in. But then he thought of the Nowhere Girls and how this faceless devil had robbed thirteen people of seeing the breathtaking sunset that now lit up the town, and Jonah was filled with a new resolve.

He turned into the parking lot of his apartment and took his designated spot. He got out of the car and flexed his legs, trying to shake off the proverbial dust. As he crossed the pavement and started walking up the staircase, he wasn't cognizant of the forest-green Jeep that was pulling into the parking lot behind him.

26

The man saw him walking up the stairs as he pointed his vehicle toward one of the visitor parking spots. His target was long and lanky, with dirty-blond hair, a baby face, and a chiseled jaw. The fact that someone so young had caused him so much strife ate at the man's core. His knuckles whitened as the grip he held on the steering wheel tightened.

After much prodding and poking, the man's source had finally given him the name of the demon who was on his trail. The man had told his source he was just going to threaten the boy to try and scare him off. But he had other plans. Perhaps it was age ebbing away at the man's cautiousness. As a younger man, he probably *would* have just heeded a menacing warning. But now, in his fifties, he was past the point of being rational. This threat needed to be eliminated.

The man had already thrown caution to the wind with his treatment of the witness. His original plan was to knock him out, drag him into his vehicle, and then dispose of him. But everything had gone awry. For a moment, the man was scared that he had lost the witness in the bevy of backyards he had chased him through. Wild thoughts of fleeing the city had shot through the man's brain as he considered the possibility he had just attempted to murder someone who escaped. When he finally caught the witness, the man was filled with such jubilation that he got carried away and killed him on the spot. As soon as the witness was dead, the man became filled with trepidation. There he was, covered in blood, next to a body in a semipublic (albeit forested) area. The man had dragged the body to a thick bush and hidden him under it while he retrieved his vehicle.

Once he had properly disposed of the body, he was consumed with a heavy sense of relief. But then he remembered his true enemy: the person who had found the witness in the first place. He had stayed up all night after he had buried the witness, fretting about what to do. Should he stop hunting Sierra Bunker altogether and just hope that he had not left behind any clues when he murdered Katie Deeds? Or should he continue obliterating every obstacle in his path and vanquish the devil who was hunting him? It was a quandary that had confounded the man.

Usually the man spent months planning a single kill and mapping out the details in his head. He had just impulsively killed someone with only a few days of preparation to remove the first immediate threat to his freedom. But that was different. The witness had *seen* him. The devil that was looking for him just *knew* of him.

What had allowed him to evade police for the last thirty years was patience. The patience to wait for the perfect time to do the deed. The patience to meticulously carve out an adequate explanation for the impending death. The patience to stalk his victim and learn everything he needed to know. If he followed through and squashed this final peril, the act would be anything but patient.

But then the man had thought of Sierra Bunker. Her wonderful face and tantalizing skin. The man could already feel the imaginary smell of her rotting corpse dancing into his nose. It gave him such pleasure, such unadulterated euphoria to picture killing the beautiful blond teen. That's what had done it. That's what had made up his mind. He had already come this far. It was time to thwart this menace once and for all.

Once his source had given him the man's name, it had not been difficult to find his address. He had already visited the complex several times over the past few days. In fact, earlier that afternoon, he had entered the boy's apartment. The lock on the door had been easy to pick. He knew that his target was not there. The blinds were drawn and the lights were off. He had just come to scope out the place that he knew he would be visiting that evening. Partly for his amusement, the man had used the boy's bathroom while he was on his reconnaissance mission.

And now here he was. Waiting. Waiting to jump on his unsuspecting prey, destroy him, and be free of this burden. He reclined in the driver's seat of his Jeep as the kid walked through the door of his apartment. As soon as he disappeared from view, the man pulled the glove box open, setting his eyes on the pistol that lay inside.

27

Jonah plopped down into the chair in his living room, simultaneously kicking off his shoes. Thoughts of Joanne Fellner consumed him. What were they going to do next? He and Wiggins were coming close now. He could feel the proverbial curtain beginning to pull back. The mystery was slowly starting to unravel before his eyes.

Jonah briefly wondered why Fellner had entrusted in him what she had refused Wiggins for so long. It hadn't even taken much to get her to talk. Perhaps Wiggins had just been using the wrong technique the whole time. She *was* a little brash and unrelenting. Fellner had likely seen it not only as a danger but as a nuisance.

As for what came next, there wasn't much that Jonah and Wiggins *could* do regarding Fellner. Theoretically, if they ever arrested a probable suspect, and the case went to trial, they could get a judge to subpoena Fellner to testify. But they still had the central problem of identifying the killer. Maybe Wiggins was trying to organize a quid pro quo. If she found out who Fellner's daughter was, perhaps she could arrange something to quell Fellner's fear for her child's safety.

Jonah's stupor was interrupted by a noise he couldn't identify at first.

Drip. Drip. Drip.

The noise was coming from his bathroom. Jonah rose from his chair, irritated at the fact that he had to get up.

Drip. Drip. Drip.

Jonah marched over to his bathroom, which was adjacent to the living room. As soon as he entered the room, he saw where the noise was emanating from: the sink faucet.

Drip. Drip. Drip.

That's odd, he thought, looking at the faucet and feeling a little disturbed. He hadn't used the bathroom since that morning, and he was positive he had turned the faucet all the way off after he had washed his hands. He moved toward the sink, reaching his arm out.

Before he could touch the handle, a loud *clunk* echoed from somewhere nearby. Jonah jumped and turned back around, looking for what had caused the disturbance. He stayed frozen for a moment. Every small noise was suddenly sinister, including the water leaking from the sink.

Drip. Drip. Drip.

Jonah looked around his apartment. He was sure that the clunk had come from the staircase outside. But what could it possibly be? Jonah was the only one who used the stairs. He focused his attention on the front door, listening intently for any noise that came from beyond it. Part of him sensed that something was awry.

Drip. Drip. Drip.

Jonah hurriedly twisted about and turned off the faucet, welcoming the silence it brought. Turning forward again, he quietly crossed the living room and stood next to the front door.

He pressed his eye against the peephole, but saw only darkness. Annoyed, Jonah flicked on the light switch next to him that lit up the porch, but there was still nothing there. He waited for a few seconds, and then turned the light back off. A deep feeling of unease was percolating in his stomach.

Thinking that the eeriness of the case had simply caused him to imagine the noise, Jonah made an about-face and walked back toward the armchair that he had just gotten up from. Right before he sat, it happened again. *Clunk.*

Jonah craned his neck back toward the door.

Clunk. Clunk. Clunk.

Someone was walking up the stairs.

Jonah couldn't breathe. He tried to slowly exhale and think rationally. Perhaps it was just Wesley or Daisy. Maybe it was even Wiggins. Trying to remain calm, he crept back in the direction of the door, taking silent footsteps. Placing both hands on the frame, Jonah leaned forward so that his eye was pressed against the peephole. Once more, he was initially thwarted by the darkness outside.

Jonah reached over toward the light switch, keeping his eye on the door. Flexing his finger, he held his hand on the switch for several long beats, waiting to turn it on. Tension made his entire body taut. Before he could convince himself to do otherwise, Jonah pushed his finger up. Light flooded the porch. This time, there was a massive figure standing there, wearing a ski mask and holding a gun.

Before he could stop himself, Jonah gasped loudly. As soon as the noise escaped his throat, there was a loud *thud* on the door as the masked man tried to smash through it.

Jonah sprinted into his bedroom. He scrambled around, looking everywhere for something with which to defend himself. The first thing he found was the baseball bat he kept next to his closet. There was another *thud* as the man slammed against the door again, trying unsuccessfully to break the lock. Jonah gripped the bat tightly against himself, frantically trying to think of what to do. Just then, he had an idea.

Jonah set the bat down for a second, jumped onto his mattress, and flipped the latch that was on the window above his bed. With his hands shaking, he pushed the window ajar, and then stepped back down onto the floor. Jonah then picked up the bat, slid behind the door to his room, and pressed his back against the wall. The unfastened window would be the first thing that the man saw when he entered the room, as it was directly across from the door that Jonah was hiding behind.

Suddenly, a loud crack rang out, followed by the sound of a heavy object slamming against the wall of the living room. The man had broken through. Jonah's heart felt like it was going to explode, and his ears were ringing. He tried to remain motionless, looking through the crack between the door and the wall.

The intruder entered Jonah's room, holding his gun aloft. Once he passed through the door frame, he froze, looking toward the open window. The man made a noise of frustration and moved swiftly across the room, taking no notice of anyone hiding behind the door. He leapt onto the bed and stuck his head out of the window, thinking that Jonah had escaped through it.

Jonah knew he only had a few seconds. He slithered out from his hiding place and quickly crept toward the man. When he was just behind the hulking figure, he began to cock the bat. As if the intruder had realized his mistake, his head started to turn. With all his might, Jonah swung, making devastating contact with the side of the man's jaw. The man howled in pain and crumpled onto the bed with the gun hanging lamely off the bed in his hand.

Jonah thought of swinging again, but he was worried that the man would come to and shoot him. He also debated going for the gun, but the masked man was huge. Jonah likely couldn't overpower him. After two seconds of watching the man roll around while holding his jaw, Jonah turned and darted out of the room, still carrying the bat.

He took long strides across the living room and ducked out of the front door. The steps of the staircase were still damp from the rain that had fallen earlier that day, but Jonah couldn't slow down, as the man would likely be right behind him. Once he got to the bottom of the stairs, he sprinted toward his car, fumbling in his pocket for his car keys. After locating them, he jammed the keys into the car door and unlocked it. Jonah chucked the bat into the back and practically dove inside the vehicle, landing hard on the driver's seat. His hands shook so badly that he had difficulty sticking the keys in the ignition, but once he did, he didn't even check to see if anything was blocking his path before he reversed. His Corolla came within inches of hitting the car that was behind him, but Jonah swerved at the last second, put the car in drive, and headed toward the nearest exit at a high speed.

Looking into his rearview mirror, Jonah attempted to get one last glance at his pursuer. However, the masked man was nowhere in sight. Perhaps he was still in Jonah's apartment, trying to recover from the swing of the bat. His car skidded on the pavement as Jonah turned left out of the parking lot and sped toward Highway 101.

Jonah was nearly hyperventilating as he stopped for less than half a second at the stop sign and turned onto the highway. He felt like he could jump out of his own skin. Thinking of how close he had just come to death, another surge of adrenaline coursed through him, causing his foot to push harder against the gas pedal.

Jonah fumbled in his pocket for his phone. His hands were sweating so profusely that the phone slipped out of his grip twice.

"Fuck!" screamed Jonah. Finally, he clung onto the cell phone and went to unlock it. However, the screen of the phone stayed black and a minuscule icon that looked like the outline of a battery flashed three times. The phone was dead.

"Jesus fucking Christ!" He couldn't even believe his luck. The one time in his life when it was imperative to have a functioning phone, the juice had evaporated. Jonah literally felt like he was going to have a heart attack. He consciously tried to slow his breathing, and he slacked his hold on the steering wheel to stymie the shaky movement of his hands. He focused only on the road, attempting to ignore the physical symptoms of his body's anxiety response.

Holy fucking shit, thought Jonah. A million ideas raced through his mind. There was no doubt that the masked man was the killer he was looking for. But how had he found Jonah? Had the man located Leighton Jones? Had he somehow coerced Jones into revealing Jonah's identity? Even so, how had the man found Jonah's address? And why had he targeted him in the first place? Jonah must have been even closer to cracking the case than he had thought.

He supposed that he should go to the police station. After all, since he couldn't dial 911, it would be the easiest way to get the police to come to his aid. But the station was on the other side of town, and he was yearning to get off the road, so that if the man was following him, he would be thrown off of Jonah's trail. The killer likely wouldn't follow him all the way to the police station, but what if he tried to run him off the road? Fear clouded his judgment. His only thought was to get to safety as soon as possible, and the longer he was driving, the less safe he felt.

With a split-second decision, Jonah veered into the next lane and turned right in front of the Taco Bell, heading down the hill toward the Agate Beach Wayside. He was going to go to Wesley's place. From there, he could call the police and make the report. Jonah looked over his shoulder once more, just to make sure that nobody turned off Highway 101 and followed him onto the wayside. As far as he could tell, there wasn't anybody behind him.

Wesley's apartment was in a towering building that was right in front of the cliff the locals called Jump-Off Joe's. Whenever Jonah went to visit Wesley, he would park at Jump Off's, and walk over to the building. Tonight was no different. After winding around the many curves of the wayside, Jonah saw the turn that led to his destination. He dipped his Corolla down the road and settled into an open parking spot. There weren't any other cars parked along the side of the embankment.

Jonah got out of his car. He felt totally numb, but that might have just been from the cold outside and not the lingering adrenaline. The wind beat against him like a drum. Jonah shut his car door, forgetting to lock it while he made his way to the large apartment building that sprouted up across the road from where he was parked. He knew that the chances of the masked man knowing where he had gone were minuscule; after all, Jonah had made his escape with the man nowhere in sight. But still, Jonah kept his wits about him in case he was somehow still being stalked.

Once Jonah got to the building, he made his way up two flights of metal stairs. Wesley's place was on the third floor, and Jonah pounded on the door as soon as it came into his line of sight. He stood there impatiently, waiting for Wesley to open the door. Ten seconds passed, and there was no answer. Jonah knocked again, but after fifteen more seconds, there was still no inclination that Wesley was home. *God damn it, Wesley,* thought Jonah. He waited for a bit longer, hoping beyond hope that Wesley was just in the shower or asleep. After a couple more minutes of dead silence, Jonah went back down the stairs.

To confirm his suspicions, Jonah circled around the building to the parking lot where Wesley had an assigned spot.

Sure enough, Wesley's blue Subaru was absent.

"Well, shit." Perhaps he would have to go to the police station after all.

Out of nowhere, Jonah felt a little weak in the legs. It was as if all the spirit that he possessed had been zapped out of him by some extraterrestrial force. He sat down in front of Wesley's empty parking spot. The fight-or-flight reaction that Jonah's body had exhibited had apparently taken all his energy. A wave of extreme nausea hit him like a wrecking ball. He felt so woozy that he had to place both hands on either side of him to keep him from losing his balance.

Small spatters of rain began to fall as Jonah sat on the sidewalk. His body vibrated so much that he felt like he had lost control of his neurological function. Anxiety-riddled thoughts zoomed through his head. What was going to happen next? Would he have to stay with Wesley until the police apprehended the man who had broken into his apartment? It was a deeply disturbing sensation to know that someone who was hunting him knew where he called home. It made Jonah feel dirty and tainted, like safety was no longer attainable. Without noticing he was doing it, Jonah rocked back and forth. He supposed he should get out of the rain, but it was somewhat cathartic to let it cleanse him of the horror that had just taken place. When he had reported on crime stories before, it had been exciting, like a dark alternate universe filled with thrilling encounters. But now that his life had been threatened, the excitement had been replaced by terror and chaos. He sat there for well over ten minutes, trying to regain some semblance of composure.

Jonah considered going to one of the neighboring apartments and knocking on the door. After all, he desperately needed to talk to the police as soon as possible. There was the slight chance that the masked man was still somehow incapacitated inside Jonah's bedroom, reeling from a broken jaw and maybe even a concussion. Perhaps the man could still be apprehended if Jonah acted fast. However, he knew that the sooner he got to the police station, the safer he would be. So instead of disturbing one of Wesley's neighbors, Jonah decided to make the trip to the precinct.

He supposed now that he had been attacked, he would no longer be able to continue with the story. Not only for his own protection, but also because he would have to tell the police why he thought a man wearing a ski mask had broken into his apartment and attempted to murder him. The case would now be in the hands of the authorities. Strangely, Jonah was okay with that. He wanted no part of this anymore. His future superseded his need for the truth. It would do no good knowing the identity of the killer if it ended up costing him his life.

Jonah lifted himself from the sidewalk, realizing that his legs had been recharged by the ample time he had spent sitting. He walked back around the apartment building and crossed the street to Jump-Off Joe's. As he looked up toward the sky, he noticed that the rain clouds overhead were moving off, allowing the stars to shine through. Jonah felt more aware of his body than he ever had in his life as he stared up at the stars, and a surge of euphoria pulsed through him. To be alive—to see the beauty of the twinkling constellations overhead after he had just came within inches of death—it was truly a miracle.

Jonah opened the door to his car and sat down in the driver's seat. His breath had finally slowed and his pulse had become steady. After a couple of seconds, a curious smell wafted into Jonah's nostrils. It was a bad odor, a mixture of sweat and cigarettes. But Jonah didn't smoke.

He only realized what had happened at the last second. Trying to use his hands to cover himself, he began to duck down, but it was too late. From the back seat, the blast rang out like a cannon, followed by the noise of splatter against the windshield.

28

Maryanne Wiggins lay in bed, trying to get comfortable. Her left knee throbbed in pain. She had already taken three Advil earlier that night, but it hadn't helped. She rolled over, looking irritably toward the clock. It was only five in the morning. Wiggins sighed. Insomnia was so commonplace for her now that she felt strange when she wasn't tired. She fumbled around for her phone, as she had fallen asleep with it next to her in bed.

Wiggins was fifty-six, but she felt far older because of her failing leg. She had torn her lateral collateral ligament while chasing a suspect when she was thirty-two. That was back when she was a detective, working for the EPD in Eugene two hours east of Newport. She had been giving pursuit to a man who had killed a young boy in a drunk-driving incident in Washington. The man had evaded police for weeks, fleeing across state lines. Wiggins had finally located him after receiving a tip from a citizen who had seen the man and recognized his face from the papers. When she was chasing the suspect, Wiggins had attempted to leap a fence, but her belt loop had caught on a hook, causing her pants to rip and her legs to land at an awkward angle. As soon as her left foot had hit the ground, her knee gave way, and she had collapsed in a heap. The suspect had gotten away, and her knee was torn to shreds. She had the surgery the following week, but the surgeon had botched the procedure, and her leg had never healed properly.

Wiggins hadn't known at the time the extent of the repercussions she would face in the years following her accident. She could no longer exercise without terrible agony in her leg. Therefore, she had gained about thirty pounds in the decades since she had wrecked her knee. The weight added even more strain on her lower left limb, and it made walking anywhere of significant distance an iffy proposition. And it was all because of the inept surgeon. Every time she thought of the stupid man who had caused her so much pain and inconvenience the last twenty-one years, her temper sparked like a lit fuse. She had considered suing the hospital, but she didn't have the financial means to hire a competent attorney at the time. Workers compensation had aided in her recovery, but had not provided enough to get her in the room with a good lawyer.

Wiggins finally located her phone and slid the screen to unlock it. There were no new messages, nor missed calls. She had been waiting up late to hear back from her friend Leonard Cohan, who worked as a clerk in the Hall of Records for Lincoln County. She had known Leonard for several years, and he often did favors for Wiggins—favors like pulling a birth certificate for Joanne Fellner's unidentified daughter. Once she had the name of the girl, she would be able to contact her friend at the DMV. If the girl had a driver's license in the county, Wiggins would quickly be able to locate her address.

Her eyes felt sandy, as Wiggins was still totally exhausted. She placed both hands on either side of her body and pushed herself into a sitting position. There was no use trying to fall back asleep. Her mind was the furthest thing from quiet. Combined with her aching knee, it was no wonder she was a near insomniac.

Wiggins had been on the police force in Eugene for nine years, from the time when she was twenty-five until she was thirty-four. She had eventually grown tired of the bureaucracy and the politics of the department, hence she had quit. After she had left, Wiggins had gone through a bit of a midlife crisis. She wasn't sure that it could be called a midlife crisis since she was still in her thirties at the time, but it was a crisis nonetheless. She had no plan, no long-term goals. The desire to apprehend criminals still burned inside her, but she didn't have the outlet or the means. Eventually, when she was thirty-five, she had decided to return to the University of Oregon where she had gotten her undergrad degree to get her Masters in Business.

As soon as she graduated in 1999, she transplanted herself to the coast. Having been born and raised in Eugene, Wiggins was more than tired of the doldrums of the medium-sized city that sat at the south end of the Willamette Valley. Therefore, she had moved to Newport when she was thirty-seven. It had taken a little less than a year to get her business started. Once it was up and rolling, it had been quite a while before her work had provided any sort of financial stability, and to get by she had had to rely on some of the money she had inherited from her deceased grandfather. But now that she had been doing it for some time, business was somewhat steady.

Wiggins rolled out of her bed and hobbled over to the window so that she could pull the blinds open. She lived in the apartment that was connected to her office. A small kitchen, bathroom, and bedroom were jammed into less than 600 square feet. It was barely enough room, even for just one person. After opening the blinds, Wiggins limped over to the mirror and saw a face that she barely even recognized. Before her injury and the subsequent weight gain, Wiggins was actually quite an attractive woman. Her pretty twenty-year-old face was the one that she still attached to her inner portrait of herself—not the flabby, wrinkled visage that was a part of her current exterior.

Wiggins grabbed a box of cereal from on top of the fridge and scrounged through her cabinets for a bowl. Unfortunately, there wasn't a clean one, so she fished in the sink full of dirty dishes until she found a bowl that had remnants of the cereal that she had eaten the day before still clinging to it. Wiggins rinsed the bowl under hot water and dried it off with a paper towel. *Good enough,* she thought. She spent so much time being overly meticulous about the details of each case that she was working on that she often skipped over things that a normal person would consider to be crucial, like eating off sparkling clean dishes.

After plopping down onto her small sofa, Wiggins ruminated on the case that she had spent more than ten years thinking about. She didn't even consider the Nowhere Girls an obsession anymore. It was more of a lifestyle. She had spent thousands of hours interviewing anyone who could possibly be connected to the victims or the killer and gathering documents that she thought might possibly help her crack the case. But after ten years, she had finally accepted the distinct possibility that it would never be solved.

The big black binder that represented the Nowhere Girls was obviously not the only thing that consumed Wiggins's time each day. Since nobody was paying her to hunt down the killer, she had to make ends meet in other ways. Much of what she did revolved around finding people who had slipped through the cracks of the criminal justice system to make them pay the piper. Occasionally, she also would bust a cheating spouse or hold a rogue police officer accountable. But throughout the dozens of other cases that she spent time on, the Nowhere Girls always lingered in the background like an evil spirit. Silent, watchful, and menacing.

Everything had changed the week before when Wiggins had

met with the kid from the paper. Her work on the case had grown stagnant for the past several months; there had been neither new victims nor leads. She had, for all intents and purposes, set the case aside. But when Jonah Carr had come knocking on her door, she felt reinvigorated. He had brought her the news of Katie Deeds, a girl whom she was certain was the newest notch on the killer's belt. Everything about her fit. Her age, what she looked like, and what she was doing when she was last seen. And finally, after waiting helplessly as girl after girl was murdered with no traceable evidence left behind, the thing that Wiggins had been hoping for all along had finally happened: The killer had made a mistake. And it wasn't a small mistake. He had left a witness behind. Someone had finally laid eyes upon the devil who had haunted Wiggins's dreams for the past decade. And Wiggins was positive that the investigation into Katie Deeds's death would yield results.

She was not hopeful on the Joanne Fellner front, even though Wiggins was currently waiting for Leonard to provide her with news about Fellner's daughter. Wiggins did admire that Jonah was so adamant about getting Fellner to talk, but truthfully, it felt like it was a waste of time. If Fellner was going to talk, she would have done so years ago. Wiggins was going to try and organize some sort of deal as a last-ditch effort to try and persuade Fellner, but she knew in her heart that it was not going to go anywhere.

Searching irritably for the remote to the flat-screen television that was plastered on the wall across from the couch, Wiggins moved her hands along each of the crevices that divided the three seat cushions. But she didn't locate the remote. Silently cursing, Wiggins stood up and walked around the living room in circles, hoping to see the wand-like device. It seemed to have vanished. If Wiggins had one mortal weakness that she knew would someday be the death of her, it was her lack of organizational skills as it pertained to physical assembly. Her whole apartment, like her office, looked like it had been ravaged by a small tornado.

Wiggins walked unabashedly to the kitchen, although she knew that the remote was unlikely to be in there. She took notice of several of the pictures hanging on her fridge and felt a pang of sadness. The faces of the sparse remaining family that she had left were staring solemnly back at her, as they did each day. Her parents had passed away long ago, and she had no siblings. The only photos on her fridge where of distant cousins, uncles, and aunts.

The absence of nearby family was far lonelier to Wiggins than the fact that she was single. There were some days when she was alone in her apartment where the solitude was almost unbearable, and she felt herself yearning to move back to Eugene. But she knew if she did that, she would let the killer of at least thirteen innocent girls get away. So she stayed on the Oregon Coast, ignoring the feelings of despair that the lack of family brought. She had a job to do, and she would stay in Newport until that job was finished or she was dead.

29

After three hours, Wiggins's phone finally vibrated. It was Leonard Cohan. Wiggins eagerly answered.

"Hello?"

"Maryanne?" asked a nasally voice.

"Leonard! Good to hear from you," she was quick to say.

"Yeah, sorry it took so long. It was more of a task than I expected it to be. The Hall of Records isn't as efficiently organized as one might think. Anyway, I finally found the certificate about ten minutes ago."

"Wonderful!"

"Do you want to come look at it in person, or do you want me to just give you the name over the phone?"

"You can just give it to me now over the phone. That is fine."

"Alright, good." Cohan sounded relieved he had avoided an in-person appointment. "The girl's name is Eleanor. Last name Fellner, obviously."

Wiggins raised one nostril and frowned in surprised. “Eleanor? That is a little old-fashioned.”

“Maybe she’s named after an older relative or something,” Cohan said, appearing intrigued by the small mystery.

“How old is she?”

“She was born in 1992. So, she is 24.”

This was about how old Wiggins expected the girl to be.

“Middle name?”

“Rae,” Cohan said simply.

“R-a-e?”

“Correct.”

“Is the father’s name on the document?”

“No. Just the mother’s,” Cohan replied. “Joanne.”

“Ah, okay. Well anyway, thank you for this, Leonard. I really appreciate it.”

“Any time! Do you need anything else?”

“No, I think that is it for now.”

“Okay.” Cohan sounded disappointed.

“I will let you know if I need another favor in the future. Thanks again. Have a good day, Leonard,” Wiggins said.

“You too. Buh-bye now.”

Wiggins hung up the phone and processed the information. Fellner must have had a child when she was a young adult. But who was the father? From what Kaitlyn Conroy had told Wiggins years ago, Fellner wasn’t exactly a nun when it came to sexual partners, so the father could be any of a great number of men. What was the most striking was that the child would have been only three when the man that Fellner had slept with had made the threat. *Despicable,* thought Wiggins.

What *didn’t* make much sense was how the killer had dealt with Fellner. It seemed remarkably risky to leave such a big loose end that could come back to bring him down. What that communicated to Wiggins was that the killer had some sort of power over Fellner she didn’t quite understand yet.

The next step was calling the Department of Motor Vehicles. One of the best things about being in the same profession for a lengthy period of time was the connections that you established, and this held true for Wiggins as a PI. She had a good friend who worked at the DMV named Ray Giles. If Eleanor Rae Fellner had a license issued out of Lincoln County, Giles could find out where she lived.

Wiggins wasn't quite sure how she was going to reassure Joanne Fellner of her daughter's safety. The best-case scenario would be if Eleanor had moved to a different town without the killer's knowledge. Then again, if that were so, it was likely that Fellner already knew about it and was still scared that the man would find her.

Wiggins found Giles's name in her contact list and called him. Giles took several seconds to answer.

"This is Ray."

"Hey, Ray, it's Maryanne Wiggins." She was a little perturbed by the fact that Giles didn't have her number stored in his phone.

"Oh hey, Maryanne! Haven't heard from you in a while! How are you?"

The two exchanged pleasantries and small talk for a minute. Wiggins asked Giles how his wife was doing, forgetting that Giles was single.

"My wife?" Giles asked, confused.

"Yeah, how is she?"

"Uhm, Maryanne, I'm not married."

"Well, don't give up. I am sure there is someone out there for you."

Giles laughed loudly into the phone, while Wiggins didn't even crack a smile. She always thought it was strange when people laughed at their own jokes.

"So what can I do for you, Maryanne?"

"It's pretty straightforward actually. I know you hate when I ask for this, but I need an address."

Giles sighed and lowered his voice so that whoever was nearby him wouldn't hear him speaking. "Maryanne, you do realize that if I ever get caught doing this for you, I could get fired?"

"I know, Ray. I wouldn't ask if it weren't important."

"You always say that." Giles sounded exasperated.

"I am 100 percent serious when I say that this is the most important favor I have ever asked of you," Wiggins said, trying to inflict weight into her voice.

The line went silent for a while, as Giles was apparently contemplating whether or not to give in.

"Well, who is it?" he asked finally.

Wiggins couldn't help but smile. She knew she had him now.

"Her name is Eleanor Rae Fellner. She is twenty-four years old. Her mother's name is Joanne Fellner."

"Hold on, hold on, let me write that down." Wiggins could hear him rustling around for a writing utensil. "Okay, how do you spell the name?"

Wiggins spelled it out slowly.

"And she is twenty-four?"

"Correct."

"What was the mother's name again?"

"Joanne."

"Got it."

"Great. So, you'll run the name through the system for me and pull up her address?" Wiggins had a hopeful lift to her voice.

"Yeah, but not right this minute. I have some other things to take care of first."

"Okay."

"Do you want me to just text the address to you when I find it?"

"*If* you find it," Wiggins said, correcting Giles. "I'm not even sure she still has a Newport address."

"That won't matter. If she was issued a license at any time from us, she is required by law to call us and request a new ID if her permanent address changes, so it should still be in the system."

"I know the law, Ray, I just don't think everyone follows it."

"Amen to that. Anyway, the question was: Do you want me to text it to you?"

Wiggins nodded subconsciously while she replied. "Yeah, that will be fine."

After thanking Giles, Wiggins hung up. She was surprised at how smoothly this had gone. She already had the name and would soon have the address of the girl, and it was likely she would quickly be able to speak with her. The only thing now was developing a plan of action to convince Fellner that Eleanor was going to be safe.

Wiggins decided to call Jonah, knowing that he was probably waiting with bated breath for an update on Fellner's daughter. The phone rang only once, and then the call went straight to voice mail.

"*Hey, this is Jonah. Leave me a message and I will get back to you as soon as I can*," said the recording. *That is odd,* thought Wiggins. He had said the night before that he would be anxiously waiting to hear from her. Perhaps he was still sleeping. Wiggins made a mental note to call him again later in the day.

Less than ten minutes later, Wiggins received a text from Giles. *The girl grew up in Newport, but moved to Moscow, Idaho, when she was twenty. That is where she currently lives. Her address is 424 Franklin Avenue in Moscow.*

Wiggins felt a mixture of jubilation and frustration. If Eleanor were living a bit closer to Newport, she would be able to travel to her house and speak with her. But Wiggins was not going to make a prolonged drive to Idaho when she didn't even know if the girl would talk to her. Also, she didn't have a phone number for Eleanor, and it would be difficult to find one. The best Wiggins could do would be to communicate to Fellner that her daughter was living in another state and hope that, one, she didn't already know and, two, that it would be enough to convince her to talk. Wiggins knew that it was a long shot.

Next up on the agenda would be calling Joe Damascus, Fellner's attorney. There was no guarantee that Damascus wouldn't just hang up immediately after hearing who was calling. After all, Damascus had a strong distaste for Wiggins after his client had claimed that Wiggins was harassing her. But Wiggins had to try to contact him nonetheless.

Wiggins didn't have Damascus's number saved in her phone, so she had to Google his name. Unlike a random citizen like Eleanor, it was easy to get contact information for an attorney. The first hit in the Google search was Damascus's business website, and Wiggins clicked on it. She withdrew her phone and dialed the number, gulping in apprehension. This was likely not going to be a pleasant conversation.

"This is Joe," said a deep voice on the other end of the line.

"Hello, Mr. Damascus. This is private investigator Maryanne Wiggins. You may remember me from our conversations regarding a client of yours several years ago."

"Maryanne who?"

"Wiggins."

"Wig—oh, shit."

Wiggins couldn't help but chuckle.

"Funny how many people say that when they see me," she said cheerily.

"Tell me this isn't about Joanne."

"I can't tell you that, unfortunately," Wiggins replied.

"Trust me, I remember you quite well. And unless you require my services for a crime you have committed, then I have absolutely no desire to speak with you. Have a nice day, Ms.

Wiggins."

"Wait, don't hang up. This is not about arranging another meeting with your client."

"I can't fathom why else you would be calling," Damascus said brusquely. "She made it explicitly clear that she has no desire to speak with you ever again."

"I know, and if we were ever to speak, it would obviously have to be of her own volition."

"And why on earth would she talk to you of her own accord?"

"Because I have information about her daughter that might change her mind."

After a long pause on the line, Wiggins heard rustling in the background, so she knew Damascus hadn't hung up.

"Her daughter?"

Apparently, Wiggins wasn't the only one who was ignorant to Fellner's offspring.

"Yes, her daughter."

"She doesn't have—"

"Yes, she does. And there is a reason she hasn't told you or anyone else about her child."

There was another brief pause before Damascus started to talk again. "I don't understand—"

"And I don't need you to understand, Mr. Damascus. I just need you give her a message for me."

"A message?"

"That's right," said Wiggins patiently, leaning on the counter in her kitchen.

"I just *told* you, she doesn't want anything to do with you."

"It has nothing to do with me. It has to do with keeping her daughter safe."

Damascus groaned. "Listen, I don't know where you got this fantasy from, or why you are trying to spread this bullshit, but I am telling you, she doesn't have a daughter. She has been my client for well over a decade. You think I wouldn't know if she had a child?"

Wiggins rolled her eyes. *Men and their egos,* she thought.

"Mr. Damascus, I don't care what you think you know. Please just pass this message along for me."

"What message?" Damascus was growing so irate he was almost yelling.

"Her daughter no longer lives in Newport. She lives in Moscow, Idaho. And the man who threatened her is ignorant of this." Wiggins wasn't 100 percent positive about this, but she did feel reasonably certain about this assertion. After all, how would the killer have any idea unless he had actively been stalking Eleanor for twenty years?

"The man who threatened her?"

"Yes."

"Wait a minute. Are you saying . . . Jesus Christ, don't tell me this man who allegedly threatened Joanne's daughter is the same one who you thought killed those girls back in the nineties."

Wiggins was surprised how quickly he had made the connection.

"That is what I believe, yes."

"Well, no then. I won't be passing any message along that perpetuates your crackpot theories."

"Mr. Damascus—"

"I am not going to feed into this. Please don't call me again."

"Just please pass the message along, Mr. Damascus," Wiggins pleaded until the call was cut off.

"God damn it!" shouted Wiggins. She chucked her phone angrily onto the sofa and limped around her apartment, pacing while she tried to think of what to do next.

She had never pictured that this was going to go anywhere when Jonah had first started asking about it. After all, she had been borderline harassing Fellner off and on since 2011. Wiggins had admired Jonah's courage, but she had thought he was wasting his time. But then Jonah had broken through, and had gotten Fellner to fill in the missing piece of the puzzle about her daughter. Things had finally begun to fall into place. Wiggins had gotten the name and the address of the girl so quickly that she could hardly believe it. But now that Damascus had refused to pass the information along, she was starting to come to the realization that Fellner was not actually going to yield results after all. Wiggins was angry that she had allowed herself to get her hopes up.

What was next? Wiggins felt in her gut that she was closer to the answers than she had ever been before. And she knew that the reason for that was Katie Deeds. The man had made a glaring mistake by allowing Leighton Jones to see him. Wiggins knew from the moment Jonah had told his story that Jones was the key to everything. He could give a physical description of the man: height, weight, and what the man had been wearing. Perhaps Jones knew even more than he was letting on. Regardless, Joanne Fellner was officially a dead end, and Wiggins's way forward was clear: She had to go speak with Leighton Jones.

Wiggins decided to call Jonah one more time, but it went straight to voice mail again. *What the hell, kid,* thought Wiggins. She was certain Jonah didn't have the day off and wouldn't still be sleeping. So why else would his phone be either dead or disabled? It worried Wiggins since Jonah had actually been the one who had found Leighton, which was a fact that may have found its way to the killer somehow. However, she tried to convince herself that it probably meant nothing and that she would hear from Jonah soon.

Being that Wiggins couldn't afford to wait around for Jonah's consent and approval, she decided to move forward with the next step she had to take. She went into her office and fished around for her notepad that contained the notes she had taken during the first conversation she had had with Jonah. Riffling through two pages, she pinpointed what she was looking for: Leighton Jones's address.

30

Leighton Jones's house wasn't upscale by any means. In fact, it looked to Wiggins like it hadn't been lived in in months. The lawn was overgrown and the bushes were wild and unkempt. And yet, it was still curious that a single man with such a dark past could afford a house on his own. It was likely that Jones didn't actually own the house; he probably just rented it from a landlord. Most people who lived by themselves in Newport weren't actual homeowners. However, the feat was still somewhat impressive.

Wiggins moved her lame left leg out of the front seat of her silver Audi and used all the strength in her lower right limb to lift herself. She limped in the direction of the house, with its dank exterior and aesthetically poor paint job. Attached to her belt was a holster that held the Sig Sauer P320 that she took with her everywhere she went. Wiggins had had her concealed-carry license since she had been off the police force. She had never actually fired her gun outside of a shooting range, but it comforted her to know she had it when she was about to interview people like Leighton Jones. The only other thing that she carried besides her phone and her wallet was the notepad that contained the copious amount of notes she had taken about Jones when speaking with Jonah.

Wiggins climbed up the three steps to the front porch, wincing as she did so while pain shot up her leg. As soon as the door was within arm's reach, she knocked loudly four times. There was no immediate sign that Jones was home; the lights inside were off and there didn't come an audible response to her knocking. She waited for half a minute and then knocked again. Still nothing.

Wiggins leaned to the side and peeked through the window that was next to the door. The inside of the house looked barren and she noticed no movement. With her gut sinking in disappointment, she decided that Jones must not be home.

What next? She had no other information on the man. She had tried to research him briefly before she left, but information on Leighton Jones was not readily available for some reason. She didn't even discover where he worked. Wiggins took out the notepad and looked for something she had written that could assist her in finding Jones. The only other thing Wiggins saw from her interview with Jonah was that Jones apparently spent a lot of time at the bar he had followed Katie home from. *Worth a shot,* she thought.

No more than ten minutes later, Wiggins emerged from her car in the Nye Beach Turnaround parking lot. It had been a very short drive from Jones's house. Wiggins hobbled her way up the sloping hill, passing a chowder restaurant to her left. On the ground, she saw a bucket full of cigarette butts that was in front of a musty-looking building. The words Rip Tide's were etched on a wooden sign above the door to the building. Wiggins opened the door and walked inside.

Blaring country music greeted Wiggins as she walked in.

There were several people sitting at the bar; most of them looked like fishermen. It surprised her a little, since it wasn't even noon. Only a couple of patrons glanced in her direction as she limped by, and the ones who did only maintained their glances for a couple of seconds. Behind the bar, an older woman with a kind face and silver hair was looking at Wiggins. Her name tag had PATTY printed on it.

"Hey, hunny, can I get you something to drink?"

"No, actually, I was just wondering if you could answer a couple of questions for me." Wiggins smiled, trying to sound polite.

"Questions? What kinda questions?"

"It is about a patron who apparently has visited this tavern frequently. His name is Leighton Jones."

Patty got a curious look on her face. "Funnily enough, you're the second person to ask me about Leighton in the past couple of weeks."

Wiggins nodded. "Was the other person a handsome young man with dirty-blond hair?"

Patty smiled. "That's him!"

"That was Jonah Carr. He is a reporter for the *News Times*."

"A reporter?" Patty had a befuddled expression on her face. "Is Leighton in some sort of trouble or something?"

"No. Well, not that I know of. Anyway, have you seen Leighton around lately?"

Patty placed her hands on her hips and looked toward the ceiling, which was covered in banners for various sports teams. She bit her lip.

"You know what? Now that you mention it, I haven't seen Leighton in several days."

"Is that unusual?"

"Very much so. Until the past week, Leighton has come to the bar almost every single night for the past seven or eight years," said Patty while nodding her head and pursing her lips.

Wiggins leaned in like she hadn't heard right. "Eight years? Wow."

"Yeah."

"And you haven't seen him at all the last few days?"

"Nope. Kind of strange now that I think about it."

"Yes," Wiggins agreed. "It is kind of strange."

Once Wiggins got back to her car, she mulled over what Patty had told her. What could possibly have caused Leighton Jones to forego the tradition he had partaken in for so many consecutive years? It was bizarre and seemed like more than just a coincidence after all of the drama that had taken place with Jones in the past couple of weeks.

Wiggins needed to talk to Jonah even more now. Together, they could come up with a plan of action. He would be eager to hear what had happened in regards to Joanne Fellner's daughter. Also, he might be able to offer up some explanation for where Jones had gone. Hopefully, he had finally turned his phone back on. Wiggins scrolled through her mobile device for his number and redialed.

Once more, his voice mail picked up after the first ring. It was eleven in the morning, and it had been three hours since she had first attempted to contact Jonah. Wiggins was growing more worried. There was no legitimate reason for Jonah having his phone off for that long, especially since he had been expecting a call from Wiggins. *Screw it,* Wiggins thought. She flipped through her notepad and found the address that she had coaxed out of Jonah during their first meeting. He might not appreciate her showing up at his apartment, but she no longer cared. Wiggins had to make sure that he was alright.

31

The man drove farther down the logging road, as rain splattered into the mud puddles that lined the sides of the gravel street. The wind was blowing the rain in every direction, and the trees that surrounded the road dipped precariously overhead. The man was still getting use to the brakes of the Corolla; they were far more sensitive than the brakes of his Jeep. He was at least twenty miles deep into the forest, and there was no sign of life; human or otherwise. After all, this road had been officially closed long ago.

The man had already disposed of the young reporter's body. He had spent hours attempting to make all traces of the kid disappear, so that if his remains were ever recovered, they would be totally indistinguishable. First, he had placed the corpse in his own bathtub, cutting every major artery. He had then filled the tub with warm water and let it drain, repeating the process several times until all of the bodily fluid had been sucked away. After he had forcibly removed every tooth from the skull with a pair of pliers, he had also shucked the skin from each fingertip. When he was done, all the DNA, dental, and fingerprint evidence had been exterminated. Afterwards, he had butchered the reporter into seven pieces, and placed each chunk in a separate garbage bag. Eventually, in the dead of night, he had gone for a drive north on Highway 101. Every six or seven miles, he would veer off onto random logging roads that took him into the forest and head east until he was well beyond any sign of civilization. He had buried each bag in a spot that was at least fifteen miles from the next, always at least seven feet deep in the ground. The entire endeavor had taken three hours. It was a tedious process, and made his attempted cover-ups twenty years ago look like child's play, but the man felt certain that he was in the clear as far as the reporter was concerned.

Back when he was a novice, he had failed to hide the bodies properly, and they had been found, resulting in him almost getting caught. And after he had changed his tactic, he had never had to conceal a body in the same way as the first girls. Hell, most of his elaborate cover-up schemes over the years hinged on the police *finding* a body. If they didn't have the remains, they would think the death was nefarious in nature. But this was different. The man didn't have time to devise a plan to make the reporter's death look like a suicide or some freak accident. He had had to dispose of the kid quickly. No doubt the police would eventually arrive at the conclusion that the kid was murdered, and then they would start hunting. But thanks to his prowess, they would never connect it to him.

With the witness, he hadn't been as meticulous when disposing of the body. After all, when he had looked into it he had found that the witness was a rapist and a lifelong criminal, not an up-and-coming reporter from a big city. Nobody would be looking for the witness. And even if he *was* reported as missing, the man didn't think the police department would allocate serious resources to finding a serial sex offender. Therefore, the man had butchered the body into several pieces in his shed, thrown them into more garbage bags, and placed those bags underneath a mountain of garbage in a landfill. The man had had to pause to admire his stroke of genius when he had come up with the idea. Who would ever look for something that was discarded in the trash?

The real problem had been finding a place to dump the young reporter's car. Once the car was safely at the man's house, he had spent hours cleaning up the mess using rubber gloves, oxygen-based bleach, and a sack full of sponges that he planned on burning. It was paramount he remove all evidence that someone had been murdered inside the vehicle, in case the police ever found it. The man had also taken off both license plates and other various items that could help someone identify who the Corolla had belonged to, including the VIN tags. He felt almost superhuman in his efficiency while cleaning up the naughty deed.

After fifteen more minutes of driving, the man finally came to the spot he was looking for. The road forked off to the left, and on the right there was a giant cliff that was fifty feet above the ravine below. In the valley were brush and blackberry bushes so tall that the man estimated the actual soil was a good twenty feet farther down. The man put the car in park, pausing while he took a deep breath. Now came the tricky part.

He opened the car door, got out, and stood next to the Corolla. Leaning his body back into the vehicle, he used his left hand to press on the brake while he gripped the gearshift. He didn't want to simply put it in neutral and push, because then the car might not dive down as far into the ravine. Inhaling deeply one more time, the man forced the gearshift back into drive and the car lurched forward. The man leapt back to avoid the back tire crushing his feet, and the body of the Corolla rushed past him. His foot caught on a root, and he tumbled to the ground, landing on his butt. From a seated position, the man watched as the car plunged over the cliff. There was an earth-shattering crash as the car landed below. Instead of standing up, the man crawled a few feet forward to see where the car had ended up. It was so firmly entrenched in the vegetation below that nothing was visible. The man let a relieved grin spread across his face. Immediately, visions of Sierra Bunker's blond hair danced in his head.

32

Wiggins's Audi careened into the parking lot. She had been speeding the entire way, and as the vehicle had gotten closer, she had unconsciously made it go faster and faster. Her grip on the steering wheel increased tenfold as she tried to regain control over the Audi when she slammed on the brake and skidded to a stop inches away from colliding with a yellow Hummer. Wiggins's face contorted with relief as she realized how close she had come to an accident. Breathing deeply, she turned into an open spot next to the Hummer.

Wiggins emerged from the car, moving as fast as her injured leg allowed. There were three different apartment buildings with British-sounding names plastered on the outside, including Stonybrook, Greenridge, and Nottingham. Wiggins quickly walked over to Greenridge, where she knew Jonah's apartment to be. There were three sets of stairs, and she moved toward the one on the left. She had to limp slowly up the staircase, as it caused immense pain in her leg. When she got to the top, she saw number 505 next to the entrance. This was the right place. Wiggins hammered on the door with her fist. As soon as her hand made contact, the door swung open.

Wiggins had to stop for a second and process what had happened. The first thought that came to her mind was that the door had been left unlocked, but then she realized that it wouldn't have opened without twisting the handle if that were the case. She pulled the door back toward her and leaned in to closely observe the lock. It was broken.

Her heart pounded. *Oh shit, oh shit,* Wiggins cursed.

"Jonah!" she yelled into the apartment frantically.

There was no response. She charged into the open room with her hand on her pistol, though instinct told her that the place was empty.

The first thing that Wiggins noticed was that it was freezing. It seemed as if the heater hadn't been running for some time. The apartment was bare, with hardly any furniture or belongings. Wiggins scanned across the living room and kitchen area, seeing nothing but the usual items you would find in an apartment: cutlery, pots, pans, a television, and other extraneous items. The whole place smelled like it had been bathed in cologne, as whatever scent Jonah wore hung in the air. Wiggins walked around the room, scoping the place for any sign of what might have become of the young reporter. There wasn't anything of note to be found in the living room, so Wiggins moved toward the door she figured led to Jonah's bedroom. It was ajar.

Nothing immediately stuck out to Wiggins, as her new surroundings just looked like a typical male bedroom. Dirty laundry was spread out on the ground and an unmade bed that looked unwelcoming sat on the right side of the floor. The room was so small that it only took Wiggins a few steps to circle around it. Above the bed, Wiggins noticed that the window was open. Being that it was raining and gusting outside, this struck her as odd. She put her unencumbered knee gingerly onto the bed and placed her face against the screen of the open window, looking down into the parking lot. All she saw below was a small line of bushes.

As Wiggins turned back around, something caught her eye. She had to do a double take before her eyes zeroed in on the disturbance. Three minuscule specks of crimson lingered morosely on the topmost white pillow. Blood.

Wiggins went numb. A tiny amount of blood on a pillow usually wouldn't be cause for concern; it could easily have come from a spider bite or a nighttime nose bleed. But Wiggins knew in her heart while staring at the blots of red that they had been left there because of something far more sinister. She moved carefully around the spot, trying not to tamper with it, as it could become viable evidence later. Though most of the time she had no problem looking at blood, it made her feel strangely nauseous knowing what it possibly signaled. Wiggins unsheathed her phone from her pocket and brought up the camera application. From every angle possible, she took a different picture.

After she put her phone away, Wiggins kept looking at the pillow. She couldn't take her eyes off the spot of blood. It was so unsettling, so bleak. She stared intently, as if imploring the stained inanimate object to recount the tale of what had happened there. As she stood, the cold bit at her skin, and she felt deeply disturbed. Could Jonah have been murdered in his own bed? If he had, there would likely have been a much greater volume of blood on the pillow. So perhaps he had been injured while the intruder attempted to drag him out of his room. For some reason, that thought was far more haunting to Wiggins than anything else.

Wiggins walked back into the living room. She began one last mental sweep, trying to find anything that might aid her. She noticed a brown notepad tossed haphazardly in front of the recliner that was by the television. Before picking it up, she pulled out her phone and snapped more pictures, knowing that she was about to possibly remove evidence. She lifted the notepad and flicked through a few pages. By the looks of it, these were the notes that Jonah had taken while conducting his interviews. Wiggins knew she shouldn't disturb a likely crime scene, but she couldn't resist. She put the notepad inside the coat she was wearing and hobbled out through the front door.

Again, taking out her phone, Wiggins pulled the door toward her so that it was nearly closed. She opened the camera app once more and took a close-up picture of the lock, making sure that it was obvious to an onlooker that it was broken. Wiggins looked at the photo, satisfied with the point it was trying to make. She then closed the application and made a call.

"Nine one one, what's your emergency?"

"Hi, this is private investigator Maryanne Wiggins. I am calling to report a missing person."

33

"So you don't actually know for sure he's missing?"

"How would I be able to know for sure? If I knew where he was, he wouldn't be missing."

Wiggins tried to keep her voice calm and measured, but the man with the receding hairline and leather skin was making it difficult.

"So you tried to contact him, but his phone was dead?" the officer asked.

"I obviously don't know if the phone was dead, but it went straight to voice mail, so I think it must have been."

The cop that Wiggins was speaking to had a buzz cut that called attention to his already massive head. His hair was light blond and his skin was red. He had a heavy build, with a combination of fat and muscle ballooning his torso. It hadn't taken him long to arrive after Wiggins had made the call to the 911 operator. Less than five minutes had passed before the dark blue police car had pulled into the lot, and Wiggins had flagged him down from the top of the stairs of the Greenridge building.

"And you showed up at his apartment after he didn't answer his phone? Seems kind of extreme."

"He was *waiting* to speak with me. He was waiting for me to call him." Wiggins was annoyed at the fact that the cop was focusing on her actions instead of where Jonah was. "And his phone was off for three hours. Anyway, why does it matter? This obviously looks like a break-in, doesn't it?" She pointed at the broken lock, trying to make the officer see reason.

"And you are his coworker?"

"No, not exactly. I am a PI. He is a journalist. We have been collaborating together on an unsolved case."

"Hmmm," said the man vaguely, looking at Wiggins skeptically.

"What do you mean 'hmmm'?"

"It's just, like I said, it seems a little extreme to just show up at his house like this just because his phone was off for three hours."

A fuse in Wiggins's brain ignited, and for a fleeting moment, she felt like slapping the tall man on his giant forehead. She let the moment pass and tried to keep her voice as steady as she could.

"Listen, Officer . . . ?"

"Casey. Rick Casey."

"Alright, Officer *Casey,*" Wiggins said in a patronizing tone. "Why does it matter that I showed up at his house unannounced? He obviously isn't here to take offense, so shouldn't you be more worried that somebody is missing?"

"Ms. Wiggins, as soon as you actually have some sort of confirmation that he *is* missing, then I *will* be worried."

"His phone is off, he isn't here, and his front door is smashed in!"

Casey shook his head irritably. "Smashed in? The door isn't off its hinges. For all we know the lock could have been broken for some time. Anyway, have you checked to see if he is at work?"

Wiggins opened her mouth, and then shut it after a couple of seconds.

"No, I haven't."

"Maybe you should go talk to Randy Marks."

"Maybe *you* should go talk to Ra—" She stopped herself and redirected her train of thought. "Wait, do you know Jonah? How do you know where he works?"

Casey started stammering, as if he had revealed more than he intended. "I don't know him personally. I mean, I know who he is. He has covered cases that I have been a part of. He works for the paper, you know. They always send people down to the department."

Wiggins looked Casey up and down. He sure was exhibiting a strange reaction. Then a light bulb turned on in her head. With a rush of understanding, she realized she had heard Casey's name before. Jonah had told Wiggins that Rick Casey was the police officer who had run the criminal history on Leighton Jones, and the one who had evidently confronted Jones and listened to the man change his story. And that meant he had also heard about the man in the ski mask who was waiting to abduct Katie. *Well, fuck me,* thought Wiggins. *That's quite a coincidence.*

Wiggins stepped towards Casey and lowered her voice a little. "You don't have to lie to me."

"Excuse me?"

"Jonah has mentioned you before. You do know him personally, don't you? You were the one who helped him find Leighton Jones. In fact, you were the one who talked to Jones for him."

"Shhh!" He looked around, making sure that there wasn't anyone around to overhear their conversation.

"Listen, Sergeant, I really don't care that you broke protocol and fed information to a reporter. I don't give a flying fuck that you ran a criminal history on a rapist, or that you interviewed said rapist. It is none of my business, and I sure as hell am not going to bust your balls about it. I just want to find Jonah."

Casey stared at her, flabbergasted. He sputtered, "I don't . . . What do you think . . . Well, shit."

"Jonah also told me that you were aware of the masked man Jones saw when he was following Katie Deeds."

"Jones never told me that," Casey said defiantly.

"But you were aware of it regardless. So you know that Jonah has been following up on this masked man."

"I don't presume to know what Jonah has been doing. Anyway, what does that have to do with this?"

Wiggins was normally good about keeping her cool, but Casey was testing her patience. "Can you not put two and two together?" she shouted while pointing at the broken lock.

For a few seconds, Casey still looked bewildered. Then comprehension spread across his face. He suddenly became amused.

"Oh, please," Casey said. "No. Just . . . No."

"What do you mean 'no'?"

"I mean, I interviewed Jones, and he said he wasn't even at the bar the night that the Deeds girl died. The story that he told Jonah was not true. He was making it up."

"Why would he—"

"I don't know. The point is there never was a man in a mask stalking Katie Deeds. She committed suicide, for Christ's sake. And I don't know what Jonah has been doing, but even if he was poking around, you think this imaginary masked man came and kidnapped him? Don't be silly. Just because the lock is broken on a door doesn't mean someone killed him. This could have happened a great number of ways. Maybe he locked himself out of his apartment one time and had to break the lock to get back in."

Wiggins rolled her eyes in exasperation. "If he locked himself out, why wouldn't he just call the landlord to let him in?"

"Maybe he lives out of town."

"So Jonah's solution was to break down his own door?"

"Perhaps he was drunk."

Wiggins made prolonged eye contact with Casey with a fierce expression on her face.

"You need to go and talk to Randy Marks."

Casey grimaced in anger. "Do I?"

"Yes, I believe you do. Even if we forget everything about the masked man and what Jonah was looking into, does this *not* look like an intruder forced entry to you?" Wiggins gestured at the door again. "Do you really believe that Jonah did this himself?"

"I have no idea. It looks like the television and all of the other valuables are still inside," replied Casey. Wiggins was sure he was trying to purposefully antagonize her now.

"Not that kind of forced entry." Wiggins gritted her teeth. Casey smiled with only his lips, but it wasn't a friendly thing. It was a mocking gesture.

"Will you please just humor me and go and talk to Marks?"

The smile vanished from Casey's face. He furrowed his brow and was apparently debating how to respond.

"Fine. But you are coming with me."

Wiggins followed Casey's squad car on Highway 101 and turned after him on Tenth Street and then down Avery Road, where the offices of the *News Times* were located. Wiggins parked in the spot that was right next to the one Casey had taken. They got out of their cars simultaneously and exchanged unfriendly glances as they both walked over to the main building.

Before they entered, Casey moved in front of Wiggins,

blocking her path. He got within several inches of her face. Wiggins could smell onions on his breath as he began talking.

"Now I know when we get in there, you're going to want to do all the talking. But if you knew what was good for you, you will not mention anything about this masked man or Leighton Jones," Casey said in a menacing whisper.

"Don't worry yourself about that," Wiggins said, inflecting strength into her voice. "And I would appreciate it if you weren't so damn close to my face."

Casey began to snarl, and it was evident that he wanted to say something. However, he made an about-face and stalked toward the office building again. Wiggins followed.

When they got inside, Wiggins was overwhelmed by the plethora of different noises that swarmed her. There was the sound of loud typing as different reporters wrote stories in their various cubicles and a million conversations were taking place—some on the phone, some in person. There was a reception area directly in front of the door that Wiggins and Casey had walked through, and a skinny brunette woman with high cheekbones and pretty green eyes was sitting behind the desk.

"Hello. What I can I do for you?"

"Hi, is Jonah Carr here?" Casey asked before Wiggins could open her mouth.

"I haven't seen him today, no. But it's not unusual for our staff to keep different hours while on assignments."

"Can we talk to Randy Marks then, please?"

"Uh, sure. He is in his office. It is at the end of the second row of cubicles," said the woman, while gesturing toward the room next to her.

"Thank you," said Casey, bowing his large head a little.

Casey and Wiggins walked in the direction that the secretary had indicated, until they were in front of a door with a plaque that read, RANDY MARKS, EDITOR IN CHIEF. Casey rapped on the door with his knuckles several times.

"One fucking second! Jesus!" the voice from behind the door yelled.

Casey looked at Wiggins with his eyes widening and his brow raising.

"Well, this sounds like it is going to be lovely," said Wiggins cheerfully.

Eventually, the door opened and behind it stood an overweight man with a weird bowl-shaped haircut. He was confused at first, but when he saw Casey's uniform, his expression changed. He squinted his eyes and sighed irritably.

"Aw, fuck. What the hell have we done now?"

Casey looked perplexed. Wiggins just stood back, amused.

"Um, hi. I am Officer Casey. This is Maryanne Wiggins," Casey nodded to Wiggins.

Marks shook Casey's hand with a sarcastic expression on his face. "I recognize you, officer. We ran a profile on you a while back. But it is a fucking pleasure to actually meet you."

"Uh, right. Thanks. Anyway, I was just wondering if you have heard from one of your employees, Jonah Carr, at any point today."

Marks flushed a nasty shade of red. "I wouldn't mind if I never heard from that little shit again."

Wiggins waited for Casey to respond, but jumped in before he could speak. "Why? What do you mean?"

Casey glared at Wiggins. "You're looking in the wrong place. Jonah Carr no longer works here. That unprofessional little twat," Marks said through gritted teeth.

"Sorry, I am not following," Wiggins said, confused.

Marks began quivering in a bout of unmitigated rage. "The bastard quit last night. Texted me at nine to tell me he was moving back to Portland. Can you believe that? Quitting over a text message. Un-fucking-believable."

Wiggins's stomach dropped.

"Not to be intrusive, but do you mind reading exactly what

the text said?"

"That's it. Just said, 'I am sorry, Randy. I can't do this any longer. I'm heading back to Portland tomorrow. I quit.' I tried calling him, but the fucker didn't answer. Can't even believe it. Thought he loved working here. But with that kind of conduct I can guarantee he will never get a job in journalism again. Quitting over a fucking text message. Unbelievable."

"How long was it between when you received the text and when you called him?" Wiggins asked as Casey stood there looking annoyed he had lost control of the interrogation.

"Shit, I don't know. I read the text when I got out of the shower. It was probably about fifteen minutes. Why the hell do you want to know that?"

"And when you called, did the phone ring or did it go straight to voice mail?" Wiggins pressed, ignoring Marks's inquiry.

"Straight to voice mail. What is this all about anyway?"

Wiggins didn't answer. Her mind was racing. This is exactly what the killer had done with Katie. He had sent three texts to Teresa Deeds from Katie's phone to cover his tracks. And if that told Wiggins anything, it was this: Jonah Carr was likely dead.

34

As soon as they were out in the parking lot five minutes later, Casey turned to Wiggins. "Well, are you satisfied?" He said it like he knew what Wiggins's response would be, like he was reading off lines of a script.

"Satisfied? What would I have to be satisfied about?"

"Jonah! I mean, I am disappointed that he left Newport, but at least we know he's okay." Casey feigned ignorance to Wiggins's position.

"I don't think he left Newport, and I sure as hell don't think he is okay," Wiggins said quietly.

Casey's jaw twisted and his nostrils flared. "Did you not hear anything that Marks just said?"

Wiggins bit her lip and lowered her voice. "I heard everything. And all it does is confirm my suspicions."

"How on earth—"

"Think about what happened to Katie Deeds."

Casey stopped in his tracks and looked at the sky in

exasperation. It looked like he was debating whether to respond. After a while, he couldn't hold in his retort any longer and pointed at Wiggins bullishly.

"Katie Deeds killed herself. End of story."

"Maybe you should do some actual police work before you jump to conclusions like that."

For a moment, Casey looked like he was having a stroke, twisting his face and turning purple, but then Wiggins realized he was just experiencing uncontrollable rage.

"Don't you fucking tell me that. Listen, you kook, I have had this badge for thirty years. And I am not about to let some nobody tell me how to be a better cop!"

Wiggins rolled her eyes so hard that she felt pain in her forehead.

"I was a cop, too, you know."

"Who the hell cares? You have nothing, lady. Because there is nothing here," Casey finished.

"Nothing here? We have a witness who *saw* Katie being stalked by a man in a fucking ski mask!" Wiggins shouted. "You and I both know that Leighton Jones would have no reason to make that up. This man abducted her, stole her phone, and texted her grandmother a suicide note. Do you seriously think it is just a coincidence that the one person in Newport besides myself who's looking for Katie's killer suddenly vanishes, and then his boss receives a text that conveniently makes it look like Jonah dropped all his career aspirations to move back to his hometown?"

"I seriously don't have the time or the energy for this." Casey shook his head. "I don't know if you think that making stuff up is good publicity for you, but I can assure you it's not. Please just drop this conspiratorial bullshit and move on."

"I take it that means you're not going to file a missing person report?" Wiggins asked in a patronizing tone.

"You are goddamn right!" Casey yelled, and he stormed

over to his squad car. Within moments, the vehicle was back on the road, speeding away. Wiggins just stared as the car disappeared from her view.

The way Wiggins saw it, she had two options going forward. She could approach another officer and hope for better luck than she had with Rick Casey. Or, she could go straight to the top. The one person who was already familiar with the case and had more weight to throw around than Casey was the district attorney, Dan Jenkins. Wiggins detested Jenkins, but she also knew rationally that he was the only other option she had in terms of jump-starting an investigation into Jonah's disappearance. She could meet with Jenkins in a last-ditch effort to get the ball rolling. If nothing came of it, she could go back to square one and probe into the circumstances surrounding Katie's death, much like Jonah had. She would speak to Teresa Deeds and other people familiar with Katie's day-to-day activities. Perhaps she would finally find a solid lead. But first, she needed to try her hand with Dan Jenkins.

Wiggins knew that the DA's office was busy, and she didn't want to talk to some secretary, so she decided to send an email directly to Jenkins instead. She stood in the parking lot of the *Times* and composed a new email.

> *Hey, Dan, it is Maryanne Wiggins. If you can manage it, I would like to arrange an appointment with you regarding a case we have previously spoken about. New information has come to light and something may have happened to one of my colleagues. This is very important and time sensitive, so please write me back ASAP so we can schedule a meeting.*
>
> *Best regards,*

Maryanne.

The Lincoln County Courthouse stood out like a sore thumb in Newport. While most of the other buildings were sprawling shopping centers that were one level, the courthouse sprung up six stories into the air. It was right next to the jail and across from an ice cream shop, which always struck Wiggins as somewhat ironic. A place where people were kept like caged animals right across from one of the great joys in life: ice cream.

Wiggins parked in one of the sixty-minute parking zones and made her way over to the courthouse. The automatic doors opened as soon as she crossed over the motion sensor, and Wiggins walked down a hallway. Once she rounded the corner, she came to a glorified security guard in full police regalia who looked mighty serious. He stood next to a large metal detector and a stack of gray bins that were intended for guests to place any items inside that might set off the detector.

"If you could please put anything you have in your pockets inside, you would save us both a lot of time," the over-serious security guard said.

"Is my gun okay?" Wiggins quipped, trying to break the ice. The stoic security guard just stared at her, ignoring her attempt at levity.

"Please don't make jokes like that, ma'am. Unless you do actually have a gun, then I am going to have to place you under arrest."

"Tough crowd," said Wiggins. She opened her coat to reassure that she was not actually armed at the moment, and then started putting everything from her pockets inside one of the gray bins. After walking through the metal detector without setting it off, the guard handed her the bin through the crevice next to the archway of the detector. She put her wallet, keys, and Tic Tacs back inside her pocket and walked toward the elevator.

Dan Jenkins's office was located on the fifth floor. He had replied to her email in less than an hour and had agreed to an appointment at four that afternoon. She could tell by the tone of his reply that he was eager to hear what she had to say, even though they shared a mutual dislike.

Once the elevator reached the fifth floor, Wiggins hobbled out of the claustrophobic area and walked down another long hallway. Just before the hallway splintered off in another direction, a doorway with a small window next to it was visible. Beyond the window, Wiggins could see Dan Jenkins typing away on his laptop.

Jenkins was a tall and slender man, with white hair that stood up like a hedgehog's spines. He was spindly and seemed to move his arms in a noodle motion when he typed. He had a large Adam's apple that seemed to bob up and down whenever he moved his neck. For some reason, he had always reminded Wiggins of a villain in an old Western film, minus the cowboy hat and revolver.

Wiggins tapped on the window of his office. Jenkins looked up from his computer screen, and his expression didn't change when he saw her. He stood and his head almost hit the ceiling. Wiggins guessed he was somewhere around six feet six. Jenkins opened the door and tried to contort his face in a welcoming manner, but he just looked like he was in physical pain.

"Hello, Maryanne. It's good to see you." He had a very soft voice that wouldn't be audible in a loud room.

"Likewise, Dan," said Wiggins in a perfunctory tone. She sat in the seat across from Jenkins's desk even though he didn't offer it.

"I have to say, I am a little surprised to hear from you. I didn't think you would ever come to me for help again," Jenkins said. Wiggins knew that he said this because of their hostility for each other, but he made it sound much more cordial than it was.

"Ah, well, I am a bit surprised myself. No offense."

"None taken. So what is this all about? You made it sound fairly serious in your email. You said something might have happened to your colleague?"

Wiggins tried to make her tone delicate. "Right, well, trust me, we will get there. However, there are other matters that we must discuss first to get you caught up on what has been happening."

"Okay." Jenkins tapped his fingers on his desk as he turned away from his computer. "Where do you want to start?"

Wiggins hesitated, knowing that Jenkins wasn't going to like what he was about to hear.

"It's our guy, Dan. From the nineties. The teenage girls. He's been at it again."

Jenkins started to smile, seemingly vexed, and he began shaking his head.

"How did I know that it was going to be about that?"

"Just hear me out, Dan. This has to do with Katie Deeds."

"The girl who jumped off . . . Oh God, please tell me you're not about to say what I think you are about to say."

"Just please listen to what I have to say." She began by telling Jenkins about Jonah, and how he was assigned the write-up for Katie's death for the *News Times.* She relayed what Teresa Deeds had told Jonah about suspecting that her granddaughter was murdered, and the oddities of the texts Teresa had received. Next, she explained how Jonah had found Leighton Jones. She told Jenkins that Jones had seen someone waiting to attack Katie (though she accidentally left out the description of the man Jones had seen), and that he changed his story when he had talked to Rick Casey. Throughout her explanation, Jenkins remained indifferent, unmoved by the evidence that Wiggins was presenting. When she was done, Jenkins sighed.

"Everything you have told me is purely circumstantial hearsay, Maryanne," Jenkins said dismissively.

Wiggins clenched her fists in fury. "Including the fact that Leighton Jones saw a man waiting to abduct Katie on her walk home?"

"A story that you said he has now changed," Jenkins said without missing a beat.

"Jesus, Dan, not you too."

"When are you going to let this go, Maryanne? We caught our guy years ago. Bobby Ray Foles was the killer. For years, you have come to me with so-called evidence that you think suggests that every young girl who has died in Newport in the last thirty years was murdered. And frankly, I am tired of you skewing the facts to fit your narrative. Katie Deeds committed suicide. To say otherwise is an insult to her memory."

"Damn it, Dan, there is a pattern here and if you can't see it, you are blind," Wiggins said through gritted teeth. Jenkins looked surprised at the fact that she was throwing barbs. Usually it took longer for them to get into a verbal sparring match.

"There is no such pattern, other than the pattern of you speaking of things that you do not fully understand," said Jenkins softly.

"Riley Reid," Wiggins said bluntly.

"Uh, what?"

"Explain to me what you think happened to Riley Reid."

"The girl who drowned at Olalla Lake in 2001?"

"That's the one. You think she randomly decided to go for a swim by herself when she left her friends to piss, even though her mother said she was a terrible swimmer?"

"Yep," said Jenkins succinctly, sounding like a petulant child.

"And what about Evelyn Sizemore?"

"We have already talked ab—"

Wiggins slapped her hand on the desk to interrupt. "What do you think happened to Evelyn Sizemore?"

Jenkins stared at her. "She ran away to stay with her

biological father in Oklahoma."

"A man who had never been in her life, and who was actually living in Florida when Sizemore disappeared?"

"Maryanne—"

Wiggins pressed more. "And Lacy Larson. What happened to her?"

Jenkins paused and pursed his lips before continuing, "She hydroplaned over a cliff after she tried to make too tight of a left turn," he said. Wiggins was a little surprised that he was continuing to play along, but she was going to use it to her advantage.

"Right, even though the skid marks left on the road indicate that her vehicle moved in a straight line, directly across from the steepest hill in Newport?"

"If you think what happened to Larson was anything but a tragic accident, you are cr—"

"Tell me about Serena Wu and Kelsea Craft."

Jenkins was becoming visibly agitated at continually being interrupted by Wiggins.

"I am not going to play this game for much longer."

"Tell me about Wu and Craft," Wiggins repeated.

"They got lost while hiking in one of the largest forests in the continental United States," Jenkins said, raising his voice.

"But Kelsea and her father had gone on hiking trips in Siuslaw dozens of times. So how come they suddenly forgot the lay of the land?"

"Like I said, it is a big forest."

Wiggins pursed her lips and nodded sarcastically. "Hmmm."

"And what about Ken Craft?" Jenkins tried to turn the tables on Wiggins with questions he didn't think she could answer.

"I think our guy killed him too."

"Bullshit," Jenkins said quickly. "A man in his forties? I thought we were talking about teenage girls here."

"He's a serial killer, Dan. He doesn't abide by the rules. Even his own rules."

"There's no way. There's just no way," Jenkins said, his voice lowering back down to a softer decibel.

"Dan, please. I implore you to look at the facts. How can you not see at all the irregularities here? Riley Reid, Evelyn Sizemore, Lacy Larson, Serena Wu, Kelsea Craft. All their deaths pose questions that you can't provide a reasonable answer to. And don't even get me started on Mariah Beckham and Wendy Gordon. A beautiful, popular teen with no history of depression who committed suicide? And a young woman falling to her death off a pier, even though the man she was with said she was walking in the opposite direction? I know we've had this conversation over and over, Dan, and I sound like a broken record, but I keep hoping one of these days you will see reason."

Jenkins began rubbing his face in impatience. "And reason would be illogically linking the deaths of seven females that are clearly unrelated to the homicides of five teenagers in the nineties that bear obvious similarities to each other?"

"Yes. Absolutely."

There was a long, drawn-out pause as Jenkins looked at the ceiling, trying to find words to counter Wiggins's argument. He shook his head again.

"I can't believe you. I can't believe I agreed to this meeting. I thought you said this was about a colleague, anyway."

"It is. Jonah Carr, the reporter who uncovered Leighton Jones's story, has gone missing."

For a moment, Jenkins's face showed surprise. Then it transformed into concern.

"He is missing? What?"

"That's right. I had pertinent information to share with him, and I went to call him this morning, but his phone was off. So, I went to his apartment, and I found the front door broken in. And no Jonah inside."

"Jesus," Jenkins replied, unable to contain himself. "Did you call the police?"

"Of course. Rick Casey, the same officer who interviewed Leighton Jones, was the one who showed up. He was more than a little unsure of the whole thing and insisted that we visit Randy Marks, Jonah's editor at the *Times*. So, we did. Apparently, last night Marks received a text from Jonah saying he was quitting the paper and moving back to Portland. After we talked to Marks, Casey refused to file a missing person report. Hence I have come to you."

At first, Jenkins just looked befuddled, furrowing his brow. Then suddenly, his face slacked, and he cracked a smile.

"So you think Jonah was abducted by the same imaginary person who killed these girls, and this boogie man sent Marks the 'I quit' text?" His concern for Jonah's well-being had evaporated.

"Listen—"

Jenkins slammed his hand onto the desk, repeating the gesture that Wiggins had done earlier, except much harder and much more viciously. Wiggins jumped a little at the noise as Jenkins stood up and placed his hands on the desk, leaning in so that he was inches from her face.

"No, *you* listen, Maryanne. You are being absolutely ridiculous. I can't even believe you would come here and ask for my help. And claiming your colleague was in danger to persuade me to talk to you, when he clearly just left town of his own volition, is grossly unprofessional."

Wiggins was left confounded. She had expected some sort of pushback, but not blatant denial of everything she had presented.

"The only thing, and I do mean the *only thing,* that has any actual relevance in all of this, is Leighton Jones's story. I can't see why he would, but it wouldn't be the first time someone made something up."

"He didn't make it up," Wiggins said, feeling emotionally defeated.

"Prove it," Jenkins snapped.

"I . . . I don't know where he is."

"You don't know where Jones is? Let me guess, he's missing too?"

"I . . . I don't know." She knew she had already lost the battle.

"I am really busy, Maryanne. Can you please leave me in peace? I don't want to hear any more conspiracy theories about teenage girls or men in ski masks."

Wiggins felt a rush of foreboding, but she wasn't sure why. Something Jenkins had just said made her skin crawl. It took a few seconds to identify it, but then she realized exactly what it was: When she had been relaying what had happened to Jenkins and had described the man Leighton Jones had saw, there was a detail she had accidentally left out.

"Dan . . . how did you know that the man was wearing a ski mask?"

35

Jenkins's face seemed to lose all its color, as he realized what he had just said. He opened his mouth as though he was about to reply, but then he closed it again.

"Dan?"

"You said he was wearing a ski mask." He spoke so softly Wiggins could barely identify the words he was trying to coagulate.

"No, I didn't."

Jenkins's eyes widened. His face morphed from a state of annoyance to something much more sinister. The expression he wore was deeply unsettling.

Silence stayed between them for what felt like an eternity. They just looked at each other, waiting for the other party to do something. The tension between them was so palpable that Wiggins felt like she may in fact be in danger, even though she was in an office at the courthouse. She irrationally started to regret not bringing her gun with her, although she knew it would have just been confiscated by the overly serious security guard.

"I think you had better leave," Jenkins whispered. Wiggins looked at him, trying to examine the darkness that lingered behind his eyes. She became aware of the beads of sweat on her forehead. Slowly standing up, Wiggins kept her gaze glued on Jenkins, and he stared right back at her. She grabbed the door handle behind her and pulled it toward her while still facing Jenkins. With one last glance into his eyes, Wiggins slid out of the room.

Wiggins ignored all the pain in her left knee as she moved along the corridor at breakneck speed. She was as close to running as she could be without actually running. For a moment, her gait seemed to lose the limp that had bedeviled her for so long. She didn't look back as she hammered the button to the elevator and got inside. With her breath ragged and her pulse out of her control, Wiggins felt like she had just finished a 100-meter dash. She knew logically that Jenkins wouldn't be chasing her, but she wanted to get as far away from him as possible. She pressed the first-floor button, and the elevator doors closed.

It was as if one giant puzzle piece had fallen into place. It all made so much sense. Jenkins had been the district attorney since the 1980s, when the first girl, Kylie Desmond, went missing. He had resisted Wiggins's theory of an active serial killer still residing in Newport every step of the way, to the point that he had become almost belligerent. And then there was Jenkins's physical stature. The figure that Leighton Jones had described was tall; Jenkins was well over six feet in height. Why else would Jenkins know the attire that the killer had been wearing? The only plausible explanation for it was that *he* was the culprit that Wiggins had sought for so long. It all seemed so obvious now.

Wiggins had considered the idea before that the killer had some sort of background in law enforcement; after all, he was an expert at evading the authorities. But this? The goddamned district attorney? It seemed like the twist at the end of an M. Night Shyamalan movie.

As soon as the elevator opened, Wiggins bolted out onto the first floor. She moved with purpose and speed that wasn't fit for someone with a lame leg. She ducked through the metal detector without even looking at the security guard, disregarding the beeping that came when she passed through. The guard said nothing, as he was clearly not worried about anyone smuggling weapons *out* of the building.

Once Wiggins was back inside her car, her knee erupted in pain. Now that she was stagnant, it was as if her leg was letting her know how flagrantly she had treated it by moving so quickly. Wiggins let a small yelp escape her lips. The adrenaline that had been pulsing through her had subsided, giving way for the pain.

As she looked through her windshield up at the courthouse, Wiggins scanned to the fifth floor. It didn't take her long to pinpoint the window that was part of Jenkins's office, and as she mentally zoomed in on it by squinting her eyes, she felt a pang of horror. Jenkins was standing right next to the window, and it appeared he was looking directly at her car. Wiggins couldn't help but feel unmitigated terror as she turned the key in her ignition and fired up the engine. She didn't even stop at the stop sign at the edge of the parking lot before speeding out onto the road.

X

As soon as Wiggins was safely back in her office above Sandcastle Toys, she began scrambling around her desk, looking for her external hard drive. Although she kept a physical copy of every document that pertained to the Nowhere Girls in her black binder, she also kept a digital copy on the hard drive, and it was easier to examine the documents under time constraints while on her computer.

"Shit!" Wiggins cursed. In times of peril, it was often a

great inconvenience to be as unorganized as she was. But it wasn't something she could just turn off. Being unable to collocate anything successfully was part of her makeup.

Finally, she found the hard drive and plugged it immediately into her laptop on the desk. There was one document that she sought on the device. But first, she opened a search engine and typed "Dan Jenkins, new district attorney." It took her five minutes, but eventually she found an archived article from *The Lincoln City Gazette* with the headline, "Dan Jenkins, New Newport DA, Hopes to Put a Stopper on Petty Crime." The article had been put online in 2008, but according to the website, it was from 1980. Four years before Kylie Desmond went missing. So, he had been in his position for the entire timeline of the case.

Wiggins then put in her external hard drive and pulled up the correct folder she needed. It was divided into twelve different subfolders: Kylie, Felicity, Shelly, Jenna, Cara, Riley, Evelyn, Lacy, Serena, Kelsea, Mariah, and Wendy. Each of the subfolders contained everything that pertained to that individual case, and Wiggins clicked on the one for Kylie. In the folder were dozens of documents, and Wiggins scrolled down until she found the one she was looking for: a transcript of an interview she had conducted with Dan Jenkins. It didn't take her long to locate the passage she was seeking.

> *MW: Why are you so certain that Bobby Ray Foles killed Kylie? DNA evidence does not point toward Foles. Her skull was found in an abandoned car and dismemberment is not part of his MO. All his victims on the Highway of Tears died of multiple stab wounds, didn't they?*
>
> *DJ: There is no way we can prove that Kylie wasn't stabbed to death. Like you just said, we only recovered*

her skull.

MW: But Foles was not even in Newport when Kylie was kidnapped.

DJ: Again, we have no definitive proof of that. He might have been. Kylie was killed on August 13 of '84. The last known sighting of Foles that month was on the eleventh in Olympia, Washington. It is completely feasible that he could have made the trip down in that time frame.

MW: Wait, Kylie disappeared on the twelfth, not the thirteenth. We don't know what day she was actually killed.

DJ: My mistake. I meant the twelfth. Not the thirteenth.

Wiggins looked up from her computer screen. This interaction with Jenkins had always struck her as odd, but now it felt nauseating. It wasn't just a slip of the tongue. He had said it with such conviction. And he had used the verb "killed." Not *disappeared.* Not *abducted.* Killed. Could it just be a coincidence that he had used a different date to reference what had happened to Kylie? Or was he so proud of his own work that he had to tell the truth about the date on which he had murdered the girl?

Wiggins thought of Jonah, and a wave of grief immersed her. She wasn't sure how far the sprawl of this case went in the Newport criminal justice system, but it may have made its way as high up as the district attorney's office. Therefore, she was powerless to do anything more about Jonah's disappearance. It made her feel angry and helpless to think of the battered door to his apartment and the small speck of blood on his pillow. She was certain the young man had been killed, and there was nothing she could do about it.

However, a sense of triumph was also intermingled with her feelings of grief about Jonah and fear that Jenkins might come after her. For the first time in fifteen years investigating this case, Wiggins had something she had never had before: a prime suspect.

36

Wiggins was more paranoid over the next two days than she had ever been in her life. When she woke up in the morning, she hurried to look out her blinds for any unusual activity and spent at least ten minutes staring out of the window. This was something she repeated more than thirty times over the course of forty-eight hours, although nothing meaningful ever came of it. The most daunting thing she saw was a seagull shitting on her car. There were no tall men in ski masks nor any vehicles parked nearby that she didn't recognize.

She wasn't sure Dan Jenkins would have the guts to attack her now. After all, if he was the killer, he had knowingly let her probe his work for years and done nothing about it. And why had he murdered Jonah, but not come after her all this time? Was it because Jonah had found a material witness to his crime, and as far as the killer knew, Wiggins hadn't? But by that logic, she had just revealed to him that she *did* know about Jones. Also, she had just seemingly confirmed his identity right in front of him. So was he going to try and kill her now too?

While locked inside her apartment, Wiggins spent a hefty amount of time fretting over her next move. She wanted to stake out Jenkins's house, but if Jenkins *was* the killer, spending time in his immediate vicinity didn't seem like the most practical of endeavors. She went back and forth on it, knowing it could yield clues but possibly be dangerous.

On the other hand, Wiggins still had a desire to speak to Teresa Deeds. Perhaps Teresa would be able to confirm or deny whether she had ever seen Jenkins around Katie. Therefore, at the tail end of the second day she spent cooped up inside her apartment, Wiggins fished around until she found the notes she had taken from Jonah's apartment. She flipped her way through the bevy of pages until she found one that said TERESA DEEDS in thick font at the top. Scrolling mentally through the notes, Wiggins eventually found Teresa's phone number.

After a brief conversation, Wiggins scheduled an appointment with Teresa at two p.m. the following day. Teresa had seemed more than willing to agree to an interview, and she mentioned Jonah twice while speaking to Wiggins. "What happened to that kid? The reporter from the *Times*?" she had said. "You better go speak to the reporter," she then remarked later in the conversation. It pained Wiggins to try and maneuver around the topic of Jonah, but it would be detrimental to share her suspicions with Teresa about Jonah's whereabouts.

Later that night, Wiggins was again waffling about whether to go to Jenkins's house. *If he killed Jonah, there is no reason to think he wouldn't do the same to you,* thought Wiggins. *But what if he is about to go stalk some other girl?* It was such a conundrum. But she knew if she didn't do it, it would eat at her until she found answers a different way. And avoiding potential danger when there could possibly be more lives at risk seemed foolish. Therefore, Wiggins draped her coat around her shoulders, holstered her pistol, and limped out toward her Audi at nine p.m.

Wiggins had been to Jenkins's house when she had interviewed him in the past. It was located at the top of Ninth Street, which sloped up until it became a very steep hill. At the top of the hill was an upscale neighborhood, with many of the houses containing shiny new decks and multiple stories. The headlights of Wiggins's car illuminated the wide street, and she winded up the hill until she came to a roundabout where she knew Jenkins's house to be. It was a prodigious three-story structure located in the center of the roundabout, and it was covered in an appealing off-white color. The windows were huge, and the lights were on behind them, indicating that Jenkins was indeed home. Jenkins was unmarried, and it always struck Wiggins as odd that he had such a mammoth house when there was only one person living in it.

Wiggins parked her car along the sidewalk in front of a house that was two homes over from Jenkins's place and turned off her headlights. The radio, which was playing classic rock, shut off with the engine, and silence flooded Wiggins's ears. She had the eeriest of feelings as she turned her head toward Jenkins's house, knowing that a serial killer could possibly be within twenty feet of her.

She sat in the dark, with the cold biting at her hands and ears. Wiggins didn't want to risk turning the heater on because the lights on the dashboard would also start and give away her position. The only noise inside the car was a faint clicking, as the fuel injectors inside the engine shut off. Rubbing her hands together, Wiggins tried to get comfortable, knowing that she would be spending a lengthy amount of time in the same position.

As the hour wore on, her sense of unease greatly increased, although nothing significant was happening inside the house. The reflection of what was possibly the television screen was dancing on one of the upstairs windows. Every once in a while, a shadow would move from inside, but no doors opened and no lights turned off. A light breeze outside moved the bushes that lined Jenkins's deck, and every time a strong gust made them sway even further, Wiggins would feel a leap of excitement at seeing movement, but then she would always realize that it was just the brush. After a while, Wiggins caught herself beginning to look at her phone to break up the boredom of sitting outside of a house doing nothing. She had dimmed the screen of the phone so that it wouldn't call attention to her location.

Oh, what the hell am I doing? thought Wiggins. Even if Jenkins was the guy, it was highly unlikely that she was going to catch him sawing somebody in half next to his window. Perhaps if he had randomly gotten up and left, Wiggins could have tried to follow, but there was no use sitting around and watching a man while he was probably catching up on *Game of Thrones.* Frustrated with herself, Wiggins turned on her car and flipped a U-turn on the roundabout, heading back in the direction of her apartment. All that she had done was waste an hour.

X

The man was feeling something he never felt before: impatience. As he stared greedily at the picture of Sierra Bunker hanging in his shed, his stomach turned over in longing. He couldn't stop thinking of what it would be like to see the girl's face drain of color while the life seeped out of her. He realized it was totally irrational to think like this. He had already killed three people in less than a month. His thirst for blood should have been quenched. But it wasn't. It was like eating a delectable meal when you were starving: You couldn't just stop after a couple of bites. Perhaps that was why he was feeling restless. He had never allowed the darkness inside of him to take over like it had in the last three weeks. And it felt like he was unable to control the primal urges that drove him to kill.

The man knew logically that it would not be pragmatic to

take her if he had an underdeveloped plan, and at the moment, he barely had any information on the girl at all. All he knew were the names and occupations of her family members and a rough idea of what her day-to-day schedule was like. It was far from a lot to go on.

Standing next to the wooden table, he looked down at the thirteen random items that were placed on top of it: a lighter, a tampon, and other various articles of his pleasure. All were trophies taken from his female victims. He had not taken items from the witness or the reporter. Killing other men was not something that gave him a sexual thrill, and thus, he did not want to spend time dwelling on it.

There were so many things that could go wrong if he tried to add another object to the table by killing the girl. The boyfriend remained a problem. He spent all his time with the girl. And what if the police did start to look into what happened to the witness? What if they pieced together that the reporter who had apparently absconded to his hometown wasn't really back in Portland? Even the incompetent Newport police would think multiple deaths in such a short period would be suspicious. It would be much smarter to let things blow over, in case an official investigation was started. But his carnal desire for blood and death was so overwhelming. The unyielding impulse for a subsequent body wouldn't dissipate. As the man stood in his shed looking at a photograph of the beautiful blond girl, he was beginning to lose control.

37

Wiggins was sitting in a room that smelled like an odd concoction of lasagna and cat piss. The old woman in front of her seemed to be shaking. Wiggins briefly wondered if she had Parkinson's disease.

"Sorry about the clutter," said Teresa Deeds. "I have never been one for cleaning."

"No worries. I feel right at home in clutter." Wiggins chuckled.

Teresa laughed along with her and sipped from the mug in front of her that contained some sort of fruity-smelling tea. After the laughter ceased, Teresa's face sagged into a morose expression. She looked miserable.

"So how are you?" Wiggins put her hand over Teresa's. Wiggins had never had a family member murdered, but she had experienced severe loss. When her mother had died, a part of Wiggins had been broken beyond repair.

The austere, stern-looking woman looked through her

thick-rimmed glasses, on the verge of tears. She squeezed Wiggins's hand. "This has been the worst month of my life. And it is really not even close."

Wiggins nodded. She didn't want to say anything. She knew words could not encapsulate the pain that Teresa felt.

"I think the worst part of this whole thing is being in the dark. There's no closure at all. Especially after what the kid told me a couple weeks ago."

"About the man who saw someone waiting to attack Katie?"

"Yeah. It makes my stomach upset just thinking about it." She took her hand out of Wiggins's and put it on her belly.

Wiggins picked up her pen, primed to take notes on the page that she had placed in front of her. "Have you considered going to the police with what Jonah told you? To try and get them to look into it?"

Teresa glared at Wiggins. "Of course I haven't. He already told me the guy changed his story. Plus, the last place I will be looking for help in is the Newport Police Department."

"Why do you say that?"

"Look at the way they handled this mess! They jumped to conclusions and didn't cover their bases. And the kid said they sent somebody to talk to the witness. They just accepted that he made up the story, no questions asked? Why would he do that? What reason would he have to do that?"

Wiggins shrugged her shoulders. "I don't think he would make it up. But they can't really force him to talk. So all they have to go on is the hearsay of a reporter. At least from their point of view."

Teresa sighed and seemed to transition back to sadness and away from the fiery irritation that had taken hold for a second.

"What have you been doing about the whole thing then?" She didn't want to offend the old woman, but she also couldn't fathom that Teresa would just sit on what she knew.

"Well, I have been in constant contact with my daughter

and her husband, planning the funeral. They are devastated, obviously. Every time I talk with Mary on the phone, she tells me how much she regrets Katie not coming down with them to live in California. It is almost as if she's blaming me in some way for Katie's death. But out of the two of us, she is the one who is acting irresponsible. She can't even bring herself to come up here. Thinks it will be too painful. Imagine how I felt. I had to look at the damn body." Teresa was becoming angry again.

"Right. I more meant regarding the suspicious circumstances surrounding Katie's death," Wiggins said, trying to steer Teresa back on track.

"Oh, right. There isn't much I can do, is there? Can't trust the police. That man changed his story. It's funny, I was actually considering contacting a private investigator the last couple of weeks, but I wasn't sure how to even do that."

"It is a good thing I called, isn't it?" Wiggins beamed.

"I guess it depends on what you know. And what you want to know."

There was a perfunctory lull in the conversation, as Wiggins fretted over how to tell Teresa what she was thinking. She knew that Teresa would not like what she was about to hear.

"I guess the first thing I need to express to you is that the witness is, for now, a dead end."

Teresa's mouth fell open, and she looked incredulous. "Wait, what? Why?"

"He has disappeared."

"How?"

"I have been to his house twice, and he wasn't there either time. And from asking around, it seems as though he hasn't been seen around town either."

Teresa frowned as though she were concentrating. "What could have happened to him?"

Wiggins shook her head. "He could have skipped town. Or something else."

"Something else?" Teresa looked horrified.

"I don't want to speculate. Point is, he is not here to talk to."

"Then why did you want to talk to me?"

Wiggins pursed her lips. This whole interview was a lesson in walking on eggshells and trying to avoid beating around the bush.

"Mainly, because of this," Wiggins said, as she reached into her coat and pulled out the picture that she had printed out at Fred Meyer earlier that morning. Dan Jenkins's gray hair and creased face smiled back at Teresa from the picture. It was a photo that Wiggins had found online that he had taken for the DA's office. He was wearing a black suit and tie and was standing in front of the American flag.

"Who is this?"

"Dan Jenkins. He is the district attorney."

"Uh, okay," said Teresa cautiously.

"Have you ever seen this man around your daughter?"

The question prompted silence. It was suddenly like they were inside a library.

"Are you saying… the district attorney?" Her skin was suddenly quite pallid.

"I'm not saying anything," Wiggins responded quickly. "I am just asking if you ever saw him around Katie."

"No, I have never seen him around Katie," Teresa snapped. "I've never seen him before in my life. Happy?"

Wiggins looked up at the ceiling. "No, I can't say I am particularly happy."

Teresa nodded sarcastically and brought her mug to her lips. For several moments, the only sound in the room was the old woman slurping on her fruity tea. It almost seemed like a nervous tick, as it went on for far too long. Finally, when she was done chugging the tea, she set it back down on the coffee table in front of her, determined to not make eye contact with Wiggins.

"Can you think of any older men you have seen around Katie?" Wiggins asked halfheartedly. She knew she was grasping at straws now. She had hoped that Teresa would recognize Jenkins.

"No. Well . . . not per say."

Wiggins perked up.

"What do you mean?"

Teresa waved her hand dismissively. "Just her boss. Anthony Mason."

"How old is he?"

Teresa thought for a moment. "Maybe in his fifties?"

"Okay." Wiggins wrote it down. "So what about him?"

Teresa frowned, looking nonplussed. "What do you mean what about him?"

"I assume there is a reason you brought him up."

"You asked to know about older men in Katie's life." She looked at Wiggins as though she were a particularly brute chimpanzee that was having trouble communicating to its handler.

"And he was the one who stuck out. Why?"

Teresa clenched her jaw. "It's just, he always gave Katie the creeps."

Wiggins's heart skipped a beat. "Why?"

"I don't know. I think he just did some inappropriate things. But she put a stop to that real quick."

"What kind of inappropriate things?"

"God, I don't know." A fleeting look of mild repugnance appeared across her face. "One time I came home and he was over here talking to Katie, and when I came in he acted like I was interrupting something. She insisted he was only dropping off her schedule, but it just kind of rubbed me the wrong way."

"He came to your house?" Wiggins asked in disbelief.

"Yeah, to drop off her schedule."

"What kind of things would Katie say about Mason?"

"It was just an off-hand comment here and there. Like he would say something sexual as a joke, and it made her uncomfortable. She would just say, 'He is such a creep sometimes,' and things like that. I don't think she ever felt threatened by him. She worked for him for three years, so . . ."

Wiggins underlined Mason's name emphatically. Teresa seemed to notice this action, and started waving her hands.

"Now wait a minute! Anthony Mason may have overstepped his bounds a few times, but he sure as hell is not a killer. Don't even start with that."

"I believe you." Wiggins tried to sound sincere. But she knew that she would be making a stop at Mason's Coffee in the near future.

The bell rang, announcing Wiggins's presence in the small shop the following day. It was a peculiar little building; it looked more like a miniature museum than a place that sold coffee. With weird paintings hung haphazardly on the yellow walls and a bunch of wooden tables packed inside, the room made Wiggins feel a little claustrophobic. She looked around for a middle-aged black man she knew to be Anthony Mason, but there wasn't anybody inside except for a pretty brunette who was standing behind the espresso machine.

"Hello!" the girl chirped, greeting Wiggins enthusiastically. Just from the tone of her voice, Wiggins could tell that the brunette had likely already consumed several shots of espresso.

"Hi there," Wiggins, said noticing how old she sounded in comparison to the perky barista. "Is Anthony Mason around?"

The girl looked a little crestfallen for some reason. Maybe she was hoping Wiggins was going to order a coffee. "No, he isn't here right now. He should be in later this afternoon."

Wiggins raised her chin into the air. "Ah."

"Do you want me to take a message for him?"

"No, no." Wiggins waved her hand. "He doesn't know who I am."

"Well, who are you?"

Wiggins frowned at the girl, a little taken aback by her nosiness. When she saw Wiggins's expression, the girl became flustered.

"I'm sorry, I shouldn't have asked that."

"It's fine. My name is Maryanne Wiggins. I'm a private investigator."

The girl's eyes expanded.

"You're a PI?"

"That's right."

"This is about Katie, isn't it?"

Wiggins felt a mixture of exasperation and curiosity. It was irritating that the girl was being so invasive, but it was also intriguing that she had already guessed why Wiggins had visited the shop.

"What is your name?"

"Brittany."

"Well, Brittany, why would you think this was about Katie?"

Brittany looked unsure if she wanted to keep talking. Apparently, she couldn't contain herself.

"Because I don't think Katie killed herself."

There were at least ten seconds of dead silence, as Wiggins looked at Brittany in awe. Judging by the surprised look on her face, even the perky young woman seemed surprised by her own forwardness.

"Why do you think that?" Wiggins's pulse began to rise.

Brittany looked toward the door, making sure there weren't any customers heading in. She then made piercing eye contact with Wiggins. "Katie was an arrogant bitch. She thought way too highly of herself to commit suicide."

Wiggins couldn't help but be astonished at this. She didn't

know much about Katie, but from Jonah's notes and her interview with Teresa, it was a revelation to hear someone call the girl an "arrogant bitch."

"So you two worked together? I take it you didn't get along then."

Brittany cackled. "Well, let's just say that we weren't exactly besties."

"So, if she didn't commit suicide, what do you think happened to her?"

Brittany again looked around, checking to make sure that nobody was coming. When she spoke again, her voice had dropped several octaves.

"All I know is, Anthony Mason threatened to kill her a couple of months ago."

Wiggins felt a thousand goose bumps rise on her arms. She tried to keep her voice steady as she responded, "Brittany, I think you better come sit down over here. Let's talk."

Brittany looked at Wiggins in perturbation. "I don't know if I should. I'm in the middle of my shift."

"It won't take long. I just need to take notes, and it's pretty hard to do when we are both standing."

Brittany looked toward the door yet again, as if she was waiting for Anthony Mason to burst in at any second. Her lips rubbed against each other as she fretted over what to do.

"Fine. I'll give you ten minutes. And if a customer comes in, I won't be able to talk anymore," Brittany said sharply.

"Of course. No problem."

"And you aren't going to tell Anthony I talked to you, are you?"

"Not if you don't want me to."

"I don't," Brittany said the instant that Wiggins finished her sentence.

"Okay then. I won't."

Brittany nodded and came around the counter, and Wiggins noticed how short she was. Her waist was tiny, which was a stark contrast to her giant breasts. She had rounded cheeks and unnaturally tan skin, as if she had spent an inordinate amount of time in a tanning booth. Brittany pointed toward the nearest table, and Wiggins hobbled over to it. They each took a seat, and Wiggins took out her notepad.

"How do you spell your name? And what is your last name?" Wiggins noticed a shift in Brittany's expression. "Don't worry. It is just for organizational purposes."

"Uh, okay. My name is spelled B-R-I-T-T-A-N-Y. And my last name is Kelley. Aren't you going to ask—?"

"We will get there, I promise." Wiggins scribbled down Brittany's name. "I just need a bit more background first. So how long have you worked here?"

"About a year."

"And Katie has been here the whole time?"

Brittany seemed to scowl as she thought of Katie. "That's right."

"Why didn't you two get along?"

"She was just so stuck-up. I hated her. After the first couple of months, Anthony hardly ever scheduled us together. And when he did, it was pretty much always a shit show."

"What do you mean?"

"We pretty much would always end up arguing. God, I fucking hated that girl." Brittany raised her hand to her mouth. "Sorry."

"Don't apologize for cussing." Wiggins waggled her finger. "I don't give a fuck about that."

Brittany chortled, and her laugh was like nails on a chalkboard. Wiggins made a mental note to not be funny for the rest of the interview.

"Did Anthony ever take sides? Did either of you ever get in

trouble?"

"Oh, he took sides alright." Brittany's nostrils flared. "He talked about firing me on two separate occasions."

"And I am guessing he didn't do the same to Katie?"

"Nope. Katie was his favorite. Actually, he was kind of obsessed with her." Brittany contorted her face in disgust.

"How do you mean?"

"I mean he was infatuated with her. He wanted to fuck her the moment he set eyes on her."

Wiggins felt a small pang of disgust in her chest.

"But he is in his fifties, isn't he? Surely she wouldn't be interested."

"I don't think she was ever interested. But that didn't stop it from happening, did it?"

Wiggins froze, the pen in her hand coiled in midair.

"Are you saying they *did* sleep together?"

Brittany nodded ardently, as if she had been waiting for months to tell someone. "Yep. They had sex at least five times over the past year."

Wiggins was fairly repulsed, but also somewhat confused. "Didn't you and Katie hate each other? Surely, she didn't share this with you."

"Nah, she told Corinne, our other coworker," Brittany explained when Wiggins looked thrown off by the new name. "Corinne was the one who told me."

"I see." Wiggins was furiously writing down everything that Brittany was saying. "So if she wasn't interested, why did she keep sleeping with him?"

Brittany smiled, as she was about to divulge the juiciest bit of gossip yet.

"It wasn't exactly her choice, see. He was blackmailing her."

"With what?" Wiggins asked quickly.

"He caught her stealing money about a year ago. He told her

he was going to fire her if she didn't fuck him. Well, actually I don't think he came out and said that, but he definitely implied it."

Wiggins thought on this a bit before asking another question. "Katie slept with a fifty-year-old man just to keep a minimum-wage job?"

Brittany glowered at her. She looked affronted. "There is nothing wrong with this job. With the tips, sometimes we can make up to fifteen dollars an hour."

"Apologies. I meant no offense. It just seems like an extreme thing to do. Couldn't she have just gone and been a barista somewhere else?"

"No, that's the thing. Anthony has a ton of connections. If she turned him down, he would have spread it all over town that she was stealing, and she probably wouldn't have been able to get another job."

This made sense to Wiggins, but the story seemed strange. You would think if Mason were to partake in an activity that required him to be surreptitious, he would have pleaded with Katie to keep the whole thing concealed. But that was the nature of small towns. Even if you thought you were being furtive, nothing was ever a secret for long.

"So, you heard Anthony threaten to kill her? How did that come about? And was he serious?"

"Oh, he was serious alright. This was a month or so back. I came into the shop on my day off to pick up my check. Katie and Anthony were in the back, and they didn't hear me come in. They were yelling at each other. I came in in the middle of it, but I heard her tell him to go fuck himself, and then he said, 'I will fucking kill you, you stupid cunt.'"

Wiggins cringed. "Do you have any idea what they were yelling about?"

Brittany nodded before continuing, "I got my check from the drawer before they even realized I was there, and then I left.

To this day I don't think Anthony knows I overheard the whole thing. Anyway, Brittany told Corrine that she had said to Anthony that she was done with their whole arrangement and wasn't going to be blackmailed anymore. Apparently, he didn't take too kindly to that."

"But he didn't fire her?"

"No. But I know that she didn't sleep with him anymore after that. Corinne said that the last couple of weeks before Katie died he was starting to get clingy, telling Katie he loved her and all that. She wasn't sure what to do and had started to cut off all contact with him that wasn't work related."

Wiggins closed her eyes for a second. "So you think he killed her because she refused to see him?"

Brittany looked a little jolted by the fact that Wiggins had just come out and said it.

"Listen, I don't know what happened. All I am saying is it is strange, alright? This guy threatens to kill her, and then a month later she dies? And right after she tells this creep that she won't fuck him anymore? Is that not suspicious to you?"

Wiggins bobbed her head in agreement. "It definitely is. The question I have now is, why are you so eager to dish on this guy if you hated Katie? Also, if you think he could kill Katie, why are you still working for him?"

Brittany started to fumble over her words as she attempted to answer. "I- I'm in the same boat as Katie was. If I quit right now he is going to ask me why. And if I don't have a logical answer, he will spread something around about me not being a good worker or something. And what am I supposed to say? 'I think you probably murdered Katie so I don't want to work here anymore'? As for your first question . . . I mean . . . I don't know. I . . . I think, well, if he did kill her, then people need to know."

Wiggins considered the girl. She was probably nineteen or twenty and came off as someone who was yearning for gossip without thinking of the consequences of spreading the news. A young, small-town girl in other words.

"And why didn't you go to the police with this?"

Brittany looked a little unnerved. "I don't know. I just think they would have treated me like . . . like a conspiracy theorist or something. I mean . . . I just thought they would think I was crazy."

Wiggins nodded. It was human nature to keep quiet if you thought you were going to be scorned for voicing your opinion, so she didn't want to acerbate and harass the girl about it.

"Well, thank you, Brittany. I definitely appreciate the information."

Brittany's eyes went back and forth apprehensively. "What are you going to do with it?"

Wiggins looked at her for a few seconds. "To be honest, I am not quite sure."

As Wiggins walked back to her car outside of Mason's Coffee, she felt overwrought and confused. Teresa and Brittany had just thrown a giant wrench into the investigation. Yesterday, Wiggins had felt positive her killer was Dan Jenkins. He fit the characteristics of the man she was looking for to a tee. Middle aged, had been in Newport for decades, and he somehow knew about the ski mask that the killer wore. But now, Wiggins was lost. If this were a regular homicide, she would assert that Anthony Mason was her guy. A scorned, infatuated lover who had threatened violence against the victim? That fit perfectly in an ordinary murder case. But this wasn't an ordinary case. Was Wiggins to believe that Katie's death was not connected to the other girls? That it was just a crime of passion carried out by a hurt lover? It felt foolish to say that Katie had nothing to do with the other girls. But Anthony Mason was such a good suspect. And now Wiggins was in a quandary.

Once Wiggins got back to her car, she pulled out her phone and scrolled through her contacts. She wanted to make the call as soon as possible to her source in the police department. She had already considered going to him about Jonah, but after the interview with the district attorney, she was concerned that Dan Jenkins would get word of it. If he was the killer, Jenkins probably wouldn't appreciate Wiggins spreading around the news of Jonah Carr to other officers at the police station.

It probably wouldn't take long for Detective Albert Amos to run a criminal history on Anthony Mason, but Wiggins didn't want time to be an issue regardless. After she found Amos's number, she pressed her phone against her ear and listened to it ring.

"Y-ellow?"

"Albert?"

"Yeah, who's this?"

"Maryanne Wiggins."

"Oh! Hey, Maryanne! Long time no see!"

"Isn't that something you're supposed to say when you can actually see somebody?"

"Hell if I know," Amos quipped, and Wiggins laughed.

"How have you been, Albert?"

"Been good. Lots of politics and bureaucracy to deal with around the station. Normal cop shit, you know?"

"I hear ya." She and Amos had known each other since Wiggins had first moved to Newport. Normally she wouldn't consider a contact a friend, but she did indeed maintain somewhat of an amicable relationship with Amos.

"So what can I do for ya?"

"Just wondering if you can run a criminal history on a possible perp for me."

"Sure thing! What's the name?"

"Anthony Mason."

"Anthony Mason? The guy who owns the coffee shop?"

Amos sounded perplexed.

"That's the one."

"What the hell did he do?"

"That's what I am trying to figure out."

There was a brief overture, and Wiggins could hear Amos inhale to gather air before responding. "Yeah, I'll see what I can find out."

Wiggins thanked Amos profusely and ended the conversation. He said he would get back to her within the hour, which was good. Wiggins didn't have the patience for anything longer than that. Wiggins drove over to McDonald's to grab a bite to eat and scarfed down a Big Mac in the parking lot after circling through the drive-through.

Thoughts of Dan Jenkins and Anthony Mason dashed through her mind. It was hard to believe that after so long with nothing, she had discovered two different people capable of committing these murders in the span of three days. Whether the killer was Jenkins or Mason, he had definitely made big mistakes this time. That was why Wiggins had found two suspects so fast after years of nothing. The killer had finally made a series of egregious errors with the Katie kill.

But then again, there was a chance that Mason had killed Katie but not the other girls. And if he somehow actually was the serial killer that she sought, why did he have a direct connection to Katie and none of the other victims? That part didn't make sense. But then again, he had literally threatened to murder the girl. There couldn't be a more blatant lead than that.

Within twenty minutes, Wiggins's phone vibrated. She was pleased to see that it was Amos.

"Hello?"

"You aren't going to believe this."

"What?" Wiggins's voice caught in her throat.

"Anthony Mason has only been arrested once. It was in 1983 for battery."

"And who was the victim?"

"Kylie Desmond."

38

Sierra was pissed. It was raining, and she was soaking wet and standing alone outside of the high school. Kyle was supposed to pick her up after volleyball practice, but he was nowhere to be found, and he wasn't answering his phone. She looked around for his truck, hoping that he was going to show up at the last second. But she knew better. Kyle had probably forgotten about her. It wouldn't be the first time.

She knew logically that relationships in high school weren't the pinnacle of human interaction, but Sierra couldn't help but get wrapped up in Kyle. The way he smelled, his muscular torso, his aloof attitude toward anyone he came across. It was intoxicating. She frequently told Kyle she loved him, but up until the last few weeks, she wasn't sure she believed it. Now she was certain that she did. And, like all bouts of love, heartache had ensued. They argued all the time. It was generally the result of Sierra having some sort of unrealistic expectation of how Kyle was supposed to act. But this was the second time he had forgotten to pick her up after practice. It was hardly asking the world of him.

Sierra shoved her phone into her pocket and zipped up her rain jacket. Thankfully, Kyle's house was only a couple of blocks away and well within walking distance. Her heart fluttered nervously as Sierra thought of the heated exchange that was about to take place when she finally saw Kyle. He would probably make up some bullshit excuse, and Sierra would spend the next day or two angry with him. They had a well-established routine, and Sierra was following the script.

The clouds overhead clung together like packed sardines, and the torrential downpour was only getting worse. Sierra began to shiver as she walked down Eads Street in the direction of Kyle's house. *Hopefully his parents aren't there,* thought Sierra. She didn't think they would be home from work, but if they were, it would certainly make things far more awkward.

Sierra swerved to avoid a deep, muddy puddle on the sidewalk. "Fuck," she said out loud, as she had to go out slightly into the street to weave around the puddle. The traffic on Eads was somewhat congested as parents took their children home from school. Several cars sped by as Sierra walked along the edge of the road, coming too close for comfort to where she was walking. Once she had made her way past the water, Sierra hopped back up onto the sidewalk.

Pulling out her phone to see if Kyle had texted her yet, Sierra was left disappointed once she saw the blank screen. *Some boyfriend I have,* she thought. Unconsciously, she stomped her feet as anger coursed through her. Several loud smacks rang out as Sierra's feet disturbed the water that was running along the road into the drain behind her. A strong gust of wind blew from straight ahead and inflated the hood of her coat. *This is fucking ridiculous, Kyle,* thought Sierra.

Eventually, Sierra turned right on Tenth Court. The smacking of her feet turned into crunching as the pavement underneath her became gravel. She steadily became aware of how numb her extremities were from the wind and rain. Trying to tuck her hands into her pockets, it took her several attempts to get her arms to cooperate, as her fingers barely had any feeling in them. Sierra kept her head down and listened to the sound of her rhythmic footsteps. *Crunch, crunch, crunch.* It almost formed a beat. *Crunch, crunch, crunch.* Sierra stomped along, letting her anger ebb away at the gravel. *Fuck you, Kyle,* she thought. *Crunch, crunch, crunch.* Eventually, Sierra came to another puddle in the middle of the road and abruptly stopped walking. For some reason, even though she had stopped, she heard two more crunches.

Sierra quickly turned around, thinking somebody must have been behind her. But when she faced the opposite direction, there was no one in sight. Sierra scanned everything that was in her line of vision, looking for where the noise had come from. All she saw was a cluster of trees to her left and a series of small houses to her right, and at the end of the road where Tenth Court connected with Eads, there was a single vehicle parked off to the side. Nothing out of the ordinary.

Thinking she must have imagined the noise, Sierra started walking again. The crunching of her feet resumed and a squelching sound was suddenly emitted into the air, too, as the shoes that she was wearing had become waterlogged. "Fuck me sideways," said Sierra. Not only had Kyle forgotten her at practice and made her walk to his house in the rain, but his inaction had likely ruined her favorite footwear.

As Sierra pressed forward, she saw movement out of the corner of her eye. She turned quickly to her right, staring at a clump of thick blackberry bushes at the base of a tree where she thought the motion had occurred. But everything was completely still. *What the hell,* she thought. Perhaps there was an animal scrambling about, and that was what had caused the crunching a few seconds earlier. Regardless, Sierra started walking very quickly. It was as if some sixth sense was telling her to keep moving. Her breathing had become ragged, as the cold weather seemed to have compressed her lungs.

Up ahead, Sierra could see the outline of Kyle's two-story house. On the second story, the light of the middle room was on, indicating that Kyle was indeed at home. *Oh, you're in for it now, buddy,* thought Sierra. Her anger returned, and she discarded the thoughts of potential danger that had invaded her consciousness for the past several moments.

From behind her, the sound of tires moving along the road reached her ears. She looked over her shoulder to see what was causing the commotion. The same vehicle that had been parked at the corner of Eads was driving straight toward her, moving at a glacial pace. It startled Sierra; she had no idea that there was anyone inside the car when she had looked at it before. As it got closer, she saw that it was a green Jeep. Sierra was about to turn back around, but then the most peculiar thing happened. The driver of the Jeep flashed the headlights twice in her direction. She froze, staring at the outline of the person in the driver's seat. Perhaps it was someone that she knew. But she had a distinct feeling that that wasn't the case. Something in the deep recesses of her brain warned her of danger. She turned back around but stayed frozen, listening for movement. There was no noise of anyone approaching. After ten seconds had passed, she decided that she was safe, and continued walking toward Kyle's house.

Without warning, a pair of muscular arms shot out from behind her and enclosed around her midsection, compressing the air out of her diaphragm. She was so shocked she didn't even think to scream before one of the hands covered her mouth. Within an instant, Sierra was dragged into the blackberry bushes next to her. Pain erupted from her arms as the needles of the plants scraped against her. Partly from agony and partly from uncontrollable fear, Sierra let out a muffled scream with all of the air left inside her. Suddenly, something heavy bludgeoned her over the head, causing her to stop yelling as disorientation flooded her senses. Sierra's vision went blurry, and she lost her sense of direction. Before she knew it, she was on the flat of her back on the ground and a large figure in a ski mask was straddling her. She tried to find the will to scream again, but the blow to her head had robbed her of her voice. The large masked man shoved what looked like a scarf so far into her mouth that she almost gagged. She tried to reach up and remove it, but the man easily overpowered her with his strength, and pinned her arms to the side. Within moments, he was wrapping a thick coil of rope around her arms. Sierra tried to make a noise of distress through the gag, but all that came out was a muffled moan. The man slapped her so hard across the jaw that she became disoriented again.

After her arms were securely tied into place, the man squatted over Sierra, using his weight on her legs to keep her from moving. She tried to lash out, but it was no use. He had rendered her immobile. The man covered her mouth again, ensuring that no noise came out. Sierra was expecting him to wrap his hands around her neck and strangle her, but for some reason, he just held her in place. Sierra looked up, and with a rush of panic, she saw the outline of the man's smile under the mask.

He put his finger to her lips. "Shush."

Sierra could do nothing but lay there helplessly, even though every cell in her body was begging for her to escape.

What was the man waiting for? He kept Sierra firmly in place, leering down at her. Sierra cocked her head back, and through the brush, she could see the shape of the Jeep parked on the road beyond. She looked back at the masked man and suddenly understood his plan. He was going to try and transport her to the Jeep. The man cradled both arms underneath her body, and lifted Sierra into the air. She teetered precariously, hoping beyond hope that someone would come to her rescue. Once she started traveling through the air, horrible thoughts shot through Sierra's brain. Was he going to kill her? Was he going to rape her? Was he going to keep her shackled up in a shed for days, assaulting her at his leisure? Another surge of adrenaline gushed through her body, and she regained a bout of strength. One thought stuck in her brain, and she was going to expend all her energy trying to obey the command: *Don't let him get to the Jeep. Don't let him get to the Jeep.*

Pretending to lose consciousness, Sierra abruptly closed her eyes and went limp. Sierra felt the man's momentum stop. The brief hesitation was all she needed. She thrashed about wildly, moving her body in a worm-like motion. Her knees collided with the man's chest, shifting his center of gravity and propelling one of his legs into the air. The man tried to put his airborne foot down and regain his balance, but it was too late. He fell backward and landed in the mud with an enormous thud. Sierra rolled out of the man's grasp and began kicking her legs wildly in his direction. She felt her foot make contact and heard a wail of agony. Sierra looked over her shoulder and saw the man rocking backward with his hands clasped over his nose.

She knew she only had a couple of seconds. Using her forearms to push herself up, Sierra stood and sprinted into the woods and away from the masked man with her arms tied and the gag still in her mouth. It was difficult to run without the motion of her upper limbs to help her, and she had no idea where she was going, but she didn't dare stop. A loud sound of brush being disturbed let Sierra know that the man was in full pursuit behind her. She screamed again through the gag, but the pitiful noise was hardly enough to alert anyone to her presence. A million thoughts hurtled through her mind as she continued to run as fast as she could through the forest.

With an expeditious turn of her head, Sierra looked for the masked man, but she didn't see him anywhere. She knew he couldn't be too far behind, but it appeared Sierra had momentarily lost him. The problem was, she had no clue where she was. She pushed farther and farther into the thick collection of trees, getting more lost by the second. To try and further throw the man off her trail, Sierra made an abrupt dip to her right and moved in a new direction. She egged her legs on, and within ten seconds, she had traveled at least a hundred feet farther.

In front of her, Sierra saw a massive fir tree that eclipsed a good chunk of the forest beyond it from view. Making a split-second decision, she circled around the tree, and abruptly stopped running. She crouched down and brought her bound arms closer to her face, removing the gag from her mouth. Oxygen rushed into her lungs, and she couldn't help but gasp as she regained her wind. Sierra immediately regretted the noise it made, and she clasped her hand over her open lips.

It was very difficult to go from running as fast as she could to keeping completely still, but that was exactly what Sierra was attempting to do. She crouched down, convinced the thumping of her heart was going to give her position away. She tuned her ears to the forest around her, trying to absorb any noise of someone approaching. But there was none. The only sound she heard was that of her own breath seeping through the spaces between her fingers. It wasn't much of a hiding place, but Sierra didn't have any other option. So, there she crouched. Waiting. Watching. Listening. Beads of sweat dripped off her nose, and her head throbbed. Every second felt like an eternity. Sitting in the silence, it was as if the devil himself was closing in.

39

"Hello?"

"Mr. Desmond?"

"Which one are you lookin' for? Kenny or Brendan?"

"Either, I guess," Wiggins said with a shrug of her shoulders, forgetting the person on the other end of the line couldn't see her. "But I prefer Kenny."

"You're talkin' to him," Kenny said in a raspy voice.

"Ah, terrific," Wiggins said, although her tone of voice suggested she didn't find speaking to Kenny terrific. "I don't know if you remember me, but my name's Maryanne Wiggins. I am a private investigator. I spoke to you years ago regarding the death of your daughter."

"Oh . . . yeah. I remember you," Kenny replied solemnly.

"I'm sorry. I know you were probably hoping you would never hear from me again—"

"No, no . . . It's just, every time someone wants to talk to me about Kylie, it brings all the pain back."

"I understand, and I'm sorry." This is why she hadn't been looking forward to speaking with Kenny again. It had already broken her heart the first time having to listen to a bereaved father talk about his lost daughter. The fact that the man was in a wheelchair made it all the more gut wrenching.

"This won't take long. We can just talk about it over the phone."

"Ah." Kenny wheezed. "Okay."

Wiggins took a deep breath. "It has to do with an incident that took place the year before your daughter disappeared."

"Eighty-three?"

Kenny sounded puzzled.

"That's right," said Wiggins. "It was eighty-three."

"What about it?"

"Anthony Mason."

There was prolonged silence in response to this. Then, Kenny growled before speaking. "Why the fuck would I want to talk about him?"

Wiggins was startled by this reaction, but regained her composure. "Well, in 1983 Mason was arrested in Newport for ba—"

"Trust me, I know. And if he hadn't been arrested I would kicked the shit out of him myself. Fuckin' bastard."

"It sounds like you could give me a bit more background on the incident, which is why I am calling. So, what happened there exactly?"

Kenny didn't answer immediately. For a moment, Wiggins thought he was going to withhold the information. But then, after a tiny interlude, he launched into a detailed response.

"I want to say he was twenty-two or twenty-three at the time. Anyway, Kylie was just a kid. She had just gotten her first job working at the Agate Beach Golf Course. It was just a summer job, you know? Picking up balls on the range. Mason was an assistant manager at the golf course at the time. Kylie's boss. Anyhow, after a few weeks of working together, he seemed to take a liking to Kylie. And Kylie was shy, right? So she liked the attention. But she thought she was just making friends. He had other things in mind."

Kenny inflected this last sentence with such menacing anger that Wiggins got a little ruffled herself.

"So what happened?"

"Basically, one night after work, Kylie stayed late and was hanging out with Mason at the clubhouse or whatever the hell you call it. And they were the only ones there, so Mason went behind the bar and was giving Kylie drinks. Creep was trying to get her drunk. Anyway, he tried to make a move on her, and she wasn't havin' it." Kenny wheezed. "So she told him to back off. Things started getting heated, and he pushed her. She fell and hit her head on a table."

"Holy hell," Wiggins said without thinking.

"Yeah. I was hoping the fucker would do some major time for it. But he pleaded no contest and somehow only got a six-month sentence. The rumor was he was friends with the DA or something."

Wiggins rubbed her temple as she tried to recall whether or not Dan Jenkins had been the DA in 1983. "Damn."

"Yeah."

"So have you ever considered that he might be . . . You know. The guy?"

"What, her killer? Well, yeah, he fits the bill alright. But it couldn't have been him. He was serving his sentence when Kylie disappeared."

Wiggins sighed and bowed her head, feeling crestfallen. "Oh."

"Yeah. Sorry to burst your bubble about that. I realize now that you must've been callin' me because you were considering him a suspect."

"Like you said, he does fit the bill."

"Right. But he doesn't fit the timeline. I still mentioned him to police, but I mean, even though I hope the fucker rots in hell, he ain't the guy."

"Yeah, I understand. Well, anyway . . . I appreciate the information."

"Yeah, no problem. Hey, did that reporter ever come talk to you? It's funny that you called. I was just talkin' about you not too long ago when that reporter came by. I gave him your card."

Wiggins tried to suppress the guilt she felt while thinking of Jonah. "Yeah. We met in person not too long ago."

"Great! Anything come of it?"

"Not really." She didn't want to get Kenny's hopes up in case she didn't actually catch the killer.

"Ah, darn. Okay," Kenny said, sounding disappointed. "I guess since I let you down about Mason, that makes us even."

"You didn't let me down, Mr. Desmond. I appreciate you talking to me at all. I know this is difficult for you to speak about after all these years."

"It sure is. But I know you are just trying to help. You are really the only one who has still been invested in this after so much time has passed."

"I still appreciate your time."

Wiggins thanked him again and ended the conversation. Her mind promptly started feasting on Dan Jenkins and Anthony Mason once more. It had to be one of the two, didn't it? They were both such perfect suspects.

There was Jenkins, a man who had been in a position of power with the ability to directly manipulate the case since its inception in the eighties. He also somehow knew that Katie's abductor had been wearing a ski mask and had either had an inexplicable slip of the tongue or had inadvertently tried to correct Wiggins on the precise date of Kylie Desmond's death during their transcribed interview from many years ago. If it was the latter, that meant that he knew her exact time of passing.

Then there was Anthony Mason, a person with a direct connection to two of the victims and who had a history of predatory behavior and verbal abuse. Not only had he extorted sex out of Katie on multiple occasions, but he had literally threatened to kill her a month before her death. And was it just a coincidence that Mason had also been arrested for assaulting Kylie Desmond in 1983, a year before she disappeared? He fit the general timeline as well. Mason had been in the area for well over thirty years.

There were obvious holes in each of the theories, however. With Jenkins, it seemed a little hard to fathom that he could commit serial murder while working in the courthouse. The killer was meticulous and had obviously spent a copious amount of time hatching his schemes. Not only did it seem like someone would have noticed if Jenkins were going on constant murderous escapades, but it also seemed unlikely that he would logistically be able to kill all those girls. He was incompetent at it, but his job did require a workload that was time consuming.

With Mason, the obvious flaw in the idea was the fact that he was in prison when Kylie Desmond disappeared. That eliminated one of the two major connections he had to the case. Could it have been possible Kenny had just mixed up the dates? That Mason had been released from prison earlier than he thought? She would have to double-check that.

Wiggins had to go back to Mason's Coffee and try to talk to Anthony Mason himself. Brittany had said that he would return that afternoon. Wiggins had gone back to her office to briefly take care of other matters and that was where she had made the call to Kenny. A couple hours had passed, and she was ready to go back to the shop and try and confront Mason.

Fifteen minutes after her phone call with Kenny, she emerged from her car again, and headed back toward the coffee shop. The clouds in the sky looked dark and dreary, and Wiggins was considering the possibility that another storm was coming.

She zipped up her jacket and limped through the front door to the coffee shop.

The familiar sound of a bell greeted her, and she was satisfied to see that a tall black man was shuffling behind the counter next to Brittany. Brittany looked up at the ding, and her face quickly transformed into an expression that looked like she had smelled something revolting. Wiggins had not told Brittany that she would be returning to the shop to see Mason in person, and she looked afraid that Wiggins would divulge the information that Brittany had shared with her.

"Can I help you?" Brittany pushed as much sourness into her voice as she could.

"Yes, hi. Can I get a medium mocha, please?"

Brittany appeared relieved that Wiggins had ordered something. At once, she shifted back into her perky persona.

"Yes, of course!" she said brightly. Brittany quickly rang up Wiggins, and Wiggins handed her a five-dollar bill.

"It will be ready over there in just a few seconds." She handed Wiggins her change.

Wiggins went to the right side of the counter, waiting for her drink to be set out. She was directly in front of Anthony Mason. His bald head reflected the light above him. He didn't even look up as Wiggins shot him a disingenuous smile. He seemed to be absorbed in restocking the syrups and sugar trays in front of him.

"Hello," Wiggins said, sounding a little like Mrs. Doubtfire.

Mason looked up and raised his bushy eyebrows. "Uh, can I help you?"

"She asked me that same exact question." Wiggins pointed at Brittany. "I'm glad you are all so concerned with helping people. The world needs more of that."

Brittany snorted, laughing through her nostrils. Mason frowned at Wiggins.

"Lady, do you *want* something?"

"Are you Canadian? You seem far too polite to be American," replied Wiggins sarcastically.

"What the hell are y—"

"I'm here to talk about Katie Deeds."

Silence filled the coffee shop. Mason looked ominously at Wiggins, digesting what she had said.

"And who are you?" Mason narrowed his eyes.

"Maryanne Wiggins."

"That's great, but I more meant what do you *do*?"

Wiggins smiled pleasantly. "I'm a private investigator."

Mason appraised Wiggins carefully and then frowned.

"Why do you want to talk about Katie?"

"Because she was murdered, and I think you might know who did it."

A shocked silence swallowed the room once more. Brittany, who was stirring in the chocolate for Wiggins's mocha, let her mouth drop as she looked over at Wiggins. As for Mason, his frown became a repugnant snarl.

"How dare you."

"Excuse me?"

"How dare you disrespect her memory like that."

"I didn't disrespect—"

"How can you even say that? 'She was murdered.' What is wrong with you?"

"I can say it because it's true. Someone saw a man waiting to abduct her on the night of her death." Wiggins kept her calm, but the look on Mason's face reflected that of unbridled anger. A few seconds passed when Mason rolled his eyes.

"Bullshit."

"Far from it, actually," Wiggins responded cheerfully.

Mason pointed aggressively at Wiggins with his index finger. "That's ridiculous. Someone saw somebody waiting to kidnap her? And what? Just let it happen?"

"The witness in question fled the scene, yes."

There was another lull, and Mason flashed an imposing, mocking smile in Wiggins's direction. "Lady, how can you even have the nerve to do this?"

"Do what?"

"Come into my place of business and start this crap. I don't know what kind of two-bit private investigator you are, but if what you just said was true, you think it would have gotten past the police?" asked Mason furiously.

Brittany had gingerly set down the mocha in front of Wiggins without making eye contact with either of them. She was doing her best to look down at the counter, as if it was truly mesmerizing.

"I have proof—"

"I don't give a *shit* what you have. Do you know how much that girl meant to me? And for you to do this. Rub this in my face like this. It's so goddamn disrespectful!" Mason shouted.

Wiggins tucked her hair behind her ear and clicked her tongue sarcastically. "So I take it you don't care to listen to the rest of the evidence I have amassed?"

Mason glared back at her for a solid five seconds before responding. "Get out of here."

Wiggins smiled. She had expected abrasiveness, but not the outright fury from Mason. She looked him dead in the eye. "Okay. Talk to you soon," she said softly.

Mason continued to stare at her, and his eyes bulged. Wiggins turned around without even grabbing her mocha and walked out of the shop.

40

When Wiggins got back to her office, she started hashing out a plan. It seemed prudent to follow up on Mason somehow; perhaps looking for threads of connections to some of the other victims would be a good place to start. Therefore, Wiggins dialed the number of Tara Reid, the mother of the sixteen-year-old girl who drowned in Olalla Lake in 2001. Out of anyone she had spoken with regarding the Nowhere Girls, Tara was the only one who consistently followed up with Wiggins. Wiggins heard from her at least once a year, and she felt like she owed it to the woman to contact her first to identify a possible suspect. Wiggins knew it was a long shot; it seemed very unlikely that Tara would remember Anthony Mason ever popping up in her daughter's life. But she had to give it a try. Wiggins pressed the phone against her ear and listened to it ring.

"This is Tara."

"Hi, Tara, it's Maryanne."

"Hello, Maryanne," Tara said in a high-pitched voice.

Wiggins could tell that Tara had gotten anxious with anticipation as soon as Wiggins had told her who was calling.

"How are you?"

"I'm okay. Keeping busy with work."

"How's work been?"

"Oh, fine," Tara said. Wiggins could tell that she was deliberately giving short answers so that Wiggins would get to the point.

"I assume you are anxious to know why I am calling, so I'll just get to it. I need you to look at a picture for me."

"A picture? Of what?"

"A man."

There was a faint shuffling on the other end of the line.

"A suspect?" she asked with her voice full of nervous excitement.

"That's correct."

"What's the name?"

"Anthony Mason."

"The coffee shop owner?"

"That's right."

"That's your suspect?" Tara asked dubiously.

"Correct." She already knew by the tone of Tara's voice that Mason had no obvious connection to Tara's late daughter.

"Hmmm. I don't remember him ever interacting with Riley or anything."

"Do you know what he looks like?"

"Uh, I don't think so. I've never met the guy; I just know his name."

"Do you think you could meet up and look at his picture for me? Even though you don't remember him knowing Riley, maybe seeing what he looks like will jog your memory of something. And there is some other information I want to share with you."

"Other information?" Tara perked up. "Regarding what?"

"It's difficult to explain over the phone. A lot has happened regarding the case in the past couple of weeks, and I want to update you on it all."

"Wow. Okay. Yes, of course. I'm out of town for the next couple of days on a business trip. Do you want to meet for lunch this Saturday?"

"That sounds great. Thank you so much." Wiggins felt like leaping for joy. Tara had always been the easiest informant to work with over the years. She wasn't private, nor was she too overbearing about Wiggins's work.

After agreeing on a time and place with Tara for Saturday and ending the conversation, Wiggins grabbed her laptop off her desk and went through the door that led to her apartment before plopping down on her couch. She rarely utilized her office for actual work, instead using it simply for appointments with clients. It was much more cozy and easier to do research in the living room of her apartment.

Flipping open the laptop while getting comfortable on the couch, Wiggins searched Dan Jenkins's name. Even though she was now subconsciously leaning heavily toward Anthony Mason over Jenkins, she guessed she ought to do some more legwork on Jenkins as well. However, there wasn't much information on the Internet that she hadn't already scoured over since Jenkins had let slip that he knew the killer to be wearing a mask, so Wiggins only stayed on the bowels of Google for ten minutes or so.

This doesn't seem to be the way to do it, thought Wiggins as she clicked out of a web page that was a story about Jenkins donating money to some foundation for inner city kids in the greater Portland area. She didn't know what else she hoped to find about Jenkins on the Internet. Why waste time on something when she didn't know what she was looking for instead of going full force after Anthony Mason? Mason was the far more likely candidate. The only thing she had on Jenkins were two instances of him knowing a suspicious amount of information about the victims and their abductions. And honestly, could it be feasible that the District Attorney was a goddamn serial killer? Now that she had another solid suspect, Wiggins was starting to downplay Dan Jenkins and rationalize the evidence that she had accumulated against him.

After clicking out of the story about Jenkins, Wiggins typed in the website for *News Lincoln County* and perused the site for any noteworthy stories to read. It had nothing to do with Mason or Jenkins; it was just a way for Wiggins to fill the void while she thought of what to do next, and she hadn't been watching any TV or listening to the radio over the past 24 hours anyway, so she wasn't caught up on the news. The first headline she came across nearly made her heart stop.

NEWPORT TEEN ESCAPES AFTER ATTEMPTED KIDNAPPING.

After reading the sentence, Wiggins felt a lump in her throat and a massive tightening in her chest. *Jesus Christ,* she thought. With her hands shaking, Wiggins used her finger on the mouse pad to scroll down and read the story:

> *Sierra Bunker, a 17-year-old girl, was taken to the hospital for the treatment of minor injuries after a man wearing a ski mask attempted to abduct her on Tuesday evening, authorities say. Bunker was able to escape after a brief physical altercation with the man on 10th Court, just south of Newport High School. The suspect is currently still at large. Police urge parents and students to remain vigilant in the wake of this incident and to please report any suspicious activity immediately.*

The excerpt was short, but it was enough to make Wiggins feel light headed. The bulletin had been published on the site only two hours earlier, but Wiggins was still a little surprised that she had to read it on the Internet instead of hearing about it from one of her contacts. As her heart thumped against her rib cage, Wiggins pulled out her cell and called Albert Amos.

"I think I know why you're calling," Amos said as soon as he picked up.

"I take it you have my number saved in your phone now?"

"Affirmative. Unless this isn't Maryanne. Then we have a problem."

Wiggins pretended to chuckle, even though she was not in a jovial mood.

"Don't worry, it is. You think you know why I am calling, do you?"

"I am guessing it has something to do with the girl who was almost abducted by a man in a ski mask yesterday?"

"You got it," Wiggins answered. Over the years, Amos had grown familiar with Wiggins's work on the Nowhere Girls. She wasn't quite sure where he stood on the whole thing, but he never tried to get in her way. And that was why she had maintained a relationship with him.

"I'm afraid I am not at liberty to discuss the details of that at this time. The investigation is ongoing."

"I am aware of the fact you can't divulge anything that hasn't been released to the public," Wiggins replied, irritated she had to go through the whole rigmarole with him.

"Then I am not sure why you are calling."

There were a few seconds of silence before Wiggins responded.

"You have to give me something, Albert. Please."

"Sorry, Maryanne. Really, I am. But no can do. We are still looking for the guy."

"Any idea who it might be?"

"That is exactly something I can't share with you," Amos said, a little crossly.

"Where is the girl now?" Wiggins asked without missing a beat.

"She's under protective custody at her house. Why?"

"I want to talk to her."

There was a pause, and the only noise Wiggins heard was the bustling of the police station in the background.

"You can't be serious."

"Listen—"

"It's a no, Maryanne. Just . . . No. There is no way my superiors—or the girl, for that matter—would be okay with that."

"Why don't you just ask her?"

"Ask her what? Ask her if she wants to talk to an outside private investigator after she has spent hours being interrogated by detectives?"

"Tell her that I've been hunting this guy for ten years."

Amos sighed. He and Wiggins had discussed the case in detail several times before, and he seemed to have always avoided making his stance clear one way or another. But Wiggins was putting him in the compromising position of telling her what he thought.

"You have no idea who this guy is. Hell, *I* have no idea who this guy is. There is no way you can reasonably conclude that this is connected to your thing. You don't even know for sure if your guy even exists."

"Just ask her if it would be okay," Wiggins pleaded. "Please just ask."

Amos sighed again.

"Jesus, Maryanne."

"Please, Albert."

The familiar rustling noises of the police station returned to Wiggins's ear as Amos stopped to think once more.

"Fine. But I'm not going to try and argue with her. If she says no, she says no. And if the higher-ups get wind of this, they'll shut it down, so don't be surprised if it doesn't happen even if she *does* say it's okay."

"Thank you, thank you!" Wiggins felt a rush of jubilee.

"You owe me one," Amos said before he hung up on her.

X

The man couldn't breathe. As he paced on the deck of his house under the illuminated porch light, his stomach did a double backflip every time he thought of his current situation. He knew he had blown it this time. His blood lust had finally doomed him.

The man couldn't believe he had given in to the urge to go after the girl so soon. He had never done anything like that before. Sure, the man had killed the witness and the reporter without a second thought, but that was for survival. That was covering his tracks. This was something he had done because he had wanted to. And it looked like it would cost him dearly.

The man had convinced himself that he was doing the deed so quickly because he had already done a hefty amount of legwork on the girl before he had been interrupted by his source telling him about the witness. But that was just rationalization. What had allowed him to remain unencumbered as he killed for so long was the ability to ignore his primal impulses when they started to tell him to do things that would not behoove him. His scrupulous planning and patience were the ultimate ally when it came to evading police. And he had thrown thirty years of work away by finally giving in to his urges.

He had spent an hour looking for the girl in the wilderness. The man would have dedicated more time to finding her, but he came to the realization that if the girl had somehow managed to free her hands from the rope he had tied, she would be able to reach her cell phone and the police would soon be on their way. So the man had retreated. Angered beyond belief at his sloppiness and having a near panic attack as he ran back through the woods, the man had begun to consider leaving Newport for good.

And now here he was, cursing his ineptitude. The man leaned against the railing of his deck, looking up at the sky. He wondered if this was going to be one of his last days looking at the sky as a free man. *Cut that shit out,* he told himself. Negative thinking was never productive, but especially now when he had to remain calm and come up with a plan. All was not lost.

The man knew that he would not be able to touch the girl now. Not only would she be under the watchful eyes of the police for the next few days, but she would likely spend the rest of her life looking over her shoulder, and she would probably never walk alone again. It would be very difficult to apprehend her now. What was the man to do? There had been times before over the course of his killing career where he had made mistakes, but they had been relatively minor. He had never made this egregious of a blunder before, obviously. However, perhaps he could look at his past responses to turmoil as a template for what to do now. What had he done when a kill had not gone smoothly? He had gone dormant. It usually wasn't for more than a year or two, but he had laid low and allowed things to blow over. Was that what he was supposed to do?

Maybe it was time to hang up his cleats, so to speak. Maybe he had finally reached the pinnacle of his productivity and was now on a sharp decline. What did athletes do when they couldn't produce anymore? They retired. The man gazed out at the forest in front of him, imagining what it would be like to run into it and never come out. Perhaps the best plan of action would be to simply disappear.

41

"Maryanne?"

"Yes?"

"You *really* owe me one."

Wiggins rubbed her eyes. She was extremely groggy. Amos had interrupted her slumber by calling her. It was just past seven a.m. Still, she couldn't help but let anticipation build up in her stomach for what he was about to tell her.

"What is it?" Wiggins asked, attempting to remain reserved.

"She's going to talk to you. But don't mention a word of this to anybody. The only people who know are me, the officers at her house, and the girl herself. The higher-ups aren't aware of it. At least not yet."

"Terrific!" She was more excited than she had been in quite some time. "What did you tell her about me?"

"I told her you may have some answers as to who this guy is, and what his motivations are. Don't worry—"

"But—"

Amos didn't let her finish. "I told her that it may be totally unrelated. But yeah, anyway, I said there is a chance that you may have been hunting this guy for years. The girl says she hasn't slept since the incident. She probably won't feel safe until we catch him, hence her willingness to talk to you."

"I really appreciate it, Albert. I *do* owe you one. Big time. When and where am I meeting the girl?"

"Her house. The address is 206 Avery Lane. And today at noon. That's why I am calling you so early. I wanted to give you a chance to prepare. She gave me the word late last night."

"Great. Awesome. Again, thank you so much, Albert."

"Yeah, well. Now you do your part," Amos said boldly. "I have always had my reservations about your theories, but I think this situation has now offered irrefutable proof. So, if you are right, it will be the biggest case ever in this town. Go catch this guy."

"That's the plan."

The respective parties each hung up their phones, and Wiggins shifted into full gear. She had plenty of time to get ready, but she wanted to get herself focused for this all-important interview and conjure up a list of pertinent questions. So she ate breakfast, took a shower, and got dressed in less than half an hour, then spent the rest of the time readying herself for the impending interview.

Fifteen minutes before noon, Wiggins headed out to her car, carrying her pistol in the holster on her hip, as well as a notepad, her phone for recording purposes, and a pen. She knew that it was probably not a good idea to bring a gun into an interview with a traumatized teenager, but she also didn't feel comfortable going out without it, so she took it out of the holster and placed it in her glove box. It took her less than seven minutes to drive from her apartment to the address that Amos had given her. The house on Avery Lane was a two-story blue structure, with a black Cadillac Escalade and a Mercedes parked in the driveway.

Just from a single glance, Wiggins guessed that the Bunker family was very well-off. She waited in her car for a few more minutes before getting out and walking up the driveway.

When Wiggins knocked on the front door, there was a loud shuffling sound that came from within.

"Who is it?" a deep booming voice called from behind the door.

"Private investigator Maryanne Wiggins," Wiggins said confidently. Less than a second later, the door swung open and a burly man with a unibrow looked down on her.

"Hello there," Wiggins said pleasantly, holding out her hand. "I'm Maryanne. Nice to meet you."

"Officer Nick Cody," the large man said, shaking Wiggins's hand with a crushing grasp.

"Nice to meet you." Wiggins winced at the handshake.

After the two unfastened their hands, there were a couple seconds of awkward silence as Wiggins looked at Officer Nick Cody's bushy unibrow. Eventually, her fixation was interrupted by Cody asking her a question.

"So, you are friends with Detective Amos?"

"That's right. I take it he has informed you of what I am doing here?"

"He has," Cody said shortly. *A man of few words,* thought Wiggins.

"Then may I come in?"

Cody looked at her for a few seconds as though she had offered up a deeply philosophical question about the meaning of life itself. Then, after apparently deciding she could enter, he nodded and stepped aside. *A man of few words and IQ points,* thought Wiggins.

Cody led her through an expensive-looking marble kitchen and pointed her into an expansive living room with multiple black leather couches. On one, there sat a police officer. On the other, there sat three people who Wiggins supposed were the

Bunkers, although they didn't look related at all. On the far right, there was a middle-aged redheaded woman with pouty red lips. On the left, there was a squat balding man with a large gut and glasses. And in the center, there was a pretty teenager with blond hair. They all bore expressions that indicated varying types of distress. The little, round balding man was looking at the teenager, scanning her up and down as though she might burst into tears at any moment. The middle-aged woman was looking at Wiggins skeptically, as though her bleak appearance somehow reflected her abilities. And the teen, whom Wiggins knew to be Sierra Bunker, looked terrified and exhausted.

When Wiggins got farther into the room, the cop stood up and strode over to Wiggins, holding out his hand, while Cody retreated into the kitchen.

"Hey. I'm Officer Hernandez. I take it that you are Maryanne Wiggins?"

"That's correct." Wiggins shook his hand.

"Great. Okay, before we get started, let me introduce you guys."

The three Bunkers stood up in unison, and Wiggins hobbled over to them, shaking their hands as Hernandez said each of their names.

"This is Tony Bunker," Hernandez gestured to the bald man. "And his wife Celeste." He nodded to the stoic woman and Wiggins held her palm in the air to acknowledge her.

"And this is Sierra," Hernandez finished. Sierra looked at Wiggins, but didn't make eye contact.

"I bet you are surprised by my appearance, huh? Didn't expect a private investigator to look like Bilbo Baggins."

The corner of Sierra's mouth twitched, but she remained looking uncomfortable.

"Okay, let's establish some parameters," Hernandez said. "First, this whole thing is only going to last twenty minutes. Max. I don't think it is a good idea in the first place, but it isn't up to me. The Bunkers and I have agreed on twenty minutes, so that is what it is going to be."

Wiggins tried to stifle her surprise. Hernandez was looking at her as if daring her to challenge him.

"Second, if there are any questions that Sierra feels uncomfortable answering or that her parents don't *want* her to answer, I ask that you please respect their wishes."

"That sounds perfect," Wiggins said. Hernandez frowned as if he had expected her to rebel against his rules.

"Uh, alright then. The floor is yours," Hernandez said, motioning toward Sierra. Hernandez went across the room and sat down stiffly into a wooden chair.

Wiggins smiled kindly at Sierra as she approached, but the girl kept her eyes on the floor. Wiggins held out her hand. Celeste glared at Wiggins's arm as though it were some wretched thing. Sierra's torpor was broken, and she shot a furtive glance down at Wiggins's hand before clutching it.

"Hello, Sierra. It is nice to meet you," Wiggins said warmly.

Sierra still didn't make eye contact. "Hello," the girl replied in a small voice.

Wiggins sat down on the large square ottoman that was in front of the couch so that she could draw even to Sierra's eye level, and withdrew her notepad from her jacket while simultaneously setting her phone on her lap. It took her a couple of seconds to get to the Voice Memo application and start recording. She swallowed before speaking.

"I've never felt how you are feeling right now. I was a cop for a long time. But I've never gone through what you are going through. Nobody should have to go through that."

Sierra looked up into Wiggins's eyes.

"First, I want to commend you. You had the strength and nerve to escape. Not many people would be able to say that."

In response to this, Sierra sat up a little straighter. Next to her, Celeste relaxed her shoulders by a fraction. Tony's eyes shifted around the room as though he were afraid of an extraterrestrial invasion that could come at any moment.

"Since our time together is short, I'll get straight to the point. I want you to walk me through what happened from beginning to end. Tell me everything you can remember."

Celeste placed her hand on Sierra's shoulder and the girl jumped. Celeste gave Wiggins a dirty look.

"Don't you think she might be tired of telling the same traumatic story over and over again?" Her voice sounded like it had endured many cigarettes over the years.

Before Wiggins could respond, Tony spoke. "Honey, it's fine. Let Sierra decide what she wants to talk about."

Celeste glared over at Tony, but didn't respond. Sierra didn't look at either of them.

"Where should I start?" Sierra asked in a timid voice.

"Tell me what you were doing. Where you were going."

She swallowed. "I had just gotten done at volleyball practice. I was waiting for my boyfriend, Kyle, to pick me up at the high school, but he forgot about me. So I walked home. I was heading down Tenth Court when I heard footsteps behind me. But there wasn't anybody there. All I saw was a green Jeep parked down the road."

"A green Jeep? What did it look like? What shade of green?"

"Eh, I don't know. Like dark green, I guess."

"Do you know what model of Jeep it was? Or did it have anything else that stood out to you?"

"Uh, I don't know the model. The windows were tinted. That is all I really remember about it. I didn't think much of it at the time."

"That's totally understandable," Wiggins replied. "So you said the Jeep was parked. Was there anybody inside of it?"

"There had to have been. But I don't remember seeing anyone."

"Okay. What happened next?" Wiggins wanted to probe further into why Sierra said there had to be someone in the Jeep, but she thought it was best to just let the girl continue.

"I started walking farther down the road. Kyle's house was like a hundred feet away or so. Anyway, I heard some weird noises. Like some . . . rustling and stuff."

"So, did you think you were being followed?"

Sierra shuddered and shook her head with vigor. "No. I mean . . . I don't know. I just felt weird. Like creeped out."

"Right, right. Then what happened?"

"I turned around, and the Jeep was driving slowly right at me. I didn't see who the driver was, but he flashed his lights at me."

"He flashed his lights? Like he was trying to get your attention?"

"Yeah. And then I turned around because I was scared. I waited for a moment, listening for the sound of anyone coming, but I didn't hear anything. And right after that is when the guy grabbed me from behind."

Wiggins couldn't help but feel elated at hearing this. What it sounded like to her was that the person in the Jeep had seen someone approaching and was trying to warn Sierra somehow. Which meant that there was likely a witness who had seen the whole thing. But if that were true, why hadn't the person gone to the police?

"Someone grabbed you from behind?" Wiggins glanced over at Hernandez, who was still sitting stiff and looking bored in his chair.

"Yes. Right around my waist. He grabbed me and pulled me into the forest that was right next to us," Sierra said, while starting to get quieter again.

"Describe this man for me." Wiggins was paying rapt attention to every word the girl was saying and taking notes.

"He was wearing a black ski mask, so I didn't see his face."

Her voice was starting to crack with emotion.

"He w-was tall. And buff. And w-wearing a black sweatshirt and s-sweatpants. And black gloves."

Wiggins wrote this down word for word.

"What did he do after he dragged you into the forest? Were you screaming?"

Sierra nodded and her eyes glistened with tears. Celeste rubbed Sierra's arm.

"He had his hand over my mouth. And then he hit me over the head with something." She pulled her hair back from her face to show the edges of a purple bruise that protruded back onto her scalp. "It might have just been his fist. But anyway, I was kind of out of it for a second, so I stopped screaming. He tied my hands and put a gag in my mouth. It all happened so fast."

"Did the man say anything to you?" Wiggins hoped she didn't have to hear the answer.

"No, he didn't. But he was smiling at me."

A chill ran down Wiggins's spine. She shot a glance at Tony, who looked green in the face. Hernandez shifted in his chair. Celeste turned white.

"Smiling at you?" Wiggins asked slowly.

"Yes."

Wiggins lost her train of thought. The image of this monster leering down at one of his intended victims was truly disturbing.

"What happened? How did you get away?"

"Well . . . He was straddling me, kind of holding me in place for a while. Waiting. Then he picked me up in his arms and started carrying me. I pretended to pass out once he had me in the air, and it made him stop walking for a second. Then I started moving around like crazy, and I think it took him off guard because he fell backward and dropped me."

"You pretended to pass out? That was clever."

"Thanks." The corners of her lips turned up a fraction. Next to her, Celeste looked soothed.

"Anyway, continue."

Sierra looked up, and she was finally making eye-contact with Wiggins. "Right, so, once he dropped me, I kicked him right in the face. I got him pretty good. He yelled pretty loud."

"And then you ran away?"

"Right. I ran off into the forest. I ran for a long time. Once it seemed like I lost him, I hid underneath a tree."

"Why did you run into the forest?" asked Wiggins, confused.

Sierra appeared bemused by this question. "What do you mean?"

"Why didn't you run back out onto the road?"

"Because of the Jeep," Sierra said.

"The Jeep?"

"Yeah. I think that is where the guy was trying to carry me to before he dropped me."

With that sentence, Wiggins's whole world changed. Chills ran down her spine, and the hairs on her arms stood up. She was hurtling through space, unable to process anything but what Sierra had just said. She finally had the missing piece. The key to everything that had stumped her for so long. All the dots were connecting in her head as a massive piece of the puzzle fastened into place. Someone else had been driving the Jeep. Someone who was in on the plan. There were *two* killers.

42

"Have you talked to him?"

"Of course I have. There isn't anything he can do about this."

"So what are we supposed to do? Run?"

The man shook his head angrily. "That's not what I said."

This sentiment initially prompted silence.

"How did we let this happen?"

The man stared back at his partner with hate. He wanted to scream at him. Grab the nearest blunt object and bludgeon his counterpart over the head.

"Obviously, it wasn't fucking intentional," said the man sardonically.

The man's partner stood there in the kitchen, dumbfounded. Tall and hulking, he was more brawn than brain; the man was the real mastermind behind their endeavors. But somehow, someway, it was the man's own mental blunders that had gotten them into this mess. *He* had been the one spotted by Leighton

Jones. *He* had almost let Jonah Carr get away. And *he* had given in to his irrational desire to try and take Sierra before he was properly prepared.

It wasn't as though the man's partner was totally incompetent either. In fact, his sidekick had been the one who had cleaned up the messes of late. And before the past month, the pair had had a perfectly symbiotic relationship. The man was the one who did the bulk of the work. His partner usually would just keep a watchful eye, be the assistant next to the proverbial surgeon's table who handed the man his tools. Occasionally his partner would get his hands dirty, but usually, he let the man take care of things. He had done well. And yet, the man couldn't help but take his anger out upon him.

"We have to be smart here," the man said, trying to quell the inner voice that was begging him to yell. "This is going to turn into a real shit storm here soon. And when it does, we can't do anything rash or foolish. We can't just get rid of anyone who gets in our way, like we did with Jones and Carr."

"That wasn't my id—"

"I fucking know that!"

The man glowered at his partner, ready to launch himself across the kitchen and wrap his hands around the witless goon's throat. His partner stared back at him, cowering even though he was slightly larger in physical stature than the man was.

"So what are we supposed to do?"

The man rubbed his eyes with his palms, hoping that if he pressed them hard enough he would wake up from this nightmare. But alas, his confused associate was still gawking at him when he opened his eyelids. And Sierra Bunker had still gotten away.

"We have to lay low and keep our ears tuned in to what is happening with the investigation. That won't be difficult, obviously. If things start to get out of hand, then we will flee. For now, we need to keep our heads down. You need to keep busy. I will schedule as much work as I can. And just in case things *do* go south, we need to have our passports renewed in case we have to make a quick getaway."

The man's partner nodded. "Should I tell Tim and Vince that there will be more odd jobs coming their way?"

"Unless you can manage to do it all on your own, then yeah, you probably should," the man said in frustration, exasperated at his partner's inability to make even the simplest of decisions on his own. "You're the boss, aren't you?"

"Just relax."

The man threw up his arms in wrath. "Don't tell me to fucking relax. Do you realize how much of a clusterfuck this is?"

"But we need to keep calm. Isn't that what you always tell me? 'Keep a level head. Don't make any decision if you are at your highest or lowest point'?"

"But this isn't—"

"Getting angry isn't going to help you make smart choices."

The man opened his mouth, ready for a snarky retort, but then he stopped. Angry as he was at his partner's boundless naivety, he had to admit that he was right in this particular circumstance.

"We need to get rid of everything," the man said suddenly, diverging from what they had been talking about.

"What?"

"Everything. Pictures. Trophies. Plans. Anything that could tie us to any of the girls."

"Don't you think that is a little rash?"

"Trust me, I don't like it either. But it is a necessity."

His partner stood there for a second, looking around the room as if somebody else might come to his aid in the argument. "I'm not sure I agree. I . . . I just don't think it is necessary to dispose of everything we have worked so hard to collect."

There were several moments of silence as the two men stared at each other. The man knew his partner would acquiesce to his demands after some persuading. For several moments, he wondered how to frame his argument. Usually, it just took speaking in grandiose metaphors to convince his partner of his point of view. Sounding smart got you far with a lot of people, no matter how much you verbosely bloviated about nothing in particular.

The man placed his hands on his partner's shoulders. "Look at me, standing here. I'm an actor."

"What are you talking about?"

"You're an actor too. And the reason we are standing right here and not in a cell is because we play our parts well."

His partner looked like he didn't understand.

"We are going to have to act better than we ever have before. And do whatever is required of us. And right now our roles demand getting rid of everything that could come back to haunt us. Because our new audience won't be convinced that we are innocent men. And we must persuade them that we are. From now on, you must act irreproachable in everything that you do. Do you understand?"

The man's partner looked up at the ceiling.

"Yes. I understand."

43

"Are you alright?"

Wiggins looked up at the girl. Ironically, the person who had just survived an attempted kidnapping was asking *Wiggins* if she was okay.

"Yes, dear. I'm fine," Wiggins said delicately. She wanted to continue with the interview, but every cell in her body begged her to leave Sierra behind and go obsess over the newfangled idea of a pair of killers.

"So, uh, yeah, he was taking me to the Jeep, I think."

"So the person inside the Jeep who was flashing his lights at you was the masked man's partner?"

"I suppose so, yeah." Sierra shrugged.

"I wonder why the police didn't release that information."

Sierra squinted her eyes in consternation. "What?"

"I wonder why they didn't frame it in the news release as having been the work of two abductors," Wiggins said, thinking out loud.

Hernandez cleared his throat from the other side of the room.

"We don't do the news releases; you do realize that, right?"

"I do realize that, but I also realize that the proprietor of that website would speak to your PR guy about the case," Wiggins countered.

Hernandez gave a miniature chop at the air and raised his voice a fraction in frustration. "The investigation is ongoing. We're not going to give out crucial details that might hamper our ability to catch the guys."

"So the station deliberately cherry-picked the information they gave to the reporter to make what happened seem different than what it actually was?"

"We don't even know if there *is* a second kidnapper. We obviously assume there is, but we don't know who the person in that Jeep was. And if it aids us in reeling in these guys because the website puts out that it was one perpetrator instead of two, then yeah. I have no problem with the information relayed."

Wiggins didn't say anything, but she couldn't help but furrow her brow in irritation as she turned back toward Sierra. She glanced down at her list of questions and decided to skip over a few and go straight to the meatier stuff.

"Ms. Bunker, I was wondering: Do you ever have any regular contact with any older men?"

Before Sierra could answer, Celeste stampeded into the conversation.

"And just what is that supposed to mean exactly?" she asked, sounding furious.

"It doesn't mean anything, other than our guy is likely in his fifties, and he may establish some sort of contact with his victims before he tries to take them." Wiggins kept her calm.

"Victims?"

"Huh?"

Sierra's eyes widened in awe. "You said victims."

"That's correct."

"So he has done this before?"

"Yes."

"How many times?"

"Thirteen."

Instantly, everyone in the room turned their heads towards Wiggins, unable to do anything but think about what she had just said.

Sierra's face seemed to be petrified in an aghast expression. "Thirteen?"

"Yes."

"So . . . what does he do after he kidnaps them?"

"He kills them."

"Oh my God." Sierra grabbed a fistful of her blond hair in anxiety. "So this guy is a serial killer?"

"Yes," Wiggins said firmly.

Another instance of overwhelming quiet dropped into the room like a bomb. Sierra was now the one looking like she might vomit. Tony was staring at Wiggins and biting his lip; sweat beaded over his bald head. Celeste rubbed her daughter's arm, seeing that she was in obvious distress. Hernandez, however, looked extremely irritated.

"Pay no attention to what Ms. Wiggins just said," the officer said, breaking the silence. "There are no active serial killers in the area. To suggest that is asinine. Don't you think you would have heard about it in the news if there was?"

"Officer Hernandez has the right to be skeptical, as I will admit, it does seem preposterous to someone on the outside looking in. But believe me, I am 100 percent certain about this. There have been thirteen cases in the last thirty-two years of young girls, all between the ages of fourteen and twenty-one," said Wiggins. "Celeste, let me ask you something. How long have you lived in Newport?"

Celeste looked a little startled by the question. "Uh, since

1990."

"So then you will remember the five teenage girls who went missing while walking alone at night on Highway 101 over a ten-year period?"

Celeste looked afraid as comprehension dawned on her face.

"That? You think this is connected to that? Didn't the police catch that guy?"

"Yes," Hernandez spoke up. "Bobby Ray Foles. Serial killer from Canada who died in prison."

"Except that they never gathered any DNA evidence corroborating the theory that Foles was the killer. And he wasn't even in Newport when the first girl went missing," Wiggins added.

Sierra's voice was barely even a whisper as she put her hand over her mouth, looking traumatized. "A serial killer was in Newport? I've never even heard of this."

Either Hernandez didn't hear Sierra or simply didn't care because he continued arguing with Wiggins.

"Okay, sure, there was a serial killer in Newport twenty years ago. But you just said there have been, what, thirteen cases? And then you say that this guy only killed five girls? There is a big difference between thirteen and five," said Hernandez mockingly.

"There are thirteen cases. Only five of them have been confirmed as homicides."

"Oh come on!" Hernandez said loudly. "You think this guy killed eight more girls without us noticing?"

"I could take you through the details of each individual girl, but frankly, I don't have the time. You gave me, what was it? Twenty minutes? Detective Amos told me that Sierra was kind enough to do this interview because she wanted to know who this guy was and what his motivations are, since I have made it my life's work to find him. So, I am telling her who he is. I'm not trying to scare you or anything." Wiggins turned back to Sierra. "I just think it is best if you have the truth."

Sierra nodded with fervor. "I think that is best too."

Hernandez reclined back in his chair and rolled his eyes. He tapped his foot in aggravation.

"Didn't you just throw a fit once you found out there were two kidnappers? But you keep referring to this person as 'the guy.' Singular, not plural. Are there two serial killers who are working together? And you just found out about this today, even though you say this is your life's work?"

"Officer, I think it is best if you stay out of this now. If I need your help, I will ask for it," Wiggins said, throwing a subtle barb in his direction. Hernandez shook his head in disgust but didn't say anything more.

"Do you think he is going to come after me again?" Sierra asked in a shaky voice.

"No. I don't. I think he is going to try and lay low here for a long time after what happened with you. But that is not an excuse to not be vigilant. Never walk alone again. Always have someone with you. Even in places where you think you're safe. I don't want you to live your life constantly looking over your shoulder, but you need to be smart. And I think you will be. You seem like a smart girl."

Wiggins reached out and patted Sierra's shoulder. Sierra cracked a tiny smile and leaned her head against Celeste's shoulder.

"Now, I have a couple of pictures I want you to look at for me. And tell me if you recognize either of these men."

From her jacket, Wiggins pulled out two folded up photos that she had printed out earlier that morning. One was of Dan Jenkins. The other was of Anthony Mason.

"Do you recognize either of these men?"

Sierra looked over the photographs. "Why?"

"Just answer the question, please. Do you recognize either

of them?"

Sierra scanned the photographs for a good long while. She brought one of them closer to her face, as if that would help jog her memory.

"Isn't that Anthony Mason?"

It turned out that Sierra was good friends with Brittany Kelley and had visited her at Mason's Coffee several times. She knew who Katie Deeds was, mortified when she realized what Wiggins was asserting about the nature of Katie's death. "So you think she was thrown off the bridge? And that was the same guy who tried to kidnap me?" Sierra had asked. Wiggins had only nodded in response to these inquiries.

As for Anthony Mason, Sierra said she barely knew the man and had only seen him a few times inside the coffee shop. However, she did describe him as a "creep." Wiggins had assumed that this was just because of hearsay that Sierra had received from Brittany. Overall, Wiggins couldn't tell how much Sierra's testimony about Mason would help her theory. The girl only gravitated toward the idea of Mason as a capable killer after Wiggins had proffered the suggestion.

Wiggins had wrapped up the interview after her twenty minutes were up, thanking Sierra for her time. She shook Celeste's hand and waved good-bye to Tony, who was still looking like he was waiting for someone to attack him at any moment, what with the sweating and manic glances around the room. Wiggins didn't think much of it, though. He was probably just concerned for his daughter's well-being.

When Wiggins was in her car she was finally able to obsess over the idea of two killers. How had she never thought of it before? It was so obvious now. This kind of intense planning and painstaking attention to detail seemed a lot more plausible under the design of two culprits. And what had happened to Sierra *only* appeared possible via the work of multiple perpetrators. She had said the Jeep was flashing its lights at her from the end of the road, but then when the masked man had straddled her in the forest, the vehicle had been waiting next to them. There had to be a separate driver.

Wiggins also wondered if this was the method they used to abduct the other girls as well. Did one of them distract the target from the forest-green Jeep while the other attacked from behind? Is that how they took Katie? If only Leighton Jones hadn't disappeared. Had he not vanished, Wiggins would be able to speak with him and see if he saw a Jeep in the vicinity of the masked man.

This newfound theory of a second killer opened up worlds of possibilities that Wiggins hadn't been able to consider before. Sure, Mason had been in prison when Kylie Desmond was taken. But what if his partner had done the deed that time, under his instruction and bidding?

The information Wiggins had gotten from Sierra also paved the way for re-interviewing past respondents, to see if they would remember anybody of significance driving a green Jeep. The first person that Wiggins would run this thread of intel by was Tara Reid. Even if Tara weren't able to offer a breakthrough upon receiving the knowledge of the Jeep and the two suspects that Wiggins had focused on, surely another person in Wiggins's black binder would be able to provide something. She had interviewed so many people in the past that it seemed more likely that someone would be able to buttress her theories rather than counter them.

So here she was. Farther than she had ever come before. As Wiggins drove back toward her apartment, her mind was still churning. Two killers. *Two.* It was almost unbelievable in its audacity. Could it be purely circumstantial that directly after Wiggins had finally found two solid suspects, she had come to the revelation there were also two killers? Or was it inevitable that she would find a link between Anthony Mason and Dan Jenkins? Two men who had been in Newport since the eighties when the case began—one of them with a direct connection to multiple victims, and the other with specific knowledge of the crimes. Two men who were vile and insolent. Two killers. Could it possibly be just a coincidence?

44

The next couple of days, Wiggins streamlined all her efforts into finding some sort of link between Anthony Mason and Dan Jenkins. She talked to several of her contacts around town, including multiple people who worked at the courthouse. But nobody could confirm the notion that Mason and Jenkins knew each other, let alone that they had spent a copious amount of time in each other's company. Wiggins figured that this was probably by design. If the two men *were* partners, they would probably have put a great amount of effort into ensuring that nobody would make the connection.

Wiggins had a checklist of things to do that she ran through as the hours passed, but nothing seemed to aid her in building a case against her suspects. She stopped in at Rip Tide's, but Patty, the bartender, said that Leighton Jones hadn't made an appearance. She checked in with Albert Amos to see if Rick Casey or another officer had filed a missing person report over the past several days, but nothing had transpired. The real wild card was Joanne Fellner. Wiggins desperately wanted to call Joe Damascus and beg him to relay the message that Fellner's daughter was safe in another state, but she knew doing that would be detrimental to her efforts. And yet, what if Fellner could confirm that the man she had slept with and who had threatened her daughter was either Dan Jenkins or Anthony Mason?

It was so frustrating to Wiggins that she was so close to answers, and yet she couldn't quite get there. She had gotten so near in proximity to solving this on multiple fronts. Dan Jenkins had let slip that he knew the man was wearing a ski mask. Brittany Kelley had said that Anthony Mason had threatened to kill Katie. For God's sake, she had finally gotten Joanne Fellner to admit that she slept with the likely killer. And yet, none of that amounted to anything. The piece of evidence against Jenkins was circumstantial at best, and she couldn't prove Katie was murdered now that Leighton had vanished, so Mason's threat currently meant nothing. The fact that he had done time for assaulting Kylie Desmond was also insignificant since he was in prison for that crime at the time of her disappearance. Fellner was too scared to talk, and her attorney refused to let Wiggins speak with her anyway. Jonah had likely been killed by her guy, but again, she couldn't prove it because of the text sent from Jonah's phone, and she couldn't force Rick Casey to reconsider looking into it. She had tried to contact Jonah's parents to attempt to get them to come to the police to verify that their son had never actually made it home, but she hadn't been able to get ahold of them. To be so damn near to a breakthrough in so many ways without any gratification was aggravating beyond belief.

When Wiggins woke up on Saturday morning, she felt resigned to the fact that her interview with Tara Reid later that day would not yield anything of significance. She even considered calling Tara and canceling, but decided to stick it out. She had nothing else to do that day anyway. Therefore, Wiggins flipped through her big black binder for anything else that might be useful to run by Tara again. But nothing stuck out.

Eventually, after a morning of scrupulously going through everything she had on Mason and Jenkins, Wiggins got ready for her lunch appointment with Tara. They had agreed to meet at Georgie's Beachside Grill. It was one of several elegant and high-end restaurants that lined Elizabeth Street on the west side of town. The place was a bit pricey, but Wiggins figured that she could indulge every once in a while. After taking a shower and cleaning up, Wiggins limped down the staircase of her apartment and walked through Sandcastle Toys, heading for her car.

No more than ten minutes later, she was walking through the parking lot in the direction of the front door. Tara had just texted her several minutes ago and let Wiggins know that she would meet her in the reception area of the restaurant. Wiggins grabbed the golden door handle and pulled the heavy door open. Inside, the building was dimly lit, but in an extravagant way. The carpets were a pleasant shade of maroon and everything in sight seemed to be covered in a layer of gold. Wiggins scanned around the reception area, looking for Tara. Eventually, she caught sight of the woman sitting on a soft-looking bench off to her right. Wiggins walked up to her and smiled.

"Tara. Long time no see."

Tara looked up and beamed at Wiggins. She was a dainty little woman with wispy brown hair and a small mouth. She didn't look at all like her daughter Riley, although Wiggins had only seen the girl in pictures. Tara was immensely short and petite and attractive in a strange sort of way for a mousy woman in her late forties.

"Maryanne! Good to see you."

The women exchanged small talk and were greeted by a host wearing all black with a gold name tag.

"Just two?" the middle-aged man with slicked-back hair said.

"That's right," Wiggins said. The host led them to a table on the far-left side of the restaurant that was right next to a giant window which gave onlookers a spectacular view of the ocean. It was pleasantly warm and sunny outside, which was somewhat rare for a late September day. The weather enhanced the aesthetics of the beach down below.

"Your server will be with you shortly."

The women nodded and took seats opposite of each other.

There was a cursory cessation as Wiggins and Tara contemplated how to start the conversation. It seemed like every time the pair met up they always said the same thing at the beginning of their talks. Wiggins would always complain about her knee causing her pain, and Tara would dwarf her sorrows by shedding light on how much she missed her daughter. After all that had happened over the past couple of weeks, Wiggins didn't feel like having this interaction for the hundredth time.

"I know you are probably anxious to receive an update on my, uh, exploits."

Tara nodded rapidly. "I will admit, the past couple of days have gone pretty slow. I don't want to say I have been waiting with bated breath because I have been trying to temper my expectations, but I am curious to know what you found."

Wiggins looked at Tara, hoping she wouldn't disappoint her.

"A lot has happened since the last time we met. When was it? March?"

"I think so."

Wiggins took a deep breath and launched into an explanation of all the important things that had taken place over the past month. She first told Tara about Katie Deeds, and how it looked like the girl had committed suicide. She then spoke of Jonah and how he found Leighton Jones, and what Jones had saw. She relayed the news of Jonah and Jones's subsequent disappearances and Sierra Bunker and how she had escaped an attempted kidnapping. Wiggins neglected to tell Tara anything about Joanne Fellner because she thought that it might drive the woman crazy knowing there was a person who possibly knew who her daughter's killer was but refused to talk. Wiggins also excluded everything about Dan Jenkins and Anthony Mason because she wanted to get Tara's untainted reaction toward the two men.

"My God." Tara clutched her chest as soon as Wiggins finished. "Oh my God."

Wiggins fiddled with the collar to her blouse awkwardly. "Yeah."

It was all she could think of to say. Tara had kept silent throughout Wiggins's monologue, but her eyes widened further and further until it looked like her sockets were that of a skeleton's.

"So wait, let's rewind for a second. That Katie girl was murdered then? There is no way she actually committed suicide?"

"No. She was murdered. I am positive," Wiggins said resolutely.

"Right. And the man who saw the guy in the ski mask—"

"Has not been seen in the past couple of weeks. Correct."

Tara looked directly into Wiggins's eyes. It looked as though she were debating something internally.

"So . . . do you think the guy in the ski mask came after him?"

Wiggins shook her head, showing Tara that she couldn't be sure either way.

"I mean, either that, or Jones skipped town. Both of those scenarios are equally likely."

"Ugh." Tara shivered. "And you think it was this same person who went after the Bunker girl?"

"Correct."

Tara's gaze shifted, looking around the restaurant as though the killer might be sitting at the table next to them and offering up a toast.

"Jesus Christ," Tara said suddenly. Wiggins was slightly taken aback, as she thought for a moment that Tara was angry at her for some reason.

"What is it?"

"After all this time." Tara shook her head. "Fifteen years. Fifteen goddamn years since Riley died, and nobody knows anything. And then all of this happens in a month? I mean, Jesus."

"I know," Wiggins concurred. "It's pretty unbelievable."

Tara took the napkin in front of her and fiddled with it absentmindedly as she thought of what to say next.

"Isn't your theory that this guy plans everything out? Like he's a schemer? How would he let himself get caught in the act like this? Like, he lets somebody see him take the Katie girl? And then he gets outwitted by the Bunker girl too? That doesn't seem like it fits . . . does it?" She was almost pleading with Wiggins, wanting to be reassured that this man was in fact the one who had murdered Riley.

"I think he *was* very meticulous and detail oriented. I think he *did* plan everything out. But he made a mistake that he had no way of avoiding. There is no possible way he could have kept Leighton Jones from seeing him hiding behind a tree waiting to abduct Katie. How could he plan on a random person following the girl home on the same exact night that he would try and take her?"

"Jones was following her home? Why?"

Wiggins pursed her lips. "I don't think I should tell you that. Ignorance is bliss and all that. Point is, he *was* following her home and he saw our guy. That was a mistake that, like I said, was unavoidable. But then he started making errors that *were* avoidable. It's almost like he over corrected, and compounded his flaws. Basically, to answer your question, yes, I do think he was a very good planner, and that was why he was able to evade the police for so long. But he made a single blunder that he couldn't have eluded and he panicked. And that's when everything started to unravel."

Tara nodded, seeing the logic. A long interlude followed Wiggins's speech, as Tara looked around the restaurant and meditated on what she had just heard. Before another word could get said, a waiter arrived next to their table.

"Hello, my name's Miguel, I'll be your server this afternoon. Can I get some drinks started for you, ladies?"

Wiggins ordered a Pabst Blue Ribbon and Tara ordered an iced tea. Miguel flashed a tremendously white smile and scampered off toward the bar to prepare their drinks. Immediately after he left, Tara turned back toward Wiggins and made fierce eye contact.

"So do you know who it is?"

Wiggins couldn't help but flash a quick smile, amused at how dramatic the moment was. Tara ignored this, waiting for Wiggins to answer.

"That's actually the main reason I brought you here today. I have a couple of pictures I want you to look at."

Tara jumped a little as she recalled what Wiggins had told her over the phone. "Ah, right! My God, I totally forgot. That was the reason you called in the first place! To have me look at the picture of Anthony Mason. When you said that you had a major update on the case on that phone call, everything else kind of went out the window. And honestly, I don't mean to poo-poo your work or anything, but I just kind of found it hard to believe that such a prominent name in the community would be the guy, so I haven't given Mason much thought."

"Yes, I expected that. Right. Well, anyway, let's look at those pictures, and if you recognize either of them, I can expand on what I have. I know Mason seems far-fetched, but just bear with me anyway."

Wiggins took out her phone. Instead of printing out physical copies of the photographs like she did with Sierra, Wiggins had decided to show Tara the pictures digitally. It saved her having to haul around anything extra. She first brought up the picture of Dan Jenkins that she had found on the web, which was of him standing in front of the American flag.

"That's Anthony Mason?" asked Tara in awe.

"No. This is Dan Jenkins, Newport's district attorney."

"I thought you said the suspect was Anthony Mason?"

"He is *one* of the suspects."

"The DA is the other?"

"I know it sounds preposterous." Wiggins expected the circumspect response from Tara. "But trust me. What I have is extremely suspicious at the very least."

"I don't recognize him. And I don't remember Riley ever interacting with him."

Wiggins had expected this, but she couldn't help but feel her stomach sinking slightly at the news. However, Jenkins wasn't the main target anyway, so she let it roll off.

"Ah, okay. I thought maybe you would have seen him around the time Riley passed away because of your experience with the criminal justice system." Wiggins cast out one last thread regarding Jenkins.

"How would I? Nobody was ever brought to trial."

"Yeah, true. I just thought maybe you would have crossed paths with him at some point or another."

Tara shook her head crossly. "I haven't." It was almost as if she were disappointed in Wiggins for not producing someone better than Dan Jenkins.

"Right. Okay. Let's take a gander at Anthony Mason then."

Wiggins scrolled through the pictures in her phone until she found the one that she had saved of Mason. It was an awkward photo taken at a charity event that Mason looked clearly unhappy to be a part of. In the picture, he was posing with a middle-aged white woman who had black hair and green eyes. Mason was making a facial expression that was supposed to be a smile, but it was so forced that it just looked like he was passing a kidney stone mid-photo. Mason's bald head gleamed in the light of the reflection that Wiggins guessed was from the flash of the camera.

Tara took a hard look at the photograph. She frowned in concentration, and Wiggins felt a flutter in her chest. It was clear that Tara recognized him.

"I totally have talked to him before. He volunteered at the Newport Marathon with me and a bunch of other people last June."

"Really? Interesting. What did you talk about?" Her voice had raised a couple of octaves as it started to strain.

Tara fanned Wiggins down dismissively. "Oh, nothing really. I can't even remember. It was just in passing. Nothing that stands out. It was that guy, though. I recognize him because . . . well . . ."

"Because he's black?" Wiggins raised her brow.

"Well, yeah." Teresa flashed an awkward grin. If there was anything that Newport lacked, it was diversity. There were only three or four black families in the entire county.

"Do you remember him at all from before the marathon? Do you recall him ever interacting with Riley in any way?"

Tara shook her head. She didn't even take a few seconds to think about it. She seemed positive that Riley had never spoken with Mason.

"No. He never did. At least, not that I saw. And . . . I have a pretty good sense of things. I know it is basic human instinct, but I have always been able to tell when there is something off about people. And he didn't give me that sort of feeling when we are at the marathon. Anyway, if he ever came in contact with Riley in front of me, I would have remembered that. And I don't."

"I understand," Wiggins replied. She hadn't put a lot of

stock into this interview with Tara anyway and had tried to shield herself from dismay, but it did feel a little disheartening all the same.

Just then, Miguel the waiter returned, carrying their drinks. He set the iced tea down in front of Tara and the beer in front of Wiggins.

"Do you know what you want to eat?" he asked with flourish. He seemed a little flamboyant and overly energetic.

Tara shrank timidly into her chair. "I think I need a little bit more time to look at the menu."

"No problem! I'll return shortly," he said.

The waiter scurried off, and Tara unfolded the menu. Wiggins could tell that she wasn't really looking at it. Her face was etched with inefficacy and sorrow. Wiggins felt guilty, even though she knew she had done nothing wrong.

"Look, Tara, even though you don't remember these men talking to Katie, that doesn't mean it's not one of them. I have some incredibly damning stuff on Mason in particular."

"I know, I know. It's just . . . This has been going on for so long and I have felt so depressed about it for the last couple of years. So I got my hopes up when you called. I know I shouldn't rule them out, but I was hoping that I would make a solid connection right away so I could be like, 'Yeah, he could definitely be the guy, he totally gave Riley the creeps this one time,' you know?"

"Yeah. But these things don't usually work like that," responded Wiggins.

"I know," said Tara. She looked out the window morosely, taking in the calm panorama of the Pacific Ocean.

Wiggins's next move was one that she considered to be on the borderline of bold and stupid. She wasn't sure what made her do it; after all, they had discussed such manners many times. But for some reason, as a last-ditch effort, she asked a question that she already knew the answer to.

"I know this might piss you off. And I know I have asked you this many times. But perhaps this time you will have a different response. Can you think of *any* older men Riley ever had a bad experience with? Or anyone who gave you a weird vibe?"

Tara smiled, but she was not amused. It was an exasperated smile; a gesture of annoyance more than anything. She shook her head with such force that Wiggins was surprised that her red earrings didn't go flying into the air.

"Of course not, Maryanne. You know I would have told you if there was somebody like that. And my answer isn't going to change no matter how many times you ask."

"The only reason I am asking you again is because I want you to consider possibilities that you haven't considered before. I know you think you have thought of everyone who it could be, but I assure you, you haven't. I want you to open your mind to anything and everything. If there is anyone involved in this thing that has *ever* rubbed you the wrong way, please don't be afraid to share it."

Tara's voice raised about six octaves until it was so shrill that Wiggins almost cringed. "I am not afraid to share it! There isn't anybody. I have thought of every possible scenario, and none of them make any sense."

"So no one that has spoken to you about Riley has *ever* made you feel weird?"

"No!"

"No one has ever given you an odd vibe, even if it didn't make sense?"

"Nope."

"There wasn't any instance of someone who made you feel weird that you didn't want to share with me because you thought it wasn't possible?"

Tara's eyes seemed to mist over as she seemed to be recalling something. "No. Well . . . no."

Wiggins froze. Maybe it was just her imagination, but it seemed like Tara had paused for a moment.

"You hesitated."

Tara leaned back as if Wiggins was accusing her of something terrible. "No, I didn't."

"Yes, you did."

"Maryanne, please."

"You thought of someone."

"No, I didn't! Well, I mean, I did, but it's literally nothing. It's silly."

"Who is it?" Wiggins asked without missing a beat.

"It is insane," said Tara dismissively. "Don't even bother asking about it. It's that silly."

"Didn't I just say to open up your mind to every possibility? Even if it seems totally far out?"

"Yes, you did. But come on. I am embarrassed to even tell you. You will think it's ridiculous," Tara argued. "And all I thought of was someone who once made me feel a little uncomfortable. But it's nothing. If I thought it was something, I would have told you about it a long time ago."

Wiggins made piercing eye contact with Tara and didn't blink. She was almost trying to intimidate her into speaking.

"What's the name?"

X

Wiggins was totally on edge as she pulled out of the parking lot of Georgie's, although she wasn't sure why. It was a minuscule thread that Tara had given her. In all likelihood, it was nothing. Just a pure coincidence. But she needed to look into it to make sure.

As she sped along Elizabeth Street and turned left back to Highway 101, Wiggins felt the hairs on the back of her neck stand. This would make a lot of sense if the name that Tara had given to her was the killer. It would explain unanswered questions that she had about Leighton Jones and Jonah. But Tara was right; it did seem unrealistic on the surface.

As soon as Wiggins got back to her apartment, she started making phone calls. She first dialed Larry Gordon, the father of the girl who had been found in Yaquina Bay with blunt-force trauma to her head. The conversation only lasted five minutes. Sure enough, Gordon provided Wiggins with the same name that Tara had after some brief questioning. It made Wiggins's stomach tighten, but it didn't necessarily confirm anything.

Wiggins then called the mother of Mariah Beckham, the teen who had been found with her wrists slit. The conversation with Beckham's mother was again short, and the woman gave Wiggins the same person whom Gordon and Tara had. Wiggins was now almost positive that she was on to something. Her hands were damp with nervous energy as she hung up and went to call the next person in line.

Throughout the next half hour, Linda Craft, Michael Sizemore, and Stu Larson all were able to provide similar information. The relatives of the Nowhere Girls weren't all able to reiterate the name, but they each were at least able to provide an accurate description of the man. As Wiggins finished the last call, she felt a sense of unyielding triumph. She knew that she had her killer. No more red herrings or false trails. The evidence she had accumulated now against the real culprit was incontrovertible.

The same person had shown up every single time. Every report that was filed when each girl had died was done so by the same individual. She had been right; the killer was in law enforcement. But unless Dan Jenkins was his partner, it wasn't the district attorney. It was a cop. And that cop was Sergeant Rick Casey.

45

"Hello?"

"Ray?"

"Speaking."

"Ray, it's Maryanne Wiggins again."

Giles, Wiggins's friend at the DMV, sighed into the phone, although it sounded like he was being facetious.

"What do you want from me now?" he asked with a chuckle.

"I need another address," Wiggins said seriously, trying to quell the attempted humor from Giles.

"Of course you do."

"The name is Rick Casey."

Giles breathed into the phone, speechless. "Listen, Maryanne, I really can't keep doing this."

"This will be the last time I ever ask this of you," Wiggins said quickly.

Giles scoffed. "Sure it will be."

"Ray, I am telling you, this is important. Lives literally hang in the balance."

For a few seconds, all Wiggins heard was the shuffling and clicking of whatever was happening at the DMV.

"Jesus, Maryanne. You really know how to make me feel the pressure, don't you?"

"I did used to be a cop," Wiggins replied dryly.

"Fine. But you better not ask this of me again for a long time."

"I won't."

Giles sighed again.

"What was the name?"

"Rick Casey."

Giles told Wiggins that he would get back to her within the hour, and she thanked him profusely before hanging up. Back in her apartment, she limped around the living room, pacing like a crazy person. After a few back-and-forths, Wiggins crossed over the threshold to her office, and went right over to the massive shelf that was lined with numerous binders. She quickly located *The Nowhere Girls* and plunked it down onto her desk with a thud.

Tara had said that during her first interaction with Rick Casey, the man had made her feel very uncomfortable. He had shown up at Tara's house after Riley Reid's body was discovered in Olalla Lake, and he had interviewed her about her daughter to get a better feel of what the girl was like and how the incident might have occurred. At least that's what Casey told Tara at the time. Tara had thought Casey tried to control the direction of the interview and totally discredit the idea that Riley's death could have been foul play. He scoffed and snorted every time Tara insinuated that Riley had been murdered, even going as far as telling Tara not to be ridiculous. The reason that Tara had never mentioned this before was because she had simply found the interaction odd; she didn't feel as though Casey could possibly be her daughter's killer. However, Wiggins suspected the interview was more sinister than Tara relayed it to be. After all, there had to be a reason Tara had remembered such a seemingly small interplay after all these years.

It had to be him. The chances of the same exact officer showing up at each crime scene and then subsequently interviewing all family members involved by random chance were infinitesimal. The work the police had done on all seven of the unconfirmed kills had always struck Wiggins as negligent. Now she had found the reason for it. Casey was the one controlling each investigation by altering the initial report to make each death seem like a freak accident or suicide. He was the one controlling the interviews with those involved and feeding the manipulated information back to the Newport Police Department. The only way it could logically fit that Casey was the first one to show up at each crime scene was if he had already known that there would *be* a crime scene.

Casey being the killer also made sense when it came to Jonah and Leighton Jones. He had been the one to show up when Wiggins had called 911 and had planted the seed to go and talk to Randy Marks. Maybe this was because *he* had been the person who had sent the text to Marks from Jonah's phone. As for Jones, the key witness had changed his story only after Casey had gone to speak with him. All of this reeked of a master manipulator directing the case in the way he saw fit. And yet, why hadn't Casey come after Wiggins? He obviously knew that she had at least been on the right track. And if he had killed Jonah because Jonah had found Leighton Jones, why hadn't he killed Wiggins too? She had personally told Casey that she knew about Jones. That part didn't make sense.

Wiggins couldn't discount the idea of Casey having a partner either. After all, somebody else *had* been driving the Jeep when it had pulled up next to Sierra and possibly Casey thrashing about in the brush. But Wiggins was almost ready to rule out Dan Jenkins. She had nothing on him. There had to be some sort of logical reason for Jenkins knowing Katie's abductor had been wearing a ski mask. Perhaps Jonah had tried to talk to him about it to get him to reopen the case after Leighton Jones had changed his story. Jonah hadn't mentioned talking to the district attorney, and his notepad that Wiggins had recovered did not contain any traces of a transcribed interview, but that didn't mean Jonah hadn't had some sort of brief phone interaction with Jenkins.

The only other thing that Wiggins counted as a clue was a slight slip of the tongue during an interview several years earlier when it had sounded like he knew more about Kylie Desmond's disappearance than he was letting on. But nothing of what Wiggins possessed was remotely substantial. And it seemed supremely unlikely that there were two serial killer partners working together in the criminal justice system.

Anthony Mason was a different story. She had accrued plenty of evidence against the coffee shop owner. He had a violent history with the first victim, and he had threatened to kill the last. Perhaps Mason and Casey worked together to pick their victims, and Kylie Desmond and Katie Deeds were Mason's personal choices. Maybe after Mason had gone to prison for assaulting Kylie at the Agate Beach Golf Course, he had sent Casey to kill the girl as revenge, and that was how the whole thing got started. It seemed a little outlandish, but Wiggins was going to look for a link between Casey and Mason.

While slowly turning the pages of the thick-hooped black binder, Wiggins grew impatient. Giles was taking longer than he usually did. She tapped her fingers on her desk, noticing how the pain in her knee had flared up because of the pacing she had done while dwelling upon Rick Casey. Forty-five minutes after their first call had ended, Wiggins's phone finally began to vibrate.

"Hey, Ray," Wiggins said after glancing at the caller ID and picking up the phone.

"Hey, sorry it took so long. Turns out you left me quite a bread-crumb trail to follow!"

"What do you mean?"

"Well, I searched Rick Casey, and I got an address pretty fast. It is 606 Portsmouth Road."

Wiggins wrote this down on a piece of paper in front of her.

"However, I saw an interesting tidbit of info linked to Casey's license. Apparently, he changed his last name in 1985."

"What?"

"Yeah. The first license the DMV issued to him was in the mid-seventies, and he was registered under a different last name, which was his birth name, I think."

"What's the name?" Wiggins's mind sped 100 miles an hour.

"Desmond."

46

So here it was. The truth staring Wiggins right in the face. She thought she had all the answers now. After years and years of accumulating hundreds of pages of documents for the thick black binder that was sitting on the desk in front of her, she was positive that she had reached the endgame. The final twist.

Wiggins had persuaded Giles to answer one last question for her on the phone call. And since he had already brought up Rick Desmond's information, the DMV employee had granted this request. According to Giles, the SUV that was registered to Rick was the exact model Wiggins had thought it would be: a 2000 Jeep Wrangler in forest green. The same vehicle that Sierra Bunker had described. Not only that, but the Jeep was also registered in someone else's name: Brendan Desmond.

After the call with Giles, Wiggins had done some brief research and spent a half hour making phone calls around the county gathering more intelligence. And what she had found was sparse but still illuminating.

Marilyn and Thomas Desmond had had three children: Kenny, Brendan, and Rick. The three brothers had lived in Lincoln County their entire lives. Two of the siblings had taken over their father's landscaping business, while the final brother had become a cop. That was all Wiggins had in concrete facts, but she had much more in theory. She believed that one of the men, Kenny, had gone on to live a life full of sorrow and heartbreak after losing his daughter, Kylie, to a brutal murder. The other two, unbeknownst to Kenny, had formed a dangerous alliance, first killing their niece and going on to terrorize Lincoln County for three decades.

Brendan, a lumbering man whom Wiggins had encountered briefly before her initial interview with Kenny, was the other killer and Rick's partner. The only reason Rick would change his surname was because the name had some sort of sinister meaning lying beneath the surface that could bring Rick down if anyone ever caught on to the connection. It meant that someone else inside the Desmond family tree had assisted in killing Kylie and all the other girls. The fact that Brendan was the second owner of the Jeep was the icing on the cake.

The man now known as Rick Casey had changed his last name the year after his niece, Kylie, had gone missing. There was no way that could be a coincidence. He had also joined the police force right after he had swapped names. It seemed likely to Wiggins that Rick had become a cop purely for the leverage he would possess in regards to the case. And it had worked. He was an excellent orchestrator, killing at will and throwing his colleagues off the trail each time he did.

As Wiggins sat in her office and thought of Kenny, she became furious. When the broken, battered man found out that his brothers had conspired to kill his daughter, he would lose any sense of purpose and goodwill he had left. Those bastards had preyed upon an innocent, kind-hearted soul who loved his daughter more than anything in the world. Wiggins's hands turned white as she clutched the desk in pure wrath, thinking of the victimized old man who was currently sitting in a wheelchair, with his spine and heart shattered. She would make his two brothers pay.

Wiggins began to wonder if Kenny had ever caught on to his brother's exploits. After all, he jointly ran a business with Brendan, so he must have been privy to some sort of suspicious behavior over the years. But he probably never even entertained the idea that his brother and business partner was a criminal, let alone a serial killer. And Wiggins had a feeling that Brendan was sort of just a crony of sorts; Rick was the one who was pulling all the strings.

As she sat staring at the black binder in front of her, Wiggins was no longer feeling triumphant. The euphoric, jovial feeling of finally cracking the case she had worked on for so long had dissipated. It was now replaced with a sense of nervousness and dread. She had spent hundreds of hours trying to decipher who the killer was, but she had never even given a second of thought to what she would do if she ever did hone in on a suspect. She couldn't call the police, obviously. She had no proof, and one of her killers *was* the police. Even calling Albert Amos seemed foolish, because it would likely get back around to Rick. What was she to do? The only thing that she could think of was to confront Rick or Brendan and try and force them into talking. But that was obviously risky. She would have to do it somewhere public, where the man she picked would not harm her. And she would have to bring her gun just in case.

Who would she go after first? Wiggins didn't dare try and bring them both down at the same time. Two burly, tall men against one crippled middle-aged woman? It would be much smarter to pick them off one by one. But which was the bigger fish to fry? Rick seemed like the alpha male. The one directing the chaos. He should be the priority.

After mulling it over, Wiggins came up with a mental

blueprint. She would call Rick and get him to agree to a meeting in some sort of public setting. She would have her phone in her pocket recording the conversation as a voice memo. And she would play hardball with the man.

Ten minutes later, she received a text from her friend Albert Amos. She had sent him a message trying to procure Rick Desmond's cell phone number. Amos had simply responded with nine digits. Taking a deep breath, she only thought about it for five more seconds before pressing the button with fervor.

Ring. Ring. Ring.

Wiggins gulped. It was so bizarre to realize that she was calling the killer that she had sought for so long.

Ring. Ring. Ring.

Would she give herself away? Her heart was thudding like an 808 drum in her chest. She had always been a good actor, but had never felt this much pressure before.

Ring. Ring. Ring.

Maybe he wasn't going to answer. Should she leave him a voice mail?

Ring. Ring. Ring.

She was going to have to alter this plan. He wasn't going to pick up.

Ring.

"Hello?"

Wiggins's voice caught in her throat. She couldn't find the words to respond, knowing who she was speaking with.

"Hello?" the voice said again.

"Is this Rick?"

"Yes, it is. Who is this?"

"This is Maryanne Wiggins. The private investigator. We spoke in person a couple of weeks back regarding Jonah Carr."

"Ahhh," Rick said, sounding most displeased.

"Yeah, I usually receive that sort of response when people realize whose calling," Wiggins said, trying to break the tension.

The line stayed quiet, as Rick apparently didn't find Wiggins amusing.

"Anyway, I have a request," Wiggins continued, unsure of how else to put it.

Rick groaned into the receiver. "I'm sure this is going to be good."

"It actually is probably not what you think. I was hoping to meet with you in person."

Rick made a strange noise that was supposed to signal his annoyance. "For what exactly?"

"I'd rather not say over the phone. But it is something that is rather important."

"It sounds like a waste of time," Rick said bluntly.

"It won't be. It has nothing to do with Jonah Carr."

"It doesn't?" Rick sounded surprised.

"Nope."

"What *does* it have to do with?"

"Like I said, I don't particularly want to divulge it over the phone. How about we meet in person?"

There was a long instance of complete silence. Wiggins was sure he was going to say no. But curiosity apparently got the better of him.

"Fine. When and where do you want to meet?"

"Oh, I don't know." Wiggins tried to sound nonchalant. "How about later this afternoon at the park by the Performing Arts Center?"

"Like what time this afternoon?"

"Oh, say four?"

"Hmm. Alright."

"Great. See you there!" Wiggins said excitedly. There was suddenly silence on the line, as Rick had hung up without saying bye.

It was still two hours until four, but Wiggins began preparing for her showdown while sitting at her desk in her office. She texted Amos again, just letting him know that she was meeting Rick at the park. She didn't divulge why, and Amos had replied with a simple, "OK." He probably thought it was a strange message, but just in case something happened to her, she wanted someone to know where she was going and what she was planning on doing.

After Wiggins texted Amos, she fiddled with her notepad, attempting to write down questions but knowing it was going to be unlike any interview she had done before. She reached out and grabbed the *Nowhere Girls* binder and flipped through the pages, trying to build up her confidence for her impending confrontation. These were the girls. The innocent. The forgotten. She had to do this for them. Finally, finding a new sense of resolve, she pulled open her desk's drawer and withdrew her pistol, making sure that there were indeed bullets inside the chamber.

Birds chirped incessantly and clouds collected overhead like congealed gray gumdrops. The grass that made up the vast fields was covered in a thin layer of dew and the trees swayed gently as they were caught by a benign breeze. Several joggers that were barely dots in Wiggins's vision circled glacially around the exterior of the park, and a woman carrying her baby in a stroller speed-walked while she spoke on the phone. In the distance, Wiggins saw the outline of a large figure with a sharp buzz cut sitting on a park bench. Rick Desmond was still wearing his police uniform. Wiggins walked slowly over to him, trying not to focus on how her leg seemed to be swelling with each step. Rick caught sight of her and gave a robotic wave. She returned the gesture. Once she was within a few feet of him, Wiggins initiated conversation.

"Hello, sergeant."

"Hello, uh . . . what do I even call you?"

Wiggins shrugged her shoulders. "Well, don't call me private. And I don't think investigator is right either."

"So what the he—"

"Just call me Maryanne. Or Wiggins, if you feel like we aren't on a first-name basis."

"Fine, *Wiggins*." Rick hurled her surname as though it were a particularly nasty insult. "I do hope this doesn't take very long. I have actual stuff to do."

Wiggins pulled out her phone, pretending to check the time. After making sure it was recording in the voice memo utility, she placed it back in her pocket upside down so that the sound receiver was poking out of her black slacks.

"Oh, it won't take long at all. I will let you resume your 'actual stuff' in no time."

Rick mumbled under his breath. Wiggins couldn't hear what he said. She assumed it wasn't pleasant, and therefore didn't ask him to repeat it before sitting in the vacant spot next to Rick on the park bench.

"Alright, I won't beat around the bush since we are on a time constraint. Here, let me get my list of questions."

Wiggins withdrew her notepad and took an unnecessarily long amount of time to flip to the page that had her inquiries.

"Okay, so . . . how are you?"

Rick let out a deep belly laugh. Her attempt to be humorous had finally gotten through.

"You know, I'm just fine," Rick replied with a big grin plastered on his face.

"That's good," Wiggins said, forcing a smile back. Underneath her facade of humor and lightheartedness, she felt very tense.

Wiggins looked down at her notepad, although nothing meaningful was written on it. She had to feign as though she was conducting a normal interview. She looked back up at Rick and pretended to proffer a kind expression.

"First, I want to apologize for the way I acted when I spoke with you before. I was a little overbearing, and I am sorry."

Rick waved his hand while still smiling.

"No worries. Water under the bridge."

"Good, good." Wiggins nodded "I'm glad. Well, anyway, let's get down to brass tacks. What kind of car do you drive, officer?"

The amiable grin that had been on Rick's face vanished and was replaced with an expression of complete befuddlement. Wiggins had said the question so abruptly that it had thrown the man for a loop.

"Why do you want to know that?"

"Just humor me, sergeant. It will all make sense here in a second," Wiggins said, taking his brusqueness in stride.

"Fine." Rick's ill mood had returned. "I drive a Pontiac G8."

"And is this car registered in your name?"

Rick scrunched up his forehead in vexation. "Again, why do you want to know that?"

"Please, sergeant."

"Alright, then. No. It's under ex-wife's."

"Why are you driving your ex-wif—"

"Because I paid all the damn money for it, that's why!" Rick spouted before Wiggins could finish.

"Okay, okay. Relax."

Telling Rick to relax was the wrong move. He turned a magnificent shade of fuchsia, as his temper threatened to rupture several veins in his forehead.

"Please tell me why this is relevant."

"Because I want to know why a 2000 Jeep Wrangler is registered in your name at the DMV."

For several long seconds, Rick remained silent while his face slowly became stony.

"How do you know that?" He said it so quietly it was more

like a hiss.

"Does that really matter, officer? I think the more pressing issue is why there is a vehicle in your name that matches a description of an SUV that was used in the attempted kidnapping of seventeen-year-old Sierra Bunker."

Rick's eyes became comically wide, and if it were any other setting, Wiggins would have laughed.

"Are you saying what I think you're saying?"

"I'm not saying anything. I am simply asking."

Rick stayed silent. He wasn't even attempting to find an answer to her question. He sat there, staring at her malevolently.

"Why did you change your name, Mr. Desmond?"

At first, Rick's face showed only blank shock. Wiggins's sudden foray into the new subject matter had again taken the man off guard. This was intentional on her part. Being blunt was a better way to ensure genuine reactions. Slowly but surely, his upper lip furled into a snarl.

"Mr. Desmond?"

"Don't call me that!" he hissed, looking around to make sure no one was in earshot.

"But it's your name."

"You think I want people to know that?"

"Why, Mr. Desmond? Why don't you want people to know?"

"Why the fuck do you think?" Rick strained to keep his voice quiet.

"Enlighten me," said Wiggins pleasantly.

"Because of what happened to my niece, you bimbo! Her death is practically taught as a lesson in Bible school in this town! Everyone knows about it, even thirty years later. She disappeared for ten years for Christ's sake! Her skull was found in a car! You think I want to be tied to that? You really believe that I want people to hear my name and think, *Oh, is he related to that Kylie girl? What happened to her was so awful.* No! I don't!" Rick spat all in one breath. His throat moved up and down like an elevator as it recovered from his epic tirade.

Wiggins took a few seconds to consider this. It was a well-reasoned, if totally rehearsed, response.

"So that's why you did it then? Not to distance yourself from the name because there was a more sinister meaning attached to it?"

Rick leaned back and raised his eyebrows. "What on earth is that supposed to mean?"

"I just think it's odd that you changed the name a year after Kylie died. And right before you joined the force."

"Great. I'm glad you think so. Is this why you wanted to meet with me? To grill me about my family history?"

"Well, that, and my first question, which you never answered. Why is it that a vehicle that matches the description of the one Sierra Bunker's abductor was driving is registered under your name?"

Rick just shook his head. He placed his hands on the wooden bench underneath him, and for a fleeting moment, Wiggins thought he was going to get up and leave.

"You think there is only one green Jeep in Newport? There are ten thousand people here. The town's small, but not that small."

"No, I don't think that. But here is what I *do* think, Mr. Desmond—"

"Stop fucking calling me that!"

"I think that there was an ulterior motive behind you becoming a cop. I don't think you did it because you sought to bring justice on criminals and keep the streets of Newport safe. I think you did it to cover your tracks."

Rick made indistinguishable noises; he was so flustered that he couldn't form a complete sentence.

"Cover my . . . what?"

"I think you killed your niece, Rick Desmond. I think you

changed your name so that no one would make the connection. I also think you killed four other girls between 1992 and 1995. They almost got you, didn't they? You were close to being caught after you murdered Jenna Eason and Cara Lee, so you changed. Oh no, I don't think you stopped killing. But you sure as hell did a lot better of a job of covering your ass after that. I think you started making the deaths look like accidents, and in the cases of Mariah Beckham and Katie Deeds, suicide."

Rick's mouth twitched as he glowered at Wiggins. His face was contorted in a mixture of anger and consternation. But he didn't say anything.

"I think that you were the first one who showed up when each of the other eight girls turned up dead because you were the one who killed them, and you were the one who wanted to make sure that nobody would ever figure out what you did. Hell, you want to know what I think?" Wiggins raised her voice by a fraction. She didn't know where this sudden disposition of strength was coming from, but it was aiding her in taking down her prey. Rick recoiled as though she were about to strike him. He fumbled over his words, trying to respond. Wiggins ignored this and continued.

"I think you murdered Katie Deeds too. I think you made a mistake, and weren't aware that Leighton Jones was following her home that night. I think that once you came to the realization that he was the one who saw you hiding behind a fucking tree in a ski mask, you went to Jones's house and tried to persuade him not to talk. But then, after you thought it over, you decided to remove the threat altogether. You killed Leighton Jones, didn't you, Mr. Desmond?"

Rick's face was so red that he looked like he was about to combust. "Wha . . . I . . . This is ridiculous!"

"And then Jonah Carr got on your trail. I think he made you feel the heat, didn't he? And that's why you killed him. You were the one who sent that text to Randy Marks from Jonah's phone, weren't you, Mr. Desmond? And you were the one to show up when I called with the address that Jonah was missing from because you had just been there to kill him the night before."

"Stop. Please stop." Rick covered his ears.

"I think you're a real sick fuck, Rick Desmond. Was it your niece that started all of this? Did you catch yourself having unspeakable thoughts one day? You spent so much time around her when she lived with you and Kenny that you couldn't help but be overcome with thoughts of longing, could you? Your perverse sexual attraction toward Kylie reached a boiling point, until one day you imagined what it would be like to watch her die. Did you get hard thinking about that, Mr. Desmond?"

"Enough!" Rick screamed at the top of his lungs.

Every one of the other park goers around them looked in their direction. Rick reminded Wiggins of a caged animal. In one motion, Rick pushed himself off the bench and began storming off. The move was so abrupt that it caught Wiggins by surprise. She watched as he marched away, and she felt a sinking feeling in her stomach. The prospects of getting a confession right off the bat were never good, but she thought she would get more from the man than this. Wiggins almost debated getting up and following him.

Suddenly, before Wiggins could take any action, Rick stopped in his tracks. He stood like a sentinel in the middle of the sidewalk. He turned around slowly and glared at Wiggins, looking demented. Without warning, he prowled back in her direction. It was Wiggins's turn to feel a pang of fear. She grasped the pistol that was inside her hidden holster and pointed the muzzle of the gun in Rick's direction without removing it from behind the curtain of her coat.

When he was within two feet of Wiggins, Rick stopped and put one hand on the back of the bench. Goosebumps ran down Wiggins's spine as the man leaned in so close that she could feel his breath on her neck. She kept her gun pointing right at his sternum and her finger tightly wrapped around the trigger. The adrenaline pounding through her was urging her to pull, but she didn't. She simply waited for what Rick was going to do.

"Keep walking down this path and you'll end up in the same place as them," Rick whispered into Wiggins's ear. He said it so soft and low that there was no possible way her phone recorder would have picked it up. Before Wiggins could respond, Rick whipped about and walked off again. Within a minute, he was out of sight, and Wiggins was left on the park bench with cold sweat on her arms and every cell in her body possessed by fear.

47

Wiggins sat on the park bench for a good ten minutes trying to calm herself. Her fingers were tingling as blood rushed to her more vital organs, a physiological byproduct of the fight-or-flight response, unable to delineate actual danger from perceived danger. She took out her phone and ended the recording. It only took her a few moments to scroll through the digital file and find the segment where Rick had essentially confessed to his crimes. But, as Wiggins suspected, his whisper was so muffled that it was inaudible. *Damn,* she thought.

Should she go to the police? Surely Wiggins had enough to persuade them to look into Rick. But she didn't want to go to Amos and put him in the compromising position of either ratting out his colleague or throwing Wiggins under the bus. Perhaps the best idea was to find someone who worked for Internal Affairs at the station and run the theory by them. Maybe even submit an anonymous tip.

As Wiggins rubbed her left hand against her thigh over and

over, as if the motion somehow aided her in dispelling the unpleasant feelings of anxiety, she felt her phone vibrate. A quick glance at the screen showed her that the call was coming from a private number.

Wiggins felt her gut clench. Was this someone calling to harass her? An agent of Rick's perhaps? Maybe it was even Rick's partner in crime and brother, Brendan, calling to further the threat that Rick had issued. Wiggins agonized over whether to pick up the call. Finally, she pressed the phone to her ear and took the call.

"Hello?"

A robotic automated voice answered her.

"*Hello. You have a collect call from an inmate at Coffee Creek Correctional Facility. Will you accept the charges? Press 1 to accept. Press 2 to ignore.*"

Wiggins almost leaped off the bench. She nearly pressed the wrong button out of sheer excitement.

"Hello?"

"Is this Maryanne Wiggins?" a wheezy voice asked.

"Yes, it is."

"Well, shit. I guess there is no going back now, is there?" Joanne Fellner coughed.

"Joanne?"

"Yeah, why? You field a lot of calls from women's prisons?"

"I've received my fair share," Wiggins retorted sarcastically. Fellner let out a guffaw that was wrought with gravelly phlegm.

"Can't imagine what your line of work must be like."

"And I can't imagine what living in a women's prison is like," Wiggins said, a little surprised at how she was maintaining her usual dry wit even after being shaken to her core by Rick.

"It really ain't bad, I'll tell you that. Just got to find yourself a good cucumber."

"I don't even want to know," Wiggins said quickly. Fellner laughed again. The woman was already showing more levity and warmness than she ever had to Wiggins before.

"So what can I do for you, Joanne?"

There was a tiny respite as Fellner seemed to be working up the courage to say what she had planned on saying.

"Joe gave me your message about Eleanor. How she's safe. At least how she is in another state."

Wiggins waited, but Fellner let silence ensue.

"And?"

"And I've changed my mind."

Wiggins felt her stomach do several cartwheels. Perhaps she wouldn't need a confession from Rick after all.

"About what, Joanne?"

"I'm sorry that I kept this a secret for so long. I couldn't risk Eleanor's safety. But . . . you were right all along. I know who killed all them girls," she whispered.

"You do?"

"Uh-huh."

"Didn't you tell Jonah Carr that you didn't know the man's name? That it was just a random stranger you met at the bar?"

"That was a lie."

Wiggins's ears were so in tune to the phone call now that she felt like she could've heard a pin drop.

"Who was it, Joanne?"

The longest silence yet followed this question. Wiggins wondered if Fellner was still there.

"It was Eleanor's father."

Wiggins clasped her hand to her mouth in disbelief.

"Her *father*?"

"Yeah."

"Were you still seeing him at the time?"

"I *was,* yeah."

Wiggins closed her eyes as one more thread of the mystery

was unraveled. This made so much more sense. Fellner hadn't just been protecting her daughter. She had also been holding out because she didn't want everyone to know that the father of her child was a killer.

"Who is it, Joanne? What's his name?"

"Brendan. Brendan Desmond."

X

Wiggins closed her eyes. *Of course,* she thought.

"Brendan Desmond?"

"That's right."

Wiggins felt a rush of joy mixed with annoyance. How could she have missed it? Retroactively, it seemed so obvious. How could she have been so shortsighted to think that Fellner was just a random stranger who had stumbled onto the pictures of Cara Lee and Jenna Eason? Hindsight was 20/20, but it seemed patently stupid to have missed this for so long.

"So you and Brendan were in a relationship? How long were you seeing each other?" Wiggins attempted to push past her self-loathing.

"Oh, about three years. He got me pregnant a year after we started seein' each other."

"And you never noticed anything suspicious during your time with him? Up until you found those pictures and the bloody shirt? Or is that part not true either?"

"No, that part is true."

"Tell me exactly what happened regarding that incident."

"Uh, okay. I was over at his house. We still weren't livin' together even though we had been together for so long and had a kid. I had a separate apartment where me and Eleanor stayed. That bastard kept givin' me this shit about not bein' ready. But we had been together for three years at that point, right? And we had a goddamned child. If he wasn't ready then, when was he ever going to be ready? Once I found out what he was really doing with his time, that made a lot more sense though. He probably didn't want me and Eleanor living with him because he was busy huntin' all those girls, right? That twisted bastard."

"So what happened the night that you found the shirt and the pictures?"

"Oh right. I was over at his house. I had a babysitter that night for Eleanor. But anyway, we had just fucked and Brendan was taking a shower. So, I decided to make myself something to eat in the kitchen. When I was walking through the hallway I stepped on a loose floorboard. It seemed weird because it was such a nice house, right? So I bent over to see what was up with it, and it came out without any effort at all. In the tiny space below there was a bloody white blouse and a little box full of pictures of those two girls. Eason and Lee."

Fellner paused after saying this and swallowed loudly into the phone receiver. Whether it was to simply clear her throat or because she was getting choked up with emotion, Wiggins couldn't be sure.

"It only took me about a minute to figure it out. I mean, all the little things that I couldn't make sense of before suddenly made perfect sense. All that time he spent away from me and his daughter. All the shady behavior. God, for the longest time I thought he was cheatin' on me. I always was so scared of that. But now I would give anything for him to have just been cheating on me," Fellner said with a humorless laugh.

"Anyway, when I put two and two together, I was so shocked that I just sat there staring at the pictures. Couldn't even stand up. When Brendan got out of the shower, he found me there. God, I'll never forget the look on his face. He was so scared. I was too, obviously. To find out that the father of my kid is a . . ."

"Killer," Wiggins finished for her.

"Yeah. I mean . . . it's almost kind of funny now, you know? How ridiculous it was. It was so unreal. Can you imagine what it is like to uncover that about someone you thought you knew? Let alone someone you figured you were in love with. I mean . . . God damn."

Wiggins shifted around uncomfortably. "So what did you do?"

"Nothin'. I just sat there. That's when he said it."

"Said what?"

"He told me to leave. And never come back. That he never wanted to see me or Eleanor again. And that if I ever told anyone what I had found, he would kill me and my baby."

"Jesus," Wiggins replied in disgust.

There was a prolonged break in the dialogue. Joanne apparently needed more prompting before she continued.

"So you left? And you thought he would make good on his threat? Even though it was his own daughter?"

"Yeah, I left. And I mean, of course. He seemed to have no problem killin' his niece, did he?"

Wiggins thought of Kenny, fractured and maimed in a wheelchair. She immediately began to get angry again, realizing how Kenny had been victimized by his two brothers. Brendan Desmond, like Rick, was truly a monster.

"That was the worst part of it all," Fellner continued, and Wiggins was shook out of her brief stupor. "Realizing that the man I loved was the one who did that to Ky . . . Kylie."

With a sinking feeling, Wiggins realized that Fellner was crying. Part of her was feeling sympathetic, but she was also plagued with a bout of sudden confusion. Why would Fellner be reacting this way over Brendan's erstwhile niece whom she had never met?

"I'm sorry, Joanne. I know it must be difficult to realize that your boyfriend had killed members of his own family," Wiggins said tentatively. It was a stab in the dark; she had no idea why Fellner was so upset.

Between sobs, the woman started to form a muddled

sentence.

"H-his family? W-what about m-my family?"

"Your family?"

Wiggins was totally bamboozled. What on earth was Fellner talking about? After a few moments of being completely perplexed, it suddenly made sense. For what felt like the tenth time in the past two weeks, Wiggins was blindsided yet again by another shocking turn of events.

"Wait . . . Kylie Desmond was your *daughter*?"

48

Wiggins sat at the park bench in disbelief, holding the phone to her ear. How could it be been possible?

She never heard Fellner answer her question. All that reached her ears was the melancholy tones of the woman continuing to sob uncontrollably into the receiver. Wiggins took a moment to let Fellner cleanse herself of grief. Then, after Fellner regained some semblance of composure, Wiggins repeated her question.

"Kylie Desmond was your daughter?"

"Y-yes," Fellner said timidly.

Wiggins's gut leapt. The self-loathing she had unleashed on herself over not realizing that Brendan was Eleanor's father paled in comparison to what she was feeling now. How could she have been so stupid? Joanne Fellner was her key witness. How could she possibly have neglected to find such a vital connection, and to the very first victim no less? She *had* done a bit of legwork trying to find Kylie Desmond's mother, but not nearly enough. Nobody seemed to have any idea it was. The inkling that Wiggins had gotten at the time was that Kylie was the product of a one-night stand. Kenny Desmond had told her as much and had added that Kylie's mom had been "out of the picture" for years. But now, on the other end of the line, there she was. Joanne Fellner. Feeling hatred toward her own ineptitude, she pressed forward in the conversation.

"So is Brendan the real father?"

"No, no, no. Of course not. Kenny is."

Wiggins leaned back into the bench. "Okay, I seem to be missing something here."

Fellner sighed into the phone. She had apparently not realized that this was going to come up. When she launched into her explanation, she was talking inexorably fast, as though she were hoping to get it over with as soon as possible.

"I met Kenny at the bar in 1970. I was only sixteen at the time. But back then, nobody cared about that kinda thing. Either of those things, actually. I looked older than I was so nobody ever knew or cared that I was too young to drink. And Kenny was only twenty. Honestly, the age gap never mattered to us. And *my* parents sure as shit didn't care what I was up to," Fellner said, resentment in her tone.

"So . . . you hooked up with Kenny?"

"Yeah. I was young and horny and so was he. And at that age you're so naive and just excited to be with an older guy, right? So, I let him do whatever he wanted."

"And I'm guessing what he wanted was to not wear a condom," Wiggins said dryly.

"You're good at this."

"He got you pregnant?"

"Yup. And I didn't even realize it until I was well into my second trimester."

"I bet your parents weren't thrilled about having a pregnant teenage daughter."

Fellner laughed. “Yeah, you could say that. My dad wanted to kick me out, but my mom wouldn’t let him. I even had to drop out of school and everything to take care of Kylie. When I was eighteen, my dad refused to let me live there anymore. I didn’t have a place to stay, and I couldn’t take care of a two-year-old on my own. So, I gave her to Kenny. And he raised her after that.”

“But he knew about Kylie before then, right?”

“Oh yeah. He was payin’ child support for the first two years.”

“And you didn’t ever try and maintain a relationship with Kenny after the night you hooked up with him, did you?” Wiggins asked, although she knew the answer.

“Oh God, no. No, we both knew what that night was.”

Wiggins rubbed her knee. The uncomfortable bench she sat on was doing no favors to her legs.

“So how did you meet Brendan?”

“Well, when Kylie disappeared, I went over to meet with Kenny to talk about the whole thing. And that’s how I met Brendan. It was the first time I had been over to Kenny’s house in twelve years. He had full custody and never let me see Kylie. Thought I would be a bad influence on her. But I came over then because . . . you know. She was gone.”

Fellner’s voice caught again.

“But I thought you didn’t start dating Brendan until the early nineties?” Wiggins tried to keep Fellner focused on the task at hand.

“We didn’t. I met him in eighty-four. But we didn’t start really talking until ninety-two. I ran into him at Rip Tide’s one night and recognized him. We started talkin’ about Kylie. He pretended to be all sympathetic and shit. Here I was thinkin’ that me and this guy were bondin’ over someone we had both loved and lost. But he was just usin’ it to get me on his side. God, it makes me sick now. Knowin’ that that sick bastard was the one who killed her all along."

"And so Brendan got you pregnant with Eleanor a year after that?"

"Right."

"Did Kenny have a problem with that?"

"If he did, he didn't get in the way of it. But he never came and saw Eleanor. Honestly, I think Kenny just thought I was a whore and didn't want anything to do with me. He had to take care of Kylie, but he sure as hell wasn't going to have a relationship with his niece if he didn't have to."

"So Eleanor and Kylie are half-sisters," Wiggins said, more thinking out loud then anything.

"I guess so. But Kylie was dead before Eleanor was even born."

Wiggins wasn't sure what to say to this. It was a deeply unsettling and morbid thought.

"So that's why you were so afraid of Brendan? You were certain that his ultimatum of killing Eleanor wasn't an empty threat because you knew he had already murdered your other daughter?"

"Exactly."

Wiggins nodded subconsciously, even though she was aware that Fellner couldn't see this gesture.

"So why now, Joanne? Why are you finally coming to me with this after all this time?"

"I knew you were going to ask me that."

"It just seems strange. I have given you many opportunities over the years to speak to me about this. And I know you feared for your daughter's safety. But it seems like me telling you that Eleanor lives in another state wouldn't totally expel that fear." She was trying to be tactful; she didn't want to make Fellner reconsider her stance in case she would have to testify in the future. But she also didn't quite understand what had motivated Fellner to talk.

"I mean . . . it definitely helps. If Brendan doesn't know where she is, he would probably have a tough time finding her. I was the one who raised her, and I had no idea she was in Moscow freakin' Idaho. I didn't even know there *was* a Moscow, Idaho."

Wiggins chuckled. "True. It isn't exactly New York City. But still. I feel like there must be more to it than that."

Fellner took a few seconds to answer. "Truthfully, it was something that reporter said. The one you sent to talk to me."

"Jonah Carr. And I didn't send him. He insisted upon it."

"Whatever. It was something that he said that made me start thinkin' about it."

Wiggins felt her stomach contract in guilt.

"What did he say?"

"He told me that the families of all the other girls have been feeling exactly what I fear the most for years. And I know that seems, you know, obvious. But I had never thought about it in that way before."

"In what way?"

"It's not like I hadn't thought of the other girls before. But thinkin' about it like that. That those families have been feelin' the same way I felt about Kylie. Except worse, because they have no idea who did it or why. And I can't imagine losing another daughter. Losing Eleanor. Because I raised her, you know? So . . . that is my biggest fear. Losing her. And all those other families already felt that when their girls disappeared."

"I guess that makes sense," Wiggins replied, but her tone was unable to conceal what she really thought. Fellner was right; all of this seemed like conclusions she could have arrived at on her own without Jonah's help.

"And don't get me wrong. I've wanted to bring that piece of shit down ever since I found out it was him. I guess I just decided it was time to do what I should have done all along. I'm still scared for Eleanor. But it's time to make this right."

Wiggins felt an indomitable sense of resolve. She knew Fellner was firmly on her side now, and that might be her trump card if this case ever went to trial. She still hadn't brought up Rick; she was fairly sure that Fellner remained ignorant to the fact that Rick was Brendan's partner and the likely alpha male in the partnership. Perhaps she would run the idea by Fellner later. It seemed like it would overcomplicate things if she brought it up now.

"Well, thank you, Joanne. I appreciate you coming forward. I know this must have been difficult for you."

"I figured it was time."

"I assume you know what this means for the future?"

"Huh?"

"If I apprehend Brendan and the police arrest him, you will have to testify in open court."

"Oh, that. Yeah, yeah, I know," Fellner said, as if Wiggins had simply reminded her to mow her lawn.

"So you will do it?"

"Yeah. As long as you're sure that son of a bitch will go down if I do."

"I am."

49

When Wiggins got back to her apartment, she was dwelling on her intense interaction with Rick and her revealing conversation with Fellner. She had come so far in the past hour that it was totally surreal. Having received what was essentially a confession from one of her suspects, buttressed by a witness's damning evidence against the other culprit, she was now sitting pretty. It was going to be tough bringing them down, but at least she was a hundred percent certain who the two killers were.

What next? Go harder after Rick or begin to pursue Brendan? Surely after she got one, the other would soon follow. But it would be immensely difficult to corner Rick now. The only thing that she could feasibly do would be to bring the whole thing to an Internal Affairs officer and hope for the best. Brendan was the much lower hanging fruit. The most logical plan of action would be to meet Brendan and try to force a confession out of him like she had done with Rick. Rick obviously would have told Brendan what she had put together, but if she could somehow surprise him, she might be able to coerce him into confessing. Therefore, after hobbling around her apartment for a while, Wiggins made up her mind that she was going to have to call the Desmond household.

Every few seconds she looked out of the window anxiously, as if Rick would suddenly appear outside. She still had her gun on her person, and fiddled with it every time she glanced out of her blinds. Her hands were sweating a little as she grabbed her phone after one last gander out the window, making it difficult to dial the number that she had saved on a sticky note.

"Hello?"

Wiggins recognized Kenny's voice.

"Hey, Kenny. This is Maryanne Wiggins again."

"Who?"

Wiggins couldn't help but smile.

"Maryanne Wiggins. The private investigator. I called not too long ago asking you about Anthony Mason."

"Oh, right, you. Sorry, that was stupid of me. Not good with names," Kenny said with a wheezy laugh.

"That's totally fine! I won't hold it against you. I'm a pretty ordinary person, so it's not surprising that you don't remember me."

Kenny chuckled again.

"Hey, so is your brother there?"

"Brendan?"

"Well, I'm not talking about Rick."

"Rick? Wait . . . How do you know that Rick is my brother?"

"He told me."

"He did? That's funny. I was under the impression that he would use any means possible to deny that we are related."

"Anyway, yes, I mean Brendan."

"Why do you want to talk to Brendan?" Kenny asked with apprehension.

"Oh, just have a few questions I want to ask him about the case." Wiggins kept her voice light. She was planning on telling Kenny her suspicions, but she preferred to do it in person instead of over the phone.

"Questions that I can't answer?"

"Well, without getting into too much detail, I need to hear from him specifically."

"Hmm. He ain't here right now. Do you want me to take a message?"

"Actually, do you know when he might be home? Perhaps I could talk to him in person." Wiggins thought her request was likely to be met by annoyance. But Kenny expressed no sign of irritation.

"Uh, yeah, sure. He will be home in about an hour probably. You could come over then? Unless you're too busy."

"Actually, that would be perfect!"

"Great. Should I let him know you are coming?"

"That's okay actually. You don't have to. This meeting isn't that important. It will probably last like five minutes tops. Don't want him to think it is a big deal or something and get all weirded out." Wiggins hoped beyond hope that Kenny would agree not to text Brendan. If he knew she was coming, Brendan probably wouldn't show up.

"Okay. That's fine."

Wiggins felt her chest swoop in excitement. "Okay. See you in a bit."

X

Wiggins drove along the winding Bay Road, looking at the soft fall sun glimmering on the water to her right. The light was peeking through an otherwise gray sky, portioning the clouds in half. The trees to her left were larger than normal, as though they were reflecting the impending confrontation that Wiggins felt she was about to have with Brendan Desmond.

She was much more afraid now than she had been to go and speak with Rick. No matter how twisted of a person he was, Rick was far too intelligent to physically harm Wiggins in a public setting like the park where they had met earlier that day. But this was different. Brendan was a wild card. She had no template to predict how he might act when cornered and confronted. Also, she was meeting him in the privacy of his home. Kenny would be there too, but he was a crippled old man in a wheelchair. What use could he be if Brendan decided to lash out? She knew this whole thing was undercooked and possibly foolish. But she was desperate. She had to corner her new enemies before they cornered her.

As Wiggins turned and pushed her Audi up the steep hill where she knew the Desmonds's house to be, she mentally recited the names of the Nowhere Girls in her head. *Kylie. Felicity. Shelly. Cara. Jenna.* It helped build Wiggins's confidence as she got closer and closer to her target destination to remember whom she was fighting for. The innocent and forgotten. Wiggins's heart pounded like a bird trapped in a cage as she rounded the final corner and the posh, luxurious house came into view. She was expecting to see a forest-green Jeep parked in front of the Desmond home, but alas, there wasn't one there. The driveway was empty. She parked on the left side of the concrete, allowing room enough for another car. Before getting out, Wiggins looked down at her waist, making sure the pistol that she had brought with her was attached firmly to her hip.

Moments later, she was hobbling up the wooden deck in front of the house and knocking at the door. There was a small shuffling from inside the house, and in seconds, the door swung open, revealing Kenny Desmond's grizzled visage. He wore a filthy jean jacket and black sweatpants. His musty beard looked as though it had accumulated a copious amount of dust, and Wiggins wondered when the man had last taken a shower. He moved forward in his wheelchair, flashing a big smile.

"How-dee. Come on in, uh . . . what was your name again? I'm kidding," Kenny said as Wiggins opened her mouth. "Just wanted to see your reaction, *Maryanne*."

Wiggins beamed brightly. "I'm glad I finally made an impression."

Kenny giggled again, and then beckoned Wiggins inside.

"Come on in. Brendan won't be much longer, I don't think."

Wiggins nodded. Kenny wheeled himself into the kitchen and immobilized his chair in front of the kitchen table. He nodded at the empty seat across from him, indicating to Wiggins that she should take it. Next to the table on the counter, there was a coffee maker that was brewing a fresh pot of joe.

"You can just wait here for him. I can keep you company if you'd like."

"Whatever you prefer."

Kenny nodded and gazed out of the kitchen window. He fiddled with something in the pocket of his pants, like he wanted Wiggins to inquire about something.

"Do you have something you want to ask me?"

Kenny jumped a little when Wiggins addressed him. He apparently had been having an intense internal debate over whether to say what was on his mind, and Wiggins's question had jolted him out of his stupor.

"What? Well, uh, yeah, actually. I know you kind of hinted at not wanting to share the details of why you want to speak with Brendan. But I am afraid curiosity has gotten the better of me. I just can't imagine why you would want to talk to him, or what help he would be to you."

Wiggins had been expecting to run into this sort of reaction from Kenny. He was likely experiencing some cognitive dissonance about his brother. Perhaps his gut instinct had clued him in to the person Brendan truly was, but he couldn't rationally come to terms with it. She had already mentally prepared what she wanted to tell Kenny about the situation.

"Listen, Kenny, I don't want to scare you, but I think you may have the wrong idea about Brendan."

Instantly, Kenny's pleasant expression morphed into a scowl. He leaned forward and squinted at Wiggins as though he was seeing her for the first time.

"What are you talking about?"

Wiggins gulped. There was no genial way to say what she was thinking.

"I think he may know more than he is letting on . . . about Kylie. And . . . . the others."

"The others? What do you mean?"

"The other girls."

"Why would he know anything about th—"

Kenny abruptly stopped and a look of sudden comprehension dawned on the man's face. There were a few seconds of silence, and then he burst into a barrage of laughter.

"Brendan? Are you kidding me?" He threw his head back and propelled a deep belly laugh out of his diaphragm. "No way. You aren't serious, are you?"

Wiggins mentally started scrambling. She had prepped herself for a variety of different responses, but amusement was not one of them.

"I know it sounds ludicrous."

"Well, yeah!" Kenny said, still chortling.

"But just hear me out—"

"That's okay, actually," Kenny said firmly, raising his hand to silence her. "I don't need to hear it."

"No, listen. A vehicle that matches the description of one that was used in the attempted kidnapping of Sierra Bunker is registered under Brendan's name, along with Rick." She was butchering her attempt to convince Kenny of his brother's guilt, and she knew it.

"Wait, Rick? Are you saying he is in on it too?"

Wiggins opened her mouth for a second, but then, after mulling it over briefly, she decided to hold her tongue. Apparently, her silence was just as telling as speaking would have been.

"You've got to be kidding me!"

"Listen—"

"Maybe I should text Brendan and tell him not to come home yet. Perhaps he should wait until the men in white coats come and take you away," snapped Kenny.

Wiggins narrowed her eyes, surprised at the ill-mannered reaction.

"Now listen, Mr. Desmond. There is no need to be rude."

"I'm being rude, am I? Says the woman who just came into *my* house and accused my brother of killing my own fucking daughter."

The curse word cut through the air like a knife. Kenny had turned a startling shade of red, as he was possessed by anger. It was a tad frightening to see a man who was usually so benign and kind be thrown into a state of such fury.

"Mr. Desmond, please remain calm. I'm not accusing anybody of anything yet. I am just trying to explain to you why I want to talk to your brother, since you asked."

Kenny looked like he was about to respond, and then fell silent. For several long seconds, the only sound in the room was that of the coffee maker dripping coffee into the pot.

"I think you had better leave."

He fiddled in his pocket again, and Wiggins assumed he was reaching for his phone to text Brendan not to come.

"Kenny—"

"Do you realize how much I loved that girl? I miss her every single day. And he won't say it, but I know Brendan does too. And for you to come here and make accusations like that . . . Really, you should just leave."

"Please, Mr. Desmond. I really need to explain a few things."

Wiggins stopped as Kenny had looked out of the window, ignoring her. The man moved his wheelchair forward a bit to get a better view.

"Well, looks like you are saved by the bell. He's pullin' in now."

Wiggins looked out of the window, overwhelmed by nervous energy. The harsh reaction from Kenny had shaken her confidence, and Wiggins felt a little underprepared to confront the killer who was pulling into the driveway. Wiggins craned her head around and used her right arm to push her body upward a little, fully expecting to see the Jeep come into view. But for some reason, there wasn't a car in sight.

Out of her peripheral vision, Wiggins saw movement. She was about to turn when she caught a glint of silver. Wiggins saw the blood spurt up before the pain came, but once it did, her eyes bulged as a wave of incontrovertible agony crashed over her. From far away, an odd sound reached her ears. It took Wiggins a moment to realize that it was her own screaming. As she looked down at the table, she saw that her right hand was pinned against it, and the hilt of a large butcher knife stuck out several inches into the air from the back of her palm.

Kenny sprung up from his chair, with one hand still on the knife that had stabbed the woman in front of him. Even through her unyielding pain, Wiggins stomach dropped as Kenny stood powerfully on his own two legs, leaving his wheelchair behind. He wasn't paralyzed.

"I imagine this is a bit of a surprise now, isn't it?"

50

The man was filled with triumph. Finally, something had gone right. The last threat had willingly walked into the lion's den. And she had never even suspected him. The man had been waiting for this moment for a long time. A chance to unveil his true identity to someone else. And here he was, basking in the glory. Finally, after years of lingering in the shadows, the man had revealed himself to be Kenny Desmond.

He quickly darted across the kitchen and fumbled around in his sweats again. Wiggins was still screaming in utter torment with her blood spilling all over the table. Before she realized what was happening, Kenny had taken out a zip tie and fastened her left hand to the hilt of the knife that was deep in the flesh of her right, rendering her immobile. Once her arms were fastened, Kenny reached around her waist and grabbed the pistol attached to her hip. He brandished it in the air for a few seconds with a maniacal smile plastered to his face, before sitting down on a wooden stool across from her while kicking his wheelchair to the side.

"You know, you give yourself far too much credit, Maryanne *Wiggins,*" Kenny said loudly. "I thought you were going to be a problem the moment I met you. But you know what? You're so goddamn bad at what you do that you never got close enough to the truth for me to actually do anything. Until now. How does that make you feel?"

Wiggins tried to subdue her screaming, but the pain was too much. She let out another piercing screech.

"Bitch, you better shut the fuck up, or I will just get this over with now. Here." Kenny stood and shifted things around on the counter, looking for something. Within moments he had opened a drawer and taken out a filthy rag, which he balled up and shoved into Wiggins's mouth.

"There. That is *so* much better."

Wiggins continued to moan through the gag and felt dizzy as she looked at the knife embedded in her hand. The bleeding was getting more profuse and the pool underneath her arms was slowly increasing in diameter.

"You know, I had never planned to keep this whole act up for this long." Kenny pointed at the wheelchair. "But man, you really got to me when we first met. Before then I figured, hey, if anyone ever comes sniffing around again, I won't have to sit in this goddamn chair pretending to be broken like I did back in the nineties. The likelihood of any of the same cops showing up to interview me again is what? One in a thousand? And even if they did I would have just said I proved the doctors wrong and learned to walk again. But then your fat ass came along and made me realize this was going to have to be a permanent disguise."

Wiggins looked up into the man's eyes. She felt numb, like she was out of her body entirely. Like she was already dead.

"You know what the best part is? I still went out. Fuck, in the month before I killed the Deeds girl, I must've walked over that bridge a hundred times, planning it all out. And none of you people noticed. None of you dumbfucks who think you're all so smart noticed that a guy who was supposed to be a cripple was walking around town, perfectly healthy." Kenny's voice was filled with self-satisfaction. "I mean, there aren't a lot of people *who* recognize me . . . but still . . . you have to admit, the fact that nobody I talked to back then noticed me walking on my own two legs is pretty goddamn hilarious."

Wiggins tried to move her bleeding hand, and a pain shot down her arm, making her grunt. Kenny waved the gun aloft in the air while he spoke, and Wiggins wondered if he was going to shoot her.

"Brendan ain't comin', by the way. I told him to let me do it. This was too tempting to let him take care of it, like I did with your boy Carr . . ."

Wiggins looked right at Kenny, feeling like she was about to pass out.

"Don't get me wrong. I sure as hell *tried* to kill him myself. But that motherfucker clocked me with a baseball bat. Pretty sure he gave me a concussion. Good thing Brendan was waitin' in the Jeep for him, like I told him to be. Followed him all the way to Jump Off Joe's. Shot him in plain sight. Not the way I would have done it, but then again, I did kill Jones about a hundred feet away from a house in a rural neighborhood." Kenny chuckled.

Wiggins's eyes bulged when she realized Kenny had just confessed that he and his brother had killed Leighton and Jonah. Between the immense pain emanating from her hand and the giant amount of information the man was revealing, she was experiencing sensory overload.

"Good thing I had Rick to help me out when *you* reported Carr missing. It is nice to have an ace in the hole when you do the naughty things that I do," Kenny said sardonically. "Oh yeah, Rick has been a real asset all these years. Cleaning up me and

Brendan's messes. Honestly, I can't believe he continued to protect us all this time. Kept tellin' me time and time again that if I kept killin' he wouldn't be able to help me anymore."

Wiggins looked up, pierced by the truth that Kenny had just revealed. Rick, though he was an accomplice, wasn't one of the killers after all.

"Weird thing, huh? The fact that three brothers can be raised in the exact same way by the exact same people, and two of them end up going on a murderous rampage while the other goes on to be a cop." He laughed like it was the most ironic thing in the world. "Then again, he let it happen all this time. He let me and Brendan keep killin' and kept us in the clear. What does that make him?"

Kenny stood up and walked over to the kitchen window, drawing the blinds. The light that had been flooding into the room was extinguished, and the man began pacing back and forth while continuing to speak.

"As much as Rick does what he's told, Brendan's under my thumb even more. Yeah, he gets his hands dirty sometimes. But only if I tell him to. And shit, I do all the *real* work. I gather all the intel. I go out and take the girls. Most of the time, he just stays in the car. Not really sure what he gets out of it, but hey, I think the watchers are sicker than the fuckers, don't you?" Kenny gave her a malevolent smile.

Wiggins rocked back and forth slightly, as waves of queasiness and pain dominated her senses. She tried to listen to what the man was saying, but he was so erratic and scatterbrained that it was hard to keep up.

"But yeah, we got a cop on our team," Kenny said, going back to Rick. "How many serial killers can say that? It's good to have the authority of the law on your side."

The he widened his eyes, making the man look even more crazed. Apparently, he had remembered something that had excited him.

"Shit, you know how far up this thing goes? We had Rick sharing secrets with the district attorney. The goddamn district attorney! Can you believe that? I mean, nothing of real significance. Just little details here and there. He never knew that Rick was the brother of the fucking killer." Kenny cackled. "But once Rick warned him about what that Jones guy saw, he was real worried this thing would get reopened, and he kept askin' Rick to make sure to keep it all under wraps. Seemed more concerned with the image of the department and the city than the fact that he had let a killer run wild for thirty years."

Through the agony and adrenaline pumping through her system, Wiggins felt her stomach tense up in anger at the mention of Dan Jenkins.

"And you know what? I have run wild. *Wild*." He placed his hands on the table and leaned in until he was only inches away from Wiggins's face. He whispered, "And now I'm going to tell you something that you have been wanting to hear for years."

Kenny looked at Wiggins in sick pleasure. He stayed silent for several long moments, letting the anticipation build up before speaking.

"I killed them. *All* of them," he hissed. He was so close that Wiggins could smell the cigarettes on his breath.

"My daughter. She was the first. Can you believe that? My own daughter. You know I used to do whatever I wanted to her, right? Hell, at the end, she *wanted* to die. But I kept her around for a reason, you know? She served a purpose. She was my and Brendan's favorite toy. I was actually a little sad when we finally killed her. She was so much fun for all those years."

Wiggins wished in that moment that he had stabbed her in the ears rather than the hand. She didn't want to hear anymore.

"Yeah, little Kylie Desmond was my first." His smile radiated pure evil. "Shelly Schwartz. Felicity Sanders. My second and third. Jenna Eason. Cara Lee. Fourth and fifth."

As Kenny named each of the girls, he raised an additional

finger on his hand in a counting motion. Terror continued to spread through Wiggins's body. She knew that when he was finished with his story, it would be her turn.

"But then, something unbelievable happened. The police almost did their fucking jobs. Can you believe that? I was *this* close to being caught. What with Brendan shackin' up with Joanne and almost blowin' this whole thing with those pictures, and the fact that the cops got to the bodies quicker than I intended, things were coming apart. They almost put it all together. That's when I knew things had to change."

Kenny cleared his throat, towering over Wiggins. Now that he was standing up, Wiggins noticed how tall the man actually was. He leered at her, baring his yellow, rotten teeth.

"Strangling them was my thing, you know? Hell, that was my *drug*. There is nothing more satisfying than squeezing the life out of another human being. Watching the light in their eyes extinguish. God, it makes me hard just thinking about it. And you know, there is always that final moment where they realize that there is no escape, and they submit. That's my favorite part. When they finally let go."

Wiggins was starting to try and devise a plan. The sharp edge of the knife that was stuck in her hand was also deep in the wood of the table. Even if she could free it with her own strength, there still was the matter of having to evade the psychopath in front of her who was wielding a gun.

"But then, when things started to go south, I knew I had to change. The killer that the police were lookin' for had to disappear entirely. Oh no, I could never stop killing," Kenny said with a perverse grin. "I had to evolve. I had to expend all my energy concocting ways to make my kills seem extraordinary. I had to make it so that every officer who ever even contemplated homicide would get laughed at by his colleagues for suggesting something so outlandish. Only a conspiracy theorist could catch me."

Seemingly out of nowhere, Kenny slammed his free hand onto the table with fervor.

"My God! I almost forgot. I have to show you something. You will *love* this. Here, I will be right back. Don't you go anywhere, darling!" He winked at Wiggins. The man quickly scampered off through a door on the other side of the kitchen.

As soon as he was gone, Wiggins began struggling with her hand. When she moved, she was rocked by unfiltered torture and let out a muffled scream through her gag. She tried to grip the hilt of the knife with her left hand, but Kenny had zip-tied it in such a way that she would have had to be double-jointed to grasp it. Before she could do anything, Kenny burst back into the room, carrying a wooden box that had some strange markings carved into the side of it.

"This was Kylie's." He held up the box. "She used to keep little trinkets that she had collected over the years in here. And now I do the same. I told Brendan a couple days ago that we were going to have to get rid of this stuff. But I couldn't bring myself to do it."

Kenny opened the box and dug around until he found what he was looking for, and his face lit up. He pulled out a small pack of what looked like Big Red gum.

"I took this off Riley Reid. I'm sure you know all about her. The girl who went for a swim in Olalla Lake and drowned? She had it in her purse."

Wiggins felt the beads of sweat roll down her temple. It was as if her body was working with all of its might to mitigate the bleeding but couldn't quite manage it.

"I waited for hours for her to separate from her pack of friends. I knew eventually she would make a trip either back to the parking lot or to an outhouse. They all were drunk, you know? Somehow those kids had scored a bunch of beer and were drinkin' all day. And they all were running back to the cooler to get more beer or goin' to a Porta Potty to piss out all of the beer they already drank. And that's where I planned to take her. When she was alone. And God, it worked out *great.* You should have seen the look on her face when I came out of the woods. Caught her with her pants down. Literally."

Kenny threw his head back and guffawed at his own play on words.

"Anyway, yeah, I made quick work of it. Forced her in and just kept her head underwater until she was gone. Pretty clever, right? What with the alcohol in her system that they found during the autopsy, of course they thought the bitch had just gone for a drunken swim and swallowed too much water."

Wiggins bit down on the rag in her mouth. The pain in her hand was only matched by the fury in her heart.

Kenny placed Riley Reid's gum back where it had come from and riffled through his box of goodies again. Within moments, he had located something thin and white that he grasped between his index finger and his thumb.

"This here tampon belonged to Evelyn Sizemore. Young girl that ran away to Oklahoma, remember? She was the easiest out of all of them. Mom that didn't give a shit about her. Dad that lived in another state. That story practically wrote itself, don't you think?" asked Kenny arrogantly, raising his palms in the air. "Getting the postcard was a little tricky, but the rest was *easy.* I took the girl when she was walking home from school one day. And since the story I was tellin' didn't require a body, I could kill her however I wanted to. Guess how I did it."

Wiggins knew the answer, but since she had a gag in and she wasn't going to play Kenny's games in what were likely her last moments alive, she didn't even try to summon the words.

"You better believe I strangled her." Kenny flashed his disgusting smile. "Dumped her body in the Pacific. Amazing what people won't find if they aren't lookin'."

The man placed the tampon back in the box and grabbed the next item. It was a dangly silver earring that looked to be ingrained with some fake diamonds that had lost most of their shine.

"I'm assuming you already know that this belonged to Lacy Larson. Even today I still can't believe I pulled that one off. When I thought up the whole thing, it seemed so ridiculous. Cutting her brake lines? I think I even laughed out loud when I first thought of it," Kenny said as though he were talking about the weather. "But I got the idea when I saw what kind of car she drove. It was an old one, right? Cutting the brakes would actually work like it does in the movies. But it was just pure luck, pure happenstance that she decided to park her car at the top of the steepest hill in town on a night I was stalking her. It was kind of a spur-of-the-moment thing. Sometimes, you just got to have a little luck."

With an unnecessary flourish, Kenny placed the earring gently back in the box. Wiggins was starting to feel extremely dizzy, and she wondered if she was going to faint. The chair she was sitting on was flimsy and wobbled precariously as she began to lose her equilibrium. Within moments, another item was dangling in front of her face.

"Can you guess who this compass belonged to?" Kenny wiggled a black compass under Wiggins's nose while he rummaged through the box with his other hand. "Oh, or how about this water bottle?"

Wiggins saw a light blue plastic Dasani bottle in Kenny's left hand.

"If you guessed Kelsea Craft for the compass and Serena Wu for the water bottle, you are fucking *right*!"

Wiggins closed her eyes.

"Those two were probably my favorite. I'm not sure why. There wasn't anything spectacular about how they died. Shot 'em both point blank with a pistol deep in the Siuslaw Forest. The dad too. That was my first time killing a man. But that wasn't why they were my favorite. I don't even *know* why.

Maybe just the scheme. Making it look like one last hiking trip that had gone wrong. I mean, Oregon west of the Cascades is ninety percent forest anyway. Some people are bound to get lost in the woods, aren't they? Even hiking savants like Kelsea and Ken Craft."

Wiggins looked at Kenny curiously. The man wasn't just taunting her. It was as if he was excited to be able to pour out his life's work with another human being other than Brendan—as if all the pressure of his secret-keeping had been building, and he was relieved to be able to break the dam.

Kenny set down both items and retrieved a brown leather bracelet from within the depths of Kylie's box. He moved through the case linearly, so Wiggins had a good idea who the next person he spoke of would be.

"Mariah Beckham's." He brandished the bracelet. "And man, this one almost cost me. Little cunt put up a hell of a fight. Scratched the bejesus out of me. Didn't realize it at the time, but I left some blood behind. Rick had to work his ass off to get me out of *that* one."

Wiggins looked around the room. It was only now, at the end, that she wished she had worked with a partner on this. Someone who could be able to rescue her from this nightmare. But alas, she knew she was alone. The cavalry wasn't coming.

"Once I finally overpowered her and put the gun to her head, it only took her a couple of minutes to write the suicide note that I wanted. Can you imagine what that must be like? Realizing that once the task at hand is done, your life is over? Actually, you probably can imagine what it's like, can't you?" Kenny said with a booming laugh. "Anyway, once I cut her wrists, I got blood all over me while she was trying to escape. I just held her in place, waiting for her to bleed out. It didn't take long at all."

Kenny threw the bracelet back down with an inordinate amount of enthusiasm and grasped a new artifact that Wiggins couldn't quite see. It took her a moment to identify it as a golden necklace.

"Wendy Gordon. Wendy fucking Gordon. After her, I felt invincible. If I could get away with that, I could get away with anything. You see, the police thought that the trauma to her head came from the rocks in the bay after she got wasted and tumbled off the dock, right? But it was me. It was all me. The idiot was about to get back in her car, and she was trashed. Drinking and driving, can you believe that? Some people's kids.

"Anywho, even *I* didn't realize how easy it would be to kidnap a drunk girl. She was too toasted to fight back. Knocked her out in seconds. Transporting her was a bit tricky though. It is a damn hazard to walk on those rocks under the pier with 120 pounds cradled in your arms. But all I had to do was make sure she was facedown in the water. She was out cold. Died like that." Kenny snapped his fingers. He flashed another ugly grin and went back to foraging through his medium-sized box.

"I won't bother you with most of this other stuff. You and everyone else know all about Shelly Schwartz, Felicity Sanders, Jenna Eason, and Cara Lee. But there is one last thing I want to show you. This here is the grand finale. Ready?"

Kenny drummed his hands on the table. "Drumroll, please!" he said. Once he was finished with the theatrics, he reached back into the box one last time and pulled out a bright orange lighter.

"The woman of the hour! Your friend and mine—Katie Deeds!"

Wiggins looked at the lighter grimly. It was so disturbing and morose to see such a beautiful young life reduced to such an inconsequential and inanimate object. Kenny made a motion that reminded Wiggins of a parent feeding their young child by pretending the spoon is an airplane.

"This little fucking lighter is going to be all that's left of this whole shit storm. Not you. Not Carr. And sure as hell not Katie. She is rotting under the ground right now. Nobody will ever know how close you came. But let me make this abundantly clear . . ."

Kenny moved forward so that his nose was nearly touching Wiggins's forehead. She could smell his foul breath, and his lips curled back onto his teeth in a snarl.

"You had nothing to do with this. It wasn't your moxie that got you here. It was my own stupid fucking mistakes. Do you understand?" He grabbed Wiggins's hair. He pulled her back by the scalp, cocking to get more force and then slammed her forehead into the table. The blow was so hard that Wiggins didn't even scream; it seemed to knock all the wind out of her lungs.

"It was *my* fault that Jones saw me, do you hear?" Kenny shouted. "*My* fault that I didn't know he was there. *My* fault that he told Carr. *My* fault that Carr almost got away. *My* fault that we didn't clean up our mess as well as we should have. *My* fault that I tried to take Sierra Bunker, and my fault that she got away. None of this has anything, *anything,* to do with you."

Wiggins's vision was blurred. She felt like she was going to lose consciousness soon. That wouldn't be the worst thing in the world. Perhaps he would kill her after she passed out. She could only hope that he wouldn't wake her up to continue her physical and psychological torture.

"Hell, it was actually a pretty good plan, don't you think?" Kenny went on, apparently unaware of the fact that Wiggins was no longer paying attention. "Making it look like a girl with a history of impulsive behavior jumped off the bridge after a night of drinking? And sending those texts from her phone? I thought it was one of my better ruses, to be honest with you. But all it took was one domino to fall. And then the whole thing came apart. Funny how life can sometimes do that to you, don't you think?"

Suddenly, Kenny gripped the hilt of the knife that was stuck in Wiggins's right hand. With one swift motion, he ripped it out of her flesh and dropped it onto the table. For a split second, Wiggins felt only shock. But then her body was flooded with agony as a fresh wave of blood spilled out onto the table. Through the gag, she screamed continuously for at least ten seconds. Kenny laughed sadistically. He waited for her wailing to stop before he started speaking again.

"It's just me and you, Maryanne Wiggins. You are the last barrier to my freedom. Just like I thought Jones was, and Carr too. The only difference is: I got no satisfaction from their deaths. It was necessity. It was for a greater purpose. But this one? This one is for me."

Wiggins looked into the man's eyes, groaning at the pain in her torn hand. The moment was close now. Kenny slowly raised the gun that he had taken from her and pointed it at her chest, with one last pernicious and taunting smile. Wiggins shut her eyelids, and though she was not religious, she silently prayed. *God, please forgive me,* she thought. She wasn't quite sure what she was begging forgiveness for. But it was the only thought she could muster. She heard the sound of the shot and felt her rib cage rip open simultaneously, and the color black rushed in.

51

Kenny stood towering over Wiggins's body, feeling an enormous sense of relief. This ignominious disaster that had plagued him for the past month had finally come to an end.

When the woman had called him to try and arrange a meeting with his brother, Kenny hadn't even planned on killing her. He had thought she just wanted to speak with Brendan to gain a different perspective on Kylie's death. But then, when she had revealed she had finally caught on to his brother's murderous prowess, the man had no other choice. He had to do it. And though he had gleaned a substantial amount of satisfaction from shooting her, the solace he had felt knowing he was finally in the clear outweighed any other emotion. His only regret was that Wiggins had left so much blood on his table.

Kenny looked at the mess in front of him and sighed. *This one is going to take hours,* he thought. And though the kill itself was exhilarating, the cleanup was always a hassle. Not even a killer liked to haul around a dead body. He looked at Wiggins's ashen complexion. The woman's body was slumped forward onto the wood. Judging by her wide hips and pudgy belly, moving her was going to take more strength than he possessed in his own two arms. *Son of a bitch,* he thought.

Reaching into his sweats, Kenny quickly enclosed his dirty fingers around his phone and walked out of the kitchen, leaving the body behind. He scrolled through his contacts and found Brendan's number. In his other hand, he still carried the gun, although he barely even noticed it now.

"Hello?"

Kenny walked through the front door and onto the deck in front of the house.

"You are not going to believe the day I just had."

Kenny explained everything that had transpired in the last ten minutes. He recounted it as if it were a thrilling tale he was sharing with a buddy. He had expected Brendan to be ecstatic, but he was not. Quite surprisingly, the man's brother seemed very distressed.

"How did she find out?" Brendan asked worriedly.

"Huh?"

"How did she find out that I am involved in this? How did she even find out that Rick is our brother?"

"Why does that ma—"

"It matters because if she could fucking find out, then somebody else can too!" Brendan shouted.

The man paused for a second, taken off guard by this reaction.

"You need to relax, Brendan."

"Don't tell me to fucking relax! This isn't good, Kenny! Every time you think this shit we're in is over, something else happens. How do you know she hasn't been working on this with someone else? How do you know they aren't going to the police right fucking now?"

"Shut up and listen," he yelled. His sense of relief and

jubilation had dissipated and was replaced by fury at his brother, laced with an underlying sense of dread as Brendan had actually voiced a fear that was somewhat plausible.

Kenny rubbed his forehead, trying to press out the ill feelings he suddenly possessed. "She was working alone. I know she was. And to answer your original question, she found out that you were involved because she went to the DMV and saw that the Jeep was registered to you and Rick. And she got the description of the Jeep from the Bunker girl."

"But there had to be a reason why she would do that! There has to be some sort of explanation for why she would want to know what kind of car I drive!" Brendan said, sounding incredibly stressed.

Instead of lashing out with more anger, Kenny tried to be a more calming influence now. "Listen, we can figure all that out later. We may not be completely out of the woods yet, but we have solved our biggest problem. And besides, I wasn't just calling you to share the happy news. I need help moving the body."

"Jesus," Brendan muttered.

"Where are you anyway?"

"I'm trimming some hedges for Oceanview. Was trying to take care of a couple of contracts before the weather starts to get worse," Brendan replied, referring to their landscaping business. "Tim and Vince aren't here helping. It is just me."

"Come back to the house. I need you."

Brendan sighed loudly. "Fine. I will be there in a half hour."

"Good." He hung up the phone.

Although he tried to pretend that Brendan was just blowing smoke, Kenny's brother had struck a chord. He had communicated legitimate concerns. What if the woman had been working together with someone else? She had been in contact with Carr after all. There was no guarantee that she didn't have someone else's assistance too. Also, what *had* led Wiggins to go to the DMV and research what kind of car Brendan and Rick drove? As much as he wanted to believe that he had finally tied up all the loose ends, he felt a distinct sense of foreboding as he walked back into the house.

When Kenny crossed the threshold to the kitchen, his heart nearly stopped. He swiveled his head around the room, thinking that his eyes were playing tricks on him, but all he saw was more visual confirmation of the impossible. He looked frantically in all directions. *No, no, no,* thought Kenny as panic consumed him. It couldn't be. He stared at the chair on the other side of the table. Wiggins's body was no longer there.

52

Wiggins charged down the sloping hill toward the forest, inhaling air that she had thought she never would breathe in again. Her wounded hand was pumping through the air, gathering more speed for her legs. The injury was still throbbing and bleeding, and she was certain she had at least three broken ribs and internal bleeding from where the bullet had struck. But, somehow, someway, Kenny had missed the heart that was still beating wildly inside her chest, and she had only lost consciousness for a short time.

Every time her foot landed on the ground, Wiggins's knee and entire torso screamed in protest, but she didn't dare stop. For all she knew, Kenny was right behind her, watching her get closer and closer to the trees. She wasn't sure exactly how long she had been unconscious, but when she woke up, she had heard Kenny speaking on the phone on the front deck. She had only listened for a short time before removing her gag, snatching the knife that had penetrated her and tucking it into her coat, and then bursting through the adjacent hallway. She had quickly found a sliding glass door that led to the backyard and pushed it open, attempting to run to freedom.

As Wiggins passed a small white shed that was very near the forest, she briefly thought of calling the cops. She didn't want to stop running, and she sure as hell couldn't speak on the phone while moving as fast as she was. In a split second, she mentally made a note to find a hiding spot in the trees and try to silently dial 911.

Just a few more steps. Wiggins was almost there. She was starting to feel tears build in her eyes in complete exuberance. After being inches away from death, it looked like she was going to escape with her life. She saw the shape of three giant coniferous trees three feet in front of her.

A deafening sound boomed from behind Wiggins, and one of the trees in front of her exploded in a shower of slivers and falling leaves. Her ears rang; she chanced a quick glance back while still running. Thirty feet behind her, Kenny sped forward with the gun pointed in her direction and an expression on his face that reflected the murder in his heart. He pulled the trigger again, and this time, Wiggins felt the heat of the bullet whizzing by her head before it crashed into another tree. She let out a shriek of terror and ducked into the forest.

Zigging and zagging through roots, brush, and trees, Wiggins inflicted more damage to her already battered body by scraping against blackberry bushes and bark. To try and throw Kenny off her trail, she made an abrupt turn to the left and stampeded toward what looked like a small stream that likely ran down the hill and into Yaquina Bay. She leapt over the water, knowing that the splattering of her footsteps would alert Kenny to her precise location. When she landed, her leg gave out, and she tumbled onto the ground.

While scrambling back onto her feet, there was another loud reverberation, and mud splattered across her face. She looked behind her and saw Kenny bolting in her direction with his jaw twisted in fury. He fired two more rapid shots in succession, but Wiggins had already dove to her left to avoid them, landing on her belly. She was in a compromising position and waited for blackness to encase her once more, expecting to hear one last shot. Instead, she heard a distinct click. Wiggins craned her head around in Kenny's direction. The man had abruptly stopped and looked confused. With a leap of joy, Wiggins remembered that she had only put six bullets in the chamber.

Once Kenny realized what the problem was, he screamed in fury and glared at Wiggins, who was only a few feet in front of him. She stood up and raised her non-injured fist, bracing herself for hand-to-hand combat.

Kenny saw her stance and smiled.

"Big fucking mistake."

"Try me, motherfucker," Wiggins hissed back.

Kenny danced forward and swung his fist wildly. Wiggins ducked and admonished a hard punch to his gut. Kenny doubled over in pain, grunting as the air left his diaphragm. Wiggins then blasted him with a massive uppercut, knocking him backward. Once he was off balance, she kicked as hard as she could in between his legs. The blow to his groin caused Kenny to crumple to the ground.

Wiggins stood above the man in triumph, preparing herself to hit him again. However, before she could strike, Kenny barrel-rolled out of her reach and clambered to his feet. Once he was standing, he reached into his jacket and pulled out one of the largest knifes Wiggins had ever seen.

"I almost forgot about this one!"

Wiggins's eyes swelled in horror. There was no use trying to fight him now. She made an about-face and hobbled back in the direction she had come. Kenny attempted to charge after her, but his foot caught on a root, and he sprawled forward onto his chest.

"Fuck!" Kenny screamed.

While Kenny struggled to get back to his feet, Wiggins was able to put a substantial amount of distance between herself and her pursuer. She ran diagonally, trying to make her way around the largest trees in the forest to obstruct his view. It seemed to have worked, as Wiggins chanced another glance over her shoulder and didn't see Kenny sprinting in her immediate vicinity. As she came back toward the edge of the backyard, Wiggins remembered something crucial. Kenny wasn't the only one who was armed with sharpened metal. Still running, she fumbled around in her coat and pulled out the knife that had penetrated her. She tore through the grass, realizing that she didn't have much time until Kenny caught sight of her again. Her eyes scanned the panorama around her and stopped on the white shed that she had passed earlier. A perfect hiding spot.

X

Kenny finally exploded out of the forest, covered in newfound scratches, and a shiny bruise on his jaw from where Wiggins had punched him. Loathing drove him forward, flushing his face red. He couldn't believe she had taken him down so easily. If not for his anger, Kenny would be overwhelmed with embarrassment. *That fucking bitch,* he thought. *That nasty woman.*

Kenny's stumble cost him dearly. Wiggins had disappeared. He frantically looked left and right, wondering if she had set a new course. Surely she wouldn't have been able to make it back up to the house in such a short amount of time, and he didn't see her anywhere in front of him.

"Where the fuck are you?" Kenny whispered out loud.

He did a double take once his line of sight passed over the shed. *Of course,* thought Kenny in delight. He crept forward, hoping that the woman would think that he had gone up the hill toward the house. As he edged his way around the white structure, he noticed something that made his heart do a cartwheel. On the door of the shed, there was a bloody handprint. *Not as clever as you think,* thought Kenny with joy.

Readying himself for the impending confrontation, Kenny wielded the knife into a position that would make for optimal slashing. He wasn't going to stab her. He was going to simply gash her and watch the bitch bleed out. *This ends now,* thought Kenny, beginning to press his hand against the door. He took a deep breath, ready to be free.

With one gargantuan slam of his fist, the door swung open. Kenny leapt forward, brandishing the knife wildly. But all that his weapon cut was air. It took him a couple seconds to realize that the shed was empty. He stood looking at the only thing that was inside: a table. It didn't make sense.

Kenny only realized his mistake when it was too late. The bloody handprint had been planted. He began to turn around, but he already felt the presence behind him.

"This one is for the girls."

The knife plunged deep into his Adam's apple. He coughed up blood and reached up toward his throat, but even in that moment, he felt his body weaken. Darkness seeped into his eyes, and the last thing Kenny Desmond ever saw was Maryanne Wiggins standing over him with a scowl on her face.

53

Beep. Beep. Beep.

An interesting noise. Surely it was part of the dream.

Beep. Beep. Beep.

She had been envisioning a white shore that precluded a luscious forest. One that was much more welcoming than the hell she had escaped from.

Beep. Beep. Beep.

She wondered if she had died and the beach line was the edge of the afterlife. Perhaps it was just a vivid vision of her subconscious.

Beep. Beep. Beep.

With a loud grunt, Wiggins was thrown out of her dreams with a start. The first thing she saw was a woman in scrubs bending over, fiddling with a plastic bag filled with water. Great. She had literally just been pulled from paradise to arrive back to reality with an ass in her face. She groaned loudly to let the nurse know that she was awake.

Beep. Beep. Beep. The noise Wiggins was hearing was the heart monitor that was placed precariously next to her.

The young woman, who looked to be twenty-one or twenty-two, turned around with a smile. She was beautiful; light brown skin and perfectly shaped teeth enhanced her pretty face. Her scrubs were noticeably too large for her petite body.

"Hey, honey! How are you feeling?"

Honey, eh, thought Wiggins. This nurse was new; Wiggins had been in the hospital for four days now, and she had not seen her until now.

"Well, everything hurts, but psychologically, I am fine."

The nurse grinned even wider. "That's half the battle."

I wish it was only half, thought Wiggins. The nurse continued to smile at her for a few moments. She truly was beautiful. A sobering and relaxing thought crossed Wiggins's mind. This was exactly the type of girl that she had saved by killing Kenny Desmond.

When Wiggins had called the police after shoving the knife into Kenny's throat, she was consumed by physical agony like she had never felt before in her life. The pain in her hand was only dwarfed by the indescribable hurt coming from her ribs. Perhaps it had been the adrenaline that was quelling the feeling while she had eluded Kenny, but as soon as he was dead, the pain had made it difficult to even draw breath. The 911 response had taken over ten minutes, as the Desmond household was out in the middle of nowhere. Once they arrived, she had tried to stay and talk to the police and give them a detailed account of what had transpired, but the paramedics had forced her to take a ride to the emergency room. Wiggins had only given her testimony to the cops after surgery when they visited her in the hospital.

It turned out that Wiggins had two broken ribs and a punctured lung, coupled with nerve damage in her hand. She had gone under the knife so that the surgeons could remove the bullet that was still lodged against the back of her rib cage, and after a successful operation, Wiggins had spent a day in the ICU. The doctors had told her that the bullet had traveled only inches away from her heart. She assumed that this was supposed to make her feel lucky to be alive, but she was actually more confused than anything. Why Kenny had aimed for her chest anyway was a mystery. If it had been her, she would have pointed the gun at her head. Perhaps Kenny didn't want to scoop her brains off his kitchen floor.

The police had transported Kenny's body to Bateman's Funeral Home shortly after Wiggins left in the ambulance. The cops who had interviewed her at the hospital said that their forensics guy had confirmed that Kenny had died within seconds of being stabbed. *Shame,* Wiggins had thought at the time.

In the days after, KATU news had reported that the police had found evidence linking Kenny and Brendan Desmond to all five of the unsolved cases from the nineties, as well as eight other girls who hadn't originally been filed as murders. Therefore, each of the last eight cases was being reopened as a homicide and likely would be forensically tied to Kenny in a matter of days. The families of the girls had been notified by NPD as soon as the story had broken.

As for Brendan, he had never shown up at the Desmond household. Authorities reported seeing a forest-green Jeep speeding in the opposite direction when they were traveling down the bay road in response to the 911 call, although none turned around in pursuit, as they had more pressing matters to attend to. Wiggins suspected there was probably a police scanner inside of the Jeep, and Brendan had fled when he heard that the address that was beckoning a large swath of police activity was his own home. It didn't matter though. As far as Wiggins was concerned, they would catch him soon enough.

Rick Desmond had been placed under arrest less than twenty-four hours after Kenny had been killed, charged with thirteen counts of conspiracy of murder, as well as fourteen counts of obstruction of justice. It was likely that he was looking at spending the rest of his life in prison, although with a slight possibility of early parole. Although Rick had never personally touched any of the girls, Wiggins considered his enabling and covering actions to be just as bad as his homicidal brothers.

Nothing had been confirmed yet, but when Albert Amos had relayed all this information to Wiggins, he had also said that it was rumored that Dan Jenkins was going to resign as Newport's district attorney. It would be tricky for Internal Affairs to establish a strong connection between Jenkins and Rick Desmond, but Jenkins's name would forever be tied to the slog of the Nowhere Girls anyway, so it was probably best for all parties to move on. At the very least, Dan Jenkins was guilty of laziness.

As for Jonah Carr and Leighton Jones, Albert Amos had said the police were working diligently to establish a connection between the men's disappearances and the Desmond brothers, but nothing had happened yet. They were still looking for the bodies. Amos had reassured Wiggins that they would find something eventually, but she wasn't convinced. To placate her, Amos had been able to get ahold of Jonah's parents and had informed them of what Wiggins said had happened to their son. Unsurprisingly, the devastated couple relayed that they had not heard from their son in weeks. Wiggins was glad she wasn't the one who had to make that phone call. Although she had barely known the man, she doubted that she would ever fully get over what had happened to Jonah. In her mind, the blame for his fate lied squarely on her shoulders.

As for Wiggins herself, she had mixed feelings about the case being all but over. She was deeply satisfied with the fact that she had finally brought the monster she had sought for so long to justice, but she was also worried about the future. What she had made her life's work was now completed. What was she to obsess over now? What would motivate her day in and day out? The monotonous drivel of catching cheating spouses or other meaningless tasks that made up the work of a PI? She was also in a great deal of pain, even though the doctors had given her several doses of morphine. There was some pain that drugs just couldn't alleviate. Although she was triumphant over the part she had played in the case, she couldn't say she was fully happy or content.

As the young nurse continued to fiddle with the IV that was hooked up to her arm, Wiggins saw movement coming from the open door. Through the entryway came a frail-looking old woman who had glasses perched on the edge of her nose. Teresa Deeds looked like she had aged several years even though it had only been a couple of weeks since Wiggins had seen her.

"Hello," Teresa said timidly. Her eyes shifted back and forth as though she were afraid she would catch a disease.

"Teresa. Good to see you." Wiggins's throat scratched. Her voice was straining from lack of use, as the only people she had talked to over the past few days were Amos, the nurses, and the other cops.

The young nurse who was changing the IV bag looked at Teresa and back at Wiggins.

"I'll give you two some privacy," she said and ducked out of the room.

Once the nurse was gone, Teresa eyed Wiggins up and down like a hawk.

"You look like shit. But at least you're still kickin'."

Wiggins laughed, and when she did, it hurt her ribs.

"Not the best greeting I have ever received, but I appreciate the honesty, I guess."

Teresa chuckled and pulled a seat up next to the bed that Wiggins was laying on. It took her several long moments to get seated.

"Jesus, even sitting down is a workout when you're in your

eighties!"

Wiggins wanted to laugh, but held it in to save her torso.

Once Teresa was comfortable, she set her eyes upon Wiggins and wore a curious expression on her face.

"The news said you were the hero of this whole thing."

Wiggins couldn't help but roll her eyes. "The last thing I would ever call myself is a hero."

"No one else was even looking anymore. They all thought that that Bobby guy had killed those girls in the nineties, and hell, you busted open eight more cases that weren't even on the cops' radar," Teresa said resolutely. "Face it, without you, those brothers would still be out there killing."

"One of them still *is* out there, even if he isn't necessarily killing."

"You know what I mean," Teresa said, sounding annoyed.

"Yeah. I just don't think I'm a hero."

"Whatever you are, I wanted to come here to thank you."

"I appreciate it, Teresa."

Teresa looked over her shoulder at the door, making sure nobody was in earshot.

"In my eyes, you are the only cop who's worth a damn!" she said fiercely.

"I'm not a cop."

"You're as good as one. You already did more than any of them will ever do in their whole careers!"

Wiggins sighed, but she didn't answer. She was never very good at receiving praise.

"The point is, thank you. Thank you for doing everything you did."

"You're welcome."

"Hell, even that reporter was looking at me like the men in white coats were going to show up and take me away when he first interviewed me. Although he really was the catalyst of this whole thing. How is he doing anyway? I tried calling him, but it went straight to the recording machine."

Wiggins cleared her throat. Every time she thought of Jonah she felt a stab of guilt mixed with sadness.

"He's dead. Brendan Desmond killed him."

Teresa's face showed pure bewilderment. Eventually, she started sputtering.

"My God! Brendan Desmond? The one that got away? Did Jonah get too close to solving the whole thing or what?"

"Yeah, I think he did. Brendan and Kenny both knew it was only a matter of time before Jonah busted them. So they took matters into their own hands."

Teresa brushed a strand of rogue hair out of her eyes and shook her head. "Christ! Do the police know? They didn't say anything about him on the news!"

"Yes, they know. They are in the process of investigating it. It won't be long here before it is reported by the local media."

Teresa still looked flabbergasted.

"Oh my God. I was just talking to him a couple weeks ago. That makes my stomach hurt. He was . . . so young. I can't even . . . believe that."

"Tell me about it," Wiggins replied with her voice still thick.

There was a long interlude of silence between them. Teresa shook her head and frowned.

"Just when I thought this nightmare was over."

"It *is* over," Wiggins countered.

Teresa shook her head. "Well . . . it will never truly be over."

As soon as she finished this sentence, Teresa started to weep. Wiggins was caught off guard at first, but then realized that the woman was just expressing her grief over losing her closest family member. Wiggins would have offered a consoling hand, but her nearest palm was wrapped in several layers of bandages.

"I'm so sorry, Teresa."

Teresa fanned her hand downward, trying to subdue the sympathy from Wiggins.

"Don't be sorry. If it weren't for you, I would have never gotten any closure at all."

Wiggins smiled kindly, trying to show that she appreciated Teresa's gratitude.

"It helps to know that you saved somebody else from experiencing this pain." Teresa pulled a handkerchief out of her purse and blew her nose.

"If I had been a bit faster I might have been able to save a few more families from experiencing the heartache."

Teresa shook her head in exasperation.

"Look at you. Just took down a serial killer and still won't even take any credit. Can't tell if it's humility or just stubbornness."

"Probably a little bit of both." Wiggins smiled.

Teresa wiped another tear from her cheek.

"I wish Katie would have gotten the chance to meet you. She would have liked you."

Wiggins didn't say anything to this. She didn't know what to say.

"It still doesn't even feel like she's gone. It feels like she just left and will be back any day now."

Wiggins looked at her and tried to muster an expression of strength.

"Back? I can already feel her in this very room. And I know you will carry that with you wherever you go. She will never truly be gone, see."

X

The wind blew with such force that the seagulls perched on the railing in front of the cliff had to spread their wings to maintain their balance. Although the rain was not falling, the sky was overcast and bleak. Down below, the ocean tossed and turned in its restless sleep. A flock of gulls was assembling over an empty parking spot that was lined with bread crumbs that passersby had tossed. Next to the birds, three cars were parked: a Dodge Durango, a minivan, and a black Audi.

Wiggins reclined in the driver's seat, ruminating on the weather. It would probably start raining here any minute. She zipped up her jacket and opened her door, carrying a bulky object in between her arms.

It had now been three weeks since Kenny Desmond had shot her. Every time she moved, she still felt a healthy amount of pain in her torso. Her hand was still wrapped in bandages, causing Wiggins to have trouble doing even the simplest of tasks. But she was alive. And that was something that she did not think she would be able to say when Kenny had revealed that he was the one she had been searching for the whole time.

Brendan Desmond had still not been caught. His vehicle had been sighted briefly in Ashland near the California border, but Brendan was able to continue to evade police. Several days later, the Jeep was found abandoned in Chico, California. The locals had been encouraged to report any sightings of the man, but none had come. It appeared, for now, at least, that Brendan had vanished. Every time she thought of him, her stomach boiled in anger. She would not rest until he was caught. Not after what he had done to Jonah.

Now she stood next to her car at Jump-Off Joe, likely only feet away from where Jonah had died. She looked at her surroundings and felt odd. It wasn't grief that consumed her. Rather, she felt transcendent and strange—like she was looking at the scope of the whole case from this cliff on the brink of the Pacific, and not just at what happened to Jonah. Perhaps it was the height from which she was looking down at the ocean, but she felt like she had finally risen above the mystery and was gazing upon each of the Desmond brothers' victims in silent reflection.

Wiggins trudged toward the edge of the cliff, limping as she went. In her arms she carried the black binder that was full of articles that pertained to the case. It was rather heavy; or perhaps she felt that way because she had never carried it this far before. She had already turned in electronic copies of the documents to the police and saved the files on her computer. The binder symbolized what she had dedicated her life toward the past fifteen years. But that part of her life was over. And thus, the large notebook had become superfluous. With a long exhale, she moved as close as she could to the cliff without having to worry about tumbling over and held the binder out.

"I'll never forget," Wiggins said, and with one last, deep breath, she released the binder and watched it tumble into the ocean below. Newport would never again let the Girls fade into obscurity. And they were nowhere no longer.

97046948R00242

Made in the USA
San Bernardino, CA
21 November 2018